In

*(Seren*

By

Charlene Namdhari

This is a work of fiction. Names, characters, places, and incidents are either the product of the author's imagination or are used fictitiously, and any resemblance to actual persons living or dead, business establishments, events, or locales, is entirely coincidental.

**Incognito**



Cover Art by TRC Designs

Editing by Malia

Developmental Editing by Nikki Malan

# Acknowledgments

**TO MY HUBBY AND THE Kids**

Thank you for putting up with me during this rollercoaster of a book. I LOVE YOU!!!

**TO NIKKI AND JEN (TWO super-duper awesome woman and my pillars of strength)**

This was one emotional ride with Trent and Zayne. Thank you to you amazing ladies for standing by my side, taking my late and long calls, holding my hand, listening to me rant, sharing my pain, all the late-night reading, just being there for me, and BELIEVING IN ME. I couldn't have done it without you.

You're special and I APPRECIATE YOU.

**TO CRYSTAL ERENTZE**

Welcome to my small team of special people, for jumping in at the last minute and helping me with all the late-night reads, listening to me talk nonsense, the constant motivation and BELIEVING IN ME. You're awesome. THANK YOU!!

**MARILIZE ROOS**

Welcome to my small team of special people and THANK YOU for jumping in and helping me with all the last-minute, late-night reads, advice and suggestions. I really appreciate the help.

**TO TRC DESIGNS**

Thank you, Cat Imb, for my beautiful covers, more importantly, your efficiency, constant willingness to help with my changes and just your friendly approach. You're fantastic, always.

**TO MY READERS AND BLOGGERS**

Thank you so much for taking a chance on Incognito and giving your time to read and review this taboo book. I'm genuinely grateful.

# Trent

**SEVEN YEARS AGO...**

"You've got this."

I glanced at my wife over my shoulder. She laid propped against a multitude of pillows on the bed, braiding the second of her two plaits. I loved that look. It reminded me of those first days when I met the pretty, withdrawn eighteen-year-old sitting on the curb outside Nicky's, the local diner, waiting for her father to fetch her. She'd waitressed there after school.

I'd just turned twenty-two and had a bit of a rebellious streak in me. When friends and I rode in on our bikes, the noise disturbed her reading. Something about those blueish-gray eyes drew me to her. Maybe it was the mystery I read in them or the lurking sass behind the innocence when she stared at me dead-on. Even though I tried for a few days, she wouldn't give me the time of day until I scared away boys from her school who'd attempted bullying her into giving them her notes. Turned out, she'd seen me as the bigger bully because I wouldn't leave her alone and only earned my first genuine smile a month later.

"Trent?" Krisha threw a cushion, hitting me square in the face and yanking me out of my reflections. "Did you hear me?"

Smiling, I nodded. Five years later and she still retained the same simplicity except her pregnant state had added a little maturity. Dark circles beneath her eyes, the only indication it'd been a rough one, especially the last month. I sighed. "My place is here with you, Pixie." Giving up on the tie I'd been knotting in front of the mirror, I crossed the room and eased myself down gently on the bed, next to her. "This is a crucial time for you, I shouldn't be leaving you alone." She had a whole three weeks to go before she gave birth, but the twins became a handful for the last three months and Krisha's doctor had ordered her off her feet.

She palmed my cheek with a soft smile. "I'm not alone. Carol's here remember?" she coaxed, referring to my grandmother. "You've put this off long enough, Trent. They're about to hand that deal you've wanted to someone else. This is yours for the taking. And it's only an hour and a half flight."

"That's two hours too far." I nuzzled her neck. "And other deals will come."

"You're using me as an excuse," she scolded.

I pulled back, grinning. "Why would I do that?"

"Because it means putting away your motorcycle, cutting your hair, and wearing a suit every day for the rest of your life," she teased. "And we both know you hate that Chartered Accountant role. Your place is in the kitchen as weird as that may sound to you."

Turning on my side, with my head on her thighs, I rubbed her belly. "First, there's nothing weird about it, you love my cooking. Second, even if I sign this deal, nothing stops me from riding my bike. Lastly, there's nothing wrong with wearing your hair long with a suit. The only difference is I make it look good." I winked.

Laughing, she stroked my shoulder-length hair. "Such arrogance. You're going to be a daddy soon and there will be no more motorcycle—"

I faked a shocked look. "What's wrong with them riding a motorcycle." I rubbed her stomach. "Hear that boys, your mommy's already laying down the rules and you haven't even popped out yet."

"Popped out?" She punched me lightly on the chest. "This is not one of your ovens." She rubbed her stomach. "And who said anything about them being boys?" We'd chosen not to know the sex of the twins, relishing the anticipation yet constantly teased each other about what they'd be. "It's a girl and a boy." I shook my head, and she clutched my hair in a firm grip. "Agree it's a boy and a girl else there's no sex for a year."

Grinning, I raised a brow. "Notwithstanding we haven't had any in the last four months, I'd like to see you try, Pixie." Pushing up, I straddled her while supporting my full weight on my flat palms on either side of her. "This body belongs to me, baby and you know I can make you beg."

"How can I forget." Laughing, she cupped my face and pulled me closer for a kiss. "I love you," she whispered against my lips when we broke apart.

"I love you, too." My eyes locked with hers, I drew in a labored breath. "You're the beat of my heart..." I kissed her brow. "And the whisper of my soul." I kissed her lips.

"And you're the air in my lungs..." She kissed one cheek. "And the light of my smile." She kissed the other cheek.

This was how we said goodbye every morning. By reciting our wedding vows.

"Now go before Drake is convinced you're too chicken shit to keep your word." She pushed lightly at my chest.

Chuckling, I dropped a quick kiss to her brow. "Take care of mommy, boys." I kissed her stomach then slid off the bed. "Ring me if anything happens, even if it's a twinge, okay?" She nodded. Taking a moment to study her face, I couldn't stop the hammer in my chest. My heart was begging me to reconsider but I knew she'd push me to go. I didn't want to cause her any more stress. Sighing, I turned away, knotted my tie, and reached for my jacket. "I look good?" I asked after slipping it on.

She made a show of running an appreciative gaze over me from head to toe. "Always." She pursed her lips and blew me a kiss.

Smiling, I returned the gesture. "See you later."

I was at the door when she stopped me. "Hey, handsome." I turned. "Twins are a handful. I don't think you'll have time for sex."

"I'll always make time to fuck you." I laughed when her cheeks bloomed with the rosy blush my crudeness always elicited. Five years together and she still hadn't gotten used to my dirty mouth.

Downstairs, I found my uncle, Drake, greeting my grandmother. She lived with him but insisted on staying with us for the last month to take care of Krisha.

"You ready?" he asked when he noticed me on the bottom stair.

"As ready as I can be."

"Good, let's go."

"Thank you." Forty minutes later, I smiled at the hostess who'd just served me a drink. Flying first class was great, taking my uncle's private jet, even better. A luxury I intended indulging in when the time was right. We were by no means lacking in status when compared to my uncle's family name but with twins on the way, my life was about to change, which meant I needed to tier priorities accordingly.

"How's Krisha doing?" Drake asked.

I glanced away from the cloud-peppered blue sky outside the window. "Her doctor seems to have the high blood pressure under control. Still, there are good days and bad ones." I exhaled a slow breath. "I haven't admitted this but having grandma around has been a huge help. There are days I'm just too distraught watching Krisha uncomfortable or in pain. Grandma's been a pillar of strength to the both of us."

"You're almost there." My uncle, the man I'd looked up to in my father's absence, gave me an understanding smile.

"I guess." I swirled my drink before taking a sip. "Her doctor tried to schedule a cesarean. Krisha is adamant she wants a natural birth." The pregnancy had taken its toll, more so on her. I stared out the window, wondering for the umpteenth time if it was wise to leave her during this critical time.

"You needed to do this, Trent." Drake drew my attention as though reading my mind. "You've wanted to open a restaurant since you were twelve. I still remember the first time your mother helped you pretend Christmas dinner was taking place at some fancy restaurant."

"Yeah." I laughed, remembering how I'd pestered my mother to let me do the setup that year and despite her reluctance, she'd relented. I'd subsequently shocked not only her but all fifty guests that evening by bringing a winter forest into our dining room. Drake was right and this was my chance.

Over the years, I'd searched for a small family-owned restaurant that wasn't only popular with the locals but tourists as well. The idea was to build into the whole family-orientated dynamics while adding my flair to the design, menu, and setup with the help of the existing owner. A touch of old and new. It had to be an established restaurant and hugely trusted to deliver on service offerings. After a year of procrastinating, the right offer fell into my lap. The owner was ready to sign given he'd lost his only son and at his age, too sickly to continue the family tradition. I'd presented the idea to him during a family retreat to Brenton but never got round to finalizing the discussion. Because like Krisha stated so emphatically every time she could, I was chickenshit to venture into something I was inexperienced at. Both she and Drake pushed me until I called the old man, who was on the verge of signing it over to someone else.

"Congratulations, you're officially a restauranteur." Drake clapped me lightly on the back a couple of hours later. "And looks like you're moving to Brenton."

I surveyed the restaurant we stood outside and smiled. "I've done it, Krish," I whispered. "Now comes the easy part, I guess."

Laughing, Drake nodded to the driver of our waiting car. As I followed him into the vehicle, my phone buzzed. Fishing the device out of my pocket, I panicked as Krisha's number flashed across the screen. "Krish?" I answered in a rush, dread squeezing my insides.

"Trent, you need to come home, quick. Krisha's been admitted," my grandmother's worried words spilled across the line and with it the oxygen to my lungs fishtailed, leaving me breathless.

My fingers tightened around the phone. "What happened?" I failed to keep the telltale tremble out of my voice, drawing Drake's immediate frown. "She wasn't supposed to get out of bed."

"She'd gone to the bathroom then complained of pain. Easton drove her to the hospital," she explained referring to Krisha's brother. "Trent?" I could hear the fear in that single word. "She was bleeding."

"No!" My heart crashed against my chest this time taking my ability to think. I shook my head, trying to breathe.

Drake took the phone from my clenched fingers. His words became a blur as sweat pooled in my armpits and clammy fingers bit into my bouncing knee. I glanced at my uncle through the sudden tears as he cut the call. Words weren't needed, his expression said it all.

"Drink," he ordered, shoving bottled water into my hand when my chest heaved for the third time and I pulled in deep breaths to prevent the threatening nausea.

"I'M SORRY, TRENT, KRISHA'S in a critical condition. She doesn't have much time."

I shifted my blank stare from the floor to Krisha's doctor. By the time we'd landed and gotten to the hospital, she'd delivered the twins. My excitement at seeing them came to an abrupt halt when Dr. Gina walked out of the delivery room asking to speak to me, her expression grave. Now, she stood a few feet from me with Drake, Easton, and grandmother at my rear after I'd indicated it was okay to speak in front of them. "I don't understand. You told me you had the blood pressure under control." Anger laced the words I forced out through my clenched jaw. Pain from having gnashed them together all through the flight back radiated through my face and down my neck, tightening every moving muscle.

"It wasn't the blood pressure."

"What are you saying?"

"The internal bleeding was too much, whatever we tried, wasn't enough. Perhaps if she'd allowed us to go with the cesarean..." She trailed off. "We've got a specialist flying in to assist. He's handled cases like this before. But I'm afraid he might not make it in time and she's barely conscious."

The warm blood running through my veins turned icy at the notion hitting me full frontal. "A-are you saying my wife is d—dying?" I struggled to get the words out. Next to me, Drake touched my arm, gently squeezing. I shook my head. "It can't be." I dropped my head forward, pinching the bridge of my nose, hoping to stop the tears but they burned the back of my lids, relentless and unforgiving.

"I'm sorry. I tried," Dr. Gina repeated, her sigh heavy. "But Krisha knew the risk. I warned her from the onset there'd be complications with her delivery if she went with the natural birthing."

My brain stopped processing for a moment, every part of my body frozen while my thoughts tried to catch up, tried to comprehend what Dr. Gina had just said. "She knew?" The doctor nodded. "But..." the words wouldn't come. "Why?" I choked out the single word.

"She knew how much you wanted a baby, Trent." My grandmother touched my arm. I turned to look at her. "After that first miscarriage, this pregnancy was more important to her than her life. It was why she endured it all. To give you the children you wanted."

My heart stuttered, threatening to stop beating. I remembered her devastation when we'd lost our first child three months into the pregnancy, more so when the doctor informed us Krisha would never fall pregnant again. She'd just finished school and although the news shocked us, we'd already begun planning our lives together.

"This is not what I wanted, not—" Pain crushed my windpipe, strangling my words.

"Go to her, son." Drake pointed to the delivery room.

I stared at him, knowing what he wasn't saying out loud. This couldn't be goodbye. Not yet. He gave me a gentle nudge. Nodding, I made the journey to that door, each step heavier than the one before, my heart, my body, my mind reluctant to face the inevitable. I couldn't lose her. With bated breath, I pushed through the door and stumbled, my eyes immediately drawn to the steel bed in the middle of a cold, sterile room that smelled of clean chemicals yet an agonizing taunt of death itself. I shifted my gaze, taking in my wife's deathly pale looks, a debilitating reminiscence of her former self, being kept alive by beeping machines and clear tubing.

Burning tears trickled down my cheeks, searing my skin with the very essence of pain. I tried to swallow down the rock lodged in my throat, my jaw screaming from being clenched too tight. Wiping my eyes, I choked on a sob, trying not to let the sound out, so she wouldn't hear yet in my heart I knew she could hear everything, including the beat of my heart as it boomed in my ears. When I stood near the bed, I stared down at the woman who'd given me every form of happiness for the last five years. She would've appeared peacefully asleep beneath the blue blanket tucked around her up to the neck, had it not been for the sweat beading her forehead and upper lip or the distinct paleness to her skin. Her nostrils flared on a fragmented pulse —she was trying hard to breathe.

"Krish." My voice shook as trembling fingers reached out to caress her cheek.

She opened her eyes, her smile accompanied by a slight wince she failed to mask. "Hey, daddy," she whispered.

Smiling through my tears, I leaned down and dropped a light kiss to her lips. "Hey, mommy."

"I was right." She attempted a laugh but winced instead.

I blinked back the tears. "Yes, Pixie you were right. A boy and a girl."

"Are they okay?" She turned her head slightly. I followed her gaze to the incubators that held the twins. "Can I see them?"

Nodding to the nurse I hadn't noticed when I entered, she wheeled the incubators closer. Gently, she lifted the twins, placed one in each of my arms, taking care to help me get comfortable holding them. Then she moved around to elevate the bed a little. Staring at the sleeping bundles, a small laugh of incredulity pierced my tears. I leaned against the edge of the bed and held them as close as possible to Krisha. "They're perfect."

With deep breaths I could see she was struggling to take, she withdrew her hands from beneath the blanket and traced the tips of her fingers over their facial features as though committing their faces to memory. "They are perfect." She kissed the brow of the baby closest to her. I moved so she could do the same to the other. "Promise me, you'll take good care of them."

My head bobbed and shook at the same time—what she was asking, painfully obvious. "Krish, I can't lose—"

"Promise me, Trent," she cut in with an encouraging smile, the one she always used when I argued a point. She'd never shown me anger, ever. "I need to know that everything will be okay—you will be okay," she continued in that quiet voice I'd come to love.

A sharp tug in my chest, pulling from the deep recesses of my heart. The tears fell harder. I glanced down at our children and nodded. "I promise."

As though she sensed my loss of composure, the nurse took them from my arms and placed them back in the incubators. I sat down on the edge of the bed. "Why didn't you tell me?"

"Don't." Krisha linked her fingers with mine. "I gave you what you needed," she whispered. "And I'll do it again."

"I can't lose you." Sliding down next to her, I pushed my face into the crook of her neck and didn't hold back the tears. Her scent, a mixture of orange blossoms and gardenias, filled my nostrils. I inhaled deeply, storing it in my memory forever.

She ran slow fingers through my hair like she always did at night. I could hear her breathing, short and deep like she was forcing back the tears. "You're not getting rid of me so easily." Her soft laugh was strained. "Trent?" Reluctantly, I leaned back on one arm to look down at her. "I want our daughter named after my mother. Would you do that for me?' When I hesitated, she shook her head. "I want my name to stay here..." She pointed to my chest. "In your heart where it belongs. Our daughter needs her individuality, not my shadow. Promise?" I nodded. "And our son—"

"Nicky," I whispered.

She smiled before her lids fluttered closed. We'd decided to name our son after the diner where our journey together began. Some might consider it silly, but it was her wish. She'd planned on not taking her shift that afternoon and according to her, fate stepped in. Puffy lids slowly lifted, locking with mine as tears leaked down her temples, disappearing into her hair. "I love you."

I palmed her cheek, dropping soft kisses to her lips, nose, and each eye unable to stop my tears. "I love you too, Krish."

"I want to hear my name on your lips one last—"

"Don't, Pixie." I shook my head hard, trying to pause the pain squeezing my heart, twisting my insides, knowing she was saying goodbye. I wasn't ready to.

"Trent." She cupped my face in quivering hands. "It's not goodbye. I will find you again. Believe," she whispered. "Fate will bring us back together. I don't know how but you will find me again, I will come back to you in some form or the other. You're the air..." she paused, pulling in deep breaths. "...in my lungs—"

"No. Please, Pixie, you can't—"

Her grip tightened on my face. "Let me say it, I need to say it, okay." I nodded. "You're the air in my lungs..." She kissed one cheek. "And the light of my smile." She kissed the other cheek. "Say it," she murmured."

I stopped breathing. Every tiny cell in me ached, a blistering pain that seared my lungs, pausing the air I desperately needed but didn't want. I couldn't say the words.

"Please, you have to," she choked on her breath between words.

"You're the beat of my heart." I kissed her brow. "And the whisper of my soul." I kissed her lips.

She smiled. "I'm right here." One hand moved from my face to my chest. "And I'll always stay there until you need me no more."

"I'll always need you."

"But you will let go when the time is right. Promise." I nodded. "Hold me, h-handsome."

Her voice cracked on the last word and for the first time since walking into the room, I accepted I had to let go. Whether I could or not, didn't matter, I had to give her the peace she needed. Gently, I placed an arm around her chest, eased my face in the crook, and silently cried, letting her even breaths fill my ears until I could hear nothing until she left me.

One minute I was lying next to her, feeling the fade of her pulse beneath my touch, the sigh of her breath as it became her last, and the very next a blurred vision of chaos. A screaming alarm, a flashing light, a whining beep, all yanking me out of my desolate oblivion, giving me hope at the same time lengthening the distance.

"Sir,...Sir...Mr. Shaw! Sorry, you have to leave now." I glanced down at the pale hand gripping my arm following it up to the face of the nurse who'd seen my despair. "Mr. Shaw, you have to leave. She's coding...it's her heart...you need to leave," her voice rose in crescendo.

I yanked my arm and turned to my wife. "Krish...Krisha...Open your eyes baby..." I screamed.

"Get him out of here now!" the bark resounded around me at the same time I was shoved backward.

My feet followed of their own accord, my eyes however remained, watching her vacant stare...Krisha's vacant stare before the doors closed, signaling a final goodbye, taking the love of my life, the mother of my children and my best friend.

# Zayne

**THREE AND A HALF YEARS Ago…**

I glanced at the ringing phone, half tempted to ignore the damn thing before picking it up. Recognizing the number, fury sparked an immediate line across my brow. I hit the answer button. "Yeah?"

"Long time." A voice I hadn't heard in a while rasped through the speaker. "Forget your old acquaintances?"

"Told you to forget I fucking existed, didn't I," I sneered, ignoring the hopeful familiarity from the other end.

"When have you known me to follow rules? We're two peas in a pod, remember." I didn't respond. "It's been hard as fuck trying to track you down. Seems like you're not adept at hiding anymore?" I didn't miss the cold taunt.

"Maybe I wanted you to find me. Scores to settle, remember?" my reply equally icy. "Quit thinking so hard, you're giving me a fucking headache," I mocked when he didn't respond. "What the fuck do you want?"

"Got a new client for you. A hard limit but I know you like a challenge and the client is willing to pay double. I'm gathering intel now." He paused. I figured he was gauging my interest and continued when I said nothing. "The client sees the target as a threat to their life and needs the job done fast. Will send you the info in a few."

I gnashed my teeth. "I'm not interested."

There was a brittle curse on the other side. "Look, I know I fucked up. But it's not my fault the last client fucked up. This client is good business. I've had him checked out, double and triple, and you're the best man for the job."

Staring out the window, I watched the waves crash against the shore, gripping the phone tight. Yes, they fucked up, got lazy checking out the client's full details, but I held myself accountable, I'd never left a job unfinished, ever—my golden rule. I was a man of my word. "Still not interested."

"For fuck's sake, how many times do I have to apologize."

"You need me, remember," I snarled.

He knew I was right. A strangled sigh came across the line. "He got cocky and I'm sorry he rubbed it in your face. But his man was good, played his part well, and led us on a wild chase around town. We didn't see the cyanide thing coming."

"Did you find him?"

There was a long pause from the other end. "Not yet."

"It's been a while and still nothing. Losing your touch," I scoffed. "You're a bunch of fucking idiots. A simple man, a nobody, screwed you over and took me for an even bigger idiot because you let him," my steel-lined words dripped with sarcasm. "And I'm still waiting for the how." Nothing much caught me off guard, and if by some miracle it did, somebody would die. I'd make sure of it.

"And again, I'm sorry. I still don't have an idea who leaked your name or why. But I can guarantee it will never happen again."

"You're fucking right it won't," the threat open-ended. I should tell him to go fuck himself. It wasn't like I needed the money, I had plenty of that. Only, I craved the adrenalin rush, relished in the chase. I had the looks of a prince but the heart of the fucking devil. No one saw me coming. The win was inevitable. Rule number two was simple. If you planned on fucking with me, you better make damned sure I'm dead. What the client hadn't understood was that I wasn't one to let sleeping dogs lie. I'd catch him when he least expected it. Him and his mole. I'd already set the bait. He'd bite. Eventually. Time was on my side.

"You there?"

I grunted a response. Still trying to calm the fuck down. "Fuck up again and I'll serve your balls on a silver platter to that ugly as fuck Pitbull you love." I cut the call and a second later, the phone pinged with an incoming text. Opening it, I watched the picture slowly download.

"Who's that?" came a husky voice.

I glared at the woman peering over my shoulder. "The last person that snuck up on me, sweetheart, hasn't been seen in a long time." Her eyes widened as she backtracked into the bedroom.

Note to self, don't fucking bring strange women you meet at a bar back to your room, and if you do, make damn sure they leave right after you fucked their brains out. I grinned. I'd been called everything from sweetheart to asshole since junior high, I didn't give a shit. My third rule was just as simple as the second. You liked me or you didn't. Either way, I didn't give a flying fuck. There were two kinds of women in the world, those you fucked and those that fucked you. Pun intended. Sadly, I had the benefit of meeting both.

Shaking my head, I read the rest of the message, took note of the time and location then dropped the phone and crushed it with my boot like I always did. That way I stayed off the grid, found, only when I *wanted* to be.

Three hours later, I strolled past hospital reception and headed for the elevator. As the doors opened to the private ward on the ninth floor, I stopped short. A couple of flustered nurses were either hurrying down the hall or talking in earnest. Something was up. In all the time I'd visited, I'd never seen this much activity.

I walked over to a nurse closest to me. "What's going—" An ear-splitting shriek pierced the air. Not much scared me but the haunting ferocity spiked the hairs on my arms and had me sprinting to her room—to the woman I'd been visiting every day for the last couple of years. "She's aw—" I froze at the entrance, my excitement immediately replaced by shock at the scene unfolding in front of me.

Nurses and doctors floundered around the bed, trying to hold the woman down. Arms flailing, she mumbled repeatedly, her words a string of incoherent babble. A second later, her body jack-knifed as if her chest had met the current of a defibrillator. Her high-pitched scream filled my ears, "let me go!" She fought their hold, trying to escape. "No!" Her retaliation so strong, another nurse joined the others, pinning the thrashing arm she'd gotten free. "They're coming for me!" she shouted. "Let me go. Please," the pleading tone wrenched a guttural curse from my throat. Her head shook violently from side to side. The reaction squeezed my black-ened heart, cutting off the air to my lungs. I struggled to breathe. I'd seen a lot of fucked up shit in my life but nothing quite like this. I couldn't decide if she was in pain or just frantically trying to get away from her memories. Who was coming for her?

Kicking out her legs, her body arched off the bed before crash-ing back with a loud snap from holding her body stiff. That, I'd seen before. If she continued, it could lead to muscle paralysis that would take weeks to heal. Having just woken from a coma, it would have double the effect. Giving no thought to my action, I took a step toward the bed at the same time her lids flew open and her gaze connected with mine. She froze for barely a second before her entire body started shaking and she screamed at me. "No. No. Noooo," the repeated word bounced off the walls with the force of a wrecking ball. "Get away from me!" she howled, the fear in those gray eyes palpable. I backtracked, palms up, my expression apolo-getic. It made no difference. The shuddering intensified.

"Sedative, now!" the attending physician's stern command sent a nurse scurrying to the trolley.

I watched as they prepped the syringe. Winced when the needle pierced the skin on a hand almost gaunt from being in a coma. Felt the burn in my arm when she jerked against the pressure. My stomach roiled at what thoughts zipped through her confused mind right now. My body stiffened at the thought. Did she see us as monsters in the dark? Waking from a coma was a process on its own without the added scare of being held down. Her eyes met mine just as the sedative took hold, and heavy lids closed.

A couple of seconds passed before quiet settled over the room. Nothing but the beep of a heart monitor and the oxygen tank filled the space. Dragging both hands down my face, I left the room and leaned against the wall waiting for her doctor to exit. He did, five minutes later.

"What the fuck was that?" I pounced as soon as he walked out.

The fifty-something, gray-haired man looked at me, his face riddled with concern and exhaustion. "Honestly, I have no idea."

I glared at him. "Don't give me that, doc. That woman's been in a coma for the last three and a half years, surely you've seen this before?"

Slowly, he shook his head. "I understand your frustration, Zayne but I've never seen a coma patient react that way. While it's not conclusive, the only likely reason for her reaction is memory loss."

"Memory loss?" I stared at the man I'd interacted with over the last few years since I'd brought her to the hospital, and they'd induced a coma to protect her brain. Only, she hadn't woken as they expected until now.

"When she came to, she couldn't remember her name. We barely managed to explain the coma before panic set in. Eventually, I calmed her enough to explain that it was probably temporary and once she's fully recovered, it would return. She drifted off to sleep and woke from what I can only assume was a nightmare relating to the trauma she'd suffered. Coupled with memory loss, it must've been a frightening experience."

A nurse approached with a file for him to check. Waiting while he chatted to the nurse, I shook my head in irritation, again wondering what had this woman so terrified that even my face, one she'd never seen before, had her screaming her lungs out. I was no relation, merely someone who happened to be in the right place at the right time. A month later, when no family came forward to claim her and police reports produced nothing, I'd stuck around. To date, I still wasn't sure whether my motives were selfish or simple heroism. Three and a half years of visiting her sleeping form, I'd grown attached, something I never did. I couldn't afford any alliances that could become my weakness, leave me vulnerable. Perhaps a comatose patient proved no threat. Yet here I was, waiting for an explanation to her dramatic-induced awakening with the bated breath of a lover—something I'd never be.

"As I was saying, Zayne." The doctor turned back to me. "Put yourself in her place. You've just woken from a coma with no memory, pure and utter darkness filling the spaces in your mind, there's no telling how you'd react." He sighed. "We just have to wait until she's calm enough for us to question her."

Raking a hand through my hair, I paced a few steps before coming to a stop in front of the tolerant doctor once more. "Giving her a sedative so soon after coming out of a coma. Would that not have any repercussions? Put her back into a comatose state?"

He shook his head. "It's a mild sedative, just to calm her reflexes not put her to sleep."

"So, she's awake?" I was still talking as I walked toward her door.

He caught up with me just as I reached the threshold. "I wouldn't, Zayne."

I turned to look at him. "Let's assume she has memory loss, how would you introduce yourself? She just woke, tests and specific assessments need to be done to ascertain her level of understanding. Give her some time, a day or two. I promise the minute I'm sure it's safe, I'll call you. You're her only point of contact until we know better. If anything, I'm sure she'll be excited to meet the man that saved her life and has been taking care of all her hospital bills."

"Fine," I muttered, irritation pulsing in my veins. She was awake, I deserved to meet her, find out what happened. Offer some reassurance. I walked away. Whether I liked it or not, there were only so many situations within my control, others would just have to wait. For now.

# Ashrika

**THREE AND A HALF YEARS Ago...**

"There's this secret place I go to where everything stands still. Time, life, death. A place where memories don't matter and expectation is just a word. When I'm there, all that matters is that I exist. Me. Alone in a place I created. I know. I understand. No rules, no judgments, no questions. There's no past, no future, just me and the present I create each day. There's no reason to doubt what I forgot or what will follow."

"Does it make you happy?"

I turned away from the window I'd been gazing out of and glanced at the fifty-something man in the blue shirt, navy pants, and red tie. A month ago, he never existed—technically I never existed. Today, I had a name—a name I didn't immediately react to because I either didn't know it was me, they called or I didn't know who they were if I happen to turn in their direction. "I wouldn't say happy, doctor. Just a sense of peace."

My psychologist smiled at me. I'd been seeing him every second day for the last month. "Does it remind you of anything?"

"Like what?" I took a seat in the leather chair opposite him. We were in the studio apartment of the rehab wing. While it wasn't spacious, it was my haven, my measure of comfort and help lay just beyond a pine door, the only entrance, if my anxieties took a turn for the worse.

"Sometimes the images we create in our heads are an actuality of a real place. I'm just asking if it triggered anything."

"Well, if it did then it's certainly a beautiful reality I'm missing out on, don't you think." I could hear the sarcasm in my voice but by now Dr. Landers had learned to ignore it. He understood losing one's memory was not an easy task to mediate. Thankfully, as he'd claimed a couple of times, I was far less antagonistic than some of his other patients.

"Are you ready to go out then, meet the world?" Just the thought of stepping out those doors caused immediate nausea to take up residence in my belly. Slowly I shook my head. "It's been close to a month since you woke from that coma, my dear. And while I'm glad you're eating well and exercising, I think you need to face the reality that an entire world exists outside these doors. The sooner you face it, the better." A vigorous shake of my head followed by me clutching the seat of the chair in a death grip. My expression must've relayed my unease because his hand shot up and his lips widened in a warm smile. "Okay, we'll give it another week then?" I nodded. "What about meeting him?"

"Who?" I knew to whom he referred but ignorance had served me well over the last week or so. One nurse playfully referred to me as a small child discovering the world for the first time. Yet, her kindness every time she looked at me, showed she felt sorry for me. Even though I had no recollection of who I was, I hated people feeling sorry for me. Maybe I was a badass girl before. That idealism seemed to resonate perfectly with my reluctance to either follow instructions or dictate my desires since waking, with a forcefulness the hospital staff hadn't anticipated. They were accommodating regardless and often ended their shifts with gentle well-wishes that the next day would bring back my memories.

"The man who saved you, who's been paying your hospital bills and who's visited every day you've been in that coma. I understand your first meeting was hysterical, but don't you think by now you should be able to handle at least one of his visits? He deserves a kind smile or two, even if you don't want to speak to him."

I stared at the doctor, remembering that first moment I woke. My panic-stricken response to the hospital staff around me when I couldn't remember a simple thing like my name. The anxiety persisted for who knows how long and I eventually drifted off to sleep. Then he appeared and having just woken from a dream—a nightmare actually— of being pulled into a black hole by unknown hands. I gave no thought to who he was or that his features hadn't registered in my distraught brain and I'd blatantly screamed for him to stay away. My terror got significantly worse and had the doctor asking him to stay away. He'd done that and according to the doctor would wait for me to invite him back. So I had a savior, in more than one way, and I had no idea what he looked like.

"Next week?" I asked with a hopeful smile.

Dr. Landers removed his horn-rimmed glasses and set them on the notepad sitting atop his lap, his contemplative gaze on me. "You can't stay here forever, my dear."

"I know." My heart clenched as hot tears burned the back of my lids at the thought that no one had come looking for me.

"He's offered to take you to his home, to take care of you."

"But he doesn't know me, right?" He nodded. "Then why would he want to take care of a stranger?"

Dr. Landers' laugh was low. "As much as you're inclined to believe that only sick men live outside these walls given your injuries, there are good ones too. Kind strangers willing to go out of their way for someone they rescued but don't know, is rare and an opportunity you should seize." He exhaled on a long sigh. "You've been through a traumatic ordeal, Ashrika." The name was still foreign to me. When the doctor asked me to select one, that name sprung to mind with no recollection whatsoever. I would never know if it was my real one or not. There was no one to ask. Blinking, I refocused when he began speaking again. "I would rather release you into the hands of someone I know, even partially, than let you go out alone unless you decide otherwise. We might not know your age, but I can safely deduct you're an adult. So, you're capable of making up your mind."

I lifted my shoulders in a slight shrug. "Just one more week and I'll make a decision, please?" My voice begged him to understand and fortunately, he was the sweetest person I'd met since waking.

He put his glasses back on with a low laugh. "One week, then I'm deciding for you." His scolding came with a gentle smile and had me smiling in response. "Until then, let's work on getting you to walk out of this place without having a panic attack."

I nodded. "Baby steps?"

He rubbed his jaw, his expression thoughtful. "You've been in a coma for close on four years, Ashrika, I'd be remiss if I suggested anything more. I want you to try something for me, okay?" At my nod, he continued, "I want you to go outside from tomorrow. The second you leave that threshold," he gestured to the door, "I want you to concentrate on counting your steps."

"Counting my steps?"

"Yes. When you reach a number you can't go beyond, you turn and count the steps back to your door. Every day, I want you to go twenty steps further or a number you're comfortable with. Can you do that for me?"

I drew in a deep inhale. "What if I can't make it out the door?"

"I will assign a nurse to watch over you and." He set his notepad aside and stood. "I understand your fear, sweetheart but if you don't push yourself into overcoming it, you'll never recover. Don't see your memory loss as a hindrance, use it to bolster your confidence."

"How?"

"What you don't know can't hurt you, but it can direct you into believing it can. Am I wrong in thinking you want to live beyond these walls?" I shook my head. "Then, you'll get there, only if you keep trying. Come." He held out a hand.

I frowned. "Where?"

"We're going to attempt those first steps together." When I hesitated, he offered me a gentle smile. "Believe, Ashrika."

With another deep inhale, I stood and reached out to take his hand. Together, we walked toward the door. Part of me wished I could go home with him. But he was my doctor and I didn't think it was right to burden him with such a request. For now, I had to work up the courage to not only venture outside that door but meet my rescuer, who'd been nothing but understanding.

"ONE THOUSAND AND SIXTEEN," I stopped counting, stood still, and surveyed the area around me. It had taken a week, but I'd done it—I'd taken one thousand and sixteen steps from my apartment to the street outside the gates. While the counting had helped to block out my surroundings and concentrate on walking, now that I'd stopped, I felt the first stirrings of panic at the base of my spine. Slowly, it wound its way upward, heating the back of my neck and thickening the sudden growth in my throat. I glanced around, desperate to get out of the open, away from people walking about and who weren't even looking at me.

"Cut it out, girl, you can do this," I said under my breath. Although this was the furthest I'd ventured, the dread I'd kept at bay for the last week had already started a slow ascent from the pit of my stomach, heading unchecked for my heart, pumping blood faster than I thought my lungs could keep up with. My eyes darted in all directions, landing on a coffee shop a few feet away. Keeping my head down, I made a beeline for the entrance and dropped into the first available table. My body shook. I stared at my trembling hands and clasped them together in the hopes the quivering would abate.

The rate of my heartbeat escalated to a speed that I feared if it persisted, I'd suffer a heart attack. Judging by the sweat dripping from my face into my hands, I'd probably internally combust before the heart attack had a chance to detonate. Forcing myself to calm down, I drew in slow, deep breaths as Dr. Landers had shown me. Epic fail. I jumped when someone stopped by my table and touched my hand.

"Hey, honey, are you okay?"

Nodding furiously, I swallowed and risked a glance up at the smiling waitress. "W-water, p-please," I stuttered.

She stared at me before the tenderness in her smile intensified. "Sure." As she turned away, she glanced over her shoulder. "Deep breaths."

Keeping my eyes downcast, I gulped, wondering if she'd picked up on my anxiety. No shit. I was sweating like a pig and if that wasn't an indication of my panic-stricken state, then the hard pants were a dead giveaway. She returned a couple of seconds later with a glass of water. I grabbed it with both hands and guzzled it down, giving no thought to the contents spilling from the sides of my mouth and wetting my dress. My hand was shaking so badly that when I held the glass out to her, it slipped through my clammy hands. The shattering glass exploded into fragments as it hit the floor, the noise echoed and a hundred pairs of eyes stared my way. Or rather what felt like a hundred pairs. My head swung in all directions in sharp snaps, the heated whispers catching my ears.

I shot to my feet, swiping the cutlery on the table in my rush. The clatter ricocheted through my body, startling my frazzled nerves. I jumped, not recognizing the yelp escaping my lips, "Oh, God."

"Hey, honey, it's—" the waitress reached out a hand.

I shrieked again, shoving at her hand. "Leave me alone." I backed away. Oh, God, they were all coming toward me. They were closing in. "Please..." I pressed a hand to my chest. The rapid rise and fall beneath my fingers was a clear indication I was hyperventilating. I backed away, straight into someone at my rear, sending something flying from their hand. I screamed at the sudden racket.

"It's okay, honey," her soothing voice trying to coax my racing heart, my waitress took another tentative step toward me.

Covering my ears, I shook my head vehemently, tears now blurring my vision. "No," I screeched. "Stay away. All of you." I stammered between hard breaths. Gasping for air, I clutched my throat. Black spots began to darken my vision. I shook my head to focus. "Please," was that me whispering? Someone said something behind me. It didn't register. I shook my head again, the haziness now full-blown, blanking my sight. "Help..." My vision went black as darkness closed in on me. I felt the weight of my body being dragged down. Desperate to let go, I welcomed the obscurity, the oblivion, nothing, the peace.

"Should we move her?"

"No. Let her come to first."

"What do you think happened?"

"Should we call her doctor?"

"No. Let's just give her some room. She needs air. She's had a panic attack."

Several voices filtered through my head, the last one in particular, filled with undisguised concern and oddly familiar, stood out. Deep, husky, and commanding. Was he a doctor? A policeman perhaps? The take-charge attitude lining his words indicated his experience in these kinds of situations. What situation was that? Me making an ass of myself by passing out. I kept my eyes shut. If I opened them, what would I see? Was I ready to face the concerned gazes, the pity, the shame, the curiosity? Would they take me to the hospital if I didn't?

"Hey, can you hear me?" that voice again. This time, soft, calming, tender. I felt the heat of his palm on my skin as he rubbed my arm in gentle circular motions.

Slowly, I opened my eyes and stared up at compelling irises that were neither green nor brown but a combination of both. Golden specks, framed with thick dark lashes added to the gentleness oozing from them.

"Hi. Are you okay?" the deep whisper trickled through a rush of warm air that brushed over my face.

Stupidly, I just stared, taking in the jet-black hair that strangely reminded me of satin and crowned by flecks of gray at the temples. A sharp nose and square jaw lined by a neatly trimmed salt and pepper beard completed the perfection of an extremely handsome man. While my senses were still learning to distinguish between various scents, I was consciously aware of just how good he smelled.

Full, pink lips parted in a slow smile. "Are you okay?" he repeated.

It was only when I moved slightly, that I noticed I was lying with the top half of my body in the crook of his muscular arms cradling me like a child while the rest laid on the floor. Startled by the stranger's nearness, I jerked upright, bringing me into a sitting position.

"You had a panic attack," he explained when I glanced around. Anxiety once again gnawing at my insides to find several curious stares on me. "If you let me, I can take you back to the hospital," he offered, his voice still the epitome of serenity.

I studied his expression for a full minute. Although wary, I saw no threat there yet still couldn't place where I'd heard his voice before. Something about the man's attractive face was strangely magnetic, almost soothing. I felt safe, protected. Immediate calm settled over me. I nodded.

Rising to his feet, he leaned down and offered me a hand. He was tall and I couldn't help noticing the way his black suit and dark shirt molded his powerful build. I might've been in a coma for a while and still adapting to everything, but it seemed like there was nothing wrong with my libido. I was drawn to this man—a random stranger who'd saved me—someone I might never see again. Maybe it was just the sexually potent pheromones he was giving off. Still, I couldn't explain the bizarre tingling sensation snaking over my suddenly heated skin.

"Come on," he coaxed, mistaking my admiration for hesitation.

The second our fingers connected, I shivered. The feeling like a buzz of static electricity passing through my body. Outside, he held open the passenger door to a sleek car. What make, I had no idea except that it looked very sporty. While the hospital was just around the corner, he didn't see the need to walk and gestured for me to get in. Inside, I inhaled deeply. Was it possible to describe a man's cologne as delicious? Whatever it was, the manly fragrance filled my nostrils. When he slid behind the wheel, he hung his jacket on the back of his seat then looked at me. "Comfy?" I nodded. In total contrast to the amount of time it had taken for me to arrive at the coffee shop, it took ten minutes to reach the hospital parking, sign in at the front desk and walk to my apartment.

All through the trip, I said nothing until we reached my door and Dr. Landers appeared out of nowhere. "Hello, my dear. Heard you had a bit of an adventure today?"

Laughing, I opened the apartment door and invited them in. When we were seated, I turned to Dr. Landers "It wasn't a nice one," I whispered cognizant of my savior's gaze on me. He'd chosen to stand at the window making me all too aware of his presence—a quiet, dominating one compared to all the people I'd met since waking, not like there were many.

"Well, it's a start, panic attack and all." Dr. Landers chuckled. "I see you've met Zayne."

"Zayne?" I looked from him to my savior and back again.

Dr. Landers frowned. "You haven't introduced yourself, I take it," he addressed the other man. "Ashrika, this is Zayne Morrone, the man that saved you."

It was my turn to frown. "As in today?"

"No, my dear. He's the man I mentioned to you. The man who found you and brought you to the hospital and who's—"

I gasped, unsure how to react or what to say. I hadn't practiced for this meeting. Winging it, it seemed, worked well, considering I was on my back and out of it for the second time we met. *This* man was my rescuer? This man who looked like he belonged on the cover of some fashionable magazine was my rescuer. "You're the person who's been taking care of me?" I asked, seeking clarification for my overwhelmed mind.

Zayne's smile was slowly becoming a very potent feature—I could be wrong, but I had the feeling that it was a rare occurrence and wondered what his laugh would sound like. "Yes. I'm glad you're finally awake."

"How did you know I'd be at that coffee shop today?" I was suddenly curious to discover everything about him, more importantly how he'd found me. I was still learning to estimate ages and given his salt and pepper look, complemented by his mature features, I put him in his late thirties. I could be wrong.

"I didn't know you'd be there." With infinite slowness, he rolled up the sleeves of his shirt, dragging my eyes to the thickly sinewed arms. I balked at the sudden rush of heat through my lady parts. Okay, it seems my body thought that corded arms were a thing to tease a woman into arousal. I resisted the smile. "I was supposed to visit with you today and stopped there to pick up some of those chocolate almond butter cookies you like."

That was so unexpected, I didn't know whether to smile or laugh. "How do you know I like those, seeing as this is your first visit?"

"He's the reason you like them, Ashrika." At my confused look, Dr. Landers added, "the first time you tasted those cookies, Zayne had sent them with a nurse and when you said you loved them, he made sure you got a fresh batch every day."

"Oh," it was all I could manage. "Thank you."

"You ready to come home with me, Angel?" Zayne neared my seat and stood looking down at me.

"Angel?" I met his gaze head-on.

He nodded. "It fits." My confusion must've shown because he added, "let's just say you were as much an angel to me as I was to you."

"I don't understand."

"You don't have to." I wasn't sure if his tone was dismissive or not, but his next words changed the topic. "I'm ready to leave when you are."

The words registered, spurring a sudden knot in the pit of my stomach and had me breathing faster. I twisted the skirt of my dress in my fingers. *Shit.* I wasn't ready for this, was I?

"I'm not a threat, Ashrika and I'm not going to hurt you." The unexpected statement had me glancing at him.

"Was my expression that obvious?"

One corner of his mouth twitched slightly, the only indication he found my question amusing. "I can practically hear you panicking."

"I'm fine," it came out wooden and his brow shot up, surprising me he could pick up on the lie so easily and I didn't even know him...yet. Feigning ignorance, I shifted my gaze to Dr. Landers, waiting for him to intervene.

His smile was filled with understanding. "We did discuss this, dear. And you promised me a week, remember."

My insides twisted. Yes, I knew this day would eventually arrive, but nothing had prepared me for the likes of Zayne Morrone, I didn't think anything ever would. While appealing, there was just something about him—an enigmatic mystery. He didn't strike me as a sharing man—well, sharing of information that is. Exhaling on a slow breath, I looked at him. "Where would I—we—be staying?" For some reason, my stumble amused him. A hint of a smile crossed his lips then vanished just as quickly.

"I'm taking you to Manhattan. I have an apartment there I think you might like. New beginnings so to speak."

"I haven't even explored this town, I don't see what difference Manhattan would make to me." Aware of the underlying sarcasm to my words, I cringed.

He cocked his head to one side, studying me in a manner I found mildly pleasing and at the same time unnerving, my curiosity growing in folds about the man behind the name.

"I have rooms there as well, my dear, so you can still see me whenever you want." Dr Landers reached across the seat and gently squeezed my hand.

I startled when Zayne dropped to his haunches next to my seat, his expression as serene as the blue sky in the window behind him. "I'm not going to force you into anything you don't want, Ashrika," his voice held a gentle lilt to it, almost hypnotic in its delivery. "But I am going to keep you safe. When you're ready, I'm willing to give you my name and anything else you might need to live without the worry of whether your memories will return or not. All I ask is that you trust me that I have your best interest at heart. Would you?" Amber eyes stared at me, the sincerity in them undisguised.

I'd be a fool to say no to whatever he was offering me, if I did, there was no other avenue to explore. No one had come looking for me which meant I'd need to start a new life, new memories, and looking at the man staring up at me, his smile genuine, that wasn't such a bad idea after all. He was giving me a lot more than my thank you could suffice. I nodded on another slow exhale, not sure if I'd ever be ready to take the next step but I had to. Zayne straightened and moved away to chat to Dr. Landers, leaving me with my thoughts which right now resembled a bird mustering the strength to fly against the wind. There was no predicting that outcome until the journey ended.

# Trent

**PRESENT DAY...**

I parked the car, cut the engine and stared out the windshield. The size of the diner in front of me had me wondering if I'd arrived at the wrong location. My gaze shifted to the neon sign situated front and center above the door to the mid-size building. Nope. I was at the right place. The tinted windows killed my idea of a furtive inspection.

Grabbing my mobile, I moved to open the door when the device buzzed in my hand. I glanced at the name flashing across the screen and answered. "Rayden?"

"Hey, Trent."

"Jesus, man what happened to you? You left the wedding without a word and disappear for almost a month with no contact. You had your father worried, have you called him?"

"Yeah, I'm sorry. I'll call him after I'm done chatting to you." There was no mistaking the tiredness in his voice and I didn't blame him. He'd had a rough couple of months.

"What gives?"

"Zena's alive."

"What?" I glanced at my phone as though I hadn't heard right then put it to my ear again. "That's a sick joke."

Rayden uttered a caustic laugh. "That's what I said. Where are you? I'm heading to your place."

I stalled, debating whether I should tell him. "Enigma," I muttered at length.

"Finally decided on giving New York a taste of your culinary expertise?" He laughed. Considering it was one of Zena's favorite restaurants, his calm surprised me.

"Ray, what do you mean Zena's alive?"

I heard Rayden blow out a heavy breath. "Trent, I'll tell you everything when you get home."

"Cool. I'll see you there." I disconnected the call and drummed my fingers on the wheel, wondering about my cousin's abrupt announcement. Two and half years ago, Rayden's girlfriend was killed in a car accident, traumatized and grieving, he withdrew from family and friends, taking a sabbatical, and traveling Africa. Only, his return home had brought with it a truckload of drama that none of us could have anticipated.

Sighing, I climbed out my Lamborghini and studied the diner once more. A few months ago and after a year of deliberation, I'd mentioned my intention to franchise my global restaurant to the Manhattan market. Rayden had suggested I convince the elusive chef from Enigma to come work for me. Apparently, they served some of the best meals in the city. When his father seconded the idea, I was convinced.

Now, staring at the diner situated along the New York dockyards, I was a little skeptical. I owned a Michelin five-star chain. Would a chef serving diner food hold up in my kitchen?

"Never judge a book by its cover, Trent," I repeated my uncle's advice.

Wondering if I was wasting my fucking time, I shook my head, opened the door into the restaurant, and paused. Not only was I surprised by the classy décor of light brown and gray finishes enhanced with touches of green, but the distinct aroma of citrus, pecan pie, and rich coffee beans sang to the restauranteur in my blood. Grinning, I took another step forward as a pretty brunette approached me.

Her smile wide, I didn't miss the quick slide of her eyes over my suit-clad body before coming back to rest on my face. "Table for one?" I nodded. "This way, please."

Following her, I glanced around the empty restaurant, catching the reserved markers on more than a few tables with a creased brow. "Quiet night?" I asked, taking a seat at the table she indicated.

"No. You're a little early." She checked her watch. "Another forty-five minutes and all these tables will be filled."

"Regulars?"

"Some. I'm guessing it's your first time here?" She touched my hand resting on the table. Her smile an open flaunt.

Any other day I would've flirted but I was here on business. I nodded. "Do you always reserve tables?" I sat back, creating some distance.

"It's a first-come, first-serve basis but we're a little accommodating for the regulars." She smiled. "I'm Tia, I'll be your server tonight. Can I get you something to drink?"

"Any chance I can meet the chef?"

"Getting ahead of yourself, aren't you?" At my frown, she uttered another laugh. "It's your first time, you haven't tasted any of our dishes yet and you want to meet the chef?" She ran an assessing gaze over my face. "You're too handsome to be a food critic."

I laughed at her assumption. "What can I say? I'm an optimistic man?"

"Unfortunately, she isn't one to meet the guests."

"She?"

"The chef"

A female chef. Nice. Might be easier to sway. "Even if I'm willing to try everything on the menu?" I pushed.

Her eyes widened. "Everything?" I nodded before her body shook with laughter. "That's a lot of food."

"Maybe I'm keen to see how good your chef is?"

She offered me a placating smile. "Let me see what I can do. Have a look in the meanwhile." She gestured to the black leather-covered menu in front of me before walking away.

Curious, I opened the menu and although not extensive, I was impressed with the choices. A sudden burst of laughter had me lifting my head. I glanced toward the group of five ladies chatting behind the counter that separated the bar and service area from the dining tables. Judging by the level of noise and clinking champagne glasses, they were celebrating.

"Where's—"

"Finishing off her set up," one of the ladies responded before Tia could finish.

"That woman's going to be the death of me." Tia set her glass down with a snort, strode to the swing door that probably led to the kitchen, and held it open. "Babe." She shouted. "Get your butt out here, now." I grinned, liking her sass. She went back to the group and I wondered which one of them was the chef. The door opened a second later, and a woman stepped out.

I continued watching as she fidgeted with her belt, thick, dark hair shielding her face. Then she lifted her head. "What the—" my gasp was so potent, it had me shooting up from my seat.

Raw emotion slammed through me, forcing a white-knuckle grip on the edge of the table to keep me upright. Oblivious to my shock, she smiled at her friends. Every inch of my body quivered under the strain. Bile surged upward, roiling my stomach as nausea clenched my throat. My heart pounded and I could feel beads of sweat forming in places I'd only ever felt during brutal gym workouts. Another second and our gazes collided.

"Krish," a familiar name I hadn't uttered in a long time, blew through my lips in a soft moan, yet loud enough to drown the deafening boom of my heart and stuttering breath. Paralyzed, I stared, my gaze possessed by her every move—every detail of her. A ball of thick anguish rolled through my body, congealing in my throat, choking me. I struggled to breathe. My thoughts jumped from one to the other—a jumbled mess. I tried to slow them down, to make sense of what I was seeing. I failed. Was the room spinning? I had the sudden urge to drop to my knees as a blurry fuzz invaded my sight. Jesus, was I blacking out?

Without thinking, I took a hurried step forward. Filled with unstable nerves, I stumbled and my thighs hit the table in front of me hard, rattling the wine glasses and silverware. They all turned at the noise, but I couldn't tear my gaze away from her. Her eyes drifted over me in a quick appraisal, her smile morphing into a frown. I waited for that spark of recognition. Nothing. Long, dark lashes fluttered downward, hiding those luminous grays and cresting my disappointment.

"Fuck," I cursed under my shuddering breath. I had to get out of there before they noticed my trembling body. My gaze riveted on her, it took conscious effort to move, each step more laden than the last. Bumping into another table, my arm shot out, catching the wine glass before it rolled off the table. "Fuck," I cursed, as frustration and shock raced to take first place over my frantic emotions. Stumbling out the doors I made it to the car without further embarrassing myself—without giving in to that persistent urge to sink to the floor and understand the illogical vision I'd just seen.

Leaning my palms on the roof to steady myself, I closed my eyes and blew out a slow, shaky breath. Did I overact? *Of course, not*, I immediately counted. It's not every day your wife, or rather your dead wife turned up breathing air and smiling. One look into her eyes stole my breath and then a sudden wave of despair crashed over me. My shocked brain on repeat, how? How could my dead wife be alive? *How?* The word bounced on an echo through my brain.

Only when the car roared through the dockyard gates and traffic evened out into a light stream, did I question my baffled brain.

Impossible. I repeated the word like a protective mantra. I didn't believe in ghosts and I sure as fuck didn't believe in the doppelganger shit I'd often heard my aunt, Tamara, go on about. Why the fuck had she not recognized me? Yes, seven years was a long time between people, but we were never just people, we were married, we loved one another, she was my soul mate, fuck, I thought I was hers.

I made the usual two-hour trip back home at a record-breaking speed. Yet, I was nowhere near to an answer when I pulled the car to a halt outside my home. The urge to move evaded me and left me staring out the windshield, stunned and disorientated. I had no idea how long I sat there, my fingers drumming a haphazard beat on the wheel until the main door opened.

Rayden stood there, his brow creased in question. "What's up?"

I climbed out of the vehicle and as I mounted the front stairs, my seven-year-old kids, Neha and Nicky, came bounding out the door. Without thinking, I knelt and grabbed them both in a desperate hug—thankful that reality, once again, made sense. I hugged them tight until they both squirmed.

"You're killing me, daddy." Neha giggled.

I loosened my hold and leaned back, running a gentle gaze over their curious expressions. Even though they were twins, I found it strange how much Nicky looked like his mother—he had her dimples when he smiled—the knowledge stole my breath, every time. "I love you both so much." I palmed their cheeks with each hand.

"We love you too, daddy," they replied in unison. It never failed to amaze me just how in sync their answers always were.

When they turned and entered the house, I straightened and grasped my cousin's outstretched hand in a quick shake. "Why the fuck do you look like you've seen a ghost?" Rayden smirked.

Cupping my nape, I stared at him unsure if I should tell him or not. *Fuck it.* "Because I think I might have."

His brow shot up. "You're fucking with me?" He laughed then sobered when he caught the dismal shake of my head. "You're serious?"

"I need a drink, stat." Rayden followed me into the house and only when I downed the three fingers of whiskey, did I look at my cousin. "Jesus, Ray, I have no idea what the fuck I saw, but I swear she's the exact image of Krisha."

If my cousin widened his eyes any further, they would've popped out of their sockets. "As in your wife?" His tone just as dubious as I felt. I nodded. "When? Where?"

"Enigma."

"Does she work there? Patron?"

"I think she works there." I poured another drink, this time I sipped it slowly.

"Did you speak to her? Say hello at least?"

I let out an incredulous laugh. "And say what exactly?" I stepped away from the bar and handed him a glass. "Excuse me, but are you my wife? Who, by the way, died at childbirth, seven fucking years ago?" I gritted out the last part then pulled in a frustrated breath.

"Are you planning on going back?"

"Given the shock to my system, I'd probably die from curiosity if I didn't, but I need to play it by ear." Did I have the courage to face a dramatic past in the making? Even as the thought left me, I still couldn't get over seeing Krisha's face again. I had a feeling my dreams tonight would be haunted by her face until I met that woman again. "Enough about me, how are you doing?" I downed my drink and cocked a brow at my cousin.

"I'm good."

"I'm the last person you need to bullshit, Rayden. Have you looked in the mirror?" If anyone knew him well, it would be me. While I hadn't retained the Princeton surname after my father divorced my mother, I was extremely close to Rayden and his family. I studied his withdrawn expression. He was a good-looking man but there was no mistaking the dark circles under his eyes or the consistent droop to his usually smiling mouth. I sighed. "Look, I know discovering your father was in love with your new girlfriend and then walking away takes guts but using your old girlfriend as an excuse to overcome the pain, isn't—"

"I'm not." He stared at me. I frowned. "I left the wedding because I got a call from Zena."

"Christ, Rayden, you seriously believed that? It could've been a prankster—"

"I thought the same thing then I got another call from her. Fuck, Trent." He raked a hand through his hair and I sensed his annoyance. "The desperation in her voice, it nearly killed me." He blew out a frustrated breath. "I've been working with some people to find out the truth. My gut tells me she's alive."

Slowly, I shook my head, wanting this news to be true just for him to smile again. "It's a long shot, Ray, and even if she was alive, how?" I'd just seen *my* dead wife, I should be the last person asking that question.

He shrugged. "That's what I'd like to know. Someone's looking into the body that was found in the car. There's a possibility it might've not been her."

I frowned. "Say you're right, why?"

"No fucking idea. One of the guys I know works for the FBI, he's checking what strings he can pull to get me some information." He took a step toward me with a resigned sigh. "What if you were thinking about Krisha at that moment you saw that woman?"

"Why now then?" I smirked, shaking my head. "Why not the year after she died? Or last year, or the one before. I've thought about my wife often, why specifically now? I know what I saw."

"Maybe you were just hallucinating."

"And you're chasing a fucking ghost, enough said," I snorted. We glanced at each other and burst out laughing. "Jesus, how the hell did we end up in this fucked-up situations?"

"Who the fuck knows." Rayden shook his head. "Maybe it's a sign." I cocked a brow at him. "Maybe you should consider tying the knot again."

"Now you sound like grandma." I widened my stance and leaned back against the bar counter. My father's mother lived with Rayden's family and whenever I visited, she never hesitated to remind me that I was still of marriageable age. At thirty-three, I should think so. I snorted a laugh at the thought.

"You haven't had any serious relationships since Krisha—"

"Yeah, I'm not interested in anything serious."

He studied me for a long moment. "Don't you think the kids need a mother?"

"Nope." I downed the rest of my drink. "I'm all they need."

"Would the sight of Krisha's *ghost* change that notion? Maybe it was another sign telling you that she'd want you to move on, marry again."

I took a deep breath, one I reserved for when grandma or anyone else tried to tell me what Krisha would want me to do, and shrugged. "Life doesn't always go according to plan. Fate is a mean motherfucker, but I've accepted being single. It's best for my kids. And what the fuck is up with you and signs?"

"I'm just desperate to believe in the unbelievable right now, I guess. A month ago, we were both normal men and today we're facing weird-ass situations that don't make sense. Do you blame me?"

Rayden laughed and I grinned. "I agree, fate is twisted but what about what's best for you?"

I didn't answer because it wasn't important. Instead, I stared out the window into the darkness beyond, wondering about the impending changes I could see coming. All I wanted was for my kids to grow up knowing the love of a parent. I wasn't interested in bringing someone home that would either pretend to love my children or worse still turn abusive toward them. It was a risk I wasn't willing to take. The world was already full of shit, I didn't need to add my kids' livelihood to that pile.

"Trent?"

I shifted my gaze back to Rayden's somber features. I got the feeling his so-called calm I encountered from the call earlier that evening, had hit rock bottom. Something was on his mind. "What's up." Looking at me, he exhaled on a huff. "Want to talk about it?" When he still made no move to speak, I gently pushed, "Is it about Zena?"

"There are some things that both mine and her family don't know about us," he blurted before his jaw snapped shut. I got the distinct impression he regretted his words.

"I'm not even going to remind you who you're speaking to, Ray." He knew what I meant. There might be a seven-year gap between us, but it didn't stop us from sharing the filthiest of shit.

He stepped away and raked a hand through his hair. "Fuck this shit," he cursed then swung deadpan eyes back at me. "You know the worst thing about losing a loved one?" I frowned and he continued, "you get to fucking mourn the living crap out of yourself, but you know what's worse?" He paused. "Finding out that loved one is alive." I opened my mouth to agree having gone through the motions of seeing Krisha again, I understood. He shook his head, stalling my words. "But it's got nothing on not knowing where the fuck she is. Jesus, Trent, I'm stuck in a perpetual fucking realm of the unknown. Questioning myself over and over about whether she did the disappearing act to get away from me..." He was ranting now and I let him. "Some shit went down the week before she died...disappeared and even though I convinced her it was okay, it looks like I fucked up."

Turning away, I poured him another drink, stuck it in his hand, and pointed to a chair. "Sit. Let's talk."

Much later, after Rayden finally took my advice and hit the sack and I tucked the kids in, I retired to my study for a nightcap. Giving no thought to my actions, I powered up my laptop and hovered my mouse over the folder titled 'Krisha.' The last time I'd opened the folder happened the evening the kids turned three.

It had taken me almost two years after their birth to accept her death. Each time I opened the folder, memories surfaced, hard and fast, and with it, emotions I'd worked at hiding, especially around the kids. That evening I finally found the courage to say goodbye, begging her to understand that I wanted her to remain in my heart through memories and not photographs. Still, I hadn't felt grief this strong since then. It occasionally simmered on the surface, accompanied by a dull ache behind my breastbone when anyone brought up Krisha.

Leaning my elbow on the armrest, I rolled a finger over my lip, uncertain I wanted to go down this road. *But she's my wife.* A second later, I right-clicked. I smiled at the image of my adorable wife at her prom staring back at me. The first time I met her, it was that wary expression mixed with irritation that captivated me. To date, I still couldn't describe the authenticity behind it or how it radiated the realism of her quiet personality, followed closely by her eyes and the way they lit up like that first radiance of dawn when I kissed her. She'd been an innocent, easily manipulated, flower child, I was the bad boy biker-type with tattoos and long hair. An unlikely couple but she'd come into my life at a time when I'd chosen recklessness as my guilty pleasure and changed that, giving me a new lease on life.

I smiled remembering how her father had run me off his property when I arrived on my motorcycle to take her to the dance. It took us a few dates before I convinced him that I cared for her and swore to love her until death parted us, something I never saw coming.

Sighing, I flicked through the images and sat back in my chair staring at the last photo I'd taken of her standing—a month before the complications began and she'd been ordered to stay off her feet until her due date. I reached out and traced a finger over the image. Memories of those last few hours before she gave birth tightened my stomach muscles. The thought of losing her had taken away my joy over welcoming my kids into the world. Thinking about it, an anvil of pain speared my heart, the weight so dense, it grew in my chest and radiated out to my limbs, burning into every pore. I swallowed to curb the tears.

"How's it possible, Krish?" I tilted my head, studying the dark hair, lustrous grays and dimpled smile. I couldn't have been mistaken. "Maybe I was just distraught with the uncanny resemblance." Shaking my head slowly, I loosened my shoulder-length hair from its tie and raked a hand through it. *"Go back, Trent, and confirm it was no mistake."* Rayden's earlier words rang in my ears. "If it's you, how's that possible?" Even as I repeated the question, the rationality behind the thought sounded implausible.

"Daddy?"

I looked up and smiled. With her stuffed bunny tucked under her arm, Neha stood at the doorway. "Come here, Pixie." When she reached me, I scooped her up onto my lap. "What's wrong? Is Mr. Snuggles not sleeping again?" I took the bunny, kissed it, and nuzzled her neck with its snout.

She giggled. "He's angry with you." She stuck out her bottom lip in a serious pout.

I faked a hurt look. "Really? Why?"

"You promised him that Princess castle he saw on the tele last week, remember?"

I grinned, loving the personification of her stuffed toy. Turning the animal, I stared at it. "I'm sorry, Mr. Snuggles. I was going to buy you that castle, but you've been a bad—"

"Why?" Neha's soft wail cut me off, those brilliant blues taking on an immediate shimmer.

Biting the inside of my cheek to keep from laughing, I replied in a stern voice, "because he's up after bed-time."

"But I've been a good girl." She shoved off my lap and with her arms crossed over her chest, she went to stand on the other side of my table with her back to me.

"Neha, come here, baby." I used my playful tone. Scrunching her lips in a fierce pout, she turned slightly and shook her head. "I'm sorry."

"You're not a nice daddy."

Laughing, I shot off my chair and lunged for her. Squealing, she scrambled around the table, trying to dodge me. I managed to grip her by the waist and tickled her sides making her giggle and squirm to get free. "Daddy!" she shrieked. "Let me go!" Laughter bubbled from her. When she finally sagged against me, I scooped her up in my arms and nuzzled her neck.

"Your Princess castle will be here tomorrow." Grinning, I dropped into my chair once more.

"I love you, daddy," she squealed, throwing her hands around my neck and kissing my cheek.

"I love you too, Pixie."

"Why do you call me Pixie?"

I studied her earnest expression and smiled, realizing I hadn't told her why. The nickname had come naturally the first time I used it—after her first step and she'd wobbled to me, her lips wide in a toothless smile. "I used to call your mommy Pixie."

Excitement widened her smile. "Really?" I nodded. "Why?"

Memories of our initial meeting surfaced. "The first time I met your mommy, she had long hair. I was naughty and every time I saw her, I'd pull on her ponytail when she refused to talk to me."

She covered her quick gasp. "You were a bad daddy?"

Laughing, I tweaked her chin. "When you fall in love one day, you'll understand."

"Yuck. I'm not falling in love if boys are going to pull my hair. The ones in my class are gross." She wrinkled her nose.

"Okay." I grinned, glad that I still had years to go before I had to worry about my daughter losing her heart. "About two weeks later, your mommy cut her hair and I was angry."

"But you didn't know her."

"Well," I paused. "Not really and she didn't want to be friends." I chuckled at the memory of following her after school every day with my motorcycle. She'd walk with her friends, her cheeks always rosy when I threw mischievous comments her way. Then she cut her hair and I saw red. Our first kiss hadn't gone down gently. I took without asking.

"Daddy?" Neha shook my jaw bringing me out of the memories with an impatient snort. "Then what happened."

"I asked her why she cut her hair to look like a boy and she called me stupid, saying it was called a Pixie cut. Then I kissed her and told her she'd be my pixie for the rest of her life."

Neha giggled. "Can I cut my hair like mommy?"

"If you want to." I tugged lightly on her braided hair. "But you'll have to see how short it is first before you decide." I kissed the top of her head, knowing she loved her long, black hair. She sat for hours in front of the mirror playing dress-up and making various hairstyles. I had to judge every one of them when I was home. Lord help me if I didn't like one of them, she'd pout for days.

She turned and stared at my laptop screen. "Why are you looking at mommy's photos?"

All the tickling had caused tendrils to escape her braid. Loosening her tie, I finger-brushed her hair and braided it again "Just remembering mommy today."

She looked up at me. "Do you miss her?"

"Lots."

"Sometimes I wish she hadn't gone away." She stared at me, her expression wistful.

"Me too, Pixie." As she snuggled against my chest, I kissed the top of her head, growing confident by the minute that the woman I'd seen at the restaurant, was my wife. Even though the question 'how' remained at the forefront, I intended to find out the truth. Closing the folder, I made up my mind to go back. It was the only way I'd know for sure. "I'm going away for a couple of days."

"Will you be back soon?"

I pushed her bangs back from her eyes. "Of course, baby. There's just some work I need to get done." I kissed her brow.

"Can you read me a story, please?"

"Sure." Scooping her up into my arms, I headed upstairs. "...and they lived happily ever after," I finished the story thirty minutes later with a quick tickle.

She giggled, pushing my hands away. "Daddy?" she spluttered between laughter.

"Yes."

"Do fairytales come true?"

I sat back on my knees and stared at her. This morning, my answer would've been a simple no. Now, I didn't know what to believe about the way the universe worked. Whether fairytales came true or not I couldn't say but I hoped so, for the sake of my kids. "Fairytales don't come true but nothing stops you from creating your own."

"How?"

I shrugged. "Believe in what you want, work toward it and you'll achieve it."

"What if I want a fairytale to come true for someone else?" She fidgeted with the ears of her bunny.

"Like who?"

"You." Her eyes met mine, brilliant with laughter.

"Me?" I moved to lie next to her.

She turned on her side, her nose inches from mine, and her finger traced the shape of my jaw. "Because I want you to meet a princess and live in a castle."

Surprised, I palmed her cheek with a soft smile. "You and Nicky are my happy ever after, baby. I have my castle right here with the two of you."

"What about a mommy for all of us?"

My brow shot up. This was the first time she'd mentioned me bringing home someone as their mommy. I dated occasionally but nothing permanent. "Do you want a mommy?"

Slowly, she nodded. "Then I can do all the girly things my friends do with their mommies."

"What about me?"

"You can't do girly things, silly." She shrugged.

"I don't want a mommy."

I pushed up onto my elbow. Nicky stood at the door, his lips curled in a fierce scowl. "Hey, champ." Gesturing for him to come closer, I patted the bed. He did as I asked, crawled onto the mattress and knelt between me and Neha. "You don't want a mom?" He shook his head. "Why not?" I glanced between my two children, wondering why I'd never thought to have this discussion before.

Neha's eyes immediately glazed with tears. She opened her mouth to say something, but I stopped her, "It's okay, Pixie, let him speak. What's up, champ?"

Surprise gave me pause when his eyes brightened with tears before he leaned closer, his words soft. "Mommy won't visit my dreams anymore if you bring someone else home. You always told me she watches us from heaven. I don't want to hurt her by loving someone else as a mommy."

Shock sliced through me, stilling my heart at the same time the tiny hairs at the back of my nape stood. Almost like an invisible hand had caressed my neck. It took a few moments for me to regain the ability to react. I clenched my teeth to keep my tears at bay. Sitting up, I stared at him. He'd never displayed any kind of emotion toward his mother's absence in his life before.

"N-Nicky," the single word caught in my throat, struggling to breach the seam of my lips. I swallowed against the lump, reached out and pulled him to my chest, squeezing him tight. When I glanced behind him, tears were rolling down Neha's cheeks. I held out a hand and she scooted into the circle my arms created. I embraced them for a long while until I could trust myself to speak without breaking down.

"Look at me, Nicky," I said when he sat back and dropped his gaze to his fidgeting fingers. Slowly, he lifted his eyes to meet mine. "No one will replace your mom, champ. And no matter what, she will always live here." I touched both their chests. "In your heart and here." I touched their heads. "The memories I helped you create with everything I shared about her, is something no one can steal unless you let them or it's by force. Will you remember that?"

They nodded then Nicky asked, "If you bring us a mommy, will we like her?"

Laughing, I pulled them both back into my embrace. "*If* I do, champ," I replied, hoping that just maybe I'd be able to give my children the perfect mother they needed. Their own.

# Trent

ELEGANT HANDS PLACED a steaming cup of coffee down in front of me. Coming face to face with her, I thought I would be prepared for this meeting, but one look at her heart-shaped face, almond-curved gray eyes and dark curls that were pulled back in a tight ponytail, had me frozen. Trapped in a moment that was unreal at best, before I watched perfect plump lips move. "Here you go, hope you enjoy."

"Thank you," I finally managed. The slightest nod was the only response I got. I opened my mouth to ask her name, but she'd already turned away. "Krish," I called out, hoping to get a reaction, praying she would turn, show me some recognition. *Come on Krish, turn.* Disappointed, I watched as she walked off, not giving me a second glance. Fate was intent on playing tricks. She stopped to speak to another waitress. Deep in conversation, she rolled her fingers over the pendant that hung from her neck, it was something she did when she spoke directly to people—something I'd noticed over the last few days. Maybe a nervous habit she'd picked up in the last seven years.

The entrance door opened. She turned as a customer walked in and while I was jealous at her engaging smile, I couldn't help noticing one distinct difference. Where Krisha had a slight gap between her front teeth, this woman's lips parted to reveal a row of perfect white teeth.

I sat back in my seat and sipped my coffee. "You're not my wife, are you," I whispered above the rim of my cup. Probably. But gaps in the teeth are easily fixed, a part of me argued. Take a walk, Trent. Another part of me urged. Maybe I just needed a break from over-thinking a situation that had a possible explanation. Only, I had no one to ask.

"Back again, I see. Our food must be really good." Tia offered me a small smile as I slid into a seat two hours later.

"Would my return visits now warrant a meeting with the chef?" I'd been there so often, I should take up residence if they'd allow me.

She laughed. "You don't give up, do you?"

I shook my head. "Not when I want something badly."

Her brows pinched together in a frown. "I hope you don't plan on taking this obsession outside the restaurant?"

"You make me sound like a stalker."

"If the shoe fits."

I sighed. "No threat intended. I'm just a curious person."

She seemed to contemplate my words for a moment then shrugged. "Okay, what will it be?"

"A coffee for starters." Despite the delicious aroma wafting from the kitchen every time someone pushed open the swing doors, I couldn't think of food. I was hellbent on getting information about their chef. "What about her name then?" I tried before Tia turned away.

She smiled. "Her name is Rika."

I hid my disappointment, unsure why I expected to hear the name I wanted. "Rika?" Tia was gone before I could ask anything further. Was I living in some stupid time warp?

# Ashrika

"HEY, RIKA, I NEED YOUR help, please."

I glanced up from the finishing touches of the pecan pie as one of the servers, pushed through the swing doors, her hands piled high with dirty dishes. "What's up, Leah?"

"We're kind of swamped out there. Tia hasn't returned from the market and Nina called in sick. We need help if you can spare the hands."

"Whose tables?"

"Tia's."

"Sure. Dean?" I glanced over my shoulder at my sixty-something Sous chef, with his beautiful black skin, muscular build, and infectious smile. "Dean, you don't need me, do you?" While he usually handled lunch and I dinner, we often alternated just to get a feel for the menu and offer each other suggestions.

"Nope, Sweetpea. Got it covered."

Blowing him a kiss, I exchanged my chef's coat for an apron and entered the dining area. The noise of idle chatter and laughter hummed with the clink of knives and forks, it was music to my ears. Still, the lunchtime rush was crazy. An hour later, calm had settled over the floor and the tables were easier to manage. As I set down another order of drinks, I looked up in time to catch a newcomer entering the restaurant. He paused to finish his call. The foyer was a little darker and the sunlight filtering through the windows around us shadowed his appearance making it difficult to discern his facial features.

"Who the hell is that?" Debbie, the new waitress, whispered over my shoulder.

I was about to reply I'd no idea when he started walking toward a table. His stride slow, confident, an almost regal swagger that suggested he was aware of our admiration and unfazed by it before sliding into a seat at one of my tables.

I recognized the man Tia had called Mr. Ballsy and chuckled at the name. Apart from wanting to meet me his first day there, he'd abruptly left without ordering anything and became a regular over the last two weeks. But it wasn't the reason I remembered him. That day, I'd joined the girls to celebrate Nina's engagement and caught sight of the man. He'd shot up out of his seat, his gaze locking with mine briefly before his warm smile morphed into one of pure iciness or shock, I couldn't tell. Then, he'd walked out without a backward glance.

Initially, I didn't think anything of it until he returned. With each visit, I sensed his gaze on me and when I'd turn around, it was to catch him staring. Strangely, the look in his eyes baffled me. They graced me with a sensual caress, something akin to warmth as though he knew me. Though I saw no reason to reciprocate his mysterious smiles, I found myself speculating if he knew me—if he was connected to my past in some way. Admittedly, the man's curiosity intrigued me.

As I approached his table, I had to agree with Tia. He was a looker, and I couldn't help wondering why he'd wanted to meet me in the first place. Pretending interest in my notepad, I studied him beneath the shield of my lashes. There was an imposing presence to the way he carried his tall, athletic build. While there was nothing sexier than a man in a gray suit and black button-down, one with hair long enough to be pulled into a small ponytail and the evidence of tattoos that began on the back of his hands, kicked up my pulse a notch. I suddenly wasn't sure if the aircon was turned up full blast as an inexplicable burn scorched a blazing path from my nape down.

I balked when I noticed his penetrating gaze pinned on me. It felt like more than the typical stare of a diner trying to attract a waitress. Almost like bait on a hook, they were reeling me in, promising the allure of unknown indulgences. Shoving aside my mental visions of what pleasures he'd inflict on a woman's body—well, mine in particular. I pasted a small smile on my face and stepped closer, my nostrils immediately assailed by a masculine scent that was rich and spicy with an underlying freshness.

Squaring my shoulders, I forced calm into my body, barely holding in the need to inhale deeply. "What can I get you?"

Deep probing eyes, the color of a perfect raindrop on a bluebell stared up at me. Even though he didn't answer, the slow slide of his gaze over my body, from head to toe, told me what was on his mind. Warmth unfurled in my chest. I felt like I'd just woken from an extended hibernation, eagerly anticipating something. What? I had no freaking idea.

"What I want." His smile was slow, almost deliberately wicked. "Isn't on the menu." The deep, velvet tone glided over me like the tender stroke of a lover's touch and had me wondering how my name would sound, slipping through those perfect lips.

I shivered. The abrupt action startled me. Wiping my suddenly clammy hand down my apron, I gripped my pen tight, trying to regain the loss of control. Handsome or not, the man held a dangerous impact on my emotions, and I didn't even know him. I lifted my gaze to find him watching me. My cheeks heated. A ghost of a smile curled his lips, confirming he was aware of his effect on me.

"I think what you want, is served on the other side of town. You'll find an interesting variation on the street at negotiable rates too." My tone bordered on brusque.

Maybe I was overcompensating for my body's reaction. Yet I couldn't stop staring at his thick, full lips rimmed by a neatly trimmed beard. His husky laugh echoed an unusual sound that coursed through my already hyped-up body. *What the hell's going on?* I'd never reacted to a stranger this intensely before.

"That may be true but I'm sure it wouldn't be as tasty as what I'd find here?"

Matching his cocked brow with one of my own, I added a slight smirk to my lips. "Since I'm not privy to your tastes, I can neither agree nor disagree. However, if you insist on eating here, I suggest you stick to the menu." Despite my friendly tone, I maintained a level of firmness he wouldn't miss.

I waited while he made a show of contemplating my words. His gaze dropped to my breasts, watching my chest rise and fall with each exhale. I was suddenly self-conscious. Could he make out the lines of my red lace bra beneath my white blouse? Was it thick enough to hide my unexpectedly hard nipples? Trying not to squirm, I fingered my half of a heart pendant attached to a thin gold chain.

"Gorgeous and feisty." He rolled his tongue over his bottom lip. My eyes followed the action and I salivated at the thought of the pink wetness sliding over mine. God, where was this coming from? "Two of my favorite dishes." Those blue eyes roamed over my face, challenging me to smile. I resisted with effort, dropped the pendant, and positioned my pen over the notepad. His gaze latched onto my chest again like a snake that had just spotted prey. I was about to give him a piece of my mind when he said, "nice pendant." Surprised, my brow shot up. "What happened to the other half?" Mistaking my hesitation for my reluctance to answer, a languid smile played around his lips. "As long as it's not broken."

I frowned. "What?"

"Your heart."

I stared at him, unable to read the look in his eyes. I shifted from one foot to the other. "Order please," I squeaked, irked by my own lack of control I had over my voice.

His sudden grin burned a hole right through my stomach. "Recommend anything?" Slowly, he licked his lips, his gaze riveted on me, trying to make me squirm. I wasn't about to give him that satisfaction.

"I'm pretty sure Tia's filled you in on our offerings, so if you don't mind?" I muttered, not bothering to keep the impatience out of my voice. The man was clearly a player, one who obviously commanded attention and took without asking. Fortunately, I wasn't in the market.

At first, he seemed taken aback, and then the warmness in his smile intensified. "I'll try the pecan pie. I believe it's the best in town."

I shrugged. "Wouldn't know, I don't eat what I cook." A stretch of the truth but he didn't need to know that. Wary of newcomers, I hated the strong feelings the man elicited in me without lifting a finger.

"Why don't you eat what you cook?"

I glanced up from my notepad. "When I know the answer, I'll be sure to inform you."

With that, I turned away. Warm hands gripped my wrist, catching me off guard. I gasped, looking down at the strong fingers halting my movement. My heart hammered in my chest. The beat so frantic, it drowned the sound of my uneven breaths. *Oh, God.* Why was he touching me? What the hell was that searing heat radiating up my arm? Adrenaline-infused fear staggered my breathing. I freaked out on the inside. Silently, I congratulated myself on my restraint not to yell as my eyes sparred with his, demanding an explanation for his conceit. But those thousand hues of blue cut through me like a warm knife through butter. If it wasn't for his hesitant smile, I would've believed his intentions were immoral.

"Coffee, please."

He released his hold, and I caught my breath, feeling the immediate loss of warmth. Baffled, I arched a brow then walked away followed by his low chuckle. I could feel his gaze on me, scorching with their intensity. Somewhat intimidated, I snagged Leah's attention as I entered the kitchen. "Table twenty needs a coffee and a slice of pie, please."

She wiggled her brow, her smile mischievous having seen who sat there. "Too hot to handle?"

"More like too cocky."

"That guy?" She hung out her tongue, mimicking a panting dog. "OMG, Rika, his voice alone would give a woman an orgasm."

She wasn't wrong on that account, but I wasn't about to place myself into a situation I knew I'd struggle to get out of. The girls were constantly trying to involve me in the lurid details of their latest sexual conquests. "Whatever tickles your fancy." I grinned. "He's all yours," I called over my shoulder as I entered the walk-in refrigerator to start dinner prep, hoping the cold would chill my flustered emotions.

Yet one thing was undeniable—whatever the man's interest in me was, my body melted with just his stare alone, not to mention his touch. I felt him in my gut, on the little hairs standing at the back of my neck, on my sweat-slickened skin, and deep between my thighs. Shaking my head, I reached for a packet of peas and held it to my brow.

"Who the hell are you?" I asked the empty room. Either my non-existent sex life was seriously begging me for attention, or that man wrote the book on how to seduce a woman without touching.

I was so not ready for this.

So not ready for a man like him.

As I began picking items off the shelves, my little inner voice warned me I'd never be.

# Trent

AMUSED, I WATCHED RIKA walk away. The stiff set of her shoulders told me I'd annoyed or unsettled her, either way, she'd failed to convince me I did not affect her. Under her plain black and white uniform that did little to hide her sensuality, her incredibly sexy body had yelled for me to kiss her or perhaps more. She'd displayed all the signs—flushed cheeks, evasive eye contact, frequent lip biting, a nervous shift from one foot to the other, her tight grip on the pen and notepad, and not forgetting the fidgeting with her necklace. Those actions conveyed a direct contrast to the feisty responses spilling from her lips—nowhere near to the woman I knew, but I was drawn to it and I wanted more. It had taken extreme effort to not pull her down and latch onto her perfectly plump lips.

*Fuck.* I shifted in my seat to avoid adjusting my crotch. Since discovering the woman I'd loved more than life itself might be alive, my dick had taken over my thought processes, leading me on a fucking unlikely pussy chase I hadn't planned on. Then again, plans tended to go astray when the heart was involved.

Despite not getting anywhere, I'd persisted and with each visit, I got to see more of Rika. Although she kept her distance, just watching her tempered the erratic beat of my heart. And as if my luck had turned, I was surprised when she approached to take my order. While I couldn't get a smile out of her, I found her smirk—just a small pouting of pink lips, a narrowing of silver eyes, and a slight tilt of the head—so subtle, yet sexy as fucking hell. If that wasn't enough to bolster my curiosity, the sight of her pendant left me momentarily dumbfounded, confirming I was on the right track. Krisha's parents had gifted her the pendant on her nineteenth birthday. Spurred by the coincidence, my plan to hire Rika took a back seat as my focus shifted to how my dead wife had returned from the grave without me knowing.

"Back again, Mr. Ballsy?"

I looked up to find Tia at my side, her brow raised above a no-nonsense grimace. "Hi." I laughed at her choice of name since I hadn't offered one. "The name's Trent."

"I like Mr. Ballsy," she retorted. I grinned. Her gaze on me, she scraped back a chair and sat. "So. Are you going to tell me the real reason you've returned every day? I know the food is good, but I doubt anyone would want to eat all three meals here every day for almost two weeks."

Grinning, I sat back and stared at the pretty woman across the table. Something told me that her rash mouth more than made up for her petite frame. "I happened to be in the neighborhood."

"Yeah, and my uncle's the next president." She scowled. "Cut the bullshit. You're intent on snagging Rika's attention and something tells me it's not just a case of blue balls. So?"

I threw my head back in a loud laugh. "What's your fascination with my balls?"

"Don't flatter yourself," she huffed. "Answer the question."

"She's a beautiful woman—"

"And?"

I leaned forward deciding to go with the truth—well, some of it. "I want to offer her a job."

"You?" Her tone almost accusing, she didn't look convinced.

"I own The Crystal Oasis."

"As in the global franchise?" I nodded. "You're shitting me." I laughed at her surprise. She eyed me for a moment, her expression openly suspicious. "I must say you've got balls—"

"Yeah, two and they're monster size." I lavished her with a mischievous smile.

She didn't bite and instead muttered, "are you always this arrogant?"

"No. I just know what I want." I shrugged.

Slowly, Tia shook her head. "You've got some nerve. Walking in here, pretending to be interested in the food—"

"I pretended nothing, Tia." I ran an index finger along my chin, keeping my tone light. "I did ask to meet the chef my first day here."

She blew out a frustrated breath realizing I was right. "Well, you're barking up the wrong tree."

"Why?"

"Rika will never leave this place."

"Want to take a bet on that." I raised a brow, and she dared to laugh. "I always get what I want."

"Is that so?" She crossed her arms over her chest, the action matching her defensive expression. "I'm almost tempted to accept the challenge."

"Why do you sound so convinced I'd fail at enticing Rika to leave here?"

"One reason being she loves this place, it's her home."

"Zayne!"

The sudden shout had me glancing away as Rika rushed around the counter and into the arms of a tall, good-looking man. I hadn't noticed him enter and continued watching as he enveloped her in a bear hug, picking her up off the floor. A stab of jealousy pierced my heart. My insides tightened, wishing to be on the receiving end of her embrace and bubbly laughter.

"And that there is the other reason."

Attempting to rein in my resentment, I looked at Tia. "Is that her boyfriend?" She didn't answer. "Husband?" I choked on the word, earning a frown from her. I hadn't noticed a ring on Rika's hand then again, I hadn't actually looked.

"I need to get back to work."

Tia walked away leaving me cursing and fisting my palms with the agony of not knowing Rika's relationship status. As if she sensed my anguish, my gaze collided with my wife's. I smiled. She didn't return the gesture but tilted her head almost like she was studying me. Was she just as curious about me as I was about her or was my earlier taunting a bit too much?

"Remember me, Krisha," I begged, stupidly wondering if the universe had delivered her back into my life, if it would be keen to let her remember me. She turned away and I pulled in a deep breath. "Guess not." I reached for my ringing mobile. "Yes." My frustration spilled through that single word.

"Trent? It's Chris. I've got a copy of those records you wanted."

I straightened in my seat. Chris was a nurse at the hospital where Krisha had given birth. I'd asked for his help to get me her records. "Thanks man, anything out of the ordinary?"

"Sorry, buddy, but nothing I can see that would hint at her walking out of this hospital alive. Her gynae listed the prior complications and all the technical terms associated with her death. It's all straightforward."

"Then how?" the question more for myself than Chris.

"Unless the doctor was involved which is unlikely, there's no other reasonable explanation."

"Doesn't mean just because you can't explain something logically, it can't happen," I muttered.

"Maybe it was a nurse that was involved? I'm pulling at straws here but the day it happened, was there anyone around your wife who appeared a tad suspicious?"

I wracked my brain trying to remember. "Honestly, I can't recall anyone remotely suspicious—wait a minute." I stopped as a memory flashed. "There was a nurse with her when I walked in. She'd helped me hold the kids."

"That's normal. Was she the last person with your wife?"

My heart clenched at the memory—of watching Krisha take her last breath. Then I remembered, she hadn't. "She was. I thought Krisha had gone but she went into cardiac arrest and that nurse sent me out of the room. After that, it's all kind of blurry. Fuck it."

"I understand your frustrations, Trent. Even if she's alive. Why?" Chris had been a friend since college, and I always appreciated his frankness. "Why would she fake her death, supposing she did? If she didn't, what reason would someone have to keep her from you?"

"I've been asking myself that since the first day I saw her." Had we not cremated Krisha, the possibility of digging up her grave would've been non-negotiable. Now, I had no idea if we'd cremated my wife or some other lost soul. "Guess I have a lot more investigating ahead of me."

"Have you tried the direct approach?"

I sighed. "Considering she doesn't recognize me, I doubt I'd get any answers now. I just need to bide my time."

"Probably for the best. What about asking the people around her?"

"The less they know the better, for now." I shifted my gaze from the view outside. Tia was headed toward me. "On second thought I might just ask someone."

"Great. I have to run, but if I find out anything new, I'll call you. I'll also look into that nurse and see if there's anything there."

"Thanks, Chris, I owe you."

Tia stopped at my table, her expression thoughtful. "Why do I get the feeling there's more to your desperate attention than just a mere job offer?"

Smiling, I picked up the coffee refill she set down in front of me. I shrugged, relishing the rich taste of the black liquid then looked away as Rika exited the restaurant with the guy she'd hugged. Clenching my fingers, I steeled myself from rushing after her.

"Judging by that scowl, I'd say you've just answered my question." Tia's curt statement drew my gaze. "Do you want to talk about it?"

"Do you have time?"

She glanced at her watch. "My shift ends in twenty minutes if you're willing to wait?"

"Sure." I wasn't about to look a gift horse in the mouth. She nodded then turned away as a diner signaled for her attention.

Still curious about Rika's relationship status, I glanced out the large windows facing the open water along the docks. My gaze froze on her and her companion standing to one side. Whatever their relationship, they were close, her smile of undisguised affection told me so. Envious, I watched him reach inside his pocket for something before taking her hand. "Fuck. Is he proposing?" I scraped back my chair and stood. "Not if I have anything to say about it," I muttered and headed for the door.

# Ashrika

"WHY DIDN'T YOU TELL me you were coming back today?"

"Because I wanted to surprise you." On the deck outside the restaurant, Zayne turned to face me and tweaked my nose.

I stared up at the handsome man with his dark hair tousled like he'd just gotten out of bed, black V-neck t-shirt sticking to every ridge and hard muscle of his torso. His amber eyes drooled with affection and smiled back at me. There was no denying, the man in front of me screamed power and was intimidating.

Zayne Morrone. My savior, my reason for living, my friend, the only family I knew for the last four years, and my husband. He was my one source of comfort on a bad day, my reason to laugh on a good one and never failed to treat me like a damsel in distress. Yet, an air of foreboding just added to the mystery that was him. Quiet, broody, the *speak when he wanted to* kind of guy, whom I'd come to adore.

"Did you meet anyone nice?" I teased.

He'd left on a business adventure to Japan for the last five months. I had no idea what he did for a living and saw no reason to question him. Even in his absence, I felt his presence in the form of bodyguards he had following me. While they remained invisible, I sought comfort in the knowledge they were around. That was the extent of his care and although we chatted on the phone daily, I missed him like crazy.

"And cheat on the love of my life." Despite the light smile, his words packed a punch.

"Oh, my heart." I placed a hand to my chest and fluttered my lashes. He let out a deep, sexy laugh, mock-punching my chin. "So, what did you bring me for our anniversary?" I wiggled my brows not caring that I sounded like an excited twelve-year-old. With Zayne I could be myself. There were no walls to hide behind. He knew everything about me. Literally.

Grinning, he withdrew a box out of his jacket pocket and opened it. I stared at the center stone, a mixture of pearl and green, set inside a circle of diamonds on a gold band. "Wow. It's beautiful."

"Just like you." I wrinkled my nose at the compliment. Smiling, he took out the ring, set the box on the railing, and reached for my hand. "It's a moonstone, known for new beginnings and said to encourage inner growth and strength." I gazed up at him, my smile wide. "According to the jeweler, when starting afresh, this stone is claimed to soothe those uneasy feelings of stress and instability so you're able to move forward." He slid the ring down my finger then gently kissed it.

Smiling, I admired the precious stone. "How ironic. Given I'm stuck in a—" I broke off as I glanced over Zayne's shoulder, my gaze clashing with eyes that burned hotter than blue flames. Considering he held the ability to steal the oxygen around him, I didn't doubt their intensity.

My arrogant diner raised a brow as if expecting me to respond. With what? A wave? Smile perhaps? I frowned instead, baffled by the abrupt scowl plastered across his face. If I didn't know any better, I could've sworn he was jealous. I almost laughed at the notion before his square jaw worked a smile that prefaced his deviant intentions. My body reacted with a shiver of pleasure that tingled and stirred right down to my nerve endings. His effect on me was bizarre, leaving me confused. Now that he was standing, I couldn't help noticing the way his impressive height filled out his gray suit, hinting at the broad shoulders and a masculine build beneath the expensive material.

"Do you know him?" Zayne broke the connection. I was so caught up in my introspection, I didn't notice him glance over his shoulder.

Mr. Ballsy's appearance threw me for a moment, more precisely his insane effect on me. "What? No, I don't," my reply rushed out between breathless inhales. My already warm face flushed a shade deeper.

Zayne turned to look at me. "You sure?" His lips parted in a slow smile. "Don't think I've seen you this flustered before."

I rolled my eyes more to cover my irritation with the other man's influence on my thoughts once more, yet still stole a glance in his direction. He offered me another decadent smile which under normal circumstances, I would've returned. Normal meaning, he was just an ordinary person greeting me. But with each passing moment, I had to admit there was simply nothing ordinary about him. I balked when he took a step toward us, then seemed to think better of it, changed direction and re-entered the restaurant. Grateful, he hadn't approached, I let out a breath I hadn't realized I was holding.

Zayne noticed though and cocked a brow at me. "Something you want to tell me, baby?"

Although I shook my head, I found myself responding, "I have no idea who he is. Arrived here one evening, asked if he could speak to me then disappeared. Two days later he returned and has been back every day since."

His brow creased. "Want me to speak to him?"

I shrugged. "If you want to. I'm not interested in whatever he's hoping to offer." While I uttered the words, that earlier niggle was back, its taunt clear. Mr. Ballsy didn't look like a man who gave up easily once he set his mind on something. Again, I wondered about his interest in me.

"I think I will." Zayne slid an arm around my shoulders, pulling me tight into his body.

I loved his protectiveness and felt safe when he was around. Together we walked back inside and no matter how hard I tried, I couldn't keep my gaze from straying toward Mr. Ballsy's table. I was surprised to find he'd left. Maybe after seeing Zayne, he'd given up his endeavors to meet me. Strangely, I found myself wanting him to be someone I knew with a lot more intimacy than our less than salient relationship warranted. *What are you thinking, woman?* I admonished myself as Zayne pulled my attention once more.

# Zayne

MY GRIP TIGHTENED ON Ashrika's shoulders as we entered the restaurant. I kept my expression as neutral as possible for her sake, my insides twisted at the possibility that she might have a stalker. Every precaution I'd taken over the last couple of years, could be threatened by someone from her past. The fact that no one had come searching for her before gave me some reprieve and allowed me to let down my guard. Now, all that was about to change.

Concerned, I searched the tables. My pulse kicked up when I couldn't find him. I glanced down at Rika and forced back my agitation with a deep swallow. Our relationship might've started unusually but given her past trauma, I'd protect her with my life. I was the only family she knew, and I aimed to keep it that way. She hated my vigilance, but I made a promise to keep her safe and that's what I intended to do.

"I'll see you just now, okay?" I dropped a quick kiss to her brow and headed for the door.

Outside, I scanned the parking lot and caught sight of him. He leaned against the door of a black Lamborghini Huracan, talking on his mobile. I studied him for a couple of seconds, taking in his suit-clad body as my senses pricked up. Whoever that man was, he was rich, and judging by his mannerisms, he didn't strike me as the stalker type. But I'd learned a long time ago to never take anything at face value.

With measured steps, I approached him. He looked up, noticed me, and cut the call. "What's your interest in Rika?" I didn't waste time with pleasantries.

He ran a slow gaze over me as though he was sizing me up. Although few inches taller, I put him at a couple of years younger than me, yet he reeked of arrogance, immediately scaling my wariness a notch higher.

"Not that it's any of your business but who's asking?"

I clenched my fists. I was known for my short temper and when it came to Rika it got significantly worse. I scowled at the man. "Rika *is* my business."

"Is she your wife?"

"Yes," I replied without hesitation.

"Well, then I think you have a serious problem, Mr. Whoeverthefuckyouare."

I took a step closer. "I think it's you who has the problem."

"I don't think so." The man had the audacity to grin.

"Zayne!"

Ashrika's yell had me stepping back. I looked over my shoulder. She was standing outside the door and shook her head. I knew what that meant. She'd probably read my body language and knew I was a second away from letting the arrogant bastard's face meet my fist.

"Saved by the yell." I sneered.

"I'm going to make this simple for you." My brow shot up at his nonchalance. He straightened, taking his time to adjust the cuffs of his jacket like I had all the fucking time in the world for him. "Your wife has two husbands."

"What?"

"Your wife—"

"I heard you the first time."

"Then you understand that you're married to my wife and I intend to get her back." While his voice was quiet, I didn't miss the hardened tone.

I almost punched the fucker right then and there. Barely able to keep my anger in check. "You've got some fucking nerve, arriving here out of the blue and claiming to be her husband—"

"Would this help?" He drew something out of his inside jacket pocket and handed it over.

I stared at the photo, my insides suddenly churning a shit storm on the worst possible day. There was no mistaking Ashrika's face, her distinct smile or eyes that glowed like tinsel at Christmas as she leaned into the man next to her—the man I now glowered at. "This could've easily been photoshopped." Steel lined my voice, not wanting to believe the obvious evidence in my hand.

"Feel free to get an expert opinion." He shrugged then turned away to open his car door, leaving me feeling a lot more fucking annoyed than when I'd started the confrontation.

"If she is your wife, what happened to her?" I didn't give a shit who he claimed to be as long as I got answers.

He turned to face me. "Apparently she died at childbirth."

"Died? Apparently?" I scoffed, pausing a moment to breathe deeply, because it was impossible not to feel the poisonous darts of anger and disbelief sparring in my chest, heating my blood. His blatant arrogance worked a nerve—the one I reserved for the asshole in me. "What the fuck does that mean? Is she your wife or not?" If it weren't for the photo and the possibility that he might be telling the truth, I would've told him to fuck off. I owed it to Ashrika to find out the truth.

He stared at me for a moment as if contemplating whether to share more. "Unless that woman is a ghost." He gestured to Ashrika still standing at the door. "Then, your guess is as good as mine."

Hoping for more information, I let out a frustrated breath when he slid behind the wheel, closed the door, and drove off. I stared at the taillights until he disappeared around the corner. Slowly, I turned and walked back to the restaurant.

"What happened?" Ashrika's frown cut across her smile when she noticed my expression. "You looked ready to punch the guy's lights out."

I slipped an arm around her waist and guided her back inside. "Nothing to worry your pretty little head about."

"Really? Is that all you're going to say?" She stopped short and scowled. "C'mon, Zayne, you're always shielding me. What are you not telling me?" She stared at me and my heart thumped harshly as I held my breath waiting for her to look deep into my soul, to break through those walls I'd erected to hide my true feelings. To see me as someone other than a friend whose name she used. When I said nothing, she sighed, oblivious to my internal struggle and palmed my cheek. "I'm grateful for everything you do, but I am a big girl you know. Sooner or later, you have to accept that I can handle the truth, whatever it is."

I cupped her face in my hands and dropped a light kiss to her lips. "I will never stop caring for you, Rika and I'm not hiding anything from you."

She inhaled deeply and smiled. "What did he want?"

"He wants to give you a job." Tia came up behind me and I turned, catching the understanding look in her eyes. She and I might not agree on most things but when it came to protecting Ashrika, we remained on the same wavelength. Something told me she'd been needling the guy for information and got the bare minimum, just like me.

"A job?" Ashrika spluttered. "What gave him the idea I was looking?"

"He was told you're the best in the city," Tia explained.

Ashrika bit out a laugh. "Well, fancy that! And all this time I thought the man was stalking me."

My gaze collided with Tia's once more. Her brow shot up. I figured she'd seen me approach the guy and probably wanted to know what I'd learned.

"He owns the Crystal Oasis," Tia offered.

Ashrika arched a brow, disbelief marred her perfect features. "Wait. That's Trent Shaw? Seriously? That guy owns the Crystal Oasis."

"You've heard of him?" I asked. What's wrong with him?"

"Of course, I've heard of the Crystal Oasis and its affluent owner." She laughed. "Just never saw him before. The longish hair and tattoos don't scream billionaire restauranter, does it?"

"Appearances can be deceptive." My lips twitched. "Would you want to work for him?"

Uncertainty sprinted briefly across her features. "I'm surprised you'd even ask that question."

I shrugged. "That's a Michelin five-star chain."

"So." She stepped between me and Tia, slid an arm around each of our waists, and pulled us close. "My place is with you guys. Nothing, not even a deep-voiced, Michelin five-star restauranter is going to make me move for anything. Never."

My gaze met Tia's over Ashrika's head. I couldn't hide the saddened droop to my lips. She frowned. "Never say never, baby," I rubbed Ashrika's lower back.

She looked up at me. "If I didn't know any better, I'd believe you're hoping I accept his job offer."

"Rika," Dean popped his head through the doorway of the kitchen. "I need you, Sweetpea."

"Coming." She kissed my cheek and left.

"What's up?" Tia asked the second Ashrika walked away. "You don't look happy."

I pointed to the deck. Tia followed me outside. "He's her husband."

Tia wasn't ready for my point-blank statement and stumbled. She gripped the railing to keep from falling. "What?"

"That was my response too."

"I don't understand. If he is, why didn't he just say so?"

Placing my arms on the railing, I stared down at the dark water lapping against the pillars that served as the base of the restaurant. "I think he waited for her to recognize him and when she didn't..." I was pulling at straws. "Maybe she had recognized him and was pretending not to know him."

"You think she's afraid of him?"

"Honestly, I have no idea what to think. We don't have a beginning to base anything on, except what Ashrika told us and that wasn't even enough to go on."

Tia rubbed her brow, her expression thoughtful before letting out a slow exhale. "What do you suppose we do? If he returns and questions her, she might run."

I straightened. "When he comes in again, ask him if he's willing to meet me."

"He is." I frowned at her response. "Earlier I asked if he wanted to talk about it and he said yes but I guess your confrontation made him leave. He might be back for dinner."

I ran a finger along my jaw, contemplating my next move. "Try grabbing him before he sits down. Ask him to meet us later at the club." I referred to the gentleman's club I owned.

She nodded then went back inside. I stood on the deck a moment longer deciding if I was ready to face what was coming. Raking a hand through my hair, I groaned. Who the fuck knew that my return from Japan would mess up my plans?

# Trent

"WHY THE HELL IS SHE pretending she doesn't know me?" I pushed away from the wall I'd been leaning against and glared at the man in front of me. What had he done to my wife to force her to forget me? Jealousy was a nasty motherfucker, but I doubted he'd be idiotic enough to keep me from her. Now that I knew she was alive, I would never give her up.

When Tia approached me to meet her friend outside the restaurant, I hadn't expected her friend to be the man who'd confronted me in the parking lot. Now, five minutes into the conversation and I still hadn't been given anything viable. I wanted information about how my wife was still alive. Not some cock and bull story about her being afraid of strangers.

"Believe me I'd like to help you. Give you the information you want. But I can't." Zayne seemed a lot calmer than the man I'd met earlier.

"What the fuck does that mean." Annoyance spurted through my veins. I was through playing games. "Is she my wife?" I barely managed to keep from shouting.

"She has no memory, Trent."

I swiveled sharply to look at Tia. "What?" My breathing stuttered. I could've sworn my heart stopped beating for just a second.

She stepped forward, her hand a gentle touch on my arm. "Rika doesn't remember you. I've asked."

I reared back, the movement so abrupt, her hand dropped. A surge of alarm flooded my body, mind, and soul at precisely the same time my heart resumed its persistent beat. Louder and harder in my chest. "Why just me?"

"No, Trent." Zayne walked around to stand next to Tia. "Not just you. She remembers nothing."

"Like nothing at all?" I couldn't keep the incredulity out of my voice.

"Not even her name." Tia sighed.

Every single muscle tensed, squeezing the breath from my lungs. "But she must remember some of her past, though," I muttered, clinging to hope.

She shook her head, her expression solemn. "Nothing."

For just a beat, the skeptic in me came to the fore. "Is this some sick joke you both concocted to get rid of me? What have you done to her?"

"Are you serious right now?" Zayne gritted. "Why the fuck would we want to get rid of you. Hell, I've been waiting a long time to see if someone would come looking for her. But a fucking husband and a dead wife story wasn't what I expected."

"Looking for her?" I frowned. "How long?"

"Seven years."

I cursed. "That's in line with my wife's death which right now doesn't make sense. Still skeptical, I shot Zayne a quizzical look. "When exactly did you find her?" The second the date left his lips, my body shook with the force of my anger. "That was a couple of weeks after she'd given birth—after I'd cremated my wife. Suffered her loss for—" I broke off, unable to swallow the stubborn lump that suddenly lodged in my throat. "Which means—"

"Rika is your wife." Zayne finished, his expression unreadable.

"Trent," Tia whispered. "Maybe you should sit. Let Zayne fill you in on how he found Rika. And if you still don't believe us..." she trailed off.

Trying to rein in my impatience to go see Rika, I nodded. "Okay." Leaning against the window that overlooked the main floor of the club, I crossed my arms over my chest and waited. Zayne offered me a glass of whiskey before he took a seat on the edge of his table. I tossed back the drink and set the glass on the ledge next to me before he began speaking.

"Seven years ago, this club was an empty shell. A vacant building filled with rubbish and vagrants. A couple of weeks after we'd cleaned out the place and before renovations began, I came out one afternoon to take measurements." He stared at the floor, momentarily lost in his memories. "I was just about to leave when a sound had me mounting the stairs to this room. She was lying in that corner on a dirty mattress." He jerked his chin toward the area behind his table. The blood in my veins turned cold. "Because of the lack of lighting, I assumed she was just another vagrant. When my shouts got no response, I yanked a leg and that's when I caught sight of the chain. She was shackled to the wall by both hands."

Fists clenched, I straightened, every inch of me now a block of ice. "Was she..." I couldn't say the word. Just the thought of some sick bastard touching her shot arrows of rage through my body. The hairs at the back of my nape stood.

Zayne stared at me, his expression consoling. He shook his head, answering my unasked question. "When I finally got her to the hospital, the doctor confirmed that while there'd been no sexual attack, she was heavily drugged on heroin."

"Heroin?" Disbelief spiked my breathing. I dropped into a chair. Hot tears welled in my eyes, threatening to fall.

He nodded. "According to him, she wasn't an addict. So not only was she forcefully injected with that shit, but her body was also covered in bruises. A deep gash to her head made matters worse."

With each word he uttered, pressure built in my chest, constricting my lungs and forcing my heart to pump harder, faster. "God, what did they do to her?" I blinked away the tears to focus on Zayne. "Why?"

He rolled his neck, the agony on his face unmistakable before dropping his gaze to the floor. "Someone left her to bleed to death, Trent. Using the heroin to make her seem like an addict who'd overdosed on that crap." He looked at me and I pinched the bridge of my nose, letting out a deep breath, not wanting to hear his words. But I had to. "The doctor had to induce a coma." At my frown, he let out a long exhale as though reliving the memories were killing him as well.

Tia stood, her eyes glazed with tears. "Because of the injury, it caused a swelling of the brain and given the amount of heroin in her system, they had to be cautious. The coma ensured her brain would rest while they administered the appropriate treatment. Only, she didn't come out of it."

"How long?"

"Three and half years."

"What?" I forced back the rigid curse words with effort.

Tia nodded. "And when she finally woke, she had no memory."

"Fuck." Shoving up out of the chair, I raked both hands through my hair and paced the room. "God, she must've been terrified through all of that and I wasn't there," I gritted through clenched teeth.

"You had no way of knowing, Trent," she consoled. "You thought your wife was dead."

Massaging my brow, I glanced at Zayne. "Was there any help from the cops? Any idea who was responsible?"

"The detective handling the case tried to help. Her fingerprints didn't come up on the system and we couldn't post her picture anywhere. Given the circumstances surrounding her discovery and her injuries, we were advised to proceed with caution. So, we waited."

I kept thinking I was stuck in some goddamn nightmare and any minute now, Krisha would walk through the door to comfort me back into the realm I knew. "Will her memory return?"

Tia took her seat again and folded her hands in her lap. "When he first discovered her memory loss, the doctor said it would take anything from a few days to a few years to return. Or never," she whispered the last part.

"Never," I repeated, dumbstruck. "Fuck, I need to go see her, tell her I'm back." I headed for the door.

"No." Tia sprang up. "You can't."

I pivoted and grasped her arms to prevent her from crashing into me. "Why not?"

Zayne moved to her side. "She's been through an ordeal, Trent. It took her a long time to accept her memory might not return. You can't just tell her—"

Stiffening, I pierced him with an angry glower. "I won't do anything to upset her if that's what you're worried about."

"We know that. But this might be too much too quickly for her to handle," Tia consoled, her eyes imploring me to understand while Zayne's dripped a colossal warning.

If they were waiting for me to say something, they were shit out of luck. I had no idea what to say. I just discovered the woman I loved might never remember me. What did one say to that? Worse. How the fuck do I act like a stranger around her? How do I refrain from crushing her to me the next time I saw her? A string of curse words slipped out as I sidestepped them and walked over to the drink's cabinet. "Do you mind?" I glanced over my shoulder.

"Help yourself. Lord knows we can all do with a drink," he muttered.

Tia shook her head. "Not for me, thanks. I need to leave, Zayne."

As she walked out after saying goodbye, I handed him a glass before downing mine. The stiff drink did nothing to alleviate my tense muscles. Moving to the large window that overlooked the floor below, I glanced around, taking in the scene of what appeared to be a refined gentleman's club. Earlier, I'd come in the back door as per Tia's instructions and had no idea what I walked into. At a glance, it looked like any other bar, but a deeper inspection indicated otherwise. Dark furnishing and soft lighting created an air of mystery and probably a subtle nuance to hide identities. A long bar served by shirtless men, occupied one wall while the rest of the space was cordoned into trendy seating areas. Considering the number of men in expensive suits scattered around either talking or drinking, it was a hugely popular place. Although scantily clad women danced on small podiums, clinging to poles, thrusting either their tits or ass out to gain favor, something told me it wasn't the usual strip club.

"It's a voyeur lounge. You can either watch or fuck while watching. You get the pleasure of both worlds. What you're seeing is just the entertainment area. The performance rooms are another floor down."

I turned at Zayne's explanation. "Didn't figure you for the voyeur type."

"To each his own?" His bottom lip curled slightly into something that resembled a smile, the first normal reaction I'd seen since meeting him.

"And I'm guessing with a name like Incognito, people pay a heck of a lot to keep their identities a secret?"

"We all have secrets, Trent, some more so than others." Something flashed in his eyes that had me curious about the man behind the club. Who was he? Was Rika aware of her husband's occupation? "Entrance is strictly by membership but feel free to come by any time."

"Thanks." Oddly, the digression in conversation settled my frustrated thoughts a little. It gave me a chance to regroup. I cupped the back of my neck trying to massage the stiffness. "Yesterday, you mentioned Rika's your wife?"

"She is," Zayne replied, his non-committal tone had me wondering if it was a love marriage or one of convenience.

I could've just asked but I figured the man would be abrupt in his sharing of information. Unsure how to approach that divulgence, I took a moment to consider my options. Not that I had many. "Then why did you invite me here, knowing who I am?" I asked at length.

"She needs to know her past. I promised her I'd do anything to help."

"Even if it means breaking your heart. Giving her up?" My surprise filtered through my words unsure I'd be that gracious.

"Putting the cart before the horse, aren't you?" He watched me over the rim of his glass then lowered it. "If that's what it takes to give her the happiness she deserves."

"Are you saying she's not happy at the moment?"

"No. But she needs to know she has a family."

"And you'd give her up for that?" While I was grateful for his help, I found it strange a man would just give up his wife without a fight.

He took a moment to respond, sipping his drink as if contemplating my words. "Don't mistake my chivalry for insensitivity, Trent. She's a woman I'll go out of my way to make happy. I'll give her whatever she wants, whatever she asks, to make her whole again. You have my consent for whatever it takes."

"You're giving me permission to sleep with your wife?" Even though I voiced the words, I was grateful that in a world full of morons, she'd found a man like him, someone who loved her as much as I did and if I wasn't mistaken, maybe more. Did I even stand a chance with her?

"I'm permitting you to try your best to get her memory back. I won't stand in your way, but I won't let you take advantage of her." I caught the underlying warning to his words. It was clear as daylight. "Fuck with her emotions and I swear you'll regret walking into her life," he confirmed my thoughts. "I suggest you don't take my threat lightly, I'm a man of my word." I met his stony stare head-on. While I wasn't easily intimidated, something about the look in his eyes, told me I'd be wise to take heed. Not that I intended hurting the only woman I'd loved. "There are two conditions, though." At my raised brow, he continued, "you don't mention this conversation. You don't ask her anything about our relationship."

I found his second condition surprising, seeing as she'd probably question my motives or toss me out on my ass declaring she was a married woman. "I can live with that." While I never let my guard down easily, I was curious. "Supposing it works, how do I get around the cheating aspect?" His questioning gaze made me shrug. "Would she be willing to cheat on you?" He smirked and I wondered if I was being too optimistic too quickly. The woman hadn't even given me the time of day, why the fuck would she sleep with me.

"Leave that to me," he said, pulling my attention. "Just don't go back to the restaurant for now until I say so." I waited for him to elaborate. He said nothing, instead set his glass to the side, crossed his arms over his chest, and leaned against the table. "Can I ask you something?" I nodded. "What if she doesn't remember? Or doesn't take an interest in you? Have you thought about that? You seem to think you're going to get her into your bed with a charming smile," he stated, his tone deprecating.

"Well, then I'll make damn sure she does," I retorted, not bothering to keep the irritation out of my voice. His eyes hardened at my dare, turning his amber gaze almost black. I had a feeling he wasn't usually challenged. Yet his smile was slow, almost triumphant and I wasn't sure if he wanted me to succeed or not. "So, what the fuck would be my next step." Annoyance heated my words.

He observed me for a second as though contemplating his next share then said, "A month before I left for Japan, Rika attended a regressive hypnotherapy session." I frowned. "A patient is hypnotized before the doctor takes them through various scenarios to remember their pasts," he explained.

"I'm guessing it didn't work," I muttered.

"She refused to attend the third session." Shoving his hands into his pockets, he stood and leveled me with a scowl. "Trust me, she's not as easily manipulated as you'd like to think. Once she sets her mind on something, there's no changing it."

I'd probably hit a sore point but found the divulgence intriguing. Krisha was a woman I could bend to my will with just a smile. Perhaps memory loss had a stronger effect on her personality than I expected.

He dragged a hand along his jawline gauging my reaction. "My advice. Don't get your hopes up."

"What would your response be if our roles were reversed?" I snapped. He was seriously beginning to irk the fuck out of me.

"Simple." He shrugged. "I wouldn't have lost my wife in the first place."

I scrunched my fists, a second away from letting his face meet their aggression. "I'm going to pretend you didn't just say that," I hissed on a controlled breath.

My words didn't faze him. "Just remember who needs whom, here." His tone was eerily calm, further maddening me but I held my anger in check, barely. He continued speaking, "I'll set up a meeting with you and her doctor. Let him decide the next step for you?" When I didn't respond, he narrowed his eyes at me. "Take it or leave it. Your choice."

I forced back the irritation lining my throat. "Thanks." He was right. I needed him if I intended to get anywhere with Rika.

"I'll give Dr. Landers a call in the morning."

I handed him my business card and while I headed out the club, my mind drifted over the last thirty minutes. There was no doubt that nothing would've prepared me for Zayne and Tia's divulgence. My wife was alive. How the fuck that had happened would remain a mystery. More so the knowledge that someone had gone through a lot of trouble to not only kidnap her but had gone to such lengths to ensure she'd meet her demise. Why not take her life at the hospital instead?

Yet, even though fate intervened and kept her alive, she remembered nothing. Not me, not us as a couple, our marriage, her pregnancy, her father, and everything else we'd shared. When I slid behind the wheel, I did something I hadn't done in a long time. I gave in to the tears that had threatened the second Zayne began. I was a grown-ass man, but I didn't care. She was the love of my life. Pain gutted me like a knife at the thought of what she must've gone through at the hands of a depraved fuck. Of how she'd missed out on seven years of her children's lives. I shoved my hands in my hair and leaned back in the seat wondering how I could right a wrong, how I could let her know she was loved.

The abrupt ringing of my phone had me reaching inside my jacket pocket. Wiping the tears after a quick swallow, I answered, "Uncle Drake," the formality slipped out before I could stop myself.

"Jesus, Trent, what the fucks going on. First, your message that made no sense, and now this. You haven't called me uncle in forever," Rayden's father snorted over the line. He was right. The last time I'd called him uncle was on my wedding day. As the man I'd looked to for fatherly advice, he'd subsequently labeled me a man and said I was to call him by his name. "I've been out of the country. Landed last night and got your message. You up for that drink now?" He pulled me out of my musing.

"Yeah, sure. The usual in thirty." He agreed and I shot down the street a second after the engine roared to life.

Thirty minutes later, I walked into The Red Rum bar on Fifth Avenue. It was around the corner from Drake's apartment and our usual meeting place whenever we were both in the city. He stood as I approached a table at the back.

Gripping my hand in a firm shake, he took one look at my face and shook his head. "You look like shit."

"Given what I've been through in the last couple of days, I'm not surprised." I managed a grin and dropped into a chair opposite him.

Fifteen minutes and two neat whiskeys later, he observed me over his glass like I'd just told him I was considering checking myself into a mental institute.

"You have no idea what it felt like watching her, Drake. Silently begging, hoping, praying that for just a second she'd recognize me. Not look right through me like *I* was the fucking ghost." I balled my fists to keep from hitting the table as anger poured through me, fueling my desperation. "After what Zayne told me tonight, the only thing I want is to see her, to hold her in my arms and tell her how much I love her, that I'd never forgotten her..." I trailed off as my insides churned, similar to the battering of an aggressive hurricane. Clammy fingers of fear gripped my heart, refusing to let go, tearing into my lungs, squeezing tight. I struggled to breathe. My head spun. "What the fuck is happening?" My body shook. I clenched my teeth, shutting my eyes tight as everything around me blurred to watery shadows and an echo of distant sounds.

"Trent!" Drake's harsh whisper cut through the fog of anxiety stealing my thought processes. "Deep breaths, son, you're having a panic attack." Forcing air into my lungs, I blinked rapidly trying to focus on his hand grasping my arm in a vice-grip before meeting his gaze. Concern masked his expression. "When was the last time you slept?"

"Too fucking long." I shook my head trying to remember when I'd last slept without being haunted by visions of my wife's face.

"Here, drink this." He pushed a glass of orange juice I'd no idea he'd ordered, toward me. Gray eyes filled with the usual fatherly tenderness he'd always lavished on me searched my face and I was suddenly grateful he was around, thankful for his maturity and guidance. If there was anyone who'd know how to handle this situation and calm me the fuck down, it would be him.

"Thanks." I downed the drink, enjoying the bitter freshness sliding down my throat, set the glass on the table, and stared at pulp remnants at the bottom. "I'm a grown-ass man, a father of two kids for Christ's sake, I should be handling this better." I glanced up at my uncle.

His stern features, the ones that spoke to the affluent businessman he was, relaxed into an easy smile. "It's a unique situation, Trent. I don't think anyone is prepared for something like this."

"It feels like a goddamn nightmare some sick wiseass has on a loop," I grunted. "Shit like this is supposed to happen in movies, not fucking real life. I keep wanting someone to remind me it's not real, to believe she hasn't forgotten me." I cupped the back of my neck, massaging lightly to remove the tension tightening the tendons there.

Drake sighed and rubbed his jaw. "It's a normal reaction. Chances are it's going to take a lot more out of you until you know the truth."

I understood what he was saying, and it made sense, but it still didn't calm my racing heart. "How the fuck do I fix this?"

"It's not up to you to fix anything. Let nature run its course. I've always told you everything happens for a reason, right?" he asked. I nodded, remembering the conversations we'd have every time I found myself stuck between decisions. Drake Princeton might be a workaholic, but he always had time for his family. "Trent, if fate intended a quick fix for the two of you then maybe you would've gone to that restaurant sooner, like two and a half years ago, when Rayden first suggested it. You weren't ready then. Maybe the two of you are both ready now to face the future intended for you."

I hoped like hell that was indeed the case. "I keep asking myself now that she's seen me, what if I didn't go to her—if I didn't touch her and whisper in her ear that I'd keep her safe. She might fade further away, forever, never believing I was here for her." My eyes watered. Pinching the bridge of my nose, I leaned back in my chair to stem the flow before it made an appearance.

"I understand your frustrations, but I'm inclined to agree with Zayne." Drake tossed back his drink and toyed with his glass. "What if you tell her the truth and it has the opposite effect? Seven years is a long time to go without hope even if almost half of them were spent in a coma. Would you be able to handle her pulling away from you?"

Dragging a hand down my face, I sat back in my seat. "I have to make sure that never happens." Waving to the waiter for a refill, I continued, "I don't know if I trust her husband."

"Why?"

"I can't answer that. I just get this feeling about him."

Drake laughed. "Considering the guy is willing to give you a little room to explore her feelings, I wouldn't be surprised if you thought any less of him." I frowned and he added, "You have every right to be cautious, but he's her husband. I don't think any man would be prepared for what you've just unleashed on him. Ask yourself if you'd be able to do what he's offered you." He arched a brow, and I couldn't give him an answer. "If it were me, I'd probably show you the door."

I grinned. "I guess you're right. But—"

"No buts, Trent. Suck it up and get your shit together. Love triangles are all kinds of fucked up. Ask me, I know firsthand. I ripped my son's heart to shreds and it took everything from me, let alone what it did to Sianna. If this guy's giving you a hand, don't ask for the whole fucking arm. Take it, until you know better."

Picking up the drink, the waiter set down in front of me, I held the glass out. "Well, here's to however long it takes to finding out the truth." Drake clinked his glass against mine before we drank. "I've looked at this in every possible angle of how and when she was taken and came up blank."

"Before she passed, was Krisha having any problems, minus the pregnancy complications of course?" he asked, his expression thoughtful. I shook my head. "It's a pity her father's in no state to help."

Numb, I blew out a frustrated breath. A week after her death, Krisha's father was an innocent victim in a drive-by shootout according to the police report. The bullet to his brain left him with permanent paralysis. Except for a healthy heartbeat and eyes that stared at nothing, there'd been no other sign to show he understood people around him.

"You'll have to mentally prepare yourself for the days ahead, Trent." He drew my attention. "You're going to need patience, lots of it, and time."

"I guess," I muttered, shoving a hand through my hair. "I'm scared she might never remember me, that her memory might never return."

Drake studied me for a moment then shook his head. "Eight years ago, you were scared to open a restaurant because you didn't think you had it in you. After a little push, you did. Today you're a Michelin five-star restauranteur with franchises in every continent. What did I tell you then?"

"Believe in myself and take it one day at a time. I guess sometimes the unreal *is* more powerful than the real." I sighed, quoting novelist Chuck Palahniuk.

"Exactly. And that's what you have to do now, take it one day at a time and believe in yourself. I'd caution you, though." I frowned and Drake studied me for a moment, his expression guarded. "The question you should be asking yourself is how far you are willing to go to prove to her that she's yours. Zayne's already proven his love for her just by allowing you to enter her life. What sacrifices are you willing to make? What would you do? What would it take?"

And for the first time since leaving Zayne's club, blatant reality hit me in the stomach. Just because I was her husband, didn't make her mine. I needed to throw a lot more into this. Everything from a smile to the damn kitchen sink. If all else failed, the last resort would be to lay on the charm and seduce the fuck out of her. Although the thought crossed my mind, something told me Rika was different. She was no longer the sweet, submissive woman I'd married, she'd probably make me work for it. Good thing I was up for the challenge.

"I can't answer those questions right now."

Drake smiled, toasting me. "What's meant to be, will happen."

I returned the gesture. "Speaking of meant-to-be, how are you doing?" While my drama had just begun, Drake had recently faced his fair share. "How's Sianna?" I asked, referring to my ex-manageress and his wife of one month.

"She keeps me on my toes." He smiled and I chuckled. While I didn't doubt his stamina, having a wife almost twenty years his junior, probably brought its own set of challenges to the bedroom. "Get your mind out of the gutter, boy," Drake scolded as if reading my mind. "Trust me, the bedroom's not a challenge." He chuckled. "I'm afraid my stomach has become her favorite pastime." At my frown, he chuckled. "She's enrolled at a Culinary Art School."

"That's great." She'd always displayed an affinity for becoming a chef and I was glad to hear she was following her dream.

"I now have to try all these crazy dishes she comes up with."

We both laughed.

# Ashrika

"HE SEEMS LIKE A NICE guy, Rika. Give him a chance. Just talk to him. Please."

I stared at Tia, shaking my head. When she asked to be excused for the dinner service last night, I figured she'd gone on a hot date. Now, looking at her rosy features, I was even more convinced. "Why the sudden desperation? And give him a chance at what exactly? Are you trying to get rid of me or do you have a thing for the guy?" Over the last hour, she'd been relentlessly trying to get me to speak to Trent Shaw. Admittedly, the name suited his persona.

Her eyes widened as she uttered a laugh, that sounded nervous to my vigilant ear. "No, silly. Just hear him out. And if you don't like what he has to say then tell him to get lost."

"He wasn't the reason you swapped dinner service with Nina last night, was he?" I rolled my lips to keep from laughing.

"No," she answered a little too quickly.

I winked at her. "I'll think about it, okay?"

She flipped her hair over her shoulder and replied, "Yeah, you do that."

As she walked away, I called out, "Tia?" She half-turned. "It's okay, you know." At her frown, I said, "to date him, no reason to hide."

"I'm not the one he wants, Rika." She'd already pushed through the doors before I could question her further.

Who did the man want? Chewing my bottom lip, I rinsed the carrots I'd been dicing and dropped them into a hot pan on the burner. The aroma of sizzling butter and rosemary filled the air. If the man held ideas that I was interested in his job offer, he'd be disappointed. Shoving aside thoughts of him, I concentrated my attention on the snapper ready for the grill.

"Come on, Rika." Leah blew out a frustrated breath an hour later. "It's just one outing," she pushed while Nina, Tia, Kat, and Debbie pouted on the side.

I scowled at them. They were trying to coax me into attending Nina's bridal shower. Because her boyfriend was planning to move to Chicago, the couple had opted for a short engagement. I doubted there'd ever been a wedding put together that quickly which meant she'd be leaving us soon, hence the over-the-top suggestion for a shower. Since the plan was to go club-hopping, I'd opted out. "Why can't we have it here?" I finally mumbled.

"Someone strangle me before I kill this woman," Tia muttered, taking a step toward me.

Laughing, I wiped my hands on a dishtowel and shrugged. "I'm sure you girls will have a lot more fun without a party pooper like me around."

"Please, Rika, I've worked with you for the last three years, you're like family to me. It's not enough that I have to move to Chicago, a place where I know no one, you not being at my shower slash," she lifted her hands showing me the inverted coma sign, "going away party doesn't feel right. Please?" Nina begged.

Chewing my bottom lip, I took in her distraught features. She was right. When Zayne opened the restaurant for me to keep my mind occupied and stop fretting about the memory loss, I didn't think that within a couple of months, I'd meet such great people like the ladies standing in front of me and Dean. We'd become close and apart from working well together, we trusted each other. We were family. "Fine," I mumbled, knowing I might regret that response as squeals of joy emanated through the kitchen. "God, have mercy on my soul." I grinned, earning a playful punch from Tia.

Later that evening, Tia's voice echoed down the passage. "Ri-ka?"

Figuring Zayne must have let her into the apartment, I called out, "in here." I stepped out of the bathroom as she and the other girls entered the room. "Hi."

"Oh, God. I knew it." She stopped short, pointing to my black slacks and white blouse. "Please don't tell me you're wearing that?"

"Why? And knew what?" I huffed. "What's wrong with what I'm wearing?"

"Is that a trick question, babe?"

"I'm comfortable."

"Yeah, if you're going to the freaking library," she mocked. "Take this the way it's meant, Rika, but you live in a bit of a bub-ble—correction, not a bit, a *big* fucking bubble. Move with the times, would you?"

I took in her red mini-skirt and sequined silver bra top. The other girls wore similar outfits except for Nina, beautiful in a white cocktail dress. "You got me to join you tonight and that's about all I'm doing. Take me or leave me, your choice." I tossed back.

Tia glanced behind her at the other four women and snorted a laugh. "Yeah right. Grab her girls."

"What the—" I gawked as they charged me. Hands flailing, I toppled over, my backside hitting the bed as they grabbed my hands and pinned me down.

"You'll pay for this, Tia," I glared at her.

Laughing, she shrugged. "Whatever it is, it will be so worth it."

After fifteen agonizing minutes of squirming, groaning, and cursing, they led me out of the bedroom. Against the kitchen counter with his back to us, stood Zayne talking on his phone. When Tia cleared her voice, he turned around. He did a double take, lowering his voice as his gaze glided over me.

"Ta-da," Tia announced, her hands showing me off like some freaking mannequin in a store. "What do you think, Zayne?"

Over time, I learned a few things about Zayne. He was the dark, broody type and a man who hardly spoke. His expressions usually conveyed a lot more than his words. He was someone you noticed when he entered and could quiet a room with a look. Yet, I'd never seen the current expression swathing his features. If I had to guess, it was either admiration or incredulity, perhaps sexual interest too. I was unsure about the latter. Warmth spread from my nape down, spawning sensations I'd never felt before.

I fidgeted under his gaze, tugging at the low-waisted white pants that sat so low, the edges of my lace panties peeked above the waistband. Paired with a lace bustier-style top, it was enhanced with spaghetti straps that crisscrossed over my chest. Together with the slits on the sides of the pants from mid-thigh down, it bared so much skin, I was half tempted to go grab Zayne's trench hanging near the door. Admittedly with the silver heels, the outfit screamed classy.

"Jesus, Zayne, would you please say something before she runs and hides that beautiful body." Tia broke the awkward silence.

"Stunning, baby." He dropped his phone on the counter before nearing me. His amber eyes were different in this moment, softer. The professional man I'd come to know with the hard glare was gone, replaced with a man who was looking down at me with love, and something else. Could that be lust? Was this the look he used on women for his sexual transgressions? I didn't want to think about that now or any other woman for that matter, instead, I looked up seeing the beautiful smile spread across his lips. "I've never seen you in anything––"

"Gorgeous, hot, sexy," Tia finished for him making the others laugh with her usual brashness. "Of course, you didn't. Because she's always hiding behind those godawful baggy pants and tshirts," she muttered with a threatening scowl in my direction, almost like she planned on burning my clothes. I covered my chuckle with a hand, dropping my gaze to the floor. God, I loved that woman. "And why do you insist on buying her that shit," she attacked him.

That was another thing. He was also a man you didn't demand *anything* from. Somehow Tia always tried.

"Next time I take her shopping, you can come along as the fashion expert." Although Zayne didn't smile, there was a trace of humor in his cool tone.

It had little effect on Tia. "You do that." She grinned. "Let's go girls." I had no idea what their relationship was but there were days I could've sworn he saw her as a younger sister. Strangely, I never asked, and they never shared.

As we walked toward the door, they preceded me when Zayne latched onto my wrist. I looked back. His smile was gone but something about his expression was unreadable. For once, I wished I knew more about the man behind the name I took. He'd given me everything but himself. Maybe he had his reasons, maybe not and while I never pushed, now I wished I possessed half of Tia's brash confidence to ask him straight out why he'd never sought a sexual relationship with me. Would that make me sound pathetically clingy, needy?

"Enjoy yourself, okay," his soft words penetrated my reflections.

At my nod, he tugged me closer, slipping his hands around my waist. Even though the others stood by the door, Zayne didn't seem to mind. He pressed my hips to his with a firm hand on my lower back, surprising me. He'd held me plenty of times. So why did this embrace feel so different? Standing between his spread legs, I rested my palms on his hard chest. The strum of his heartbeat kicked up a notch beneath his dark lounge shirt. A few buttons opened at the top offered an ample view of his bronze skin. I'd seen him in sweats and tanks that made me sexually aware of his toned perfection. The sudden beading of my nipples, had me swallowing. I wasn't wearing a bra and hoped like hell he couldn't see the hard buds.

Staggered by my thoughts, I moved slightly, biting my lip when I felt his arousal press against my stomach. A shiver raced through my body and I scrunched my lids tight as I tried to control the sensations I was feeling.

Was he cognizant of my body's response to him? I opened my eyes.

"You're trembling, Rika. What's wrong?" he whispered, his lips a hair's breadth from my ear, heightening my already over-stimulated body.

Eyes the color of golden honey, resembling the sun's warmth, studied my face. My body's reaction to him was all new to me. His square jaw, peppered by an afternoon scruff, smoothed into a panty-dropping smile as one brow lifted in slow sexiness, waiting for a reply. I shook my head, afraid if I opened my mouth what answer would slip through.

"You're a stunning woman, and I hope after tonight you'll remember that. Always." I blinked, unsure of what he was not saying? "Do you like the outfit?" he asked.

"Yes."

"I knew it was perfect, the second I saw it."

I frowned. "You bought it?" He nodded. The confirmation spread warmth through my chest and an ache I wasn't sure how to acknowledge. "How did you know I'd agree to go out tonight?"

"I told Tia to use whatever means necessary." At my gasp, his soft laugh, rare and husky, feathered over me. "She's right, you know. You've been hiding for way too long."

His smile remained but the look in his eyes transformed from amusement to a predatory darkness. While his expression concealed what he felt, I could feel a primal need radiating from him.

The sensation made potent by the ferocious glow blazing in those amber orbs, as if he might combust if he didn't have me. I bit my lip to control my breathing because he'd never looked at me like that, ever. Consciously aware of his hand at the base of my spine, it didn't help when he rubbed his thumb over the bare skin. It gave me pause and admittedly made me wet. His gaze dropped to my lips, so brief, I thought I imagined it before his gaze met mine again.

"It's time to live, Angel." Giving me no chance to reply, he dropped a light kiss to my brow and let me go, his hand brushing lightly over my ass as I stepped away. When I reached the door, I turned and looked at him. His relaxed powerful posture leaning up against the kitchen counter, feet crossed at the ankles, this confidant man, whom I called my husband, had a smirk across his face. He knew exactly what he'd just done, how he'd just played my body. "Be safe and have fun, Rika." He waved goodbye, letting me know that our interaction was over for the night.

Nodding, I walked out, stumbling slightly on the threshold. Whether it was from the unaccustomed heels or the effect of the swoon-worthy man I'd just walked away from, I couldn't tell.

"Oh, my God," Debbie breathed, a hand to her lower stomach. "That man is so freaking hot and he's all yours." Being new to the restaurant, she hadn't met Zayne before. She sighed and the other girls laughed. "My knees are all wobbly. I'm surprised I'm still standing."

I blushed, my laugh light and unsure about the 'he's all yours' part. Zayne had never displayed such affection before. Yes, he was always caring, tonight though, there was an unusual sensuality to his smile and his touch. Almost like a man ready to stake his claim. Was he ready to take our relationship one step further or did I just imagine the whole thing?

When we exited the building on the ground floor and stepped through the revolving doors, I was still thinking about his effect on me. Tia nudged me. "Can you at least pretend to be excited for Nina's sake?"

"What did I do?" I frowned.

Her lips curled, and she glowered at me. "Wipe off that scowl, and smile," she chided.

"I'm beginning to think I brought my mom along," I scoffed, earning me a nudge in the ribs. "I'm not scowling, I was thinking of—" I broke off for a second. "A limo?" I stared at the long black vehicle parked out front.

"You have the sweetest husband," Nina called over her shoulder as she climbed in.

"Zayne booked this?" I asked Tia.

She nodded. Then noting my surprise, groaned. "Would you just get in and have some fun? Please?"

After enduring champagne, the girls taking turns to pop their heads through the roof of the limo, screaming cheers to pedestrians, and almost getting stoned by marijuana smoke, I was surprised my head hadn't started spinning when we entered the first club.

"Jesus," I mumbled. "Is this where Manhattan's elite hangout?" I surveyed the trendy set up, noting the number of suit-clad men either sitting or standing around the spacious dancefloor filled mostly with gyrating women. Probably vying for attention.

"Breathe it all in, babe," Leah flared her nostrils, inhaling deeply like she'd just gotten a whiff of my pecan pie she loved so much. "Testosterone at its finest."

"I'll say," I laughed.

"Finally." Tia didn't hide her smirk.

"What?"

"You're laughing," she teased, and I grinned.

I followed them as Nina led the way to a table, not missing the interested glances sent our way from some gorgeous men in fashionable suits that we passed.

I had no idea how long or how many drinks we'd drank when the conversation shifted to sex. How? I had no idea and remained quiet, listening to the banter until Leah pounced on me. "Speaking of sex, what kind of action are you getting, Rika? Is he hot in bed?"

"What?"

"Aww c'mon, enough with the Mother Mary innocence, babe. Last time you mentioned you married Zayne in name only. After three years, you're either fucking him or you're not. That's a hot piece of ass to not want to."

I gaped at her, my mouth hanging open like a goddamn pendulum stuck in motion and too shocked to form a suitable reply.

"Well, judging by the way he was looking at her this evening, I'd say it's a confirmed yes," Nina piped up.

Her statement had the blood freezing in my veins. I wasn't the only one that imagined his reaction. I shifted my gaze to her. "Looking at me?"

"No, Rika, not looking, more of an 'I want to fuck her right now' look," she exhaled on a long sigh. "I'd want my man to look at me like that even after three years of marriage."

I had no idea how to steer the conversation away from me, given I hadn't quite processed the effect Zayne had on me yet.

"I think they're not," Tia surmised then she turned to me. "And if that is indeed the case, I think you should fuck Trent Shaw."

"Yes!" Leah punched the air. "He's fucking hot. You should so do him, babe."

I was now beyond shocked, stuttering I tried to find the right words. "You...You guys, um, do realize I'm your boss, right?" I tried to keep the teasing out of my voice.

"And you do realize this is a sex in the city party, right?" Tia retorted. "So, instead of fucking some random dude tonight, call the hot Trent Shaw and show the man you love a creamy-filled cock and not just sausage and eggs on a Sunday morning."

I choked on my drink. My cheeks flamed before they all broke into a fit of giggles at my expense. When I finally managed to breathe, I shook my head. "I'm not sure which is worse. You girls urging me to cheat on Zayne or insisting that I need sex? And especially from an arrogant ass like him."

"I bet he's one of those controlling dominant types in bed." Leah wiggled her eyebrows, totally ignoring my comment. 'You know, slap that pussy, type."

"And with a voice like his, the sex is probably a lot wetter than this dry Martini." Debbie lifted her glass in a salute.

"Maybe he's into the whole whips and chains stuff." Nina slapped her cheeks like a freaking ad for *Home Alone*.

"Would you girls listen to yourselves?" I barely kept from yelling. My agitation more to do with the myriad of thoughts running through my head that their teasing initiated than anger over their suggestion. "Did you even hear a word I said?"

Leah laughed. "There's a whole world waiting out there for you to explore, Rika. Looks aside, I think Trent's persistence is precisely what you need. And I'm sure Zayne won't mind you taking a lover."

Tia threw back her head and bellowed with laughter. "Oh, my God, guys, look at her face." She pointed to me. "Jesus, babe, we're messing with you. But you need to get into one of those guys' pants pretty soon."

I gave up trying to argue a point I wasn't getting across. "One of these days I'm going to have sex so hot, it's going to make your pussy jealous." I scrunched my nose at her, earning a round of laughter from everyone.

"Atta girl." She slipped a hand around my shoulders and plastered my cheek with a wet sloppy kiss.

By the time we staggered into the fourth club, a name I couldn't pronounce because my words were beginning to slur into each other, I had no idea what disastrous combinations I'd drunk. Not only had the girls kept plying me until I was drowning in alcohol and could barely stand, but they'd also dared me into smoking marijuana. I'd completely forgotten about Trent, Zayne, or their effect on me until I had the intense feeling of being watched. I scanned the club and saw nothing. Nina waved at me from the dance floor. I left them when my aching feet couldn't take it anymore. Tia had followed me back to our reserved booth. That was three dances ago.

Now, I sipped the drink Tia handed me and tapped my feet in time to the music. Another few minutes and I felt the weight of invisible eyes on me again, like static over my skin. I peered into every dim corner until my gaze connected with a man dressed in black, standing across the room. Either I was too drunk or he was too far to make out but the knowledge that he'd been watching me stirred butterflies in my stomach. For just a beat I wondered if it was Zayne. Nope. I stupidly shook my head. He wasn't the club type. Trent maybe? The immediate thought popped up. I grinned. With the copious amounts of alcohol in my system, it gave me the courage to wave at my secret admirer. Watching in anticipation, I waited for his arm to lift, but much to my surprise he didn't wave and I felt disappointed. Was I imagining this man? I broke the connection to grab Tia's arm.

"What's up, babe?" she asked.

"I think Trent's here. Or it could be Zayne. He's watching me." God, was that slur my voice? "Dark hoodie, across the room."

"Why the fuck would he be wearing a hoodie in here," she garbled. "Where?"

"Did I say hoodie? No, I meant a suit or something black? Shit. I'm drunk."

Her line of sight followed my unsteady hand in the direction I pointed. "I don't see anyone."

I looked back to where I'd seen the man only to discover he was no longer there, either I was very drunk or I was very, very drunk, but I was sure that I'd seen him. Laughing at myself I leaned into Tia.

"Maybe you're horny and looking for someone who isn't there," Tia teased. "You need to get laid, babe. Zayne or Trent, make a choice and get your fuck on."

"Why not both?" I mumbled. Mouth agape, Tia yanked at my top and peeked inside then reached for the zipper on my pants. Frowning, I shoved her roving hand aside. "What the hell are you looking for?"

"You," she replied then at my blank look, added, "what the fuck have you done with the real Rika?" She giggled. "Earlier, you bitched about cheating on Zayne. Now, you want to fuck both. I should get you drunk more often."

"Whatever." I shook the craze out of my drunken brain and shot up from my seat, teetering on my heels. "C'mon, I need to pee." I grabbed her hand as a server approached us.

She held out a tray with two drinks before setting them on the table. "From an admirer." I looked in the direction she pointed and sure enough, the man in black lifted his hand in a slight wave, his face still not visible. Optimistic that it was either Trent or Zayne, I waved back then thanked the server.

"Let's go," I said to Tia.

"Never turn down free alcohol." She held out the drink my admirer had sent over. I shook my head, tightening my thighs to keep from peeing right there. "C'mon, Rika, one last drink then we can visit the ladies."

"Fine." I took a few huge gulps of the awful tasting vodka and tonic before my bladder warned me that I needed the bathroom desperately. Scrunching my face against the bitter taste I couldn't get used to, I tugged Tia's arm. "Drink up. I need to pee as in right now."

Instead of drinking, she set the glass on the table. "I'll drink it when we come back."

The resonant bass vibrated through my body as I pushed through the dancing bodies, following Tia to the bathroom. My head resembled spun cotton wool and together with the roving strobe lights made it hard to keep her in my sight. Thankfully, I reached the passage to the bathrooms without tripping over myself. A long line outside the ladies had me cursing. "Jesus, Tia, is the room spinning?"

She giggled like the drunk she was. "No. We're fucked."

I swallowed against nausea churning its way upward. "I think I've reached my puke limit." Rubbing my throat, I propped myself against the wall, trying to stay upright. "Fuck, I've no idea if I'd feel better if I pee or throw up," I groaned, glancing over at the men's bathroom. "There's no line, I'm going in there."

Tia blinked at me trying to focus, her cheeks just as flushed as mine felt. I knew she'd reached her limit too. "Go. I'm going to text the girls to meet us out front if I can fucking stay upright for just a minute." She grabbed her phone out of her purse and held it close to her face, squinting at the numbers. "Just don't fuck Trent now if you see him in the loo, I'm not going to wait for you," she called out as I stumbled across the passage.

I flipped her the bird before I tripped into the men's bathroom door. Thankfully, it was empty. I eased into one of the stalls, squeezed my thighs to hold it in while covering the seat in toilet paper before I sat. "Oh, God, yes," I moaned as alcohol-instigated pee drained from my body. Resting one elbow on my knee I cupped my brow, trying not to fall off the seat. "How the fuck did I end up this drunk," I muttered under my breath then burst out laughing.

Two men, both sexy as sin, had no idea they were to blame for starting my drinking binge. While I'd never contemplated sex with Zayne, his actions before I left home, had me thinking about him.

As for Trent, since the girls' crude remarks about sex with him, I couldn't get the idea out of my head either and opted to drown it under so much alcohol, I couldn't think straight. Yet, once again, just their names and sex in the same sentence twisted my stomach into knots. My heart fluttered and my nipples hardened. Carelessly, thoughts of what the girls mentioned about Trent's probable dominance and eroticism sprinted through my mind. Would he fuck hard or be gentle and sensual? He looked like a man who loved to experiment. I wondered if he'd be willing to give me a try. Oh, God, I didn't just think that.

"Jesus, get a grip, woman. Now isn't the time." With the immediate buzz of arousal between my thighs, it was the reason why Tia might be right. I needed to get laid. Chuckling, I finished off and swayed out of the stall.

I'd just washed my hands when the stall next to the one I'd used, opened and a young guy stepped out. He ran an appreciative glance over my body, and I was instantly wary. He wasn't bad looking but something about his cynical expression had my heart pulsing. Not in a good way. Then I noticed his clothes. I blinked a couple of times, so damn close to pass-out stage it stirred the anxiety already rippling through me. I felt the hairs on my nape stand up, warning me something was not right. Was he the same guy that had watched me, sent over the drink?

I could practically hear his disgusting thoughts, sending chills over my body. I crossed my arms over my chest as the feeling of unease surrounded me, and uncomfortable that the rest of my body laid bare to his appalling leer.

"Must say I love the way you use the bathroom. If you moan like that in there, I can't help wondering what sounds you'd make when being fucked," he drawled.

And that right there was my cue to get out. I turned and wobbled with the abrupt sharpness of the movement. Barely managing to avoid toppling over, I grabbed the edge of the basin to steady myself.

"Aww c'mon, sweetheart, where are you going." He grabbed my wrist and jerked me back against his body, keeping my hands pinned behind me while sliding his other around my waist. "Fuck, you smell good." He ran his nose along my cheek. I cringed, gulping down the nausea.

"Let me go." I tried to push away from him, but he was a big guy and his strong relentless fingers bit deep into my wrist and hip. Adrenaline-induced panic tightened my stomach muscles, squeezing hard until I gasped for air. I tried to force calm into my mind, remembering the techniques Zayne had taught me. Slackening the tension in my body, I waited for the guy to respond. The second his hold loosened slightly, I headed-butted his chin with the back of my head. Wincing with the impact, I grabbed his balls in a grueling twist at the same time I stomped the heel of my shoe with as much strength as I could, into his foot.

"Fuck!" He jerked away, releasing his hold.

Without glancing back, I shot out of the bathroom as fast as my shaky legs could carry me. My cry punched the air as my shoulder smacked into the foyer wall in my rush to escape. My shoulder throbbed and I knew that tomorrow I would be sore and bruised. I didn't care and hurried out the main door. Breathing hard, I searched the passage for my friend. "Shit. Where did you go, Tia?" Trying to remember the way back to the girls, I headed in that direction, bumping into gyrating bodies as I stumbled along. "Damn you, Tia," I cursed when I hit another hard body. "Sorry," I mumbled without looking up. Not like they'd hear me over the loud thrum of music. "Fuck." I stopped, realizing I'd reached the other side of the bar and nowhere near to the girls. Squinting through the darkness, I scanned the floor which was futile and I changed direction trying to head back the way I'd come when someone gripped my wrist.

Dread staggered the oxygen to my lungs, stilling my heart when I glanced up into the face of the same guy. Before I could respond, he dragged me through the throng of people toward the rear door. "Let me go." I yanked my arm, but his grip tightened, hurting me. I didn't care about the pain, my inebriated head not in sync with my panic-stricken body. "Help!" I squeaked, my heaving lungs rejecting my brain's instruction to scream.

No one noticed or heard over the loud booming music. Drunk and laughing, they didn't bother. Maybe this sort of thing happened all the time. Powerless to do anything but attempt tugging on his hold, my limbs froze, refusing to subject my body to further peril. With an abrupt move I didn't anticipate, he turned and jerked me to him. Sliding his hand around my waist, he squeezed hard until I yelped. Fisting my palms, I hit his chest, using all my strength to squirm against his embrace. He merely laughed, pinned my arms to my sides, and pressed me tighter to his arousal. I gasped, panting for air. Desperation filling my body, I struggled with all my might but there was no way I could dislodge the grip of a man who had a good ninety-odd pounds on me.

"My drink deserves a kiss at least, don't you think?" The disgusting stench of beer mixed with something else, slammed my senses. I gagged. "C'mon, sexy, moan for me like you did back in the bathroom." He rolled his hips, pushing his hard-on into my stomach. "You're a feisty bitch, aren't you? But you're going to pay for hurting my nose with that head butt." He squeezed my ass and leaned forward to kiss me.

"Get the fuck off me," I hissed, twisting my head away.

He gripped my hair and yanked my head back, forcing my gaze to meet his. "Stop being a whiny bitch. You know you want this," he sneered, flecks of spit hitting my face. "We can do this here or back at my place. I'm going to fuck you so—"

I had a moment's notice of someone behind me before the man's soulless irises distended in shock, and a fist came flying over my shoulder, connecting with his nose, driving his head into the wall with a loud crack and releasing his hold on me.

"Zayne!" I whipped around my lips wide in a thankful smile which died the second my gaze met eyes the color of indigo rage. "Trent," I whispered, my voice surprisingly calm. The stare directed at my attacker wasn't the look of the cocky man I met but of a fury-induced promise to kill. Not sure if my inebriated brain was dazed, relieved, or freaking turned on—okay, the latter shocked me given I was just assaulted, I felt like one of those damsels in distress where a superhero appeared out of the blue to rescue her. Okay then. I was seriously drunk. Swallowing to purge the 'fuck me now' thoughts, I staggered away, using the wall for support as Trent reached for the guy.

# Trent

I STARED AT THE MOTHERFUCKER who'd dared to touch Rika. My deathly grip twisted his shirt, choking and keeping him upright. "You chose the wrong fucking woman to mess with, fucker." I swung my other arm wide, letting my fist connect repeatedly with his face. Next to me, Ashrika gasped. Ignoring her, I dropped the bastard, his head hitting the floor with a resounding thump. Blood spurted from his nose and busted lips. I didn't give a fuck. "Who the fuck gave you permission to touch her," I punctuated each word with a crunching slam to his face. His hands shot up, trying to defend himself, screaming incoherently. Another couple of heavy hits and the man looked likely to pass out.

People stepped aside, creating room around the fucker when a bouncer, twice my size, moved in. "It's okay, man." He touched my shoulder. I was surprised by his agreeable smile, given I'd just fucked the shit out of a patron. Why wasn't he nailing my ass to the floor for causing a scene? My expression must've conveyed my confusion because he said, "regular troublemaker." Still, I wasn't convinced. His calm didn't resonate with me. I'd seen security go apeshit on patrons that caused a problem. Before I could say anything, he gestured to Rika. "Check on your lady friend, I've got this."

Wiping my bloodied hands on the asshole's shirt, I stood. The bouncer grabbed the guy by the arm and yanked him to his feet. His face covered in blood, he peered at me, his attempt at a glare, pathetic. "Yeah, remember my face, fucker," I sneered. He teetered unsteadily, trying to say something but the bouncer led him away. I watched until they disappeared then swung around to face Rika.

Part of me angry she'd allowed herself to get caught in that trap while the other half argued it wasn't her fault. She flinched and I cursed before relaxing my clenched jaw into a smile. "Are you okay?" She blinked a couple of times as if trying to understand me. I frowned. Either she was terrified out of her mind or drunk, I stepped closer. "Did he hurt you, Rika?" I asked, as I slowly scanned her body, looking for hints of discomfort.

She shook her head. "Can I kiss you?"

I breathed a sigh of relief. The tension left my body as my frown dissolved into laughter. "You're drunk, sweetheart."

She pursed her lips, shaking her head, easily reminding me of Neha when she was trying hard to hide something she couldn't. "Nope." Unsteady, she pushed away from the wall, threw her arms around my neck, and rubbed herself against my body. "Did anyone ever tell you what a sexy as fuck man you are?" she slurred.

I was tempted to record her brazen behavior just to see her squirm when I showed it to her. Laughing, I scooped her up into my arms and she let me. "Did he hurt you?" I repeated. Instead of an answer, she leaned her head against my shoulder, her smile disarmingly sweet. "Are you sure?" I figured she'd feel the after-effects tomorrow. Not only of the alcohol but any injury he might've inflicted on her body. I prayed for that man's sake there wasn't any—I'd track him down if I had to.

I scanned her body once more to ascertain for myself, my eyes devouring her unfamiliar dress sense. I'd only ever seen her fully covered at the restaurant, nothing this revealing. Her outfit was sexy, her 'fuck me heels' even more so, yet neither held a candle to her face, beautiful, flushed, and glowing with raw desire.

"I'm sure," her soft words brushed my neck.

When I headed for the rear door, black-suited security held it open, and she snuggled her head into the crook of my neck, smelling like fresh jasmine. I steeled myself against the effect it was having on my senses, not realizing she was conducting her own sensory exploration of me.

"God, you smell so fucking good." She pulled in a deep inhale through her nose. I grinned, liking this version of her. "I could lick you right now," she followed the startling statement by running the tip of her tongue along my collar bone. I froze. She lifted her head slightly, gray spheres sparkling with blatant lust, roamed over my face before resting on my lips. "Kiss me, please."

My breathing sped up, wishing I could take advantage. Just one kiss, one taste. "You're drunk, Rika," I muttered through clenched teeth and resumed walking.

She palmed my cheek as I reached the car. "Would you fuck me if I asked nicely?"

I must have looked stupefied—only because her words were nipping at my restraint—and her pink lips parted on a lazy exhale before the tip of her tongue snuck out to rim the plump flesh, leaving a glistening trail in its wake. *Fuck.* Was it wrong that I wanted my cock in her mouth right now? Wanting that tongue to stroke my over-sensitive head before I hit the back of her throat and fucked it until she gagged on my cum. I drew in a sharp breath, glad she couldn't see that my jeans had grown a little too tight.

"Do you fuck hard?" Her gaze dropped to my lips, greed painting a small smile around her lips. "My friends say you're probably into the kinky stuff. You know, dominant in the bedroom, pussy slapping, hair pulling. Maybe whips and chains too. Would you show me, if you are?"

Stunned speechless, I barked out a laugh and then stepped back to let the car doors open upward, before bundling her into the seat, glad she didn't say anything further and relieved for the silence that followed. There was only so much temptation my hard-as-fuck dick could endure. I eased her seat back a little and her gaze met mine with a soft sigh. A second later, her dark lashes fluttered downward, kissing her cheeks and hiding those brilliant eyes. But a part of me wondered if she would ever remember what we once had.

When the door closed, I rubbed my jaw debating whether to take her home or back to my place. The aroused part urged me to take her to my apartment knowing I'd fuck her raw until I couldn't stand. The logical part, the one without a demented fucking cock directing it, pushed for me to take her home, to leave her in Zayne's capable hands. And as much as I hated that notion, I finally settled on it and rounded the car to my side.

"Is she okay?" Tia's soft question pulled me out of the carnal argument with myself.

I swung around. She stood on the curb, biting her lip. Surprisingly, she appeared a lot less drunk than her friend. Either she hadn't drunk as much as Rika or she could handle her liquor. "Why the fuck did you leave her alone?" I lashed out, my arousal forgotten.

She reared back, her expression floundering between remorse and fear. "He promised she wouldn't get hurt."

Frowning, I waited for her to elaborate. When I got nothing, I narrowed my eyes. "Are you fucking kidding me?" I snarled. Considering I almost killed the bastard, I balled my fists to keep from reaching out. "Who promised? The fucker who almost raped her?"

She slapped a hand over her mouth. "I'm sorry." She spun on her heels and hurried off before I could say anything further.

Glaring after her retreating figure, I shook my head, questioning her behavior. Tia didn't strike me as someone who'd intentionally leave a friend in the hands of a fucking pervert. Since meeting her, she'd come across as someone who cared for Rika. Drunk or not, she could've been a little more attentive toward her friend. Although I remained doubtful it was deliberate, something just didn't sit right with me, but I couldn't pinpoint the niggle. Was Zayne aware of Tia's fuck up? If he wasn't, how would he react if he found out? Pulling in deep breaths to curb my anger, I slid behind the wheel. Next to me, Rika's soft snore made me smile. Reaching out, I tucked a stray strand behind her ear. She shifted slightly, making soft noises as though displeased with the disturbance. I had the sudden urge to pull her into my arms, to hold her tight and never let go. The interruption of my ringing phone yanked my gaze away.

I answered, "Yeah?"

"Is she hurt?" Zayne's hard voice came across the line. Had Tia called him?

"No. Can't say the same for that fucker though."

"Good," he said, his tone more relief than gratified.

"You knew?" I asked, seeking clarity.

"Tia called me just now." He sounded annoyed. Was he also worried about her behavior?

"I'm bringing her home."

"You're not taking her home?" He sounded surprised.

"Do you want me to?"

"No." He cut the call without a goodbye.

The more I thought about it, the stranger I found his interactions. Maybe I should take him up on his offer. Take his wife home and have my way with her. Appease the ache that began the moment I set eyes on her again. "Fuck." I started the engine, glancing once more at my sleeping beauty. For just a moment I considered kissing her awake. Shaking my head, I eased the Lambo into the main street.

I wasn't into the club scene but when Zayne called asking if I wanted to get close to Rika, I jumped at the chance. Following his instruction four days ago, I'd stayed away from the restaurant and was desperate to see her. Despite my excitement, I had no idea what he had in mind until I steered the car toward the city at a break-neck speed. According to him, it was Rika's first time out at a club and while he could've sent a bodyguard to watch over her, he thought if I happened to meet her and sway her into letting me join their outing, he'd tackle two birds. I wasn't about to say no to the offer.

Only, I'd gone back home the night after our discussion. By the time I made the hour and a half trip into the city, Rika and her friends had already moved to their fourth club, piss drunk by the looks of things. When I arrived, Tia spotted me outside the club. Indicating Rika was in the bathroom, she took me in through a side entrance, a privilege I didn't question and suggested she wait out front in case Rika came out looking for her. I'd reached the bar area in time to catch Rika being dragged by some lowlife toward the back.

Now, glancing at her, I was glad I'd gotten to her in time. My insides twisted at the 'what ifs' and I tried to blank it out, gripping the wheel until my knuckles paled. If I had my way, the fucker would've been dead. Not caring about Zayne's plans, I intended to step up the getting-to-know-her-better bit. And I'd make damn sure, she took notice.

Admittedly it was strange having her in the car next to me, almost like driving us back home after an outing the way I'd done so many times when...*you're not going there*. I blinked the unexpected haze misting my vision. She was here now. I shifted my attention when she moved and found her staring at me with a strange curiosity, almost studying me.

"Hi." I smiled. Expecting the usual wariness, her return gesture surprised me. "You okay?" I handed her bottled water from the middle console and eased the car into a parking spot in front of the address Zayne had given me earlier. She accepted it and took a long drink. As the roar of the engine quieted, I watched the slide of her throat while she drank. Just the smallest of actions had me craving her touch. To keep from pulling her into my arms, I climbed out, walked around to her side, held out my hand, and helped her into the classy building. When she stumbled, I dropped a hand to her lower back, guiding her into the elevator.

About to pull my phone out of my pocket, Rika slammed the emergency stop, fisted my t-shirt and pushed me back to the glass wall, catching me off guard. She rubbed herself against me. Without thinking, I dropped my hands to her hips and tightened the gap. *Fuck.* Her tits, ample and firm scorched my skin as if no material existed between us. This woman had no fucking idea of the hold she had over me.

Our gazes locked, she pushed up onto her toes. "Why won't you kiss me?" she whispered, her lips a breath away from mine. "Do I not turn you on?"

Taking one of her hands, I rubbed it over my hard cock straining against my jeans. "What do you think?" She gasped, trying to pull away. I tightened the grip on her waist, keeping her hand in place. "Are you sure you want me to kiss you?" I squeezed her hand letting her feel the shape of my length.

The telltale slide of her throat the only indication of her reservation. "Yes."

"And what if I want to fuck you against the wall right now, would you let me?"

She inhaled sharply, maintaining eye-contact. Arousal painted her cheeks a soft pink. It glowed in those dilated grays staring at me as anticipation lingered on her deep exhales. I dropped the hand on her waist to squeeze her ass. She shivered, completely oblivious to how close I was to losing control. My cock jerked against her hand, the ache so intense I struggled to breathe. But this was her seduction. I wanted to see how far she'd take it.

"Is your pussy wet for me, Rika?" I removed her hand from my crotch. Cupping both ass cheeks, I pressed her forward. Her hands fell to my arms, her grip tight as my cock pushed into her stomach. "Would you open that pretty pussy for me, sweetheart? Let my tongue lap up that sweet cream you're dripping for me?"

She swallowed, her pulse a fervent tick below her chin. "Please...please," her voice shook.

"Please what, Rika?" Her gaze dropped to my neck. She trembled in my arms. I smiled. "Say the words and I'll give you what you want." Despite my need, I kept my voice low, a husky whisper she fed into, her nails digging into my arms as she pushed herself tighter into my body.

"Fuck..." she drifted off. I cocked a brow. Half expecting her to chicken out, I drew in a sharp breath when she gripped the front of my shirt with both hands and ground herself against me. "Fuck me. Now."

Fuck if that didn't sound so damn sexy that I was ready to take her right there. Reality clanged. I restrained the demand flowing through me, knowing it was the alcohol responsible for the brash woman standing in front of me begging to be fucked. Tomorrow she might not only hate me but herself as well if I took advantage. Still, I wanted her to look at me with those innocent eyes brimming with wild hunger—a need I desperately wanted to tame.

"A kiss, sweetheart, nothing more." *Yeah, right.* My agitated cock cursed my gentility.

Her head tilted, she studied me before her gaze dropped to my lips. I leaned in letting my lips brush against hers. Her lashes drifted downward, concealing her desperation. Slanting my head, I slipped my tongue between her lips, letting out a low moan when her tongue twisted with mine, her softness assaulting my senses. A delicious uncertainty flavored her kiss, taunting me to slow down and stop it before desperation consumed me.

They say the first kiss can steal your soul and I'd kissed this woman a hundred times before she became my wife and a thousand more after, somehow, this was different—sweeter, deeper, electric.

Maybe it was the absence of her taste that doubled the potency. Whatever it was, the subtle hesitation unraveled with each flick of my tongue, making me harder than a steel rod. Her soft groan teased my mouth, her tongue matching my rhythm and when I retreated slightly, she clutched my shoulders, nails digging into my skin through the material of my shirt., I pulled back, exerting self-control. Her rapid breathing matching mine and then she opened her eyes.

She took a step back, the clear reservation in place again like she was physically hesitating over what she wanted to say. "You must think I'm a slut."

I jerked back. "What the fuck?" the words slipped out unchecked, my mouth reacting on instinct before my mind could catch up.

"A married woman asking a man she doesn't know, to fuck her." She laughed. I felt like a real prick for allowing her to self-deprecate. Nausea crept up my throat. I should've had Zayne collect her from the car. I had no business pushing my own agenda in her current state. Mistaking my silence for agreement, she shook her head. "What if I told you—"

A shrill beep filled the cubicle. "Hello. Is everything all right?" a man's voice asked through the speaker above the number panel.

Before I could respond, Rika sidestepped me, stumbled to the door and hit the stop button. We ascended a second later. I waited for her to look at me, but she kept her gaze fixed on the floor, her grip firm on the rail lining the panel next to the door. Tempted to ask her what she was about to tell me, I took a step forward. She swayed and I realized she was trying to stay upright. The door swooshed open, curbing my attempt.

She teetered for a moment and when I reached out to steady her, she shoved my hand aside. "I can manage, thank you." Her smile stayed but her eyes changed into piercing shards of blue and gray.

She was angry and I didn't blame her. Even though she didn't want me to, I followed her to the large black doors of the penthouse suite. She held onto the wall for support and I couldn't help smiling at her sass despite being under the influence. When she stopped and shook her head to focus, the idea that she might've been drugged struck me in the chest like a poisoned dart. I tensed, every muscle burning with unbridled rage. Fisting my hands, I refrained from reaching out to her lest she pushed me away again.

Outside the doors, I waited while she fumbled in her purse. "Fuck it," she muttered a moment later and pressed the buzzer. It opened almost immediately. "Hi," she greeted Zayne with a childish exuberance before zipping past him on unsteady legs.

I watched her disappear around a corner before meeting Zayne's less than friendly stare. He stepped aside, inviting me to enter. I shook my head, not sure how I'd react to their personal space. "I might be mistaken but I think she's been roofied."

A muscle in his jaw spasmed, and I watched his fists clench and unclench as he fought to remain calm. "Did he touch her?" His voice cracked like a whip, failing that attempt.

"As far as I can tell, no." I understood what he was going through having barely managed to keep from killing the fucker. "Look, I could be wrong. She might just be drunk," even though I uttered the words, my insides roiled at another what if. Something didn't add up, though. The bouncer, Tia, and Zayne's behaviors left me curious. "Why do I get the feeling you orchestrated this whole thing?" the question was out before I could stop it.

The shutters slammed down over his features, giving me nothing. No anger. No disbelief. Just a blank slate leaving the observer to paint a picture of what went on inside his head. "You seem like an intelligent man, Trent." I didn't miss the steel-lined tone. Either I'd hit a nerve or insulted him. "I suggest you don't look a gift horse in the mouth." Although his words were quiet, his eyes told me he was a man who ate fear for breakfast, lunch, and dinner. He was someone you'd do best to have as an ally. I pitied his enemy, yet felt no intimidation. He'd have to try harder where Rika was concerned.

"Go check on her." Hiding the desperation to demand he take me to her, I walked away.

It was only when I sat in my car, my fingers on the wheel in a white-knuckled grip, did I acknowledge one of Drake's questions, if not the most important one. How far was I willing to go, to make her mine? Jealousy slithered inside me and I refused to acknowledge it, gritting my jaw as I maneuvered the car onto the main street, joining the rest of the night-lifers that partied until the early hours of the morning. The answer was non-negotiable. "I'll do whatever the fuck it takes. Even if she belongs to you, Zayne."

# Zayne

AS I WATCHED TRENT walking away, sour bile burned in the back of my throat, threatening to surface. Blood rushed through my veins, heating my body to beyond boiling. Someone was going to fucking pay.

Shoving aside those thoughts, for the moment, I focused on Ashrika. "Rika?" I walked into her bedroom, not bothering to knock. I'd been in there plenty of times either to say goodbye when I was leaving or to take care of her during an illness, but I'd never entered unannounced. Drunk or drugged, now was no time for a morality check. The sound of running water caught my ear and the door to her bathroom stood wide open. I paused at the threshold. "Angel?"

Hearing her moan, I stepped further in only to come to an abrupt halt. Her arms crossed over her chest, she stood under the shower, fully clothed with her long hair plastered to her face. I stared, drinking her in. Was it wrong that I burned with the need to caress her body, to make her mine, mark her until she begged me to stop? Perhaps years of pent-up sexual tension had done that to me. I was a man after all. She held the power to bring me to my knees, to make me beg. Only, I had no claim over her.

"What are you doing?" I reached around her and shut off the water. Stepping back, I blinked like an idiot, forcing my gaze not to stray further than her chin.

"I'm hot." Laughing, she pushed wet strands back from her face then dropped her hands to her sides.

My breath hitched and my gaze zoned in on her wet, transparent top. Dark brown nipples taut and visible strained against the soaked fabric as the streams of water caressed her luscious body. Once my gaze latched onto those, I could think of nothing else except how those flawless full breasts would taste in my mouth. Blood rushed to my dick. *Fuck.* Was it wrong that I had the sudden urge to force her to her knees and make her swallow my cock?

I couldn't help but follow the path of her sexy as fuck body, noticing how the slither of flesh on her stomach peppered with goosebumps. Lowering my gaze, I traced the outline of her mound, the soaked fabric of her see-through white pants clung in all the right places, leaving nothing to the imagination.

*Fuck me.*

Subtly I shifted from foot to foot, trying to adjust my rigid cock, and I was sure if she looked, she would see every ridge and slope of my cock tight against the front of my sweatpants, highlighting the fact that I was not wearing any underwear. I never wore briefs to bed, now I wished I had.

The fact that we still stood in the bathroom didn't seem to affect us. I gnashed my teeth, fighting restraint, fighting the need to bend her over the washbasin and fuck her hard.

"Fuck me, Zayne."

My head jerked up. "What did you say?" My words came out in a harsh, breathless rush, not sure I'd heard right. I grimaced, but she didn't seem to notice.

She took a step closer, her lustful gaze skimmed over my shirtless torso, falling to where my sweats hung low on my hips, lingering on my hard cock. When her glazed eyes met mine, her tongue peeked out, tracing a slow provocative lick over her bottom lip.

"I said, I want you to fuck me." Her husky laugh taunted me and had my balls pulling tight, begging for release.

She took another unsteady step forward, bringing her within an inch of my body. Her soft, tantalizing fingers trailed an unhurried path up my abs, over my chest, circling first one nipple and then dragged it across to the other. I swallowed hard, trying to control my breathing. Her sharp fingernails scraped across my skin before moving higher up to my shoulders, neck, jaw, and then traced the shape of my lips where she stuck one lone finger inside my mouth. I instinctively grabbed her hand, pushing it away, and closed my eyes.

I needed to gain my control back. The sound of her unzipping her pants had me opening them with urgency. And I watched as the wet fabric of her pants fell to the floor with a wet slap, leaving her standing in nothing but her sexy as fuck barely there, white lace panties. My brain and my dick were both engorged, and my imagination ran rampant with illicit thoughts of how I wanted to bend her body to my will. I closed my eyes, trying to unsee what stood before me. Perfection personified.

"You're drunk, Rika." I opened my eyes relieved that my voice sounded normal—cool and controlled.

Her smile faded, switching from anxiety to anger in quick succession. She stepped back. "What's wrong with me? You're my husband. Or maybe you find me repulsive, is that it?" Her usually sweet voice echoed with uninhibited sarcasm. She pinned me with a look I'd never seen before. If I had to guess, it toyed between dislike and irritation. Her chin lifted, insolence glittered in those grays. "You know what, take your fucking chivalry and go fuck yourself." She flipped me the bird and zig-zagged out of the bathroom, slamming the door behind her.

I stood there too dumbfounded to move. Her words stung. Call it hurt, call it pride, I didn't fucking care, but knowing I'd done everything possible over the last three years to keep her safe, to not take advantage of her, those words hurt. Enraged, I went after her, not caring that it was the alcohol speaking. I needed my control back in place and she possessed it. With one fucking look, one fucking smile—every fucking day.

In panties and silver heels, she stood in the darkened dining room, drinking Vodka straight out of the bottle. On her way out the bedroom, she'd removed her top giving me a full view of those creamy breasts I longed to taste. Gripping her nape, my fingers tangling in her wet hair, I spun her around. I glared at her, taking a deep breath as my chest rose and fell and my nostrils flared showing her just how annoyed I was.

"What the fuck do you want from me?" I demanded, wishing for the usual calm I always exercised with her. With my barely-restrained breathing, my words sounded more like a carnal threat. So much for getting my fucking control back.

My tall frame towered over her petite body, but that did not stop her defiant gray eyes from challenging me. Her blatant dare mirrored my growing hunger, and she fucking knew it. She wasn't in control of her faculties, and that should have been my reason to stop this insanity, but being the bastard that I was, I could never walk away from a challenge. Then she bit her lip, those perfect white teeth burrowing deep into that full, plump flesh and I lost my last vestige of control, crushing my mouth to hers. The bottle fell, hitting the floor with a resounding crash that hardly registered. Grinding my mouth over hers and forcing my tongue between the seam of her lips, I took what I always wanted.

There were times I imagined our first kiss, it would've been slow, sensual, and sweet. Nothing like the blistering heat or aggressive dance our mouths currently battled. I would've stopped if it wasn't for the way she rubbed her firm tits against my naked chest. Or her fingers slipping into my hair, tightening their grip and urging me closer, or the tiny noises slipping from the back of her throat into my mouth. I would've wanted to taste and savor. Now greedy, I plundered, explored, and stole. Her breath, her sounds, her sweetness. Touching her was like sniffing the strongest drug, whatever the outcome, it was that first glimpse of euphoria that mattered.

And I had a feeling that this would leave me on a high for a long time to come.

When I finally ripped my mouth from hers, we were both breathing hard. Her gaze trapped mine and some gallant part of me silently urged that she walked away. Not because I wanted this seduction to end. Fuck I wanted it—an obsession I never truly allowed myself—desperation I desired more than oxygen itself. But because I didn't want her to regret it the second it was over or when she woke in the morning realizing what she'd done, hating herself, hating me.

Her eyes locked with mine, she backed away until her rear bumped the bar counter. Still, she didn't speak. But she didn't have to—I'd known this woman for the better part of seven years, even if three and half of them were spent in a coma, I could read every expression of hers, every smile, every breath. We might've shared our first kiss just a few seconds ago but I was sure that I'd be able to read every heartbeat, every tremble, every sigh, if she let me. I took a step forward and she watched my feet as I prowled toward her. My desire unashamedly tangible, her hunger just as voracious filling the air between us and mocking my willpower.

*You've waited for a long time for this, Zayne, you want it.* Did she? "Turn around, Rika."

Without blinking, she turned, braced her hands on the countertop, then lowered her body to the cold marble, her back perfectly arched, her glorious ass pushed out, and her sculpted legs stretched as she balanced on her toes. I wanted nothing more than to sink my aching cock inside her pussy that had tempted me for years. Instead, I studied each angled contour of her stunning body, drinking my fill, as a man starved. The only light in the room came from the glow of the building opposite and cast varying shadows across her bronze skin. Reaching out, I dragged a slow finger from the back of her neck, trailing down over each vertebra, feeling her heated skin prickle, watching my finger disappear between the round globes of her ass, and hearing her breath hitch. I gathered her thick hair, wrapping it into a tight ponytail around my hand, tugging, until her body bent like a bow, and she looked up at me, her eyes wide in anticipation.

From this angle, her perfect mouth looked ready to swallow the full length of my cock to the hilt. As though privy to my thoughts, she licked her lips in a slow, deliberate taunt. Just the notion of fucking that tempting mouth had my cock twitching in my pants. Slackening my hold so she could straighten, I held onto her hair but inched closer until my body stood flush against hers. Sliding my free hand around her waist, I cupped her pussy, pressing down lightly enough to elicit a soft groan from her.

"Which would you prefer, Rika," I growled in her ear. "Do you want me to fuck this sweet cunt?" I slid my hand inside her panties and dragged a finger through her slit. Fuck, she was drenched. She shuddered. "Or maybe I should fuck this tight ass." I rolled my hips, letting my hard cock slide along the cleft of her ass cheeks while my finger pushed into her pussy.

"Zayne, please," she cried out, her hips bucking.

I released her hair and palmed a breast while adding another finger to her soaking cunt. Her knees buckled and she leaned back against me. Rubbing my thumb back and forth over the tight puckered bud of her nipple. "Or maybe I should slide my cock between these perfect tits and fuck you raw. Would you like that? Would you like to watch my cum spray over your chest, your face?" Her breathing sped up and her pussy spasmed. I flicked my thumb over her clit. A second later, her orgasm wrenched a sharp cry from her. She shuddered in my arms but I didn't let up. "Or maybe you want to lie over this counter and let me deep throat this luscious mouth." I pulled my hand out of her panties and painted her lips with her juices. "Lick your lips, Angel. Taste yourself." Fuck if she didn't comply right away, groaning as her tongue ran over the plump flesh. Cupping her chin, I slid my thumb into her mouth. "Suck it. Show me what you can do with that pretty pink tongue." She didn't disappoint. Latching onto my thumb, every nerve came alive as her tongue rolled over the digit. "Suck harder, Rika, show me you want this," I demanded, my voice low, my tone hard.

She groaned when I removed my thumb. Placing a palm flat between her shoulder blade, I pushed down until she lay on the counter, her cheek pressed against the marble top. The position flattened her breasts and because of the height of the bar, bunched her calf muscles into tight balls.

I admired her bowed body. "So fucking beautiful." I nudged her ass with my cock, and she moaned. "I could take you right now, Rika. Your hands pinned behind your back, your body begging for my cock while I fuck you over and over until your legs can no longer support you. Would you like that, baby?"

"Yes," she murmured.

I leaned over her, letting my hands drift from her shoulders, along the curve of her breasts, the dip of her waist and over the swell of her ass, learning every arc and line, committing it to memory. My touch roused goosebumps across her soft skin. I repeated the caress to smooth the pebbled peaks, but her body shook, her whimpers echoing against the marble. Pressing my chest lightly to her back, I groaned at the skin-on-skin contact. Gathering her hair, I moved it over her shoulder then dragged my tongue down her spine. She shuddered, pushing her ass into my crotch. I gripped the edge of her panties with my teeth and tugged downward, my hands following in its wake to reveal the satin globes of her ass. Nipping the delicate skin, I edged my tongue along the cleft before circling her puckered asshole. She cried out. Kneeling behind her, I removed her panties and spread her legs, baring her delicious cunt to me.

"Jesus, Angel, you're so fucking wet." I was wrong. The pink folds weren't just wet. Her pussy was fucking quivering, delicate, slick, and inviting me to lick, suck and eat her. Grabbing her ass in my hands, digging my fingers into the soft flesh, I leaned forward. My breath tickled her sensitive skin and she moaned. I inhaled deeply. Her scent—a mix of arousal, soap and a hint of jasmine. "Fuck, I want to taste every inch of you, baby, eat you until you scream. I want to make you come so fucking hard, you forget your own damn name."

"Zayne, please." She glanced at me over her shoulder, her hunger profound, willing me to take the next step.

"This is wrong, I shouldn't," I whispered more for my own sanity, my blood no longer simmering but a low, threatening boil teetering on exploding. A part of me knew that I was skating a fine line, a point of no return. Regardless, I wanted to throw myself over the edge. I'd earned this, deserved it. Just one little taste, that was all I wanted, needed. How could I not, she was so fucking beautiful and mine for the taking. She rolled her hips, taunting my mouth with her glistening flesh. I didn't hesitate.

I ran my tongue from her clit to her rear entrance. Fuck. Sin had never tasted so good. I should know, I was the fucking devil's master. Now that I knew the pleasure of her addictive taste, I wanted more, needed more. And before logic set in, I slid the flat of my tongue through her slickness, worshipping the honied flavor of her pussy. Hungry and too far gone to stop, I licked, swallowed, and ate her like a man possessed.

It took a few laps of my tongue before the husky sounds of her cries echoed in the room, her body trembled, and her pleading turned frantic as she rocked furiously back against my mouth, desperately chasing her release. Her orgasm built, hovering just out of reach, the need for me to push her over the edge, to give her what she required and what I desired. Biting down hard on her swollen bud, she released a euphoric scream, her orgasm exploding into my mouth, filling it with the decadence I craved.

Before I could straighten, she lifted her head slightly to look at me over her shoulder. "More, please," she demanded, yet her face showcased the very innocence of Oliver Twist himself. I shoved my tongue back into her tantalizing pussy. If I was accused of taking advantage of her state, then I sure as fuck wanted my fill. Yet, with each desperate penetration of my tongue, I was unable to get deep enough, to lose myself in her whimpers and soft moans. There would be repercussions to my actions of that I was sure.

But I suddenly didn't care. She was mine, for however long she wanted me. I fucked her with my tongue, teeth, and lips, my fingers burrowing into her ass cheeks, spreading her open to the greed of a starving man's need, her cunt exactly how I'd imagined while under all those cold showers I'd endured. Sucking her clit into my mouth, I bit down on the sensitive bundle of flesh and pushed two fingers into her pussy, curling them to find that sweet spot that would push her over the edge. She was shamelessly grinding back into my face now, her fingers gripping the polished surface to keep pace with her undulating body. Soft sighs morphed into strangled moans as her third orgasm drew close. Another touch, another stroke and she unraveled, coming hard and fast, hips bucking, knees trembling before her delighted groans echoed through the silent room once more.

When I stood and gripped her hips, she rolled her ass over my crotch. "I need you to fuck me, now, Zayne," she demanded over her shoulder, the aggression baring her unashamed need.

Smiling, I pushed down my pants and stroked my cock. As I glided the head through her drenched slit, I reached up and grasped her shoulder. She yelped. I froze recognizing pain over pleasure. "What's wrong, Rika?"

"Don't stop," she pleaded.

I leaned forward and gently touched her shoulder again, watching as she flinched. It was as if someone had just thrown a bucket of ice-cold water over me, barreling my arousal like a ten-tonner as my immediate concern for her outweighed my traitorous needs. Yanking up my pants, I turned her to face me. Her dilated pupils met my gaze. "Jesus." I tensed. What the fuck was I doing? What the fuck had I done? I suddenly felt like shit. My insides roiled as shame washed over me. I was a sick, depraved fuck taking advantage of her in this state. I stepped back, breathing hard, guilt stealing the air I needed. I had to get out of here. Gritting my teeth, I took another step back and as I did, my gaze fell to her shoulder. Even in the dim light, I made out the blue hue that tainted her flawless skin. "What the fuck?" I swallowed my emotions for the moment. "You're hurt, baby?" I leaned in closer to inspect the bruise but Ashrika pushed at my chest.

"If you can't fuck me, leave me alone," she hissed. It was the drugs talking.

Cursing, I scooped her up in my arms and she instantly snuggled into the crook of my neck. I headed for my bedroom. The second I laid her down on the bed, she locked her hands around my neck and jerked me forward. Catching me off balance, I fell on top of her and before I could react, she shoved me off her. I landed on my back and she quickly straddled my stomach, her wet pussy warm against my skin.

She raked her nails over my abs, digging deep into the taut skin, her movements intense and ferocious—as if she was furious I wasn't fucking her. And by God, I wanted to—wanted to give into that animalistic desperation to make her mine completely—to fuck her until I passed out. But this wasn't her, me, or us. She was different, her needs were different, our love was different.

I grabbed her around the waist and flipped us, using my body to press hers into the mattress. She squirmed and pushed at my shoulders. I pinned her hands above her head with one hand and cupped her jaw with the other, forcing her to look at me. "We can't do this, Angel. Not now," I whispered, keeping my voice low yet firm. "You need to calm down." She wriggled and I tightened my grip on her arms. "I don't want to hurt you, baby."

She stared at me, saying nothing, her chest rising and falling. Then I felt her relaxe against my hold, exhaustion taking over her petite body. I held her gaze steadfast, silently willing her to go to sleep. For once some heavenly body was on my side because she moaned a few times, closed her eyes then drifted off. I waited for a bit and when I was sure she was asleep, I rolled off her. Standing, I inhaled deeply, trying to control my anger. Dark and dangerous thoughts ran through my mind of what I would do to that asshole. I paced the room, my long strides wearing an imaginary groove in the floor, back and forth as I willed myself to calm down, to rationally think. But every time I stopped and stared down at the beautiful woman lying in my bed, my temper rose again, not just because of the asshole that had drugged her, but because of my own selfish actions.

She rolled over onto her side, one hand tucked under her cheek, appearing angelic, nothing like the frantic sex kitten of a few minutes ago or the stunning woman dressed to bring men to their knees tonight. That sexy as fuck outfit, with her hair curled and her smokey eyes, would forever be imprinted in my mind. Yet it was nothing compared to the beautiful woman I saw every day—simplistic in everything from clothing to makeup and it worked for her. She needed none of the fancy stuff to show everyone who she really was—genuine.

I leaned over her to conduct a thorough sweep of her body. Rage pricked my skin, taking the breath from my lungs and I internally combusted spotting the purplish bruises around the distinct nail marks on her hips.

"You're dead, fucker," I swore. Fists balled tight, I stood back and studied her sleeping form before walking to the bathroom. I returned with a washcloth and warm water. Turning her to lie flat on her back, I gently wiped her face, removing all traces of her night out. Pity I couldn't wipe her mind clean of the bastard that had hurt her, but I could sure as fuck erase him off the fucking planet. I ground my teeth trying to rein in my rage.

Once the makeup was gone, I moved further down and cleansed the remnants of her arousal. When she woke, I wanted her smelling like she normally did—jasmine with a hint of roses—distinct, fresh, pure. And as I touched her, I cursed myself over and over for what I'd done. I prayed that come morning, she'd be willing to forgive me and even if she did, I would never forgive myself.

Done, I pulled the sheet over her, kissed her brow and stood, taking a moment to drink all of her in. To the world, she was my wife. But to her, I was her best friend, savior, and reason for living. Something she'd told me a thousand times since waking from that coma and realizing she had no past, no name and no family. And I'd just poisoned that trust.

With a resolute sigh, I switched off the bedside lamp and left the room.

# Ashrika

I WOKE TO THE RUMBLE of a hundred drums somewhere in my head. Startled, my eyes flew open and I blinked against the small ray of light stealing its way through the slit in the drawn curtains. I sat up and immediately winced when my stomach churned with the abrupt movement. Dropping back, I cupped the pillow around my ears in the hopes of blocking out the sound. "Please, stop."

In dire ridicule, the alarm clock chose that moment to add to my misery. I groaned as the sudden sharpness pierced the air. Turning on my side, I fumbled until my fingers stabbed the snooze button. The sound continued though. Grumbling, I lifted my head and glanced at my nightstand from where the offending sound boomed.

I grabbed my ringing mobile. "What?" I grumbled into the phone. Rolling onto my back, I massaged my brow.

"And a smashing good morning to you too," Tia's voice sang through the pounding jackhammer that resembled my head.

"How are you so cheery this early," I groaned. "And yes, smashing is exactly how my skull feels against my brain."

And Tia being Tia, she laughed until I cursed. "You need to drink more so you can handle your liquor," she scoffed.

"Never again," I vowed.

She chuckled. "By the way, it's nine o'clock and—"

"Shit." I sat up. "The restaurant—"

"Chill the fuck out, babe, Dean's got it covered. You needed a time-out," she coaxed.

I dropped back to the pillow. "But—"

"Dammit, Rika. You needed last night and you sure as fuck need this morning, not to sober up but to rest. You're overworked never mind the boring life you insist on living."

Choosing not to listen, I ran my tongue over my furry teeth, swallowing against the rancid cotton wool feeling in my mouth. Aspirin and water would be just perfect right about now and that meant walking to the kitchen. I doubted my legs were up for the journey.

"Speaking of boring, which one of those two hot men did you end up fucking last night? Or did you do them both?"

"What?" I slapped a hand to my mouth, panicking. What did I do last night? "Which men?" I asked, my tone cautious.

"Trent and Zayne. You wanted to fuck them both, remember?"

I didn't, but that was probably due to all the shit I drank last night. "Did I actually say that?" I glanced up at the ceiling, shaking my head.

"You did and I must say, I really like you drunk," Tia teased.

"Yes, well don't get used to it, I am *never* drinking again." I grinned. It was only when my gaze dropped to the opposite wall and strayed over the *'The Starry Night'* painting, did I frown. I didn't have a Van Gogh in my room. I sat up again and conducted a quick one-eighty investigation. I paled. *Shit.* "Um, Tia, I'm going to call you back." I cut the call without waiting for her to say goodbye. Not only was I in Zayne's room, but in his bed. How did I get here? God, how much did I drink? I glanced down at the sheet covering my body. Praying I didn't see what my brain was thinking, I lifted the black satin sheet. "Oh, shit." I clasped it back to my chest, trying to unsee my naked body beneath. My anxiety now full-blown, I fanned my suddenly warm cheeks as my breathing sped up, surpassing my aching head.

Why was I in Zayne's bedroom? *Think, Rika.* What happened last night? I scanned the room for something to jog my memory.

Nothing spoke to me. Not the plush gray carpet. Or the almost black thick curtains. Not even the walk-in closet with frosted glass doors. I blew out a frustrated breath. "Ok. There must be a reasonable explanation." Like what? I took a deep, cleansing breath and paused unsure about my next move. "Ok, maybe getting out of the room would be a start." Without seeing Zayne would be ideal. I rolled my eyes. Of course, he'd see me, he lived here. Given it was after eight, maybe he'd left already. That's it. I needed to get out before I lost my mind.

Gathering the sheet around my body, I slid off the bed and tiptoed toward the door. I opened it a tad and peeked out. *Shit.* I could hear Zayne in the open-plan kitchen which stood smack dab in the center between our two bedrooms. I couldn't stay in his room forever. Maybe just until he left. What if he decided to come check on me? What if he didn't know I was in his room? *Shit.* How did this happen? Still, I couldn't remember. "You can do this," I whispered. Mustering every bit of self-confidence I possessed, I walked out of the room.

As I passed the kitchen, Zayne turned and with one hand in the pocket of his sweatpants, he leaned a shoulder against the wall. He was on his cell phone. Not talking, just listening. He glanced up and I froze. His expression unreadable, he held my gaze as one dark brow lifted. My shocked gasp faltered in my throat—a bizarre blend of pleasure and panic caused another flush of heat to creep up my cheeks. Squaring my shoulders, I lifted a hand in an unconvincing wave and hurried away on unsteady legs. Inside my room, I leaned back against the closed door and took a moment to calm the hammering in my chest. I inhaled and exhaled on quick, deep breaths.

When I was sure I could walk again without tripping over myself, I dropped the sheet and headed for the bathroom. I gazed at my reflection in the mirror. My hair looked like a bird's nest but what surprised me the most, was the makeup-free face staring back at me. Who'd removed my make-up? Tia? Zayne? Baffled, I gawked at my face staring back at me before my gaze dropped to my distinctly blue shoulder. "Shit. What the hell did I do last night?" Instinctively my hand flew up to the bruise and I pressed my fingertips to the skin. "Ouch," I winced. Twisting from side to side, I checked the rest of my body. Greenish-blue marks also tainted the skin around my waist and hips.

I stepped into the shower and lifted my face to the spray. Although the hot water was a welcome relief, it did little to dull my throbbing head. The pain intensified as I tried to recall what had transpired at the club. Blurred images of a guy grabbing my wrist and squeezing my waist filtered between the blanks. Did I hook up with someone? I gasped as vile thoughts hit me. I didn't do one-night stands. Then again, I didn't go out much and I certainly didn't drink. I closed my eyes trying to remember.

As if that wasn't enough, explicit images of sexual acts with Trent, Zayne and I, brought on by Tia's question no doubt, ploughed my mind. Vivid play-by-play of me sandwiched between their hot bodies in Zayne's bed. Zayne's lips on my neck sucking hard, Trent's mouth on my breasts—so clear, I felt the pinch of his teeth on my nipple. Two pairs of hands touching, fingering and fucking me. I shuddered.

My eyes flew open. I swallowed water the same time it went down my nose. I coughed hard to ease the burning sensation stinging my nasal passage. "God, who has such thoughts." I mumbled when I could finally speak without coughing. That I was turned on by the filthy fantasy, freaked me out, more so the unexpected need to reach between my legs and relieve the overwhelming pressure that grew there. "Jesus, what the hell happened last night" I grasped my head trying once more to remember before intermittent memories of Trent punching someone, surfaced. Did he save me? Did he bring me home? Did they fuck me? "Aargh!" Irritated, I made a mental note to ask Tia.

When I finally found the courage to leave my room, it was to find Zayne at the breakfast nook. He appeared to be deep in thought as he smeared the sour cream and chives spread over his bagel, which also happened to be my favorite breakfast, but the thought of food, had my stomach churning.

He looked up. "Hi."

"Hi." I ignored the nervous tingle sitting at the base of my spine.

Unsure what to read into his calm demeanor, I waited for him to say something. Like me walking out of his bedroom naked, was an everyday occurrence, he pulled out a chair. "Sit." I slid down into the seat. "You thwarted my plan to bring you breakfast in bed, so this is the next best thing." He waved a hand over the table.

*Breakfast in bed?* I balked. Instead of addressing the elephant in the room, he placed the bagel in front of me with my usual—a glass of orange juice. Still, I had no idea what to say.

He held out two aspirin and a glass of water. "Take this first, then eat." Although I blushed, I couldn't deny Zayne's resolute care. It was like he always knew what I needed without me asking. He took the seat next to me and reached for the morning paper. A mug of coffee sat next to his phone on the table.

"You're not eating?"

"I've already eaten," he replied without looking up.

After I swallowed the pills, I emptied the glass of water and set it down with a slight clink against the marble top, courtesy of my trembling hand. "Um...Zayne?"

He glanced up from the paper, one dark brow raised in question as his knowing amber eyes stared at me, waiting for me to ask.

"Last night." I paused. How do I ask him if we had sex without coming across like a flustered teenager who'd just lost her virginity?

"How did I... end up in your bed naked?" the latter part rushed out much faster than I started.

His expression blank, he set aside the paper and rolled his pointer finger along his jaw. I hated his ability to hide his emotions. I'd give anything to take a peek inside that intelligent mind just to see what went on in there. "You don't remember what happened last night?" he asked.

I raked a hand through my wet hair and shook my head. "Just bits and pieces."

"What's the last thing you do remember?"

"I was going to the bathroom and some guy tried to get fresh with me. After that, it gets vague. I'm not even sure if my memories of Trent Shaw, the guy wanting to offer me a job, being at the club are real."

A ghost of a smile touched the corners of his lips. It vanished just as quickly when he said, "Trent was there. He saved you from a pervert and brought you home." Zayne picked up his phone and stared at the screen, hiding his face from me.

*That's it?* Expecting more, I leaned back in the chair and frowned. "And how did I end up in your bed, naked?" This time the words came out more furious than I intended.

He glanced up. Even though the idea of him taking me to bed sounded desirable, I would've loved to have been conscious for the experience. As the thought materialized, I couldn't stop my gaze from running over his body. While I sometimes wondered if suits were made with Zayne's well-built physique in mind, wearing nothing but dark sweatpants, he was deliciously sinful. Firm abs defined his bare stomach. I'd just noticed some red marks when a perfectly toned arm lifted the white coffee mug, which he paused inches below a wicked smirk I hadn't witnessed before.

Distracted, I didn't realize he'd moved. So close, I didn't know where his exhale ended, and my inhale began. "What do you think happened last night, Angel," his husky voice rolled over me like the brush of a feather against my skin.

I shivered. "Um..." Like a bumbling idiot, I bit down on my tongue to prevent me from letting him know exactly what I wanted to have happened. Where was Tia when I needed her? She'd know what to do—well, what to say.

He gazed at me for a long moment, the tense silence nipping at my calm. I watched the wheels spinning in those brown irises. What was he contemplating?

"What do you want to hear, baby?" A muscle twitched in his clenched jaw and I had a sudden urge to run a finger over that pulse. Not trusting myself not to do so, my right hand strangled the wrist of the left on my lap. "That I ripped off your panties, bent you over the bar, and tongue-fucked you until you cried out my name to let you come?" he asked. That deep sensual tone felt like a carnal sin itself.

I wanted to gasp, but I was incapable of making a sound. My teeth sank into my bottom lip, his dirty words shocked and manipulated me, the unexpected sexual hunger had every inch of my skin burning, ready to detonate. My mind seeing the image as clear as day, my body wanting everything he just said. If he touched me now, I would incinerate. I looked up at Zayne, his dark eyes watching me, a hint of amusement evident, before he blanketed his features, the mask firmly back in place. I opened my mouth, not sure what I was going to say. He reached out and ran his finger so slowly over my bottom lip, the tingling sensation almost erotic. I wanted more, but then he pulled his hand away and I swallowed my moan of pleasure. He retreated and sat back down, as though nothing had happened.

"That's not what happened, Angel. I'm teasing you." Although he smiled, there was a distinct hardness to his tone. I blinked. Zayne had never used sexual innuendos to tease me, ever. "Trent brought you home and put you in the wrong bed. I didn't want to wake you, so I slept on the couch." He shoved a hand through his hair and stood.

My mind a perplexed whirlpool of emotions, I watched the play of the muscles in his back, all the way down to the waistband of his pants as he crossed the floor into the open-plan kitchen. If Trent brought me home and I was naked this morning—did we fuck? Was Zayne lying? Did that filthy fantasy in the bathroom play out last night? Two men? Two strangers sharing me? Or was it my warped mind's need for eroticism? *Shit.* I'd occasionally woken up drenched in sweat and soaked panties thinking about Zayne but adding Trent to that mix was another level of depravity I didn't know I craved. And something I planned to keep to myself.

"Are you going to the restaurant?" Zayne asked over his shoulder, dragging my gaze back to him.

Still battling his change in demeanor, I cleared my throat. "Yes."

"Okay. I'll see you later." He returned to my side, his countenance, as usual cool and collected. "Eat something before you leave, okay?" I nodded. He kissed the top of my head, picked up his coffee mug, and sauntered toward his bedroom.

Staring out the floor to ceiling window that overlooked a glorious Manhattan morning, I took a bite of the bagel, my thoughts still stuck in the 'what the fuck just happened' moment I couldn't quite kick. Without meaning to, I glanced at the bar on the opposite side of the large room. A tremor ran through my body at the vision Zayne's words invoked. My panties were already soaked through from earlier, so one more dirty thought didn't make a difference. It was evident that while Zayne might be broody and mysterious, the man beneath was fucking sexy if those words were anything to go by. I sighed, wondering if something would ever happen between us. Whatever the case, he'd always be my one constant.

# Zayne

THE MINUTE ASHRIKA left for the restaurant, I tossed the untouched coffee down the sink. It took me another two minutes to lace up my running shoes and hit the streets. Usually, I worked out at the gym. Today, I wanted a change in scenery, hoping the warmth of the morning sun would thaw my paralyzed thoughts. After almost fucking her last night, followed by restless sleep and her not remembering, a strange numbness settled over me—a rarity since nothing much fazed me. Then again, I hadn't attempted anything sexual with Rika before and walking away had been a hard decision. Now, a part of me wished I hadn't. Maybe then, she might understand what she meant to me. Trying to ease the tension with sexually laced teasing, hadn't helped the situation much. It made me want her on a whole different level.

*Fuck.*

Seeking punishment, I ran farther than I normally did, driving myself harder and faster, pushing until my legs cramped and my breath wheezed in and out of my chest. I staggered into the apartment, hands on my sides, my lungs burning, begging for air. I denied the request instead headed to our gym. Foregoing the gloves, I pummeled the punching bag, unaware of the force of my hits until my knuckles screamed in agony.

I threw one final punch and stepped back. Chest heaving, I stood there for just a second then let out a roar of frustration. "Fuck." Breathing hard, I fell to my knees, my head hanging, my chin touching my chest, sweat mixing with my hard pants. I felt the burn of tears at the back of my lids. Whether from pain or sentimentality, I didn't care, couldn't care because I couldn't pinpoint the exact reason why, only that I wanted to cry. I didn't. I shot to my feet instead and pounded the shit out of the punching bag until my knuckles begged for relief and my chest cried for air.

An hour later, rethinking my visit to the restaurant, I parked the car in the alley behind the club. Distance from Ashrika right now was best for my sanity. My usual control back in place, I was ready for anything, spilling blood even more so. About to climb out, I glanced in the rearview mirror and grinned catching sight of the man creeping toward the car. It seemed like my wish was about to come true.

When I stepped out, he hesitated. With my hands in my pants pockets, I leaned against the car and stared at him. Ignoring the gun in his hand and scanning the area at his rear. He was alone but I didn't miss the black sedan parked at the end of the alley. I trusted no one. My gaze shifted back to him. Running a quick study of his body, I kept my expression blank. That way he had no idea whether I was friendly or aloof. "You ever held a gun before?" I asked, cocking my head to the side.

He ran a slow gaze over my nonchalant stance, his Adam's apple bobbing despite his attempt to match my stony countenance. First mistake. "Y-yes," he stammered. Second mistake. I widened my lips in a slow smile. He flinched. "You said it would be an easy job. Scare her a little. Nothing about getting his face beat," his voice shook, his fear palpable, superseding his anger.

"He made two crucial mistakes."

"There were no mistakes," he spat. "He did exactly like you asked. Chat her up, give her a little squeeze and try to kiss her. That's it until that fucking hero arrived out of nowhere and spoiled the fun."

"Fun?" I ground my molars, my palms itched to clamp around his throat, squeeze the fucking life out of him. All in good time. "It wasn't a job then?"

He paled. "I...um...he—"

"Where the fuck is he?" I snapped. His gaze darted quickly to the black sedan then back to me. "So, what's his game?"

"He wants double what you paid him."

"Or what?"

The gun jerked in his hand. "We take you the fuck out." His attempt at a snarl came out more like a squeak.

"And let me guess. You're the asshole that drew the short straw?"

"What does that mean?" Stupidity shaded his brow in a frown.

When would wannabe fucking criminals understand the power behind wielding a gun laid in the strength of their balls, not the parody of a limp dick standing in front of me?

"I don't think you're the best man for the job, Tony."

"The fuck I am."

"Then by all means, prove me wrong." I pushed away from the car and took a step forward.

"Stay the fuck back, Zayne." He waved the gun in the air. "I'm warning you. I'll shoot."

"What makes you think I'm afraid to die?" I lifted a brow. The color drained from his face as though he realized just how pathetic his effort appeared. I shook my head. "Which begs the question, what are you going to do about that?"

He shifted from one foot to the other. "I—"

My smile was slow, sly even and one that usually baffled the men I faced down. "Go on, then. Pull the fucking trigger," I taunted.

The way I felt, after Trent's arrival into my life and the situation last night, I'd take on the fucking devil. Adrenaline pumped blood in an untamed race through my body, every nerve alive and ready for action. Fuck, I needed this. I took another step, and he raised his hand slightly, glancing at the sedan as he did so.

"Do you know the difference between a pussy and a lion, Tony?" I could see the confusion in his eyes like I'd just asked him a difficult math problem. "One gives pleasure and the other pain. Yet both can bring a man to his knees with one grasp. Which one are you?"

"I don't understand."

"It's a simple question. Are you the pussy?" I smirked. "Or the lion? Are you bringing me pleasure or pain today?"

"Pain, asshole," he sneered then blinked. "Wait. How the fuck would I bring you pleasure?"

I shook my head. *Dumb fucking shit.* The best kind to fuck with. Moving so fast, he didn't see me coming, I had him in a chokehold and cracking his neck before his next breath. I dropped his limp body. "Thanks for the pleasure." I dusted my dark suit and looked up as the back doors of the sedan opened. Jason, the fucker I wanted, sprinted my way followed by two bigger guys. They stopped short, mouths agape, and surveyed the scene.

Jason's shaky hand tried to control the other that held a gun. "You killed my brother, you bastard," he screamed.

"Never send a pussy to do a man's job." I shrugged, taking in his swollen eyes, busted lips and blue-black foundation that covered his pale face. "Nice makeover." I was impressed with Trent's skill. He'd done a fucking fantastic job of reshaping the man's face.

Jason lifted the gun and pointed at my chest. "Why the fuck did you kill him?" Were those tears in his eyes?

"He was taking too long to shoot me. I got bored."

"Bored? That's my fucking brother," he yelled.

"And your point is?" Pure acid laced my tone and for just a moment he looked flustered. It would've taken me less than a second to pull the Glock tucked in the back of my pants and put a bullet right between his eyes. The wet spot on the front of his cream pants indicated he'd already pissed himself. Now to watch him crap himself. I leaned back against my car, crossed my arms over my chest and gestured at the gun in his hand with my chin. "Are you going to play with that thing or do what you came here to do?"

The look on his face—what little of it I could see—changed to uncertainty. "I did as you asked. You didn't say some fucker will be there to save her."

"And I didn't tell you to drug her." Resisting the urge to plow my fist into his face, I dropped my hands and he reared back like a frightened child. "But I did tell you not to hurt her."

"I didn't."

"Says the blue marks on her body, you fucking piece of shit," I snarled. His black eyes grew wide. "Did you think I wouldn't notice?" He shuffled a few steps backward. "If you plan on using that," I pointed to the gun, "make damn fucking sure you don't miss, Jason. Because I can guarantee you only one of us is leaving here alive."

"Suck my dick, Zayne."

I laughed. "I'm guessing your balls are not as big as your ego. Your hands are shaking, asshole. If you're going to fucking shoot someone, never let them see your fear," I sneered. He took another step back. The men behind him wore conflicting expressions—one uncertainty and the other superiority. "The least you fuckers could do was send a worthy opponent to take me out," I goaded.

Jason's gaze darted between me and his dead brother, his decision wavering before he grabbed the gun in both hands and fought to keep his grip steady. "You're going down."

"Do you want me to stand still? Would that help?" I took another step forward and he backed away, stumbling as he hit the wall behind him. "I am right here. Shoot, fucker," I roared, spreading my arms out at my sides and sticking my chest out. "Pull the fucking trigger!" I baited, my lips wide in a sneer. Maybe my time was up. The world wouldn't miss a bastard like me. No one would worry if

I went down—there was no one to care. The woman who held my heart was lost to me. It was only a matter of time. I had nothing more to lose. "Shoot, pussy," I mocked.

It was too much for him. "Stop, please." Shaking like a goddamn tree on a windy day, he lowered the gun. The hesitant guy did an about-face and disappeared down the alley, while the other looked at Jason, waiting for confirmation, like a goddamn guard dog.

"Aww, come on, Jason, don't wimp out on me now. I'm an evil fucker, right? I killed your brother, I deserve to die, don't I? Here's your chance. Take it. Avenge your brother. Don't be a pussy. Send me straight to fucking hell," I yelled.

The door to the club opened and one of my men stepped out, weapon drawn. I held up my hand and he stayed put, keeping his gun in sight. Jason sucked in a breath, his expression ultimate surrender. This was obviously not going according to plan. His remaining bulldog took a step toward me. I raised a brow, provoking him and he visibly faltered but there was no dismissing his aggressive stare down—he wanted a piece of me.

With slow calculated steps, I neared Jason. "So, you still want me to suck your cock?"

He collapsed to his knees, head shaking in a vehement display of regret. "I'm sorry, Zayne."

I dropped to my haunches, bringing me down to his level. Tears ran down his cheeks making me want to slap the shit out of him. "Your apology is accepted." His expression brightened and dipped at my next words, "But I'll believe you, only if you shoot him." My face not wavering from his, I pointed to his so-called bodyguard. The other man cursed the same time Jason gulped. Not breaking eye-contact, I ran a slow finger over the barrel of the gun he still held in his hand. "You of all people know there's no honor among thieves, Jason. "You did come here to kill me, didn't you?" Slowly, he nodded. "That means someone has to die by your hand." I cocked a brow. He glanced up at his friend.

"Are you fucking crazy, Jason," the other man yelled.

I looked at him. "What's your name?"

"Billy," he replied, his tone bordering on hostility.

"Relax, Billy, you have nothing to fear. Jason is too much of a wimp to take you out. Isn't that right, Jason?" I goaded.

He looked at me then at the gun in his shaking hand. I watched him, fascinated to see the effect of my taunting when he pointed the gun at the other man. "I'm sorry, Billy."

"Don't do it, Jason. He's just messing with you," Billy's stern features morphed into outright fear. Keeping the gun trained on Billy, Jason looked at me.

I glanced over my shoulder at my security head. "Rogue, can you clear up a little misunderstanding for these two. Am I known for messing around?" I returned my gaze to Jason's distraught face.

"No, sir," Rogue's succinct reply made both men tense.

"You heard the man, Jason, what's it going to be?"

Jason's gun went off, simultaneously my bullet, he hadn't seen coming, ripped through his skull, splattering his brains on the wall behind him. Still on his knees, leaning upright against the wall, blood oozed from a perfect hole to his brow. The look of surprise still evident in his now vacant eyes. Next to him, Billy's body twitched until he lay deathly still.

Straightening, I stared down at the lifeless fucker. "Nothing personal, Jason, but no one touches the woman I love and lives." Stuffing my gun into the back of my pants, I turned as Rogue approached me. I looked up at the cloudless sky. "Nice day for fishing, right?" He nodded. "Take Jenson with you." I referred to another one of my men and I headed for the club entrance.

When I walked into Enigma later that afternoon, my body filled with apprehension at the sight of Ashrika leaning against the counter chatting to a diner. I might've taken care of the fucker but I deserved to stay in the hell I'd slipped into, knowing I'd put her at risk. The need to pull her into my arms and hold her there forever, beat with every inhale. She laughed and the sound tightened my blackened heart. I looked at her, the woman who was a survivor, and I was in awe of her. For the first time in my life, I wanted more. I wanted her for me, to protect her, to love and cherish her. Silently I pleaded that she would accept my unspoken invitation to love me before the possibility of her recognizing Trent. A selfish part of me wanted to tell him to get lost, to leave her alone, to let her live this new life she'd created.

But if her memory came back, she might hate me, if she thought that I had prevented her from being with the man she'd once committed her life to, before me.

"Zayne?" I turned to find Tia at my side. "You good?" Her expression indicated she understood my inner turmoil. I nodded. "Does she know?" She squeezed my arm and I frowned. "That you're in love with her." I blinked my surprise. "Don't look so shocked. I've seen the way you are around her. And if your conversation with Trent wasn't convincing enough, then I don't know what is." I arched a brow, her perception unsettling. "I never asked you this before but what's stopping you from taking it to the next level? What are you afraid of?"

As a man who scared people shitless with a look, I'd asked myself the same thing countless times. "Who the fuck knows, Tia." I cupped the back of my neck and rolled it to ease the knotted tension. "Maybe it was the distraught look in her eyes that afternoon she woke from her coma. Or the numerous occasions she gave up wanting to live every time she woke from a nightmare she didn't understand. Take your pick which one made me stop and question my attempt." Fool that I was, I'd offered her salvation, my name and my protection—not expecting to fall in love. I did. Stupidly, I'd given Trent free rein to break my heart and if she did choose him, it would break my soul too. Not the best decision ever but I'd lay down my life for her. "Vowing to keep her safe, I promised her I'd never take advantage of her."

"Falling in love is not taking advantage, Zayne," Tia retorted.

I scoffed. "All my life I've been a bastard, taking without asking but somehow, she broke through to the animalistic barrier I put up. She reminds me that I am a man capable of caring for a woman, something I'd forgotten. She came into my life like an angel when indifference was second nature..." I trailed off, shutting down the emotions running rampant through me.

"You should've told her."

"Too late now." The words tasted like remnants of bile.

Tia let out a dismal sigh. "What if she finds out why we're pushing her toward Trent?"

"Can't be helped." I hadn't slept since that night, wondering the same thing.

"I don't like keeping things from her." Tia's brow wrinkled, her worry palpable. "But it's for the best, right?"

"I can't answer that," I muttered, wishing I could. "I guess sometimes lies are worth their weight in gold if it goes toward protecting someone." I'd become adept at lying. Fuck it was my job. I pulled in a deep breath, fighting the jealousy that festered in my veins since Trent's arrival. "What if it isn't? What if we're making a mistake?" I cringed, internally. I never doubted myself. Bullshit, I had once and it led me down a road that had only one ending.

"She trusts you, believes you," Tia cut through my reflections with a smile. "She'll understand."

"Last night, I thought—" I broke off, nipping the overshare in the bud. Last night wasn't supposed to happen but it did, and it hurt that she couldn't remember. Still, it would be in my memory forever. I had a part of her, however small. Tia gave me a quizzical look but didn't push, knowing when not to. "I'm scared it might cause more harm than good," I said instead, glancing at Ashrika. She was laughing at something the diner said, so relaxed and oblivious to the turmoil churning my stomach.

"You and scared don't exactly go together in the same statement..." Tia trailed off drawing my gaze. "All's not lost, you know. She might not remember him."

"And if he pursues her into falling for him?" I shifted my gaze back to Ashrika. Every part of me felt like it was being ripped apart, shredded beyond repair. My chest tightened and for just a moment I struggled to breathe, to draw in the air needed to survive but I had to—for her. "It hurts." I clenched my teeth and looked at Tia. "It hurts knowing she might."

"Who's to say she will. Don't give up so easily. It's not like you." She reached for my hand, squeezing lightly. "And if she does, you will find love again."

"Fuck love, Tia. I'm over that shit," I snapped, more from experience than irritation. "I barely survived this love, what makes you think I'd survive another?"

"Because you're you. I know you, remember." Tia was right. She knew the real me. "You're hardcore, Zayne but you're a fighter. You can't let her see your pain. Promise."

Slowly, I nodded. "I'll allow myself to break once she's gone. Once she's handed my heart back to me in pieces."

"You don't know that she will." She persisted, the desperation in her voice urging me not to give up. "You also promised that guy at the club wouldn't—" my icy glare forced a full stop to her words. She gave me a slight nod instead, knowing why I did what I did, without the need for an explanation.

We both turned as the sound of the bell above the door jingled and Trent stepped inside. Speak of the fucking devil. I returned his nod, gauging his expression before Tia walked over to him. His curiosity from last night was still in place. As long as he didn't question Ashrika, we were good.

I turned away sharply, colliding with Ashrika. She stumbled and I pinned her between my arm and chest, stopping her fall. "Always falling for me, aren't you?" I smiled but not quick enough to hide the truth behind my words.

She opened her mouth to say something but then a blast of air, as the air-conditioner kicked in, blew a strand of hair across her face. Without thinking I reached up and brushed it back behind her ear. Her lashes drifted down at my touch. I stared at her angelic face, assailed by the memories of last night. The sound of her soft moans, the feel of her skin against my hands, and the essence of her taste. What would it be like to have her in my bed every night? I clenched my jaw to stop the groan cresting my throat.

Ashrika opened her eyes and I kept mine locked on hers, anywhere else spelled trouble. The crush of her tits against my chest already tested my restraint. There were only so many cold showers a man could endure in a day. Dropping my hand, I immediately missed the feel of her as she stepped back.

"Not hard enough it seems," she said in a voice that was half laugh, half sigh.

I wondered if she really didn't remember last night, yet glad she'd chosen to accept our breakfast discussion at face value, as mere teasing. She looked over my shoulder to where Trent and Tia remained chatting near the door and missed my curious expression. Blanking my emotions, I slipped my hands into my pants pockets, waiting for her to acknowledge him. She didn't, which meant either last night's memory of him was still a blur or she wasn't interested in him. Good.

"Come sit with me." As she took my hand, her gaze fell to my chafed knuckles. "Oh, God." Undisguised terror stole her smile. "What happened?"

"It's nothing, Angel."

"Seriously. You have cuts and bruises on your knuckles, and you act like that's an everyday occurrence?"

Her feistiness made me smile. "I just got a little overenthusiastic with the punching bag in the gym this morning."

"A little?" She arched a brow, her expression laced with suspicion before she blew out an exasperated breath, nothing like the shy beauty who walked into the kitchen earlier that morning. "One day, you'll have to tell me the truth, you know."

I covered my surprise with a smirk. She'd never really asked me any outright questions before. "Is that a threat?"

"Yes." She narrowed her eyes then turned and walked off.

Grinning, I followed. This time I didn't stop my gaze from dropping to the soft sway of her hips in white jeans and a red sweater. My palms itched to grab her, swing her around and crash my mouth to hers until she cried out for more.

When we took chairs on the opposite sides of her table in the office, she studied me for a moment. "I don't think that I've ever seen you look so preoccupied. What's up?"

"Nothing." I shrugged, forgetting just how perceptive she was to my moods. I should say something, mention last night, drop a hint, anything to ease my conscience. It was fucking difficult to concentrate on anything other than the image of her face pressed to the counter as she panted her way through multiple orgasms. Christ, I was a bastard for taking advantage of her in her drunken state. Sanity had abandoned me when I had ravished her, mercilessly devouring her sweet cunt and worse, for not telling her. For that, I was guaranteed a passage straight to hell. The fact that she loved dirty talking was unbelievable, unbearably sexy, and downright hot. I lived with this woman for so long and had no idea that her mind was saying one thing, but her body was screaming for another. The raw energy of untamed arousal, a burning need for unspeakable rough desires that got me off, got her off as well. It had been too long since I'd commanded a woman or had one whimpering for more.

"Zayne?"

I glanced up, taking in the curious expression of the woman who had my heart firmly entranced in her gilded smile. "Is it my imagination or did the lunch crowd appear larger than usual today?"

Her brow arched as if aware of my evasiveness. "You've been gone for close on eight months, it might seem a little overwhelming." She laughed then swiveled her chair to face the computer.

She was right. While I traveled extensively, it was my way of staying away from her so I could keep my promise. It was hard but doable. The second we discovered her passion for cooking, I'd opened the restaurant for her. Not only had it helped steer her away from thoughts of her identity or the family that hadn't come looking for her, but she hardly noticed my absence.

"Still not going to tell me about last night?"

"Nothing else to tell." I looked at her, my expression solemn, not giving my truths away and that under my façade, my guilt was festering like an open wound. She flicked a glance at me before going back to her screen. I raked a hand through my hair and leaned back in the seat, contemplating whether to tell her about Trent then thought better of it. Even though I dreaded it, now was good a time as any to bring up the treatment. "Rika?"

"Hmm?" she answered without looking up. When I didn't respond, she swung her gaze to me then frowned. "Yes?"

"I just wondered if you've ever given Dr. Landers' advice any thought, you know about the regressive hypnosis?"

"Some."

"Some?" I gently prodded.

"I don't know if it would help." She fingered her chain.

"Remember he said you'd need a couple of sessions." She stared at me but said nothing. "Look, it's for your own good, Rika. Don't you want to find out about your past, about who'd harmed you? Whether you have a family? And what about a simple thing like your birth date."

She chewed her bottom lip, her expression thoughtful. "I guess you're right, but I get this feeling there's something about my past that isn't nice. That maybe I'm not a good person or maybe I hung out with the wrong crowd and did something terrible that resulted in my attack. I'm scared to find out."

I leaned back in my chair and gave her a soft smile. "And what if there's something good you're missing out on? Love? Family?" The pang in my chest deepened, knowing the truth to that statement.

"If that is the case, why didn't someone come looking for me?" Her eyes glazed with instant tears and for just a moment I wanted to forget everything that had led up to this conversation and go back to the way things were before logic won.

"Hey, baby." I stood, walked around and leaned my butt on the table. "Fear will only consume you if you let it." I straightened and pulled her up to stand in the circle of my embrace. "I don't want to see your future go to waste over nothing." She dropped her gaze to the floor with a soft sob. I slid a finger under her chin and lifted it until her eyes met mine. "You know I won't let anything happen to you, right?" Slowly, she nodded. "And I won't force you into anything you don't want?" Again, she nodded and I tightened my grip on her. "Just give it a try and if nothing comes of it, then we forget about it." I coaxed, holding her against my chest, reveling in the feeling of her in my arms.

A moment was all I allowed myself before loosening my hold. Anything more and I'd capture her lips in a kiss that would require an oxygen tank on standby.

"I just want to be normal and thinking about a nonexistent past makes me feel *not* normal," she whispered, brushing away her tears.

"You are normal. Considering the hell you put me through at times, I'm inclined to think you are abnormal." I teased and was rewarded with a laugh. She punched me lightly on the chest and I faked a wince. She stuck out her tongue and for just one moment, everything else ceased to exist around us. Just me and her in an impenetrable bubble I could live in forever.

"Thank you," her soft words pulled me out of my fantasy. "For always worrying about me. Making sure I'm taken care of, for putting me first as usual."

"I will always take care of you." I paused to swallow against the emotion clogging my throat. "Never forget that, okay?"

"I never will." She kissed me lightly on the cheek.

Her scent of wild jasmine filled my nostrils, and I couldn't help the deep inhale. For once, I wish I had the courage to kiss her on the mouth instead. What if she rejected me? My heart hammered in my chest. It would be so easy to make her mine, lay claim to that enticing smile. "Every life has a story to tell, Angel. Don't be afraid to start afresh. You might love your new story."

She smiled. "I'll go see Dr Landers as long as you come with me."

"I won't have it any other way." She stepped away from me and I felt the immediate loss of her warmth against my body. "I'll give him a call and see when he can see us, okay?" At her nod, I reached for my phone lying on the table.

# Ashrika

SINCE THE COMA, I HATED hospitals. It reminded me of the bleakness I experienced those first few days after waking to discover I had no idea where I was let alone my identity. If it hadn't been for Zayne who'd found me, I probably would've lost my nerve to live and take each day at a snail's pace. The worst being my inability to move given the aftereffects of being in a coma. Not only was Zayne a godsend but he possessed the patience of an angel and refused to give up even when I did.

Now, eyeing the gorgeous man in his dark suit and white button-down, standing next to me as we rode the elevator, I smiled. Although I'd been blessed with his name and care, I often wondered why he hadn't tried anything serious. I knew I loved him, but I hadn't questioned or pushed him for anything more. Perhaps he saw me as someone he'd sworn to take care of, perhaps not. Labeling our relationship wasn't easy since he'd never given me any reason to try either. Sighing, I gave his hand a gentle squeeze. He returned the gesture, probably mistaking it for nerves.

I waited while Zayne chatted to the petite blonde receptionist. "Hi. Ashrika Morrone for Dr. Landers, please."

"If you'll wait a moment." The receptionist flashed him an engaging smile, turned to the keyboard in front of her screen and typed. She glanced up a second later and gestured to the elevator across the foyer. "Third floor. Just give your name to the floor nurse and she'll point you in the right direction."

"Thank you." He winked earning a soft laugh then headed for the elevator. He caught my smirk with a raised brow. "Can't help it if I'm good-looking." He smirked. I rolled my eyes and his lips twitched. Stepping into the cubicle my shoulders slumped and the anxiety started to work its way up my spine. "Relax, Angel." He rubbed my lower back.

On the third floor, we proceeded down the passage. I surveyed the surroundings like it was hell itself. The sterile smell of chemicals, gray walls and the odd bed wheeling past us, did nothing to help my anxiety. By the time we reached Dr. Landers' rooms, I was a nervous wreck. Even Zayne's hand at my lower back, didn't help. I took several deep breaths before we entered.

In total contrast to the vivid white and gray of the hospital passage, Dr. Landers' waiting room was tastefully furnished. Classy oak furniture enhanced by pastel blue walls, pale pink couches and some famous paintings. I never could understand my eye for historical art pieces. The office was fronted by Sandy, a short plump woman with freckled cheeks and cropped red hair and someone I'd loved chatting to on my previous visits to his private rooms. She glanced up from the file she was reading and offered us a cheery smile which put me at ease.

"Hi, Ashrika. Dr. Landers is waiting for you." her soft voice matched her friendly disposition. "Go on in." She gestured to the polished oak door.

Zayne knocked lightly then entered. "Doc?" he greeted.

I offered him a smile as he stood. A tall man with dark hair and a splash of gray at the temples, Dr. Tony Landers' cherubic face and deep dimpled smile would put any patient at ease. "Zayne, Ashrika." He nodded, accepting Zayne's hand in a quick shake. "How is my favorite patient?" He always looked at me with the affection a father would bestow his daughter.

"Bet you say that to all your patients," I teased.

"Only if they're as pretty as you," he replied making me laugh. "If you'll both excuse me for just a minute, I'll be right back then we can begin."

"Sure." Zayne nodded.

After the doctor left the room, I moved over to the large window that showcased the larger part of Manhattan.

"Do you want something to drink, Rika? I'm going to grab a soda," Zayne asked.

"No thanks. I'm too nervous to think of a drink or anything else right now," I replied over my shoulder.

He laughed, moving to my side. "You'll be fine."

"Easy for you to say," I huffed.

"I'm right here, baby." I looked up, meeting his eyes. The warmth swimming in those honey-colored browns had me smiling. He kissed my brow. "I'll be back in a minute, okay."

Nodding, I turned away as he left. I was staring out the window when the door opened barely seconds after he exited. "Back so quickly? Guess you didn't find anything to drink," I teased without turning around.

"Hello, Rika," The deep, husky greeting spiked the hairs on the back of my neck.

Recognizing the voice, I whirled around, locking gazes with eyes the color of liquid sapphire. They held me captive in the time it took to comprehend that he was there, and that it was not some stupid figment of my imagination. "Why are you here? What's going on?" I asked, surprised and not returning the decadent smile he offered.

"Thought I might help."

"Excuse me?" He took a step closer and I held up a hand, stopping his approach.

"Tia mentioned your situation—"

"Did she now?" I scowled. "Seems I should have a chat with Tia, personal boundaries and all that," I bit out, feeling a little out of sorts about the way he lit every nerve in my body on fire.

He appeared taken aback by my aggression before a slow smile made an appearance. "I guess you liked me better when you were drunk."

"What?" I stammered before realization dawned. He was referring to the night at the club. Embarrassment zipped through me. Although I covered it with a grimace, I wracked my brain trying to figure out not only how he'd come to my rescue but my subsequent behavior on the way home, something I'd done a million times since. Had I kissed him? Did he change my clothes that night? Zayne had no intention of sharing the details and I had no one to ask other than Trent. I'd rather eat freaking worms than do that. *Yuck.*

"Pleasant memories I take it."

Flustered, my glower deepened. "I'm Rika only to my friends," I snapped trying hard not to notice just how effortlessly he filled those snug jeans and a knitted sweater that did little to hide his muscular build. I had a feeling he looked even better with it off. Did I just go there? Somehow, I managed to pull my gaze away from his crotch. Unbelievable that I wanted to look.

I expected to see annoyance or anger flash across his face. Instead, a hint of amusement curled the corner of his lips. "So, what do I call you?" His eyes narrowed, but the serene expression remained. Bothered by his calm, I ignored him. "Other than cooking, do you play any sports?"

Was he seriously trying to start a conversation? Even though his nonchalance irked me, I heard myself replying, "not that it's any of your business, but no."

"You should."

Not giving him the satisfaction of seeing how he riled me, I asked, "Why?"

His hooded blue eyes swept a graceful slide over me. "It might work off some of that pent-up frustration."

"I don't have any pent-up frustration." Oh, my God, did I just growl at him. Why the hell did he rattle me so much?

"My bad. Maybe you just need a mind-blowing fuck, then?" he taunted. "I can help with that since you're curious as to whether I fuck hard?"

"What the—" Eyes widening at his audacity, I choked out a disbelieving laugh. Wait. When was I curious about how he fucked? Annoyance poisoned my thoughts, my nails bit into my palms. "You're an arrogant asshole."

He quirked a dark brow, somehow managing to look displeased and sexy all at once. "I'd caution you to watch your mouth, sweetheart, I have a cock and it's far more effective than a ball gag."

I stiffened, sucking in a startled breath. "Oh, my God—" Once again words defeated me.

That bottom lip curved in the slightest of smiles. "Then again considering what you asked me that night, I'm inclined to think you might beg me for a demonstration." Sparkling sapphires poured molten heat into my body, intense and unrelenting, goading me to question him.

*Fuck you.* What the hell had I asked him? A sudden image of him fucking me against a wall flashed through my muddled brain. *Shit.* I didn't fuck him, did I? I would've remembered. Wouldn't I? Maybe I was just overwhelmed. "Overwhelmed doesn't make you wet," I muttered under my breath, conscious of my suddenly rapid breathing and slick panties. Masking my confusion with outrage, I swiveled away to face the window, Trent's soft chuckle bouncing off my back.

*Zayne where the flip are you?*

Why would Tia think it necessary to divulge my personal life to Trent? While he didn't seem like the stalker type, for some inexplicable reason he made me uncomfortable. Not in an immoral manner though. If anything, he made me all too aware of myself.

Unconsciously, I fingered my hair to ensure its neatness. Pretending I wasn't attracted to him was hopeless. He had to be aware of my reaction to him. It was uncanny how he not only aroused my anger but the unusual heat coursing through my body. As a chef of a reasonably well-known restaurant, I'd been in the presence of plenty of strange men before and I'd become adept at steering my thoughts away from anything sexual, but none had elicited the reactions this man did.

# Trent

RIKA'S TELLTALE RESPONSES to my appearance sent a jolt straight to my cock. Not only was my body having an unusual reaction to her sass, but she was just as affected by me as I was by her. Despite my teasing, I watched her through wistful eyes. The urge to reach out, take her in my arms and remind her how much I loved her, grew with every breath. I let my gaze roam over her as the breeze from the air-conditioning unit above, riffled playfully through her long hair. I longed to run my fingers through the silky soft strands like she was doing right now.

I wondered if the kiss or me turning her down had prompted her irritation. Then again, her responses indicated she couldn't recall that night. If that was the case, I hadn't given her any other reason to warrant such coldness. Had I? Perhaps it was her way of dealing with strangers. The fact that she saw me as one meant I hadn't piqued her interest yet. The thought that this would be how we would behave around each other made me miserable. Still, I'd seen the flicker of her eyes over my body like she was curious. Maybe she battled an internal struggle to get to know me or not—a long shot but optimism went a heck of a long way further than nothing. Perhaps I had to scale my manipulation attempts up a notch, go in blunt as fuck and hope like hell it worked.

Raking a hand through my hair, I took a seat on the leather couch flanking the wall parallel to the window. I reached for a magazine and pretended to be interested in an article but from my peripheral vision, I studied her rigid form. Apart from the lighter shade of her dark hair, she hadn't changed. Same long curls dancing just above her shapely rear, smooth caramel skin, and perfect curves

I ached to touch. The tight white jeans and turquoise t-shirt gave her the innocence of a teenager, nothing to hint at a twenty-nine-year-old mother of two.

On the verge of attempting conversation, the door opened. Dr. Landers and Zayne entered. Schooling my features into a polite mask, I stood.

"Dr. Landers, meet Trent Shaw, a friend of mine," Zayne introduced me.

The doctor proffered a hand as Rika crossed the room to Zayne's side. "Mr. Shaw, pleased to make your acquaintance. Caught your recent interview on the news, must say I'm impressed." I nodded my thanks. He referred to my win as Top Businessman of the Year that I'd been interviewed for, a week ago.

"You knew he was coming?" Rika's heated whisper at my rear, caught my ear as I followed the doctor to his couch.

"I'm sorry, baby. Tia mentioned he might be able to help. He's had experience with hypnotherapy for some family member."

Even though Zayne's endearment pricked my heart, I was impressed with his ability to lie with such conviction. With his help, I'd met Dr. Landers earlier that morning and explained the situation. He'd also played his part perfectly.

"Ashrika?"

I frowned at the doctor before realizing that was Rika's full name. While surprised by how close it sounded to Krisha's name, I liked it.

"Yes, doc."

"I'm ready when you are, dear." He gestured to the long leather couch.

She walked around me, still refusing to acknowledge my presence. I took the seat the doctor indicated while Zayne dropped to a chrome stool next to the couch. Sensing her anxiety, my stomach muscles twisted as she ran her tongue over her lips and settled on the couch. Avoiding my gaze, she focused her nervous eyes on Zayne. He winked then offered her a comforting smile. Jealousy meandered through every nerve as I wished for that same reaction of comfort and trust from her.

Pulling up another stool, Dr. Landers sat and gently patted her arm. "Relax, dear, there's no need to be nervous. You've done this before. Okay?"

Nodding, Ashrika reclined fully on the couch. Dr. Landers made a few adjustments to his watch then eased a gold pendulum hanging on a chain out of the top pocket of his coat.

"All right, I want you to take a deep breath." He gave her hand another gentle squeeze. "Try your best to rid your mind of all thoughts and concentrate your energy on this pendulum, okay." Slowly, he swayed the object in front of her face.

I watched as she fixed her eyes on the pendulum, following its sway for what seemed like an eternity but was a couple of minutes. Her eyelids drooped and she appeared to be fighting the lethargy. But as Dr. Lander's soft words of encouragement filtered through the air, her features relaxed until she finally closed her eyes in surrender.

"She's gone under now." He looked at me. "Do you want to swap seats with Zayne? I nodded. We stood and exchanged seats. "I'm going to ask her a few random questions to necessitate her calm then I'll begin the in-depth ones, okay with you?"

"Yes." I clenched my fingers in anticipation.

For the next minute, Dr. Landers asked her a selection of general questions. I reined in my impatience for him to begin questioning her about the kidnapping.

"I'm going to take you to a specific date now, and I want you to remember the last thing before you woke up in the hospital." His soft statement had me fully focusing my attention on her. I didn't want to miss out on any information she might recall. Her brow creased briefly before her relaxed expression transformed into panic. Her body tensed and her fingers latched onto Landers' arm.

"Easy, dear, you're safe. No one's going to hurt you," he soothed. "Tell me what you see."

Without giving any thought to my action, I reached out and gently clasped her hand. Immediately, the tension in her body slackened and she released her hold on the doctor's arm, holding on to mine with both hands. He and Zayne gaped at me.

"What do you see, Ashrika?" Landers coaxed once more.

While her features remained calm, the rapid movement beneath her closed lids signaled she was either afraid or forcing herself to see something. I had no idea how the treatment worked, and I prayed like hell it did.

"It's dark. I can't see anything. Smells rancid...like dead fish. There's..." she broke off and tension nipped the tendons in my neck until she began speaking again. "Light. A sliver of light on my left. It...its...looks like a crack in the wall—a window. Outside," her voice remained whisper soft as though she feared someone would hear her thoughts.

"Go on," Landers urged.

"There's noise outside...sounds like seagulls and heavy vehicles...machinery—noisy. I can't tell. It's blurred."

"Do you see any people?"

"No one...my eyes..."

"What's wrong with your eyes?"

"Hurt. My hands...I can't move my hands...tired. Thirsty. Water. I'm scared, please, I need to get out...please—help me!" Her voice rose in a crescendo, her fear so tangible I felt it in the tight grip on my hand. She let go, her hands flailed helplessly as though grabbing for a lifeline. Her breathing sped up, her chest rising and falling in quick succession.

I opened my mouth to say something and Landers shook his head. "It's all right, Ashrika. No one's going to hurt you. Listen to my voice. I'm right here with you. Take a deep breath and clear your mind," he whispered, his tone gentle.

With my heart in shreds, I reached for her hands once more. Bringing them to my lips, I kissed each one softly. "Bring her out, doctor," I whispered.

"Are you sure?"

"Trent?" Zayne stood and neared me. "Are you sure you want that? She hasn't said anything yet."

My stomach muscles tightened. As much as I wanted to hear the details that led to her kidnap, I couldn't stand her pained expression. "Yes. She's scared, Zayne."

"All right I'll—" Landers began.

"I have to get out. My hands...I can see...my head hurts," Ashrika's abrupt babble cut him off.

"What's outside the window, Ashrika?" he asked, his eyes on me. I nodded.

"Nothing...it's small. Have to get...Voices, male...two of them outside. They're unlocking the door...I'm scared. No!" she shrieked. "Get away from me...Leave me alone! Help me! someone help!" Her nails bit into the back of my hands.

Her anguish ripped right through me, tearing a hole through my heart. "Bring her out, doctor," I blinked back the tears, my voice hoarse.

"No, please don't hurt me. No!" she cried. "Help me! Someone..." Her tormented sobs filled the room.

Her pleading was like a poison arrow straight to my heart. I struggled to breathe, gasping harsh pants on my exhales, I hissed, "Bring her out. Now!" I bit down on my bottom lip but the tears fell. God have mercy when I laid my hands on those bastards.

"Ashrika, listen to my voice," Landers soothed. "When I count to three, you'll forget everything except my voice. Relax, now. Slow, deep breaths." Her breathing eased to gentle rasps. "Hear my voice. When I snap my fingers, you'll wake up."

When he was sure, she'd eased out of her fear, Landers nodded to me. He waited while I wiped away her tears then counted to three and snapped his fingers. She opened her eyes and startled to find me at her side, her shocked expression hinted as much. Switching her gaze to Zayne then Landers, she frowned before her eyes fell to her hand tightly clasped in mine. Her brow shot up and I almost laughed out loud at the sass in that action. My smile was a peace-offering. Hers was non-existent. Pulling her hand out of my grasp, she slid her feet off the couch and sat up.

"Did I reveal anything that might help," she asked, her tone wistful.

Glancing at me, Landers stood and moved to his table. He lowered his large build into the leather chair and waited for Ashrika and Zayne to take their seats on the opposite side while I stood behind her. "I'm sorry, dear, while you skirted the edge of something bad happening to you, there was nothing helpful."

I watched her shoulders slump in dejection. It took controlled effort not to lean forward and kiss away her pain.

"Don't despair." Landers smiled. "This kind of therapy isn't a quick fix and sometimes it's not necessarily how everything happened. Over a few sessions, bits of information can be pieced together to get the whole picture. Eight months between today and your last session is a long time to go without prompting images of your past, not to mention that we're trying to recreate something that happened several years ago. It takes time."

She let out a low sigh. "So, in other words, I need more sessions?" Landers nodded. "Is it even worth it?"

He looked at Zayne and I, his eyes questioning as though asking to help him convince her. "You know it is, baby," Zayne responded with a squeeze to her shoulder. He glanced up at me and I wasn't sure if he was trying to convince me otherwise.

"But it could take ages," she groaned.

"Not necessarily." Landers leaned forward and folded his arms on the table, his gaze encompassing the three of us. "As I mentioned before. Our memories get stored in a secure part of our brain, call it a safe if you must. All it needs is the right combination to trigger the lock. And if cracking a safe was easy, the whole world will be filled with rich thieves." I smiled at his analogy. "Perhaps, I haven't asked you the right questions, the right combination to jar your memory." He offered her a reassuring smile. "You must understand, dear, the mind is an extremely delicate matter. If playing with it was that simple, I'd be out of a job. Hypnosis allows you to become absorbed in something your mind creates. Whether it's the truth or not, we don't know for sure. But sometimes your actual memories will try to break through, it requires patience. Jolting your memory too quickly could cause you considerable harm."

"How?"

"At our first session I told you, you were mentally fighting your demons. You'd gone through a traumatic experience without the added burden of losing your memory. While it's not entirely unlikely to uncover the truth, it's been a long time. If I rush this, I could open wounds which you'd probably do best to forget. Pure speculation, dear, nothing solid," Landers consoled.

She raked her hands through her hair, sighed and tilted her head back on the rest, allowing her gaze to clash with mine. Although she didn't look away, she didn't return my smile. I wished there was something positive I could say that would brighten her expression. We stared at each other for a long moment until Zayne's abrupt cough broke the contact. She dropped her head. "So, what do I do now? Stop living and concentrate on getting my memories back. I've lived a secluded life for the last few years, not forgetting the time I lost to a coma, trusting no one besides Zayne and Tia."

She was so quiet for a long moment after that last statement, her breathing labored, it was obvious she'd reached breaking point. I wanted to take her in my arms or perhaps touch her shoulder, offer my comfort in some way then she reached across the armrest of their chairs and laced her fingers with Zayne's. Tiny spurts of envy pricked my body, digging into it like the deadly claws of an unsuspecting predator.

"I want to move on, to live like my past never existed and perhaps consider an idyllic life with a kid or two."

Her words were like a knife to my heart, piercing and profound with each utterance. *You have two already.* I silently screamed. I closed my eyes, swallowing hard to stop from regurgitating words I'd repeated over and over on my way to the hospital—words I knew if she heard, would have her walking in the opposite direction. She couldn't trust me like she did Zayne. And yet she did, once. Hell, she didn't even know me. I'd come across like a crazy-assed stalker if her responses up to now were anything to go by. But she did know me, I just needed to remind her that our love had taken a sabbatical and it was time to bring it home, back to me.

I caught Landers' rueful expression and inhaled to ease my breathing into a calmer perspective. "Your best bet right now, my dear, would be to schedule another appointment then take it from there. If I have to offer some advice, don't concentrate too much on anything solid right now, rather scour your brain to see if you can come up with anything to help your memory. Meditation works wonders."

She uttered a low laugh. "I don't have time to myself, where would I fit in meditation."

"We could close the restaurant for a bit," Zayne suggested.

Her head swung sharply. "Are you insane? I've worked so hard for the last three years to make it one of the best restaurants on the waterfront. My memories aren't important enough to warrant its closing," she huffed.

I balled my fists, biting my lip to keep from shaking her into thinking about herself, about her past for just a moment. I admired her business tenacity but if I didn't make a dent in that rigid stance of hers, I'd be lost on her.

"Listen, Ashrika." Landers stood. "While it's entirely your decision to choose your next step, can I offer another piece of advice?" She nodded. "You've resisted enjoying yourself for a long time and while hard work helped put the constant thoughts of not knowing to the back of your mind, it's to your detriment."

"How?" I could hear the irritation in her voice.

"One day with no warning, you might break, and all that evasion could come back in a rush, turning you into someone you might not want to be. And I'm sure that's not your intention?"

Slowly, she shook her head. "I'm listening."

Landers took off his glasses and polished it with a cloth. "Instead of hard work and concentrating on 'what if's', try having some fun for a change. Go dancing. Indulge in some wild fantasy, anything positive makes an ideal stimulus. Visit Disney World if you haven't. Get out of the norm, something different to stir your memory. Do something reckless, within reason of course. You've never had a birthday party, right?"

"She never wanted one," Zayne replied instead earning a punch to the arm. "What? It's the truth." He laughed and I envied their easy relationship.

"Plan a birthday party." Landers walked around the table and held out a hand. She accepted and stood. "Contrary to the popular beliefs of snobs, laughter is the best healer, dear."

"Maybe you're right."

"Something out of the ordinary might trigger the unknown." Chuckling, Landers led us to the door.

After pleasant farewells, I walked out with them but stayed at the rear. When we reached the elevators, I stalled. "Thanks for inviting me, Zayne. I think I left my phone behind. Tell Tia I'll see her soon." He accepted my hand in a quick shake. "Bye, *Ashrika*." I emphasized her name, hoping she'd make eye contact.

She didn't and instead faced the elevator door. I'd never been this turned on by a woman who wanted nothing to do with me. She might be my wife, but the appeal was that much more enticing. As I stepped away I caught her question to Zayne. "Why was he here and why the hell was he holding my hand when I came to?"

I peeked around a large trolley filled with neatly pressed laundry, waiting to hear Zayne's response. "Landers figured that if a total stranger held your hand while you were under hypnosis, it might help."

My intelligent wife wasn't convinced, I could hear the doubt in her tone. "How?"

"Doc mentioned something about hypnosis working well with touch therapy which used vibrations or some shit like that to trigger memories. Honestly, you're asking the wrong person, Angel." Zayne groaned. "Why didn't you ask doc?" Smiling, I shook my head. I had to give the man credit for lying with a straight face. "And since Trent was there—"

"Why was he there in the first place?" she muttered. "I mean first the restaurant, then the club, and now, here. What next?"

They stepped back to allow a patient in a wheelchair and his visitors access to the elevator and waited for the next one. "What's wrong, Rika. Why don't you like the guy?" Zayne asked.

I held my breath. Curious to hear her reply, the reason for her annoyance with me.

"It's not that I don't like him," she replied.

Okay, I liked that response.

"But?" Zayne pushed.

"I just get this vibe from him."

"What vibe?"

"Like he wants to devour me."

Was that self-irritation? Had I sparked her interest? I rolled my lips between my teeth to stop my laughter,

But Zayne cracked up. "Would you let him, if he wanted to?"

"Really? Are you like serious right now?" She punched him on the arm. "He's not that—" She entered the elevator, cutting off her words.

Well, at least she had my intention down pat. There were a lot of things I wanted to do to her and devour her was just the tip of the iceberg. Shaking my head, I turned. Back inside Landers' office, I took a seat opposite him. "So, what do you think, doc?"

Pushing his specs up a fraction, Landers shook his head. "I hate to say this, son, but judging from her reaction, I'd say she's suffered a terrible ordeal and I'm not sure if I'm keen to take her back there."

"Even at the risk of her losing her family?" I leaned forward and rested my palms on the table. "What are the chances of recovery?"

"It's hard to say. Had we explored this avenue closer to the time, it might've yielded a more positive outcome. Now, not so much. It would probably take months of sessions before we find out anything concrete."

I slumped back and sighed. "Hell, doc, I don't know if I can wait any longer to tell her who I am, tell her who she is. What if I took her home and showed the family photos, our house, take her to meet her father?"

"I understand your frustrations, Trent, but I wouldn't. There's the possibility she might come out of this with a minimum of sessions and blissful on the other hand, it might be the total opposite and she'd withdraw completely. Honestly, I can't say. It's a risky gamble at best," Landers crossed his arms over his midriff and stared at me.

"Why? Wouldn't she rather know the identity of her family?"

"You're forgetting one minor problem."

"Which is?"

"You made yourself visible to her weeks ago and not revealing your identity sooner might make it harder for her to accept."

Annoyance crept over me, stealing my thought process and turning me into a disgruntled fool. Rising, I shoved my hands into the pockets of my jeans and paced the room. "What do I do, then?"

"Other than bide your time, I haven't the faintest idea."

"Bide my time hoping her memory will return while she decides to make a family with another man?" The words came out harsher than I intended. I stopped and glanced at him. "Sorry, doc."

"Perfectly all right, son."

"Maybe I should just go back home and leave her be." I resumed pacing. "The last four weeks have been a living hell. Not only have I neglected my children, but I also can't seem to focus. Every day since I've walked into that restaurant and discovered my wife is alive, I've waited for a sign, something to make me believe fate isn't a cruel motherfucker determined to play with people's emotions."

"Maybe it's her time to live another life." Landers shrugged.

I uttered a caustic laugh. "I'd walk through hell for that woman, doc. There's no way I'd give her up so easily."

"Even if she might not want you?"

I stopped pacing and stared at him, chewing the insides of my cheek in contemplation. "I always get what I want, doc. It's a motto that's held me in good stead and it will take a miracle for me to walk away from her without trying to let her know how much I love her."

"I like your beliefs, Trent but what do you have?"

"Arrogance." I shrugged at his frown. "I'll seduce her if I have to."

Landers laughed. "Something tells me I should believe you."

"You should." Even as I answered, I still wished for a sign that would show me what to do. "Still, I just wish I had something to guide my next move—" I trailed off, staring at the ceiling, praying for answers. As I dropped my gaze, it fell to a shiny object near the leather couch. I picked it up, studied it for a long moment. Laughing, I turned to face Landers. "I believe I've found my answer, doc."

He glanced at the object I held up, stood and skirted the table to my side. "Isn't that Ashrika's chain?"

"Yes. Fate is on my side."

Confusion lined his brow. Grinning, I fished a chain from my pocket then held the two half pendants out for the doctor to inspect. His eyes widened in disbelief. When I brought the two halves together and clipped them into place to form a whole heart, he gasped.

"It's a perfect match."

"We are." I smiled staring down at the two chains joined by the heart. "Seasons come and seasons go but we will always be one heart and two souls. That's what she'd told me when she gave this to me when we married." Tears glazed my eyes at the memory. "We'd been married for three years before she fell pregnant and seven months later, the complications began. "Ironically, this is my way back to her, doc."

"How?"

"You mentioned she should go out and have fun. Enjoy herself to relieve stress. If I can manipulate her outings to include me, it might give me a chance to spend more time with her. Hopefully, it might trigger her memory and if it doesn't, she'd get to know me better," I explained, my tone wistful.

"You're going to make her fall in love with you again?" Landers' brow rose with a gentle smile.

I laughed. "That's the idea."

"I don't see any harm in that. If anything, I think it might help if the truth is revealed. One question though?"

"Yes."

"How do you intend to use that to your advantage?" He pointed to the chain.

"I'm hoping it will be the reason she starts talking to me. So far, she's been reticent around me. Maybe, this little trinket will change that." I kissed the pendant.

"I wish you all the best." Landers smiled. "Honestly, I've had a few amnesia cases that had me stumped but Ashrika's is the rarest, one I pray that has a happy ending for you both. Now if you'll excuse me, I've another appointment I need to get ready for and I hope to see you soon with Ashrika of course."

"Thanks, doc, for your help and patience." After a quick handshake, I headed for the elevator. While I waited for the car to ascend, I stared at the chain. "You and I will have a date with a lovely lady, soon." I grinned.

# Ashrika

"HEY, RIKA, I'M DONE."

I looked up from stacking the last of the leftovers in the refrigerator as Leah entered through the rear door. She'd gone out to discard the trash for the evening.

"Thanks, Leah." I waited for her to finish washing her hands. "I'll lock up behind you. I'm beat and looking forward to a nice hot shower."

She dried her hands and looked up. "Sounds like a plan, if you can get rid of our last diner first."

Glancing at the clock above the door, I frowned. "Last diner? It's 10.45p.m. The kitchen's been closed for forty-five minutes already." My frown deepened. She grinned. "Please don't tell me." That look on her face was all the confirmation I needed that Trent was still there. "God, the man is persistent," I moaned. After the club incident, I forgot my discussion with Tia about giving him a chance to discuss the job opportunity. I probably would have, had he not surprised me at Dr. Landers' office. Zayne and Tia had yet to give me a suitable explanation of what Trent was doing there. It was a pointless avoidance. Puffing out my cheeks in a frustrated breath, I glanced at her. "Did you tell him we're closed?"

"I tried. Tia is with him now, but he won't leave unless he speaks to you." Leah neared me. "I know we joked about it that night of Nina's shower but maybe you should give it a try, Rika."

"What?"

"Him." Her smile wasn't the usual tease but a gentle coaxing.

"I don't understand."

She neared me. "Look, you were the one that told us you and Zayne are married in name only, right." I nodded, wondering where she was going with that. "You also mentioned he hasn't tried anything, like, you know, come onto you and stuff."

"And your point?"

"You need a change of scenery. You need—"

"Sex." Tia entered the kitchen.

"Seriously?" I stared at my friend like she'd somehow lost a couple of marbles between yesterday and today. "How did that man's intentions go from wanting to offer me a job to wanting to..." I trailed off, any sexual thoughts about him were asking for trouble. The fact that he'd become a permanent resident in my dreams since meeting him and the heated looks he sent my way proved that point already.

"Fuck you?" Tia's brow shot up before she sighed. "Leah's right. You're stuck in this place twenty-four seven—"

"Are you forgetting Nina's bridal shower and how that ended?" I scoffed.

"I'm sorry that happened, babe. We drank a lot, well, you mostly because you were trying to curb your anxieties. That said you did have *that* gorgeous man save you." She jerked a thumb over her shoulder toward the dining area with a chuckle. I glowered at her and Leah as they both giggled like gushing teens. "You never did tell us what happened after he took you home. A kiss perhaps?"

"Go jump off the pier, Tia," I grunted. While I was still blown away by his impudence at Landers' rooms, I should've thanked him for saving me instead of coming across like an insolent child.

"Oh, come on, Rika. That was just one night in like three years since knowing you. You rarely go out unless Zayne forces you," she snapped, mistaking my irritation for her forcing me to go out that night and the ensuing events.

I didn't correct her assumption because she was right. Zayne had opened the restaurant as a way for me to forget about trying to remember my past. I'd worked hard to make it a success and we'd all become more like a family than boss and employee relationships. I hardly went out unless Zayne was with me. I was something of a—

"You're a recluse," Leah finished my thoughts. "Then again." She glanced at Tia, who nodded. "While you're cheeky as shit with the men that visit here, I don't think you'd be able to take on Mr. Shaw. The man is a force unto himself." She grinned.

"I second that." Tia wiggled her brows.

I rolled my eyes. "Is that a challenge?"

They both nodded with a laugh. "Twenty bucks says you can't." Leah's usual teasing smirk was back in place.

"Did you two plan this shit?" I huffed. They shook their heads. "I'd swear you're both more worried about my pussy than I am." They chuckled like the sexual deviants they were.

"We just wanted to see how game you are." Tia gave me a cheeky smile. "You know, to take on that handsome hunk." She winked.

"Fine," I muttered, shocking myself and earning a hyped 'yes' from them. "And what's the prize if I win." Not that it mattered since I didn't intend caving to their taunts.

"Depends on what you plan to do?" Leah eyed me with open suspicion, not trusting I'd keep my end of the challenge.

I made a show of wiping an already clean countertop, giving myself a few seconds to collect the thoughts buzzing around in my head. "Talk to him," I mumbled, hoping they'd let it go.

They both looked at each other. "Nope," they said in unison. So much for that notion of escaping whatever they planned.

"A kiss to start with," Tia suggested.

My mouth dropped in surprise and my heart hammered at the thought of kissing those thick, full lips. I folded my arms, hoping to come across as not completely sold on the idea. "Can't I start with a chat and progress from there?" I still was blurry on whether I'd kissed him the night he saved me. They shook their heads.

"A kiss and we do the dishes for a month?" Leah said.

"Really? That's the best you can come up with," I retorted with a laugh. "How does that help me since we do employ busboys, remember?"

They both looked at me, their expressions contemplative. "Fine, we'll owe you, whatever it is and whenever you want to collect," Tia mumbled.

I laughed. Seeing as I was very simplistic in my needs and Zayne provided me with everything I needed, I figured that would stump them. "Fine. You can both leave."

"We'll wait until he leaves," Leah offered.

Shaking my head, I pointed to the clock. "It's late and your rides have been waiting for almost thirty minutes. Go."

"Want him all to yourself, don't you?" Tia chuckled. When I gaped at her, she added, "just don't mess up the table settings, he does look like a man who fucks hard."

"What the...seriously—" I blabbered. I could feel my cheeks burning. "Get out." I pointed to the door.

They both snorted with laughter like a bunch of schoolgirls. "Be careful, babe," Tia called over her shoulder as they traipsed out the door.

"I can handle him," I retorted.

What I didn't tell them was that I aimed to give the man a piece of my mind. Who the hell did he think he was? Taking liberties we normally didn't afford our regulars. I already had a few choice words lined up. Locking the rear door behind Leah, I headed for the internal door, pushed through and stopped short. Whatever words I intended hurling were abruptly replaced with, "holy hell," under my breath. I fought the urge to retract my defiance and call the girls back. I didn't want to be alone with this man for the simple reason that he turned me into a depraved ball of sexual energy, and I had no idea how to handle him.

*Chin up, girl.*

I hadn't been to the dining area all day and admittedly, the vision in front of me, would rival any of the lip-smacking dishes I could prepare. Mouthwatering in black pants, a black button-down open at the chest and legs crossed at the ankles, Trent leaned against the bar. His attention riveted on his phone, he didn't notice me. I took a moment to admire his tall build. The rolled-up sleeves not only showcased tattooed forearms, but deeply corded veins enhanced by a large watch on the one hand and thick leather bands on the other. Strangely, I found myself salivating at the thought of what he'd taste like.

*Freaking hell!*

While I hadn't lavished him with this much attention at the doctor's rooms, I couldn't understand my reaction to him. Granted he was attractive, but we had a lot of good-looking patrons. Perhaps it was his unerring confidence that made the difference. He carried himself like a man that owned the world and those were few and far between. Still, there was just something about him and I had yet to find out what.

He looked up, staring, as though he sensed my inner debacle. His brow shot up before those thick full lips parted in a slow smile. The breath left my body on a rushed exhale. Oh, my God. If I didn't know better, I'd swear even my ovaries yelled 'fuck me.' *Jesus, would you get a grip.* He made chocolate glazed strawberries look bland and those were my favorite.

"We're closed." I cursed at the croak and cleared my throat. "You need to leave."

He pushed away from the bar, slipped his phone and hands into his pockets, and slowly crossed the room—strike that, more like prowled toward me, a graceful predator out for the hunt, hooded eyes, daring me to run. Only, I wasn't tempted to turn tail and run—more like determined to stand my ground and meet this man head on, sexiness and all.

He stopped a foot away. Eyes the color of midnight, seductive in their slow appraisal over me. My throat tightened and my breathing labored at his sudden proximity. Stupidly, I wondered why I hadn't dressed in something a little sexier than my simple summer dress. Without breaking eye-contact, I suppressed the self-condescending snort I felt hit the insides of my suddenly dry mouth. He took a step closer and I kicked myself when I stepped back. *Shit.*

"Are you afraid of me?" His full lips parted slightly, and as his gaze lowered to my mouth, my stomach muscles began a slow churn.

"No." I silently congratulated my resolve to show him I wasn't intimidated.

He cocked his head to one side, rolling his tongue in a slow wet trail over his bottom lip as though he'd discovered something appetizing. "You should be."

"Why?"

His smile was feral. "Because once I fuck you, you won't want me to leave."

*Holy shit.* His filthy words unleashed a shameless quiver between my thighs. His gaze slid from my face to my neck, all the way down to my feet before coming back to meet mine, pinning me beneath a stare filled with raw desire.

I licked my lips and those blue orbs homed in on that action. "A bit presumptuous, aren't you?"

"Not presumption. Assertion."

I wasn't sure whether to feel offended or excited. Common sense told me I should be angry with him, but strangely, I was freaking turned on—pure, blatant arousal. Was that wrong? "Tell me. Are you always this arrogant?"

"Yes." The conviction in his tone shot tingles between my legs, making the ache unbearable. "I'm a man who delights in fine dining and right now you're on the menu. I want to taste you, lick you, fuck you and when I'm done, *you'll* want me for seconds."

Oh, my God. I swallowed, trying to ignore the sudden tingle that began at the base of my spine and shot up to my suddenly heavy breasts or that my nipples were so hard beneath my bra, they grazed the soft material. Every inch of my body buzzed with the vibrant energy he radiated. Was it even possible to feel so out of control around a man?

"I have no idea if I should be angry or disgusted with your so-called assertions," I replied with a silent pat to my back for not stuttering.

"But we both know that you're sure of one thing, though?" There was a glint to his striking eyes that I chose to ignore.

"I can't wait to hear another one of your detailed analyses." My tone syrupy sweet with sarcasm.

"That right now if I had to slide my cock inside you, the sounds of your already soaked pussy will make every damn porn movie demand a remake."

This time, my jaw hit the floor, not from revulsion but his uncanny perception. How the hell could he tell that my panties were drenched. It was ridiculous how affected I was by him. When I could finally breathe without coming across as though I were on the verge of an orgasm, I swallowed and stared him straight in the eye. "It'll take a lot more than your smug words to soak anything of mine."

His grin called bullshit, but his reply was smooth, "willing to test that premise?"

Okay, I didn't see that coming. I scoured my brain for a neutral topic that didn't hint at blatant sexual tension making up the six-foot something of sin standing in front of me. "You don't know me, yet you speak to me as though you want me to fall for you."

"Who's to say whether I know you or not?" he replied. I shook my head and gave up trying to figure out the man. He was suave, appealingly so. "Would falling for me be so wrong?"

"It wouldn't be right."

"Why not?"

"Because I'm married."

"So am I."

I sucked in a breath. The divulgence squeezing my insides with a grip so tight, I was at an abrupt loss for words. And even as I looked at him, I was unsure whether my body reacted from disdain or disappointment. "Yet, you're here trying to get into my panties when you should be home taking care of your wife," I bit out. *Shit.* So much for avoiding a sexual inference.

Without so much as a flinch, he replied, "I had something a little deeper than your panties in mind." I gulped. Yep, I was out of my league. He took a step closer, caging me against a table with his hands on either side of my hips. "She won't mind. I have a voracious appetite."

The audacity in his smile was something. It could probably persuade a lot of women to bend to his will. I should be wary, angry even. And yet I was still standing there. I inhaled deeply. It didn't help that his cologne, an aggressive mix of musk and mint with undertones of citrus, stole its way through every pore, seizing my senses and toying with my restraint.

"People who overeat tend to suffer an upset stomach," I retorted.

His chuckle was low and husky, almost like an erotic beacon intent on enticing my pussy. I hoped the subtle squeeze of my thighs went unnoticed. How the hell did women survive a simple conversation with this man, without coming across as desperate to be fucked across every damn piece of furniture in sight.

"Don't worry." A wicked smirk teased his lips. He leaned closer still, forcing my body to arch back, pushing my breasts up. My eyes dropped to his lips, a breath away from mine. "I enjoy every morsel before I swallow and trust me," my gaze flicked up to meet his, "that will include your pussy too. Only, I don't chew, sweetheart, I bite."

I gasped. The vivid visual screamed 'get the fuck out of there.' Yet, for some stupid reason, I couldn't move. "Why are you here?"

"To give you a heart."

"Excuse me?"

He dipped his hand into his pocket. "You dropped your heart at Dr. Landers' rooms." He opened his palm, revealing my gold chain.

My eyes widened. "Gosh, I wondered where I'd left it."

I reached out a hand to take it and he closed his before it disappeared into the pocket of his pants. My gaze dropped. The only way to get the chain back was to slide my hand into his pocket. Eyeing the defined erection bulging the front of his pants, I was sure he'd love my hand fishing around in his pocket.

"You only get it back if I can put it on."

"Are you that desperate to touch me," I scoffed, secretly hoping I could act natural if he insisted?

"Absolutely." His lips curled in a carnal smile like it was the most obvious answer.

"Fine." Turning away, I swept my open hair off my neck to lie over one shoulder. He took a step forward. Conscious of the heat his proximity emitted, I fought to ignore the awareness, but my hammering heart proved otherwise. When nothing happened, I glanced over my shoulder. "Having second thoughts?" I bit my bottom lip to keep from laughing but it was his darkened gaze that told me he was just as affected at the notion of him touching me as I was. I turned away and bowed my head. A second later, he reached over me. His warm breath stirred a tendril of hair on my neck. The chain was a link to my past, of that I was sure. If it wasn't, I would've told him to keep it. The second his fingers touched my nape, I nearly choked on my tongue, regretting my decision. Every nerve in my body tingled, breathing life into my body. His fingers brushed over my skin as he fumbled with the clasp. Goosebumps littered my skin forcing out a rushed exhale my lungs couldn't retain.

"Done." Before I could move away, his hands slid down my arms in a delicious slow massage. "Matters of the heart, sweetheart, are inexplicable. You never know when you lose it," he whispered into my neck.

"What would anyone do with such a little heart anyway?" I murmured, distracted by the heat of his grip on my arms.

"Wear it around his neck and keep it close to his heart." His throaty chuckle had the fine hairs at my nape standing to attention.

Without thinking I tipped my head, giving him access. He let out a low growl, nibbling his way up to my ear and bit the soft lobe before dragging his tongue back down and sucking on my shoulder. My mind on a sensory overload I barely noticed when his hands skimmed my waist, around my stomach and climbed up to cup my breasts. His fingers rolled over my nipples, hardening them to tight buds. I couldn't stop the soft whimper and thrust my hips back into his hard cock, shocking my body.

He groaned. "Say the word, and I'll fuck you over every piece of furniture in this room."

I jerked away, gulping at having thought the same thing earlier while irritated that my skin was burning from his touch. We stared at each other, our uneven breathing in perfect sync. How was I so easily swayed by a man I didn't know? I was usually so adept at keeping to myself. "What do you want from me?" the words slipped out huskier than I intended.

Despite my backbone making me deceptively taller, I still had to look up at him. Hooded eyes, the only evidence of his arousal, studied me "You already know what I want."

I shifted under his appraisal. "Do you always get what you want?"

"Yes," came the quick reply.

"Have you ever gotten a knee to the balls then?" I suppressed a grin.

He threw back his head in a guttural laugh. "My balls have met other parts of the body, never a knee, though."

"*Yet*."

He cocked a brow. "I don't think kneeing my balls would bring you as much pleasure as you on your knees sucking them."

Stunned, my eyes widened. "God, you're crass."

"I did try being nice, it didn't work."

"Nice? So you resort to being an ass."

"If that's what it takes to get you interested."

"Why?"

"I'm intrigued."

"Because you've never been turned down by a woman?" Admittedly, I'd never been this captivated either.

"That too." He grinned.

Why was I still entertaining him? *He's married.* Instead of walking away, I surprised myself by saying, "If you want dinner, that I can do. If you want something a little more horizontal, I'm not interested, well..." My gaze roamed his face and one dark brow shot up, almost daring me to give him what he wanted and just once I wanted to be cheeky with him. "Maybe not yet."

His chuckle tickled my skin. My gaze dropped to his mouth, rimmed by a neatly trimmed scruff, that had me licking my own lips, begging for a taste. By God, I was tempted. As if he sensed my dilemma, he inched closer. "Try it," he whispered, trailing a slow finger along my jaw before rolling the pad over my lips, tracing the shape. "You know you want to." His words mixed with his touch held deep sexuality. Potent. Addictive. And so damn alluring.

My chin lifted slightly, lips a breath away from his, my mind whirled. I should kiss him, just to see what it felt like. I had an inkling that Trent Shaw was like a deluxe cordon bleu dish and if I didn't get a taste I might go hungry for a very long time to come. "Dinner." I raised a brow. "Take it or leave, *sweetheart*," I whispered instead, emphasizing the endearment with a touch of sarcasm and stepped back.

Laughing, he dropped his hands and straightened. "Friendship then?" He held out a hand. I eyed him skeptically, not believing his shift from erotic sensuality to gentle warmth "So, what do you say?" He rolled his tongue over his bottom lip, seizing my gaze. "As a matter of fact, my current acquaintances say I make a good friend indeed."

Disappointed by his easy acceptance of friendship, I swallowed the feeling of arousal and smiled. "Friends." I accepted his hand and was immediately startled by the heat skating up my arm.

A sly smile curved at the corner of his lips as though privy to my reaction. "A warning, though." He didn't let go of my hand. I lifted questioning eyes to his. "When a woman makes friends with me, that relationship usually changes to love."

"And let me guess, you wrote that book?" I smirked with a shake of my head.

"See, you have heard of me."

I laughed. "Now, you need to leave."

His smile fell. "I thought we're having dinner."

"I didn't mean tonight. And I'm guessing you haven't seen the time."

"Dessert, then. Please." His blue gaze pleaded. I couldn't understand his persistence. "Consider it a mini-interview."

I laughed. "Really? You've been eating here for a while now. Were the other dishes not up to standard? And who said anything about me wanting to interview with you?"

"Call it a vested interest." He winked. "The dishes were good but I could really do with something sweet right now, present company included, if possible," he said, his smile mischievous.

I rolled my eyes, still laughing. "Fine. Follow me."

When we entered the kitchen, he glanced around. "Nice."

"Not a Michelin star grade you're used to, but it does the job perfectly."

"I've no doubt."

Moving to the dessert refrigerator, I eyed him over my shoulder.

"It's a compliment. You do know what those are, right?" His brow arched. Shaking my head, I set the dessert tray I retrieved on a counter and lifted the glass lid. He leaned forward inspecting the array of 'melt in your mouth' truffles I'd created for the next evening's dessert. "What are they?"

"Balls." I grinned and his brow shot up. "Try this." I stuffed a cinnamon-flavored one into his mouth and watched him bite down on the sweet delicacy. The chef in me cringed. "You're not supposed to bite. It has to melt in your mouth until the cream leaks onto your tong—" I broke off at the surprised look on his face. *Shit.* I walked right into that one and he knew it. One dark brow quirked up, eliciting the pure wickedness that was Trent Shaw.

"The cream is exactly what I want to get to, sweetheart." He took a step toward me and I stepped back. "Why waste time with my tongue when I can use my teeth to achieve a far more explosive result." His words matched his slow steps I was failing to dissuade. If I held my ground, he'd be flush against me and I wasn't sure

I could handle that without caving. "But you're right." His voice took on a delicious, sensual tone and my legs wobbled. The counter ground into my back, halting further movement. *Shit.* My breathing sped up. With his hands on either side, he caged me in. Leaning forward until his warm breath brushed my lips, he tilted his head slightly and when he spoke again, his voice was low at my ear. "Tongue or teeth, swallowing the cream is essentially the best part. It's thick," his tongue peeked out and licked his lips so slowly, it was hypnotic to watch. Drawing his tongue back into his mouth, my gaze still transfixed on them and the words only registering when I realized he was talking, "Sticky, and tastes like fucking heaven".

Gulping, I gave up masking my shock and accepted him for what he was. Delectable mouth porn—the type you didn't rent in secret. No, he was the type you proudly flaunted. Mortified, I watched his lips curl into a lazy grin as though he were privy to my inner thoughts, almost encouraging me to sin. That was all it took. One smile and my restraint crumbled. I imagined he'd make the first move, but it was me who moved, my mouth crashing against his. His surprise lasted barely a second before he responded. Gripping me by the waist, he lifted and set me on the counter while his tongue, skilled and devilishly hot, urged my lips to widen and slid between my teeth. I forgot to breathe and that I shouldn't be kissing him. A low growl erupted from his throat, filling my mouth as he drove his tongue deeper, thrusting against mine in wild abandon. The lingering flavor of cinnamon spice filled my tastebuds, making me greedy. Grabbing his shoulders, I inched closer, deepening the kiss.

He groaned as he left my mouth to nibble on my chin. "If you keep this up, I'm going to fuck you on this counter."

I froze as reality came crashing down, bringing me out of the daze with a sharp inhale. Shoving on his chest, I caught him off guard and he stepped back. I pushed off the counter and tried to appear nonchalant but probably looked guilty as hell. "It's late and I think you overstayed your welcome." My voice came out high and tight. I cringed. Sidestepping him, I headed for the door.

He gripped my wrist and pulled me back into his arms. His head tilted slightly, he didn't appear to be offended by my rebuke, more like he expected it. "You'll change your mind soon enough, sweetheart." His certainty pierced my willpower for just a second and I was pretty sure that if he hadn't been holding me, my knees would've buckled. Silently, I stepped back and walked away, glad he didn't push and followed me. "Can I at least give you a ride home?"

"No need. I just need to run up the stairs," I replied without looking back.

"You live here?" He reached my side.

I laughed at his incredulous stare. "Yes, I have a small place here."

"And what does your husband think about that?"

I frowned at his first reference for the night to my husband, unsure if it was intentional. "Appearances can be deceiving, Mr. Shaw," I scoffed. "It's not a dump if that's what you're asking. I'll have you know that my husband takes very good care of me," I was off on a tangent, maybe because for the first time since I discovered Trent leaning against the bar, the personification of sex itself, I remembered that by allowing his indulgence, I was cheating on Zayne. My insides resembled a failed souffle.

Trent had the sense to blanch. "That's not what I meant..." he hesitated briefly then smiled. "I mean about you staying here, all alone." The genuine sincerity in his eyes had me cringing with embarrassment.

"It's safe. And it's not my permanent residence. I crash here when I have a late night coupled with an early start." Why the hell was I explaining myself? Annoyed, I opened the door. He stepped out and turned. Hands in his pants pockets, his penetrative eyes searched my face. I had no idea what to read in there, but I got the impression he was reluctant to leave. The thought made my heart flutter as my anger made a quick exit. Remembering I hadn't thanked him yet and my response to him at the doctor's rooms wasn't exactly friendly, I inched forward. "The night at the club..." I paused, my cheeks flushed still trying to recall what happened that night. "Thank you for coming to my rescue. Did the guy hurt you?"

"Even if he did, it was worth it. I'd do anything for you."

I sucked in a breath. "But you don't even know me."

"Sometimes all it takes is a look for you to know destiny is yours for the taking," the soft words accompanied by the look in his eyes had me questioning why I was opposing the attraction. Any woman in her right mind would be open to something—anything with him. "And you're mine."

"Yours?" I croaked trying to appear composed.

"Don't fight me, sweetheart. We *are* going to end up in bed together. The only decision you should be battling is in which position you'd like me to fuck you first." His tone like the brush of satin on my skin didn't match the molten flames in his eyes. The outright 'let me fuck you right now' invite, blazed brighter than the light above the door. I shivered, wanting to prolong his departure. This man didn't mince words nor, it seemed, the signals he sent. He knew what he wanted and went after it. Only, there were spouses to think about. Even if I had a logical reason behind betraying mine—not that I'd considered it—what about his?

I had to get out of there or I was likely to take him up on his offer. "Bye."

"No goodnight kiss?"

"Goodnight, Mr. Shaw." I managed without coming across like a flustered teen.

"Why so formal, Ash?"

"Ash?"

"The color of embers after losing their heated glow." At my creased brow, he leaned closer. "The shade of your eyes." I don't think I'd ever heard anyone describe the color quite like that before and the fact he'd coined it from a portion of my name, surprised me. "One night with me and I'll fuck the spark of a Blacksmith's fire into them."

God, this man. The intensity of a Blacksmith's fire could melt metal, I dared to imagine the potency when he fucked a woman. Need speared straight to my still-aching clit, begging me to take him up on his offer. Swallowing to ease my dry mouth, I shook my head with a small laugh. "And just when I figured you were poetic, you go mess it up with your crass mouth."

"As long as I've given your wet pussy something to think about, mission achieved." He winked and was striding away before I could form a suitable reply.

Shaking my head, I closed and locked the door. Trent was beyond shocking me with his unchecked comments. It was clear he took an interest and got what he wanted or didn't bother at all. Since he'd begun eating here, I'd seen the flirty and at times wistful glances both employees and patrons sent his way. He offered nothing, not even a smirk in their direction. As I undressed, I wondered why he was so interested in me. He could choose any of those openly flirtatious women, why me? Still, the attention was both flattering and uncanny.

# Trent

"IT'S NOT FUNNY, TRENT. I know that smirk. You're trying not to laugh." Fanny McDonald, my kid's nanny huffed. "Just *look* at this." She held up a pair of slacks and pointed to the stain. "What does that look like to you.

I burst out laughing then kept trying to hold up my hand in apology. Only, my shoulders shook each time I tried. We stood in the hallway outside my study and with tomorrow being her day off, she'd cornered me on my way out.

"You're supposed to be a father and you're guffawing like a teenager." She pursed her lips, as her cheeks turned a bright red. "At my age, I don't have time for this silly nonsense, especially when it embarrasses me in front of the entire bingo hall," she scolded. "Maybe it's time you found another nanny."

I immediately sobered. "I truly am sorry, Fanny. I'll speak to him." I couldn't lose her.

While Brenton was like a mini version of Manhattan, all the nanny services I had on speed dial, had blacklisted me. They would never help me even if I offered to triple the fee. My son, Nicky Shaw, was any nanny's worst nightmare. He knew every trick under the sun to get rid of nannies and where others had failed, he'd reinvent it.

"Nicky!" My stern voice, the one I hardly used on the kids, echoed through the house. I glanced at Fanny's miffed features, trying hard to look apologetic. She followed me into the study but refused the seat I gestured to.

The fifty-six-year-old woman was a friend of my butler's wife and took the job because she needed the money. After her son had died in an accident, her daughter-in-law kicked her out. In the last six months she'd weathered all of Nicky's tricks until he accepted she was there to stay. Unfortunately, that didn't mean he'd stop trying to annoy her and it looked like he'd finally managed to do something even I couldn't help laughing at.

"Daddy?" Nicky appeared at the door, took one look at Fanny, and immediately his face fell. I knew that expression all too well—one of remorse mixed with a hint of charm and puppy-dog eyes—a family trait apparently. I grinned inwardly not wanting to upset her any further.

"Jesus, Nicky, this has got to be one of the worst stunts you've pulled," I hoped I sounded firm enough for Fanny. I stank at being the rigid parent—it was never needed. But this required a little discipline to make her stay.

"It's just a little chocolate," he counted. "I didn't know she was going to sit on that chair. Promise." I didn't believe him and judging by her sharp inhale, neither did Fanny.

"Chocolate. A little," she shrieked going red in the face and Nicky flinched.

"Calm down, Fanny," I consoled. The last thing I needed was a heart attack on my hands.

"Don't you tell me to calm down, boy," she scolded. "The entire bingo hall thinks I crapped my pants. They think I'm an old fart who can't make it to the damn bathroom in time." She held up the white slacks with the large brown stain at the rear. She hadn't washed it and I could easily see why someone would think she'd crapped herself. "Does that look like a little to you?"

More like a slab if I knew my son. I rolled my lips to keep from laughing, imagining what the poor lady had gone through. "I'm sorry—"

"Your son made me a walking—" she broke off on a deep inhale. "Do you know what they're calling me?" She scowled, her gaze darting between me and Nicky. We both just stared at her, not attempting to answer. "Fanny McShitty," she screeched.

"Shit." *Oops.* Dropping my head, I covered my mouth, squeezing hard to hold the laughter in but I wasn't fooling Fanny. She cursed and I looked at her. "I'll make it up to you."

"How?" She glared at me.

"I'll contribute toward your charity work at the community center," I offered. Her face lit up. On her days off, she volunteered at the center on various projects. "And if it helps, I'll come down to the bingo hall and explain to everyone what happened." Slowly, she nodded as if not entirely convinced by the suggestion. I went a little further. "And an extra week's pay this month?" That just about did it. A small smile evened out the wrinkles around her mouth. "Happy?"

"What about him." She pointed to Nicky. "Surely, he deserves some punishment." Nicky crossed his arms over his chest and scowled at her. "Don't pout, young man," even though she scolded him, I didn't miss her telltale smile.

Rubbing my jaw, I neared him and ruffled his hair. "What do you think your punishment should be, champ?"

"Nothing. I didn't do anything," he huffed.

"And I suppose the chocolate grew legs and decided to jump onto her chair." I cocked a brow at him. "A man owns up to his mistakes, Nicky."

"Fine," he mumbled, dropping his gaze to the floor.

"How about him washing my car every week for two months," Fanny suggested.

Nicky looked up. There was an immediate spark of interest on his face. I glanced at Fanny with a smile. I knew what she was doing. No matter what Nicky did to her, her annoyance was always short-lived. I had no complaints with her care, she loved my kids and treated them well.

"What do you say, champ?"

"I suppose," he sighed.

I chuckled, not buying his pretense. Fanny's prized possession was a 1967 Shelby GT500 and even though she got offers for the car when she had no money, she refused to sell. It was the last remaining link to her husband. The first time she drove it to work, Nicky went apeshit over the car. Even my Lambo that he loved, took second place for his affection. Her suggestion was a well-played strategy to guarantee he'd never trick her again. Somehow, I didn't believe Nicky would stop.

"Then it's settled," I said, and she nodded. "Fanny, would you excuse us for a minute, please."

"Sure."

After she walked out, I lowered by myself to my leather chair. "Take a seat, Nicky." He slid into a seat on the opposite side, rested his elbows on the table and cupped his face. "When are you going to grow out of these tricks you play on the nannies?"

He shrugged. "Why do we need nannies? I'm a big boy now, I can take care of us." Not one to sit still for long, he stood and walked around the study, inspecting this and that.

"We discussed this, champ." I folded my hands on the table and sighed. Even though I spent every minute I could with them, I wished I had more time. Was I a bad parent? Would Krisha have done a better job parenting them? "You know I can't be here every day, right?" He nodded. "Besides school, you both have all the extramural stuff that you both enjoy. Someone needs to be here to take you guys to those lessons and bring you back. To stay with you at night when I'm away."

He rolled a finger over the glass door to the toy car collection cabinet before glancing over his shoulder. "Then bring me a mommy."

I jerked back in my seat, shocked. "I thought you didn't want another mom?" I asked. He gripped his upper lip between his teeth and shrugged. "What made you change your mind?"

He opened the door, fidgeted with the Black 1968 custom Camaro then turned to face me. "What's a soul mate, daddy?"

I found his question strange. Nicky wasn't one for the mushy stuff. "It's the person you're meant to spend the rest of your life with. Your other half. Someone your heart belongs to, forever."

"Was mommy your soul mate?"

"She is—was," Although I was quick to correct my blunder, my curiosity steepled a notch higher.

His little hand scratched his head as if he wasn't sure what to say next and I could've sworn my heart boomed in my chest. "And if mommy left you, what happens to your forever," he asked, his countenance filled with naivety.

This time my heart catapulted out of my chest, beating at an irregular pace. How did I explain the affliction of love to a seven-year-old? "Sometimes we don't get our forever with our soul mate, Nicky because our destinies are still to be written. Or maybe we have to share our heart with someone new to save them because they lost theirs unexpectedly." Was I trying to convince my son or myself that faith was real? Distracted, I twisted the black leather band on my wrist.

"That's what mommy said."

My head shot up. I frowned. "What do you mean?"

He neared my table and leaned against the edge, staring at me. "I read mommy's letter again last week when I stayed over at Cal's house," he said, referring to his alternating sleepover with his friend Caleb.

"You took the letter with you to Cal's?" I asked. He nodded. I was surprised since both the kids kept their letters locked up and considered it too special to share with anyone. "Why?"

He scratched at the tabletop and I got the feeling he was hesitant. He walked away to the cabinet again. "I wanted Cal's mom to read it to me," he said without looking at me.

"Why?" He didn't answer. Sensing some inner struggle, I stood and crossed the room to him. "Hey, champ." I crouched and turned him to face me. "You know you can talk to me, right?" He nodded. "About anything." I lifted a brow, waiting to see if he'd continue.

"I—I," he hesitated.

"It's okay, Nicky, tell me."

"I wanted to imagine what mommy would sound like if she said the words to me." His blue eyes glazed with tears. "But I didn't give it to Cal's mom because I knew she wouldn't sound like my mommy." Tears trailed down his cheek and I pulled him into my embrace.

My heart ached to tell him his mother was alive and that she would come home soon. I just needed a little more time.

Nicky pulled out of my hold and swiped at his tears. "Can I go now, daddy?"

"Yes." Straightening, I watched him walk away, wondering what was in the letter. Before her death, Krisha had apparently made sure she covered all her basis in the event something went wrong during her delivery.

She'd written each of the kids seven letters and asked my grandmother to make sure they received the letters on their birthdays. I'd followed Krisha's wish and every year, I'd read them their letters except for the last one. My kids believed that at seven they deserved privacy. I'd laughed at the notion then, now I was curious what she'd written.

Raking both hands through my hair, I moved to the window. I stared out wishing I could just tell Ashrika the truth and bring her home. The visit to the restaurant two nights ago might've been a bit over-the-top seduction on my part, but not only had her responses excited me, the acceptance of my friendship, kissing me more so, thrilled the fuck out of me. It was a step in the right direction—a slow but definite one. Maybe one more meet would seal the deal.

# Ashrika

*MY EYES OPEN TO A QUANTUM of pitch-blackness, I blink rapidly until my sight adjusts to the darkness. Still, I can't make out much. I squint against the dull ache in my head, easing my tongue around my dry lips. The rancid tang of chloroform clings to my lips, filling my tastebuds. The abrupt jostle of my body and a rolling can somewhere behind my head, suggests I'm in a moving vehicle.*

*Thrusting a hand forward, I move it, from right to left, feeling nothing but empty space until the rigid coldness of metal meets my searching fingers. And with my fingertips exerting pressure against the ridge, I pull my body into an upright position. An immediate moan slips through my lips and I drop back down, squeezing my eyes shut against a wave of nausea. Covering my mouth, I inhale a few deep breaths to curb the sensation then push up once more. My hand trembles as I run my fingers through my hair, now stiff with dust. A thin beam of light catches my eye. It must be the door which means it's still daylight outside. As my eyes adjust to the gloom, I make out several objects scattered near my outstretched feet. A large suitcase, four boxes and two gas cylinders. Judging by the dimensions, I'm in the back of a moving van.*

*I glance around looking for a means of escape. Surprisingly, fear eludes me for the moment, if anything, it makes me determined to get free. Slowly, I rise, steadying myself against the ridges of the cabin wall, the swaying motion of the van makes it difficult. Certain I can move without falling over, I edge toward the door then trace the pattern of the metal frame, using my fingers to check for a lock or opening but several minutes of searching, prove futile.*

*I grit my teeth in frustration and thump a curled fist against the heavy door, yelling at the top of my voice, "Help. Somebody please help me." The cries sound hollow to my ears. I doubt anyone would hear me. Still, I scream until my throat constricts in dryness. Admitting defeat, I strike the rigid metal once more then lean heavily against the door, breathing hard as exhaustion claims my body. I refuse to give into the tears pricking the back of my lids. The dull throb of my head signals another bout of nausea and I wretch for a few seconds but nothing comes out.*

*Weaving back and forth drunkenly, I drag myself to the corner I'd risen from and drop to the single mattress and suck in air to force down the threatening nausea. Desperate, I pull up legs and bow my head between my knees. The move doesn't help. I need food and water. "No. I need to get the fuck out of here," I mutter. Where is my kidnapper taking me?*

*Kidnapped! The sudden realization dawns hard and fast. Cold fear grips my body, squeezing the air from my lungs and pricking the walls around my heart. I clench my fingers, as my breath rushes out in sharp exhales. "Please. Help me," the words squeak out. I clasp my hands together to stop the shaking before my teeth began to chatter and my body gives into violent trembling. I clutch my knees in a frantic attempt to stay still but the sudden jerk of the van flings me against the side. Groaning, I try to sit up then roll onto my back when a loud bang resonates through the cabin and a stark brightness hits my eyes. I cover them quickly.*

*"Are you awake, pretty girl," the loud bark ricochets through my body, filling me with dread faster than a speeding bullet.*

*Terror squeezes my insides and my eyes fly open as a bulky figure appears. "Get away from me," I screech, grabbing lungsful of air to fight off the approaching hands. "No!" Adrenaline jackknifes through me, and my body arches upward with the force of my gasp. Something cov-*

*ers my face, stealing my vision. Hands grip me around my thighs pressing down. I convulse, battling the weight restraining me.*

*"Relax. He's coming, pretty girl."*

*"No!" I scream, flailing about, trying to escape. "Let me go." High-pitched squeaks fill my ears. Footsteps grow louder, closer. "No," I croak, my throat sore from screaming. Strong hands grab my arms and pin my wrists. Kicking out my legs, I try to fight back, but they are much stronger, and more weight is forced on my legs, holding them still until I gasp for air. "Please," I try once more.*

*"Shut the fuck up!" His hand swings wide—*

Gunshots slammed my eardrums. My body snapped upward at the same time as my eyes flew open, darting around the room, fast and furious. *Where were they?* Panting, I swallowed the dryness clogging my throat. Lightning and thunder danced a quick tango outside my window, rattling the frames and pelting the glass roof. *It's not gunfire.* I fisted the blanket like a protective shield. I swiped the sweat trickling down from my brow and pulled on the t-shirt sticking to my clammy skin. Shaking with enough force to cause an earthquake, I reached for the phone and dialed.

"Rika?" Zayne answered on the second ring.

I fought to get my breathing under control by pulling in deep long breaths. "It's storming," I replied on a shaky whisper. He knew I hated storms. And the nightmare I'd woken from didn't help my state of mind either.

"Hang on, baby, I'm coming," he soothed.

"Okay."

I disconnected the call and hit the lights, flooding the darkened room with instant brightness that did little for my calm. Clutching my knees tight to my body, I willed the noise to end as another crash resonated through the sky. I sat back against the headboard and pulled the covers to my chest. My gaze swept the room, checking every corner, expecting God knows what to come jumping out of the shadows before it landed on a bottle of vodka sitting on the kitchen counter.

Tia brought it with her the day before wanting the low-down on Trent's visit from two nights ago. Somehow, we'd ended up with coffee, popcorn and watching a rerun of *Something's Gotta Give*, Trent and the vodka forgotten. I eyed the bottle again, but another burst of thunder rattled the windows and stilled my bravery to go get it. Gripping the edges of the covers, I held on for dear life like it was my salvation against the storm monsters. I shook so badly, my teeth chattered.

"Where are you Zayne?" I whispered, glancing around as my racing heartbeat stripped me of the rationality to believe storms were harmless unless I was outside in its direct path.

I wasn't sure how long I sat there, still as a picture until an abrupt thumping sounded too close for comfort. It took a few seconds to distinguish the pounding on the door downstairs. I cocked an ear to listen and barely made out the banging over the grumbling thunder.

# Trent

THE ABRUPT RINGING of the phone jarred my sleep-addled brain, shattering images of Krisha's smile and forcing me awake with a jolt. I grabbed the device and squinted at the time before answering, "yeah?"

"Trent, it's Zayne."

"What the fuck, it's 2.00 a.m." I grunted then realized he'd only call if there was a problem. I sat up.

"Are you in the city?"

"Yes."

"I need you to go to Rika, now." There was an urgency to his tone that had me vaulting off the bed and stripping hastily.

"What's up?" I stuck the phone between my neck and ear as I pulled on a pair of jeans.

"It's the storm," he replied the same time as lightning cut across the sky and a crash of thunder vibrated the windows. "The morning Rika woke from her coma, the city was plagued by an electrical storm. It just heightened her fear of waking to the unknown and she's developed a phobia since."

I was already walking through the door when I asked, "Why aren't you going to her?"

He took a moment to answer. "I told you, I'd help you. The club scene wasn't the ideal opportunity, but it got you nearer to her, didn't it?" I paused midstride and stared at the phone, wondering if he had any idea that I'd kissed his wife—technically my wife too, twice. "Trent?"

"I'm here." I hooked up the phone to the hands-free facility and started the car. Another couple of seconds and I was maneuvering the Lambo toward the docks, the heavy rain making visibility impossible. "Speaking of the club, is there something you're not telling me?" I asked, squinting through the rapid swish of the windshield wipers.

"Do you want to go to Rika or not?" Zayne's impatience filtered through the car, squashing my need to find out his angle.

I pulled in a deep breath. "Thanks. I appreciate the help."

"Whether you're her husband or not, just remember, Trent, there are limits to what I will allow her to go through." He cut the call before I could respond.

While anger fired up the blood coursing through my veins, I was grateful he'd taken the time to call me. Still, I had no idea why a tiny niggle warned me there was more behind the man's evasiveness. Maybe I was just being paranoid because he'd been in her life for so long. I should consider myself lucky. How many husbands would be so obliging?

The thought of her fears being so mundane yet so real, so stark, she'd begged for him to go to her, tightened the noose around my heart that had slipped into place since discovering she was alive. There was only so much I could do to prevent that noose from squeezing the life out of me. I needed Zayne. For the moment and until I could get a little more than a kiss out of Ash. And if tonight went well, the prospect of a permanent relationship looked promising. Not even Zayne's hard words a couple of seconds ago, could douse the optimism flowing through me.

Several painstaking minutes later, I pulled into the parking lot and cut the engine. Realizing I hadn't brought an umbrella with me, I pulled up the collar of my leather jacket, opened the door and after grabbing a duffel bag from the trunk, sprinted toward the restaurant entrance. The persistent rumble of thunder drowned my thumping on the door. I walked around back and pounded on the door there.

When I got no answer, I stood back, shielded my eyes against the rain and searched the windows above the restaurant "Ashrika!" I yelled, hoping she'd hear me above the roar.

The door opened a minute later. I barely glimpsed the relief on her face before she crashed into my arms, her hold a death-grip around my waist. Stunned it took a moment before I realized the extent of her fear. "The nightmare happened again." Her body shook as she cried into my chest, muffling her words. Circling her waist, I held her tight before caressing her hair in gentle strokes while oblivious to the pissing rain around us.

"It's okay, sweetheart, I'm here."

As though my voice triggered an alarm, she pushed against my chest, stepping back and gawked at me, her eyes wide. "Y-you're not Zayne." She spluttered, her response nowhere near to the woman I'd kissed in her kitchen. "How are you always popping up everywhere?"

Not sure what Zayne had told her, I offered a lopsided grin which did nothing to reshape her suspicious expression. "I was passing by and saw the lights on. I thought something had happened—"

"Passing by? At two in the morning." Her incredulity wasn't lost on me. "Where exactly would that be?" She arched a brow. I understood her skepticism. The location of the restaurant couldn't be seen from the main road.

"Can we discuss this inside?" I pointed to our drenched bodies, using the smile I reserved to charm someone.

She was having none of that. "Zayne will be here any minute, you should leave." Her gaze darted to the parking lot again as if expecting him to appear out of thin air.

"He's not coming."

"What do you mean?" She squinted at me as the rain lashed down, soaking her.

"When I saw the lights on, I called him. He mentioned your fear of the storm and I offered to check in on you."

"Offered to check in on me?" She lifted a hand and wiped away the rain that was running down her face. "What do you want?" Her distrust was unmistakable.

I tried not to laugh. "I thought we were friends," I shouted trying to be heard over the pummeling rain.

"Friends, no, you seem like a stalker, you are always—" A sudden bolt of lightning pierced the ground a couple of feet away, its resonance bone-jarring and followed by a clap of thunder. I flinched. Ash jumped, crying out as she fell backward and hit her elbows and head against the wall. Trying to right herself, she tripped, falling into a large flower bed.

"Fuck!" I yelled, reaching for her wrist to pull her up. She jerked her muddied hand from my grasp, but I didn't miss the wince. I was done playing nice. "Fuck it, woman, I'm not dying out here." Before she could respond, I leaned down, gripped her around the thighs and flung her over my shoulder.

"Put me down." She squealed then groaned in pain. "Shit, my head hurts."

Ignoring her squirming, I mounted the narrow stairway, pushed through another door at the top into the apartment. "Bathroom, Ash."

She cursed under her breath. "First door on your right."

I gave the black and white space a cursory glance as my senses filled with her sweet scent. Setting her down, I dropped my duffel and stood back. By the way she took turns rubbing her head and elbows, I figured she'd hit them hard. "Are you okay? Can I take a look?"

"I'm fine," she muttered, massaging the back of her head and then groaned when she realized she'd just rubbed mud into her hair.

"Not dizzy?" She shook her head. "Well, I'm not taking any chances and leaving you alone. Strip." I shrugged out of my jacket.

"What?" Her eyes widened, anxious and wary. She backed away from me, yelping when her elbow connected with the wall, halting any further movement.

"You're wet, I'm wet...so," I hid my teasing with a smirk, lowering my gaze to her heaving chest beneath the mud-stained t-shirt before dropping to shapely legs also slick with dirt. I moved nearer and gripped the edges of her mid-thigh t-shirt.

She stiffened, tried to slap my hands away from her thighs to prevent me from lifting the garment but cried out and quickly moved to massage her arms instead. "I am not having sex with you." Her flustered words did little to hide her pink cheeks.

"I don't remember asking you to."

"You just said..." She bit her lip.

"That we're both wet?"

"You're such an asshole," she seethed. Yet the unmasked desire in her eyes that she attempted to hide, hit me like a fist to my chest.

I cleared my throat before responding, "Guilty as charged, sweetheart, but it doesn't change the fact that in two days, my cock is going to be so deep inside your sweet pussy, you're going to be screaming to come."

She stared at me, unblinking, her brain struggling to process my words. Her mouth opened and snapped shut twice. She exhaled on a sharp laugh of disbelief, either contemplating her next words or trying to figure out if I was serious or not. "Who the hell do you think you are?" she finally spat.

"Your next fuck." I licked my lips in blatant anticipation. She opened her mouth to say something before her lips compressed into a thin line, eyes the color of the storm clouds outside. "Call me an arrogant prick if you want, but I always keep my word." I grinned at the scowl tightening her face then leaned in until my lips hovered just above hers, our gazes engaged. "If I want to fuck you, I will..." Her jaw dropped on a gasp. "Just not yet. So relax. I'm here to take care of you."

"One kiss doesn't give you permission to think—"

"One?" I tilted my head studying her flushed features. Her brow wrinkled and I got the feeling she referred to her kitchen not remembering the night at the club.

Her expression faltered as realization dawned. She licked her lips to compose her thoughts. "I don't think making me strip is what Zayne meant when he asked you to check in on me," she hissed, taking a step back.

"Maybe we have differing opinions on how we take care of a woman?"

"What's that supposed to be mean?"

"C'mon, Ash, we almost fucked, that should count for something?" I raised a brow.

"Exactly. 'Almost fucked' and 'did fuck' are two opposing extremes."

*Fuck.* I resisted the urge to snort out loud, it would just irritate her further. Watching the changing emotions flick across her face, I realized there was another discerning distinction between her and the woman who used to be my wife. Where Krisha was meek and quiet, this woman possessed a pair of brass balls that had my envious cojones vying for first place.

"Look, I need to make sure you don't come down with a cold. You're covered in mud and hurt." Inching closer, I gently massaged her elbows.

The action gave my body something to do other than pumping blood to my semi-hard cock while I thought of how easy it would be to fuck her right now. It was child's play when it came to seducing a woman. I took without asking, needing no words to get my message across. Ashrika however, needed to be handled with a little more finesse than the norm. She had to trust that I wasn't just a horny bastard even if my words claimed otherwise.

"What's it going to be?" Her eyes roamed my face, indecision apparent. "Do you want me to leave?"

The sudden boom of thunder had her glancing toward the window, her face scrunched in fear. My heart crashed against my chest at the raw panic on her face. I'd only ever seen Neha that afraid of a storm and she'd cried in my arms. This was a strong woman, but her past experiences had shrouded her memories with fear of a simple thing like bad weather. A part of me wanted desperately to reassure her that I'd never let anything happen to her, ever again but that meant divulging my identity.

"Hey." I palmed her cheek. "You're safe and I'm not going anywhere. Trust me?" I soothed, using the tender tone I used on my kids when they needed that special touch. She nodded. I traced a slow line along her jaw and over her lips. Her breath came out on a rushed exhale. I ached to kiss her, to feel her resistance melt beneath my lips, to watch her cheeks flush with arousal and her eyes darken with pleasure. "Ash, a man's touch can be sensual to elicit pleasure yet gentle with care when you're in pain. That's what I'm going to do if you let me." When I reached down and raised her shirt over her head, she allowed it. My eyes dropped to her bare breasts, perfect, creamy, and full, the brown nipples hardening to buds under my gaze. And when I slid her panties down her legs, still she said nothing.

I moved away, turned the faucet on in the shower, and nodded to her. She stepped inside wordlessly. Ridding myself of my t-shirt, jeans, and sneakers, I kept my briefs on and slid in behind her. Her eyes flew open under the water. "What are—" The shake of my head cut off her words.

She squeezed her eyes shut while I soaped her body then shampooed her hair. Despite the hot water, her skin erupted in goosebumps under my touch, heightening the burn barreling through my body. It took a conscious effort not to touch her, really touch her, or give in to temptation and fuck her against the wall, until I couldn't breathe. Unable to stop myself, I slipped my arms around her waist and brought her back tight to my chest. She shuddered when I dropped a light kiss on her shoulder. Afraid I might scare her, I released my hold and stepped out of the shower. Securing a towel around my waist, I nodded to her and shut off the water, then held a large, fluffy towel for her to step into. I dried her body with slow, caring, calming movements.

"You're a beautiful woman, Ash." She looked at me but didn't say a word. When I was done, I reached for her robe hanging on a hook behind the door and when she slipped it on, I tied the sash and dropped a light kiss to her brow. "Is your head still sore?"

"A little."

"After I change, I'll make us some coffee, okay?" As she turned to leave, I called out, "I wasn't lying, Ash. Two days."

She glanced over her shoulder at me, her expression blank. "If you're so sure you're going to fuck me, why two days? Why not tonight?"

I laughed at her bravery. "Semantics, sweetheart." I winked. She left the bathroom. Glad for the gym bag I kept in the trunk, I pulled on gray sweatpants and a t-shirt and walked out while toweling my hair. When I rounded the corner, I heard Ashrika's voice and hung back.

"Zayne." His name came out in a breathless sigh. Ignoring the jealousy taking root in the pit of my stomach, my ears perked up. "Why didn't you come?" With her back to me, she stood at the window, her phone cradled between her ear and neck while she massaged her hands. "Why did you send him?" She dragged a hand through her hair, wincing as she did so. "Yes. I fell...no. He didn't do anything to upset me."

Her quiet words confirmed she wasn't upset with my appearance yet the edginess to her tone, had panic replacing the exhilaration that raced through me seconds ago, bringing with it a chaotic dose of reality. My wife had no idea who she was. She had no fucking clue who I was. Worse still, she belonged to another man. A man who'd fucked her every day for the last couple of years while I gave up on the notion of another permanent relationship.

Stepping away, my back hit the wall as I dropped my head, blanking out the conversation. I should leave. Forget about her and let her live. She seemed content with her life right now. Zayne appeared to be giving her everything she desired. He took good care of her. I scanned the apartment, its classy décor supported that observation. I'd only fuck up everything she had going if I stayed or pushed her into something she didn't want. The question was, would I be able to stay away? Would I be able to drive into the city knowing my wife resided within the vicinity of the places I'd visit? And what if her memory returned. Would she hate me for knowing and not coming to get her?

Closing my eyes, I inhaled to still the muddled tension raging war with my head and my heart. *"Believe in yourself, Trent,"* Drake's words played in my head, reminding me to be strong. Whatever happened, I had to endure it for the sake of my sanity, my children, my love. Her soft laughter had me opening my eyes.

"No, silly. I'm fine." She laughed again, obvious joy infusing her voice.

It was obvious Zayne made her happy. How was he okay with another man keeping his wife company then? I found it strange he wasn't in the least bit concerned. Unless he doubted my capability of seducing her into falling for me or he trusted she wouldn't. "When will you be back?" It sounded like he was traveling. I could use the time to garner her interest. Maybe start by inviting her to the charity ball I had to attend tomorrow evening.

# Trent

I WASN'T SURE HOW LONG I stood there listening to her conversation with half an ear when Ashrika interrupted my reflections.

"Penny for your thoughts." Standing at the dresser, she tried lifting the hairdryer and flexed her fingers a couple of times, her grimace a clear indication she was still in pain.

"Can I help?"

Shaking her head, she walked to the kitchen and pointed to a bottle of Vodka. "Care to join me or would you prefer coffee?" Her smile was slight, but I didn't miss the appraisal as her eyes raked over my body from head to toe. I nodded. "Do you mind grabbing the bottle and two glasses?"

"Sure." Shoving aside my competing reflections, I did as she asked while she moved to a stereo system. A second later, soft music filled the air. "Let me take a look at your hands." I set the bottle and glasses on the coffee table.

When I reached out, she pulled back. "It's nothing really. Probably just numb with the cold."

"Ash, I've just seen you naked, touched your body, I think we're beyond being shy now, don't you?"

With a roll of her eyes that had me smiling, she held out her hands. I pushed up the sleeves to her robe, checked her hands, arms and elbows then gave it a gentle massage. When I looked up it was to find her gaze on me, curiosity shimmered in those gray depths. I raised a brow.

"Why do you want to be my friend, knowing I'm married?"

Her question caught me off guard for a moment. I joined her on the leather couch, poured the drinks then handed her a glass before sipping my own. "Are you saying married women shouldn't have friends?"

"Not the type that is blatant about wanting to fuck her," she retorted.

I chuckled. "Touché."

"Is it your mission to fuck all the women at Enigma? First Tia and now me. Who's next? What do you do? Ask each of us to arrange the next after you're done?"

Swallowing my drink, my insides roiled, wavering between anger and shock. "What gave you that idea?" Lips thinned, I narrowed my eyes. "What do you think? I sleep with every woman I meet. I love fucking, but it doesn't make me a manwhore and I don't believe in arranged relationships of any sort." My words came out a little harsher than intended and the blood drained from her face. I sighed. It was senseless being angry with her. She had no idea of my intentions and I was restricted by what I could offer her. I tried a less antagonistic approach. "Ash, when I saw you at the restaurant, don't ask me why but I had to meet you. Only, Tia made it clear you weren't ready to meet me or anyone else for that matter, so I forgot all about it." Her eyes widened. "Then, when I saw you at Dr. Landers' office, looking as vulnerable and afraid as a little doe that lost its mother, I thought you could do with another friend."

"Oh." It looked like my revelation left her speechless. I smiled.

"I'm sorry," she whispered.

I met her gaze head on. "For what? Assuming I'm an arrogant ass who can't control his cock or a man who takes advantage of hapless women?" Eyes the color of liquid silver roamed my face. "If it's any consolation, my marriage has been over for years and Tia is a good friend, more like a sister."

"Sister?" Her mouth opened, but she swallowed her shock. "I didn't...um...I didn't..." she trailed off unable to put her thoughts into words.

"I didn't expect you to." I pretended not to notice the mortified tinge to her cheeks by downing my drink. When I poured myself another, she held out her glass. "Nice place you've got here," I said, taking in the studio unit that had the kitchen, living room and bedroom all flowing into one big open space.

"Not a dump, right?" There were no signs of anger in her expression which gave me a measure of comfort.

"I never said it was." She eyed me above the rim of her glass. I grinned when her face contorted at the bitter taste of the alcohol. "Not much of a drinker, are you?" She shook her head. 'Then why drink it?"

She stared out the window. "Hoping it would give me the courage to handle that." She gestured to the raging weather outside.

"It's just a storm. It will pass."

"You don't understand." Her gaze riveted on the rain pelting the glass, she shook her head. "It's what I experience every morning I wake and realize I don't know who I am, my personality traits, or even my damn name. Whether I was a nice person or someone full of shit. Then I put on a brave face, mimicking a sunny day for those around me, yet inside the storm still rages." She looked at me. "Incognito." I was surprised at her mention of Zayne's club. Had she been there? What were her thoughts about it? "It's how I describe myself."

"I don't understand."

"I've hidden behind a disguise for so long, pretending to be someone I'm not. No one knows the real me, not even me. Get it? Incognito."

I concealed my surprise with a gentle smile. Wasn't I just as guilty of wearing a mask? Yes, but I hid my true self from her, for her. I cringed at the deception, more so the sadness on her face yet her voice—it held undisguised uncertainty and confusion. Barely minutes ago, I'd assumed she was happy, content. Clearly, she was going through something others couldn't see. She veiled her true feelings from everyone. Tenderness jerked my heart as anxiety kicked me in the gut. I wanted to make it all better for her. How? "I'm sure you were a nice person."

She glanced at me and laughed. "And how would you know that?"

I shrugged, not sure what to tell her. "My optimism, I guess. And judging by the person you are today, I doubt the loss of memory can manipulate a personality change." Even though I uttered the words, I didn't believe them because so far, each encounter with this woman was proving to me that her traits were different from those my wife shared. Was it a good thing or bad? I couldn't tell. Was she losing her old self to the new? I hoped not. Then again, sometimes different was better. Seven years was a long time to go without discovering the person you really were.

"Well, I wish I had some of your optimism. Refill?" I nodded, filling our glasses. "Sometimes I wonder about my past, whether it was better than it is now. Then I laugh it off accepting that what's lost, isn't coming back." A note of wistfulness filled her voice.

"Ash," I sighed, wishing to take her in my arms instead of sitting a couch length from her, watching the changing emotions on her face. Giving no thought to my actions, I moved closer and took her hand in mine. She didn't resist but glanced down at our linked fingers. "There are lots of people in the world that want a second chance at life and maybe you were given that."

She lifted her gaze to mine. "True. But I always wonder if I lost something or someone special. Then again no one came looking for me, so maybe there was nothing or no one special."

My chest tightened. I was going insane and she didn't even know it. Sitting next to her, hearing the slow cadence of her breathing, knowing that she woke every morning burdened by a past she longed to know and knowing that I could end her misery with a simple confession. Folding a leg under me, I turned fully on the seat to face her and rested my arm along the backrest. "Maybe there was someone. If your love was true, you will find your way back to each other." I palmed her cheek. "Do you know what serendipity is?"

"Serendipity?"

"Yes. When you find something so beautiful that makes your heart dance without you looking for it."

She laughed. "How is the same person so crass yet so poetic?"

"I do irritate the crap out of you, yet I make you laugh, don't I?"

"This might sound silly, considering I don't really know you." She sipped her drink as if choosing her words. "I'm not usually comfortable around men but for some reason, I think in you I found someone I can express any emotion. Anger, misery, happiness, laughter, and..." she trailed off on a sigh.

"And?"

"Nothing." She glanced away, a woman without memory had secrets. Intriguing. While I was going crazy inside, wanting to know, I didn't push for an answer. Waiting for when she was ready to share more. "Thank you for that." She looked at me again, her blush replaced with a neutral smile.

"I haven't really done anything but be an arrogant ass."

"And yet it got you into places others could only dream of."

I chuckled at the sassy lift of her brow. "Earlier, you mentioned you don't remember your name. How did you choose the one you have now?"

She lifted her shoulders in a slight shrug. "A week after I woke from the coma, the doctors asked me to choose one since they needed something to call me. At first, I looked up a couple of choices the nurses brought me and nothing stuck. Then one morning, for no rhyme or reason I uttered Ashrika out loud. They asked me if it was my name and I wasn't sure. I kept it."

"Do you think it's your real name, though? Have you had any flashbacks about it?" Considering how close to Krisha, it sounded, I figured her memory had picked something similar in sound.

"Not sure and no."

"When you rushed into my arms you mentioned it happened again, what did?"

She looked at me blankly for a moment then shrugged. "I have this recurring dream. Dr. Landers seems to think its memories of my attack that hides within my subconscious."

"Does it scare you?"

"I've learned to handle them better now, knowing it's just a dream and Landers says they might recede with time, probably when I find the happiness I seek."

My heart ached once more, wondering if I could somehow ease her into believing her life would change. Problem was, I couldn't be certain that I was the one who'd change it, for the better. Still, I planned to try.

She stood and her hands flailed as she stumbled. I jumped up, gripping her hips to steady her.

"You okay?"

"Either I'm dizzy from the knock to my head or I'm tipsy. Take your pick." She chuckled.

"I'll go with tipsy." I grinned.

She grasped my shoulders, closing the gap between us and I slipped my hands around her waist, relishing the warm feel of her against my body. The track changed to Selena Gomez's *'Feel me'* and liking the appropriateness to the moment, I swayed our bodies to the music.

Ashrika watched me for a bit then asked, "are you going to ravish my body now?"

"Do you want me to?"

"But, we're both married..." Was that regret or shame in her tone?

"And we're both consenting adults."

Her eyes lifted to mine, searching. For what, I wasn't sure. I had no idea how long we stood there, embracing each other until she dropped back to the seat, breaking the moment. Hiding my disappointment, I retook my seat and slid a hand along the backrest.

"Do you know that you're the only person that's called me Ash?" Laughing, she twisted slightly, pulling her leg under her. The action caused her robe to part, revealing a creamy thigh.

The sound and sight tightened my cock, begging for relief. "You don't like it?" I played with the soft curls on her shoulder.

She stared at me before her pink lips widened in a sensual smile. "I do like it. There's just something unique about it."

"Like you?" At her questioning gaze, I added, "you're unique."

"Are you trying to get into my panties?"

"I'm pretty sure I've stated my intentions."

"Two days?" She licked her lips. I nodded. "Why?"

"Why what?" I asked. She arched a brow. "Why do I want to fuck you?" She nodded. "I always want what I can't have," my arrogant comment didn't faze her, but I caught the flicker of interest in her eyes. Silently, I urged her to give in to the desire sweeping her body, evident by the bright tinge to her cheeks. "Whether you decide to reciprocate the gesture or not, I'll continue to seduce you and you *will* give in. I'm a man who gets what he wants, and I want you." I tilted my head slightly, my eyes on her bottom lip gripped between her teeth. "Does that turn you on, Ash?"

"Um...I...What makes you think you can have me?" Her flustered evasion made me smile.

"Because I can arouse you without even touching you. Because you may think you don't need me but I know better. Your need is only the tip of the iceberg of what you actually want."

"God, you're conceited."

"I didn't claim otherwise."

"I thought we're supposed to be friends."

"And I think we kind of blurred those lines when you kissed me." I winked. "Twice."

"That wasn't supposed to happen."

"But it did." I was pushing her to admit her attraction openly. She was a lot more resilient than I gave her credit for and far less drunk than the night at the club. It wouldn't be me taking advantage, this time, just her begging me.

She rolled her tongue over her bottom lip as if contemplating her next question. "And what makes you think you have or can?"

"Arouse you?" She flared her nostrils either to cover her embarrassment or show her indignation. "I've watched you, your reactions for *weeks*, sweetheart, whether I'm close or not and even when I've touched you, kissed you..." I brushed a finger along her lip, she shuddered.

My brow shot up.

She smirked.

"A slight tremble runs through your body. You bite your lip to try and stop it. Sometimes your nipples harden, and you jerk away, flustered. You break eye contact or shift from one foot to the other and my favorite is your cheeks turn a telltale pink. How am I doing so far?"

"Whatever," she muttered. Her expression a toss-up between a scowl and disbelief.

*What are you hiding, sweetheart?* "Have you ever explored your sexuality, Ash?"

She squinted at me, her frown deep. I could tell she was trying hard to answer the question in an evasive manner as possible. "What's that supposed to mean?"

"Have you ever allowed the sober version of the woman I met at the club to flaunt herself, to make her desires known, to fuck who or how she wants?"

She paled, her mouth opening on a gasp, but no sound came out. I'd assumed by now she'd be in touch with my brash personality, looked like I was wrong. I raised a brow, letting her know I was waiting for an answer.

"No," it was a whisper, nothing like the sassy woman a moment ago.

"Why not?"

She closed her eyes, drawing in a deep breath then another. "I—" She opened her eyes, the familiar shutter I'd come to know, firmly in place.

I decided on a different approach. "Do you know?" I leaned closer and her gaze met mine. "When a man wants a woman..." I rolled a finger in slow circles over the exposed flesh of her thigh. "He'll often make her angry..." Emboldened by the subtle change in her exhales, I slid my finger further up. "And despite her 'I hate him' stance, she'll secretly want him to come back repeatedly..." I moved the hand curled around a lock of her hair to trail a lazy path along her jawline. She leaned into my touch. "And with each visit, her panties get wetter, the ache becomes more painful and a simple touch would make her..."

Those gray irises darkened to greedy lust, pleading for me to finish that statement. I denied her the request. My finger drifted higher, inches from the warm apex between her thighs. She made no move to stop me, her throat working a swallow that pulled my gaze. Palming her cheek, I rubbed the pad of my thumb gently over her lips. Her mouth opened on a sluggish exhale before sucking my thumb in. Drawing it in until the first knuckle, her tongue coiled around the digit in its warm wet grasp shooting pinpricks of tingles down my arm, straight to my cock.

"I'm not conceited, Ash. I just have that effect on women. And right now, if I had to touch you, I know you'd be wet." I leaned in closer. "Your pussy is aching, begging for me to touch you, to run my finger in lazy circles over your clit, to slide the tip of my tongue along that wetness, tasting, sucking, biting until you beg me to let you come." Her eyes riveted on me, she stopped sucking my thumb but her breathing deepened. "I don't need to fuck you to give you pleasure, sweetheart. Just say the word." When she said nothing, I stood. "Get some sleep. I'll take the couch." As I stepped away, she gripped my hand. I glanced down at her fingers wrapped around my wrist before meeting her gaze. Waiting.

"Please."

It was the hidden desperation I'd come to expect. She wanted but was scared to ask. I wondered if it was shame that prevented her from seeking out her desires. She was married to a man who owned a fucking voyeur club, surely she would've opened up to him. Watching her though, I believed, she hadn't.

"Do you want me to touch you?"

"Yes."

"Show me." I sat down, stretched out my legs, and pointed to my lap. "Sit on me. Back to my chest, legs spread over mine."

Expecting hesitation, I was surprised when she positioned herself over my thighs, placing a leg on either side of mine and gingerly lowered herself to my lap. She perched on my knees then inched her way back until her ass pressed down on my cock. I bit down on my groan. "Lean back, Ash. I want to see everything."

She did as I asked but kept herself upright, almost rigid. Her robe fell open with the move and I placed my hands on her thighs, waiting for her to relax on her own.

Ashrika tensed a little when I brushed her hair aside and whispered against her ear. “I’m waiting.”

“Um...” Her innocence more in line with the woman I knew as my wife made me smile.

“I want you to get yourself off.”

She jerked her gaze to mine. “What?”

“Now, Ash. Show me how you want me to touch you.”

Swallowing, she reached for my hand, surprising me. She guided my fingers to her pussy. The moment the rough pads touched her wet flesh, she gasped, her ass grinding into my cock. God, she was fucking dripping and as tempted as I was to drop to my knees and lick that sweet pussy, I held back waiting for her next move.

Instead, she tensed. “I can’t do this.”

“You can.” I coaxed, keeping my voice low in her ear. “Dip my fingers in your pussy. Slick them with your juices and bring them back to your clit.” She did as I asked. Keeping my fingers on her clit, she began slow circular movements. Her body jerked with each brush of roughened pad to sensitive flesh. “Don’t rush it. Take your pleasure. Give your body what it wants.”

And as the pressure built, I leaned down and pressed my lips to her neck. Even though I wanted this seduction to be guided by her, I couldn’t resist the need to taste her skin, to remember her softness. She tipped her head to the side, giving me more access, and I dragged my tongue along the length of her neck, kissing and nibbling every exposed inch I could reach. With each sweep of my tongue, she relaxed more and more. Slowly sinking her back to my chest and tucking her head to my shoulder. Her thighs falling apart, gave her undulating fingers a wider berth and allowed me to watch our hands move between her spread thighs. When she slid two of my fingers through her folds, she moaned, flexing her hips and thrust up, her body now desperate for more. I rested my free hand on her hip, keeping her in place.

With each slide over her clit, she grew wetter and wetter and thrust up a little more. Holding my breath, I stayed still, trying not to grind against her soft ass and left her to guide my fingers as she wanted. When she moved her free hand to cup her breast, my lids slid shut. I ached to drop her to the floor and fuck the breath out of her. She moved my fingers lower to her opening and slipped two inside just a fraction. I opened my eyes when she thrust up once more and pushed my fingers deeper. Fuck, she was drenched, her thick cream coating my fingers like a second skin, and my mouth watered to taste her.

Her hand dropped from her breast. She angled my thumb to stay on her clit, keeping the pressure firm while she rode my fingers, thrusting harder and faster. Her whimpers grew into delectable moans I wanted to swallow. I knew she wouldn't last long and kissed her neck. Her pussy tightened, getting ready to come, and I feared I'd come in my pants with her. I allowed her two more thrusts and then pulled my hand away.

"What the—" she gasped, her body tense.

"The night's still young, sweetheart," I whispered against her neck as her breathing eased. She mumbled something under her breath. I chuckled. Never come between a woman and her orgasm. I was so looking forward to getting to know the new version of my wife while finding the older one. "Ready to tell me what you want?" When there was no response, I moved slightly. "Stand up."

She pulled her robe together and stood. Her brow lined in a deep frown, she kept her gaze on the floor. Her flushed cheeks the only indication of her near orgasm.

"Look at me." She did.

Her full lips mere inches from mine, slick from her tongue sliding across them, begging for me to taste. And I did. Lowering my head, I slipped my tongue between her soft lips. She needed no further coaxing. With a soft moan, she tilted her head, opened her mouth wider, and glided her tongue over mine. Letting me seduce her into surrender. I slipped my hands around her waist and drew her body tight to mine. Her hands slid up my arms and into my hair, fingers tangling in its length as her mouth grew greedy. God, I'd kissed her twice already, yet this was nothing short of sweeter, tastier, and downright delicious. Yet, as I began to learn her mouth, the subtle differences between Krisha then and now, told me she was still exploring and discovering her desires.

When I finally pulled back, I was breathing just as hard as her. With my hand on her hip, I slowly rolled a finger around her swollen lips. "I asked you to tell me what you want. You choose not to. Now I'm telling you what I'm going to give you." I lifted a brow. She nodded. I dropped my hands to my sides and took a step back. "I want you naked on that table." I gestured to the kitchen and then turned back, noticing her flaming cheeks. Was that embarrassment or desire? I inched closer, my hands lifting to the soft sash of her robe. "I'm going to eat your pussy until you're begging to come..." Her eyes widened, pupils dilating just as quickly. I pulled the knot and the lapels opened, giving me a sneak peek at the cleft between her breasts. "First, I'm going to give you a front-row seat to me jerking off..." I ran a lazy finger over the outline of one dark brown nipple. The bud tightened even as her tongue snaked nervously over her lips. My cock gave a little nod of appreciation. I flicked a finger over her nipple and she jerked, her breath fracturing. "Then I'm going to come..." She swallowed, her pulse a frenetic beat I could feel against her skin. I dragged my finger up her chest, skimmed her neck and ran it slowly over the shape of her lips. "...all over this beautiful body, painting your flushed skin until it glistens with my cum..." She gasped, her tongue darting out to lick her lips and my finger in the process.

"I'm dirty, Ash but my cock hardens at thoughts of showing a chef how enticing filthy can be." Her cheeks flamed a deeper shade of red. For each word I uttered, I took a step forward, and she a step back. We carried on this dance until I had her where I wanted. "Do you want me to fuck you?"

"Yes," she murmured.

"Take off your robe." She hesitated. "I've just had my fingers in your pussy."

She lifted her hand and slowly pushed the fabric from her shoulder, the silky material caressed her skin like a skilled lover, as it slipped down her body and pooled around her bare feet. Expecting her to cover herself, I smiled when her fingers dug into her thighs as though tempted to do so. I took a moment to run my gaze over her beautiful body, eager to lean forward and roll my lips over those dark brown nipples, to bite down on the enticing buds that were slowly hardening under my gaze. She looked at me. Urging me to touch, to kiss. Trusting me to give her the pleasure I promised and was all the confirmation I needed. Grasping her waist, I lifted her onto the table, pushing her thighs apart, my hungry gaze fell to her glistening pussy.

"Lie back, knees up." Her movements slow, she lay down. I walked around to stand where her head lay. Again, I asked, "Ready to tell me what you want?"

This time she answered, "Yes." At my raised brow, she replied, "You."

I pulled off my t-shirt. "What about me?"

Tilting her head, her gaze swept my bare chest, staying on my nipples a fraction longer. "I want you to fuck me."

"I think you want more than just me fucking you." From this angle, her nervous swallow was a lot more pronounced. "What are you afraid of, sweetheart?" She frowned then shook her head. "Are you afraid of cheating on your husband?"

She seemed to contemplate my question, thought better of what she was about to say then said, "Yes."

"I think you're more afraid of admitting your desires than cheating on your husband," I pointed out. Irritation snapped her brow into a deep line. She moved to get up. I kept her in place with a gentle hold on her shoulders. "Keep running and you might miss out," I taunted.

"I needed you to fuck me. Not lecture me on your opinions," she huffed. Did I hit a nerve?

Her sass turned me on something stupid. "Snap at me all you want, but we both know if I drag my fingers through your pussy, I'll find you wet and greedy for me to fuck you."

"Whatever." She narrowed her gaze at me. "I think I'd rather watch a movie."

"You sure about that?" I dropped my pants releasing my hard dick.

Hesitation rendered her speechless the same time her eyes zeroed in on my cock. Even upside down, her awareness was palpable. She licked her lips and I grinned, earning a smirk when she noticed me watching her. Before she could say anything, I yanked her forward until her head hung over the edge of the table and rolled the tip of my cock over her lips. The plump flesh parted on instinct followed by a soft moan when I edged in slightly, her teeth grazing the skin, her tongue darting up to lick the slit. *Fuck.*

"Changed your mind, sweet—" She swallowed me all the way to the hilt, cutting off my words. "Fuck." I gripped the table, my knees threatening to give out as she deep-throated me. Her boldness was unexpected. Krisha had always been fun but the woman she was now, was brazen almost like beneath her tentative exterior, laid hidden fantasies waiting to be explored. The knowledge was both surprising and mindblowing. Discovering my wife's new identity was going to be fun.

I watched her throat work my cock, my need escalating, threatening my control of this game I intended playing to unleash those desires. Shoving down the pressing throb to take what I wanted, to fuck that sweet, warm mouth until my cum dripped down her throat, I pulled away and heard her frustrated groan. "Not yet." I slid her body down slightly so her head no longer hung over the side.

I walked around the table, letting my fingers feather across her heated skin, from her shoulder, over the curve of her breast, painting slow circles across her stomach, and down her thigh. Lips pursed, her fiery grays followed me, yet she couldn't hide the goose-flesh that pebbled her skin. I smirked.

"Stop teasing me, Trent. I need you. Unless you're not as hungry as I am," she mumbled, her voice strained between begging and taunting.

I knew what she was doing—goading me to give her what she wanted. Clever girl. "You have no idea how hungry I am, sweetheart, so don't question my reason to fuck you." Stopping between her legs, I slipped a hand between her thighs, dragged a finger through her wet slit, rolling her clit under a roughened pad. "Or, I might leave you to starve a little longer."

Moaning, she thrust up, hoping to garner more friction. I moved my hand away and she cursed.

"Spread your legs. Show me your pussy." I gave my cock a couple of long strokes.

Surprisingly, she complied. Bending her knees, she placed her feet flat on the table and spread her thighs wide showing me every inch of her pink, wet pussy. A groan crested deep in my abdomen, thundered up my chest, and spewed from my lips. My mouth watered to taste. I gripped my cock harder, my strokes longer, faster, my eyes devouring every delicious curve, flex, and line of her body.

"Fuck, you're beautiful." Just like I remembered. "All I want to do is fuck you so hard until we both can't breathe."

A soft moan fell from her lips mingling with mine as I stroked my dick harder.

"Watch me, Ash." I cupped my balls and squeezed my cock. Then she touched herself, rolling two fingers over her clit. "Fuck," I bit out before my orgasm barreled down my spine, wrenching another sharp curse from my lips. I inched closer and she arched her back, thrusting her breasts up. "Move your hand, I'm going to paint you with my cum." She did and I groaned my release. Thick, white spurts ripped from my body, coating her stomach, her breasts, her neck. "Christ." I shuddered, breathing hard. I wiped the last droplet clinging to my cock, on her thigh.

Hovering over her, I gripped the table for support. "Perfection," I panted. She squirmed, pushing up her tits glistening with cum, her eyes brilliant with greed following my every move. I loved the unashamed lust staining her pink cheeks. Smoothing my palm on her thigh and in slow circular movements, I spread the cum over her skin. When I reached her breast, I licked the drops coating her silky skin, taking my time to bite and tease her nipple into hard buds, her soft whimpers fanning my ears. I swept a finger through a thick smear on her chin and rolled it over her lips. "Suck it."

She complied, closing her eyes as if savoring the taste. I smiled. She was fucking perfect. Rolling my tongue over her lips, I breached the seam and slipped my tongue inside her mouth. The kiss was long, hard, and deep. I nibbled and sucked the plump flesh until they turned pink and swollen.

I stepped back and when she was looking at me again, I strummed her clit and her hips bucked. My hands on her thighs, holding her open, I leaned down and dragged my tongue over her slit.

"Oh, God," she cried out.

Sucking on her clit, I gripped the sensitive nerve between my teeth, tugging on it until her hips jerked. I locked my arms around her thighs and sank my tongue deeper into her slick entrance, forcing her body to tighten.

"I need to come." She was breathing harder and faster now. I slipped a finger into her pussy in short quick thrusts while increasing the suction on her clit. "Oh, God, yes." Arching her back, her nails digging into her thighs, she pulled in sharp breaths. She was just about to come, and I pulled back. "No," she gasped. "Please."

"Not yet," I chuckled and was rewarded with a death glare.

"God, you're frustrating."

"And you want me." I winked.

"What can I say. It seems like arrogant assholes get my pulse racing," she scoffed.

"And your pussy wet."

She rolled her eyes.

Chuckling, I locked gazes with her and dragged a forefinger over her clit, through her wet slit, and further down to press between her ass cheeks. "Fuck, you're drenched, and I haven't even made you come yet." Her leaking pussy coated my finger, keeping it wet. "Has anyone fucked you here?"

"No." She squirmed when I caressed the puckered hole then pressed in lightly.

"Would you let me fuck you here?" I teased her clit with my tongue while I pushed my finger in, up to the first knuckle.

Those beautiful eyes turned darker and widened. Not from shock. From arousal. She inhaled sharply. "Please," she whispered.

"What do you want, Ash?"

"To come."

"Grab on to the edge of the table above your head." She looked confused for just a second. "It's going to be a rough ride." I winked "I might make you cry."

The second she gripped the table, I used my tongue and teeth to lick, suck and nip on her clit, while keeping my finger in her ass.

Her tortured moans grew louder by the second. When I sank my tongue into her flooded entrance, her pussy spasmed. "Trent," she cried. Her entire body jerked, and she came hard.

I wasn't done. Lapping up her cream, I pushed my finger deeper in her ass and thrust my thumb in her pussy. She twisted, trying to get free but my hand splayed on her stomach kept her in place. This time, I sucked harder and faster, my tongue a brutal dance over her clit. She bucked a couple of times when I bit down on the swollen bundle of nerves. Her whimpers told me she was close. Not holding back, I gave her what she wanted. Driving my tongue deeper and harder, I relished the sweet taste of her moans that grew louder with each sweep, each bite, each suck.

"Oh, God, Trent. Stop." She was shaking. Yet in dire contrast, she undulated—more like shoved her pussy against my face. I flattened my tongue, dragged it relentlessly over her clit before thrusting it beside my thumb still in her pussy, and fingering her ass at the same time. Her whole body tightened. I glanced up, eyes squeezed shut, her face tensed in arousal and so fucking beautiful. I gave her one last rigid suck and it took her over the edge. Her lips parted in a silent scream as her pussy spasmed for the second time. I circled her engorged clit and helped her ride the wave of her orgasm.

"Ash?" I called out when I straightened. Her eyes opened, half-lidded and glazed and sure enough, tears leaked down the sides. "You okay?" She nodded. Her legs, however, were still trembling and sporadic jerks shook her body. I scooped her up in my arms and her head lolled against my shoulder. Smiling, I carried her over to the bed and settled her into the pillows.

When I returned from the bathroom, she was already sleeping. I took a moment, to watch her, devouring her beauty, her serenity and reveling in one fact. She was back where she was supposed to be, in my arms and more importantly, in my life.

As I slid in next to her and pulled the covers over us, she snuggled into my chest, letting out a low sigh. "Goodnight, Krisha," I whispered before closing my eyes.

# Ashrika

"SHIT."

The sharp curse following the crash of something hitting the floor startled me out of my sleep. I sat up observing the scene in my kitchen courtesy of an open plan studio unit. For just a moment I blanked out trying to recall why the dashing Trent Shaw was standing in my kitchen, delicious in nothing but gray sweatpants and flexing muscles as he pushed a broom around the floor.

"Umm..." the words stuck in my throat.

He looked up, stopped sweeping and smiled. I could've sworn my heart danced a little jig of happiness. "Sorry. I was making you breakfast and broke a mug."

Then everything came rushing back and I let out a sheepish laugh. "Oh, my God, I haven't slept like that in..." I groaned. "Never."

His brow shot up on the tail of a wicked smile. "Orgasms. The best cure for insomnia."

My cheeks heated, remembering the sin he'd inflicted between my legs. Just the thought started a brazen tingle inside my pussy. I clutched the sheet to hide my embarrassment but failed. The twitch of Trent's lips told me so. "You're still here." I aimed for simpler conversation.

"I am."

"Why."

"Because you asked me to stay."

"I did?" I asked. He nodded. "I didn't beg, did I?"

"You did." He wiggled his brows with an amused smile.

"Shit," I mumbled. Notwithstanding what happened last night, I felt weird. I dropped my face into my hands, embarrassed. Had I come across like a scared little child? Worse—a wanton woman? He was probably accustomed to the wiles of classy women.

"Ash." I looked up and he smiled. "I've kissed you, painted you with my cum and eaten your pussy, and you're embarrassed about begging me not to leave you alone?"

Hot color crept up my neck once more. I tried to hide my flush and he chuckled. "Don't you have somewhere to be?"

"Other than a charity ball this evening? Nope."

I glanced to the other side of the bed noting the indent in the pillow. "Um...did we...um." I felt like a blushing teenager. His chuckle snapped my gaze back to him. He shook his head. "Why not?" the words slipped out before I could stop them. "Shit. Forget I asked that."

He laughed harder then asked, "Do you ever let your hair down?"

I frowned, brushing a hand through my hair. "It's down."

"As in fun, going out." He grinned.

"Oh." I chewed my bottom lip, shaking my head. "I did once, and you know how that turned out."

"Maybe you weren't in the right company." He shrugged. "Would you be interested in a date?"

"Date?" I laughed. "You strike me as a man who doesn't date. Just fuck?"

Instead of an answer, he set aside the broom and approached me, his steps slow in that usual confident manner he possessed. I couldn't stop my gaze sliding over his bare chest, wanting to run my hands over their tautness, my tongue even better. Climbing onto the bed, he crawled toward me, forcing me to fall back onto the mattress and straddled me on all fours.

"What you're saying is that you'd rather have me fuck you than take you out on a date?" He lowered his head until his nose hovered inches above mine. His wet hair, normally kissing his shoulder, hung loosely around his face and tickled my skin.

"Maybe."

"Maybe?" One dark brow quirked up.

I ran my tongue over my lips, and he followed the trail with his but not kissing me as I expected. "For a man who is so sexually adept as you've arrogantly pointed out, I'm surprised you haven't fucked me yet. Why is that?" I asked, my tone flippant. "I'm beginning to wonder if perhaps you're all talk and no fuck, a man who can't actually stand up when a perfectly good pussy is around to play."

"Ouch." He rubbed a hand over his crotch, "Felt that one in my balls." He smiled, not in the least bit phased by my insult. "Yet your pussy drips so easily at my touch, doesn't it?" He cocked a brow. "I must be doing something right."

"Says you," I huffed and his low chuckle tickled my skin.

"Attend the charity ball with me and I'll give you what you want."

I hesitated and he smiled. Gripping the sheet between his teeth, he moved backward, uncovering my body as he did so. When my feet appeared, he released his hold on the sheet. "Spread your legs, Ash." How did he manage to sound both demanding and pleading at once?

Anticipation tightened my stomach muscles and his darkened gaze lingered on my hard nipples before dropping to my pussy as I obeyed. Without a word, his lips dropped over mine. His tongue probed my mouth, fucking it with slow tantalizing licks. And just when I surrendered to the kiss, he moved, nipping his way down my body. Alternating between soft and rough caresses, his hands followed—touching, pinching and blazing a heated path on their way to my pussy.

"Trent," I gasped when he bit down hard on my inner thigh.

He looked at me. "Want me to stop?"

Breathless, I shook my head before he sank his teeth into the sensitive flesh on my other thigh surprised by just how much pleasure the pain inflicted. I arched my back on a low whimper, waiting for him to give me what I wanted and he did. A few seconds later he slid his hands under my ass. His grip digging into the tender flesh, he latched onto my clit, using his tongue and teeth to bite, suck and lick me until my head spun. My hips jerked in time to the cadence of his mouth and my orgasm skated down my spine. He flattened his palm over my belly, holding me down and sucked harder. Moaning, I rocked my pussy against his face, unashamedly wanton. When he slid two fingers inside me and scraped his teeth over my clit, my toes curled.

"Oh, God, yes." I gripped his shoulders. "So close," I panted. And just when I felt the burn of my orgasm, he yanked the rug out from under me. Pulling away, he sat back on his knees. "What are you doing?" I blinked. My body a trembling mess, anxious and on the pinnacle of an orgasm. His lips glistening with my juices, parted with a sinful smile. "Don't you dare stop now," I growled.

"Or what?" He moved over me, bracketing my body with his knees and hands on either side of me.

Flustered, I squirmed but he didn't budge. "This won't happen again," I warned.

Even though I resisted his charms, his soft laugh spiked the hairs at the back of my nape. "Want to take a bet on that?"

"Yes," I mumbled. He leaned closer, brushing his lips over mine and when I turned my face away, he cupped my jaw and brought my lips back to his. His tongue seared the seam of my lips, demanding entrance. I shook my head, jerking out of his grasp. "Apologize, if you want to kiss me again," I ordered.

"For what? Not making you come?" He flashed me his signature cocky smile. "I never apologize for making a woman feel so good she begs for more."

"Wow." I gaped at him. "They must've had your ego in mind when they built the wall of China."

"Sweetheart." He nipped my lip and I yelped. "Scoff all you want but when I bury my cock deep inside your sweet pussy tonight, you'll forget where you end and I begin. You *will* beg me for more."

"I don't beg and the only fucking that's happening tonight is in your dreams." I wriggled to get free of his hold and he tightened his knees against my legs. "Your problem is, you're way too used to getting everything you want."

"Of course, I am, and I always do." His breath whispered across my lips stealing the limelight to his arrogance. "Regardless, you *will* attend that charity ball with me but the only two pleas of empathy you'll hear, will be your own—begging to be fucked and pleading to come."

"We'll see." Mustering all the strength I possessed, I shoved at his chest.

This time he rolled off the bed and stood. Grinning, he looked at me. "Join me for breakfast?"

"Really? Barely a second ago you were dictating, now you're asking?"

"I'll take that as a yes then." Snubbing my scowl, he walked over to the kitchen.

Determined to ignore him, I slid off on the other side of the bed and with my back to him, I pretended interest in my phone.

Then he opened the oven door.

A delicious aroma, straddling the lines between a freshly baked cake and a grilled cheese, assailed my senses. Suddenly hungry, my stomach rumbled, and I glanced at him over my shoulder. He was setting a pan on the table.

Catching my gaze, he winked, licked his finger, and then dipped it in something. His expression the epitome of a naughty boy, he held out his finger. "Want to taste?"

The chef in me was more than curious. Pouting to show my displeasure with his tactic, I stood and grabbed panties and a t-shirt from a drawer.

I was about to slip on the tee when he said, "Don't Ash." With the sleeves halfway up my arms, I stopped and looked at him. "I want you naked."

"We don't always get what we want." I pulled on the t-shirt then followed with the panties. I ambled over to the table set with yogurt, fresh fruit and orange juice. I stared at the pan filled with something that looked like pizza. "What's that?"

"Sit and taste for yourself." He pulled out a chair, sat and patted his thigh.

The smell was now more potent, and my mouth watered. I inhaled deeply while pulling my hair into a ponytail.

"Leave it down."

"No." I dashed off to the bathroom before he could say anything. It was weird that as a chef I looked forward to tasting food cooked by others. Done using the toilet and brushing my teeth, I sauntered back into the kitchen.

As I reached for a chair, Trent shook his head. "Here." He pointed to his lap.

When I shook my head, his jaw tightened, the intensity of his gaze unnerving me a little. "Don't like following orders do you?"

"No."

"I seem to recall you following them perfectly last night at this very table."

Hot color flooded my cheeks. I barely had time to register his intent before he shot up from his seat and rounded the six-seater table to my side. He scooped me up, sat and settled me on his lap. I scowled.

"You will learn to obey me."

"I'm not a child," I snapped.

"Then stop acting like one." He waited for me to argue. I didn't. With an arm around my waist to keep me in place, he reached for the pan, set it on the table in front of me and picked up a fork. "Eat," he ordered.

"I'm surprised you're not forcing it down my throat," I muttered.

"If I'm going to force anything down your throat, trust me. It won't be food." The wicked curve to his lips told me I'd do well to shut up and eat.

Gulping back the retort, I took the fork and was amazed when it sank into whatever I was about to taste. I lifted a portion to my mouth the same time Trent sucked at my nape. I moaned as twice the sensation ripped through my body. "God, this tastes so good," I said after swallowing a fluffy, melt-in-your-mouth mix of eggs, cheese and cajun paprika, wrapped in a pancake and topped with cheese.

"So do you." Trent sucked my left earlobe into his mouth while his hands climbed to my breasts. He pinched the nipples until they pebbled. The contrasting softness of his mouth and hard fingers started swirls of need between my thighs. If I didn't get fucked soon, I'd die from a broken pussy. I grinned at the thought and scooped another bite into my mouth trying my best to ignore Trent's manipulations, I knew he wasn't going to give me what I wanted.

"If you were naked right now, I'd fuck you," he whispered against my neck.

The fork stopped midway to my mouth. I turned slightly until his gaze met mine. "So, what you're saying, is that because I put on a t-shirt and panties, you can't fuck me?" He nodded. "And not because I disobeyed you, right." Again, he nodded. Calling his bluff, I dropped the fork into the pan, pulled off my t-shirt and arched a brow.

He moved me off his lap and stood with me then dropped a soft kiss to my lips. "Nice try. I'll pick you up at six. It's black-tie, wear something pretty and bring an overnight bag or not, either way, you won't need clothes." With that, he was gone.

I stared at the closing door unsure if I wanted to laugh or curse. Overnight bag? Did the man actually think he could waltz into my life and dictate what I did or didn't do with my time? Who the hell did he think he was? *"Your next fuck."* I recalled his words in my bathroom. Shaking my head, I retook my seat and continued eating. No reason to let a damn good meal go to waste.

# Ashrika

"THIS WAS DROPPED OFF for you," Tia handed me a large, flat box as she sauntered into the kitchen.

Frowning, I set it on the counter, wiped my hands then pulled off the lid. I pushed aside the layer of white tissue paper and fingered the soft material beneath. Pulling out the beautiful gray dress, I held it up against my body.

"Wow," Tia glanced at me from across the room. "The man definitely has taste."

"Which man?"

"Oh, come on, Rika, that dress has Trent written all over it, it's classy, sexy, and matches your eyes perfectly. I'm assuming you're attending the ball, then."

"I didn't say that." I mentioned Trent's invitation earlier but wasn't expecting to receive a dress from him.

"There's a note." She pointed to an envelope sticking out at the bottom of the box. Pulling the white envelope out, I ripped it open and retrieved the note. Laughing as I read his coded words, handwritten in blue ink. The penned cursive neat and not what I expected from Trent.

"Join me tonight. I heard a Blacksmith will be in attendance if you do," Tia read over my shoulder. "I'm assuming there's a hidden meaning only you'll understand?" I nodded. "Have you started taking the pills?"

Frowning, I turned to face her. "What pills?"

"Birth control? A month ago you were considering taking them?"

Having forgotten I'd mentioned it, I laughed. "I did."

"Great, now you fuck Trent without condoms." She chuckled giving me the evil plotting face.

I slapped a hand to my brow, not sure who was more brash between Tia and Trent. Maybe me taking the pill had been out of sheer optimism with Zayne. Now, with Trent in the picture—

"So, are you going?" Tia yanked me out of my thoughts.

"I have to think about it, we're just friends. I don't want to give him any ideas," I lied remembering just how well he ate me out and knowing I wanted more of what he could offer.

"What's there to think about?" she snorted. "You're just making excuses as usual."

"He wants me to stay the night with him." My half-hearted attempt at an excuse was met by a frosty glare.

"And you're like what—sweet sixteen?" She banged her head against a wall then eyeballed me. "Jesus, Rika, you lost your memory not your ability to have sex. Grow some ovaries, would you?"

I pressed a palm to my forehead, I could definitely do with less of her sass right now. "Fine," I agreed, just to get her off my case. I planned to call Trent later and tell him I couldn't make it.

Later that afternoon I glanced up from a meal I'd just finished to find Leah and Tia watching me. "What now?"

"It's time to get ready."

*Oh shit.* I'd forgotten to call Trent. "I'm not going." I figured he'll understand something came up. Ignoring the two of them, I cleaned my counter space.

"Rika," Tia called me. I finally looked up when the silence became too much. Rope dangled from her hand. I frowned. "Remember Nina's bachelorette and how we dressed you." She swung the rope.

"Seriously? You're going to tie me up."

"If that's what it takes to get you to go tonight," Leah chimed.

Groaning, I conceded, "Fine. I'll go."

Trent was waiting at the restaurant bar chatting to Dean when I came downstairs. As if he sensed my appearance, he turned toward the entrance then he froze, his glass suspended in mid-air. I felt his gaze scorch a blazing path from my silver heels, up my body to finally rest on my face, and when his gaze met mine, it flared with unabashed desire.

I smiled. The gossamer-thin fabric draped itself elegantly over my body and crossed over my breasts with intricate straps, exposing a deep slice of plump cleavage. According to Tia, the gentle gray-suited my eyes and dark hair, which I'd left down to bounce in soft curls around my back.

Trent wished Dean a quick farewell and crossed the restaurant to my side. "If I knew you were going to look this beautiful, I would've swapped places with the Blacksmith," his smile was slow, sinfully so.

"Would he mind terribly, you know, if there were to be a last-minute change in plan?"

"Unfortunately, yes." He faked disappointment and I burst out laughing.

There was just so much more to this man I was beginning to adore. Unfortunately. "Thank you for the dress."

"My pleasure. But you didn't have to wear it." Even though he said it, his smile was triumphant but not in an arrogant manner, more like he was glad I loved his choice.

When we arrived, a long line of limos waited to offload their guests in front of the venue. I glanced out my window, taking in the scene. It had the whole Hollywood vibe to it with the red carpet and flashing cameras. I felt out of sorts amid these strangers with whom I'd be spending the next couple of hours. Zayne was a low-key type of person which suited my reserved personality perfectly. He never pushed me to attend anything fancy but never failed to suggest, offer or ask if I wanted to go somewhere or do something different, I always refused. Trent, however, was intent on pushing my boundaries to get what he wanted. Surprisingly, I was enjoying his lead.

When he opened my door, I drew in a deep breath and stepped out. "How many people did you say were attending this function?"

"I didn't." He smiled. "But I'm guessing around three hundred."

"Why does it look like a lot more?" I glanced around. People were everywhere. Chatting, laughing, posing for private photographs and selfies.

With my hand tucked in the crook of his arm, he escorted me toward the entrance. Swallowing my nerves, I hoped I'd do my heels proud and stay upright for Trent's sake. This was his event and the last thing I needed was to embarrass the man.

"Relax, sweetheart, any tighter and I probably wouldn't be able to use the arm for a while."

I looked up then followed Trent's gaze back down to where I was squeezing his arm. "Shit, I'm sorry." I eased my grip on his arm. Standing on the red carpet outside the main entrance to a stunning hotel and about to attend a black-tie event was something I'd never imagined myself doing.

"I'm kidding." He laughed. "Why are you so nervous?"

I was so out of my depth. "I don't do large crowds."

"It's just a ball—"

"Excuse me, are you minimizing my first experience?"

He chuckled. "I wouldn't dream of it, but it's just another—"

"Good."

"Feisty aren't you?"

"And you know you want me."

He looked at me, needing no words to tell me just how right I was if that hunger in his eyes was anything to go by. For just a second, I forgot about the crowds and focused on the man next to me. In a gray suit that matched my dress to perfection and a black button-down, he cut a dashing figure of power, elegance, and pure mouth-watering decadence. As we entered, cameras went off, capturing the couples ahead of us. When it was our turn, I hid my face behind Trent's shoulder. He stopped walking, pulled me to one side and circled my waist.

"Any specific reason other than large crowds?" I was still glancing around when he cupped my chin gently and turned me to look at him. "You're a beautiful woman who has the world at your feet and men eating out of your palm, me in particular." He grinned. "There's no reason to be nervous."

"I don't know anyone here," I mumbled.

"You know me."

"And what happens when you have to leave me to go...um...mingle or do whatever it is you do at these fancy functions?"

"Firstly, I wouldn't leave you alone. I'm afraid someone else might steal you." He winked and I smiled, the tension receding a little. "Second, you get to meet two important people in my life, today. So, you won't be alone."

"Really? Who?"

Trent tucked my hand into the crook of his arm, and we began walking again. "My father's brother, Drake Princeton and his wife."

"Drake Princeton, wow, that sounds so influential, so princely." I laughed at my joke. "Is he some big shot businessman? Should I curtsy?"

He chuckled. "Influential, yes. Princely, yes. Businessman, yes. Curtsy, no. Trust me, you'll love them both. Sianna is a sweet girl. She used to be my restaurant manageress in Brenton."

"You're kidding." I stopped short. "Your manageress is married to your uncle. How did that happen?"

"Long story." He grinned. "I'll fill you in as we walk around."

A waiter approached us with a tray of champagne flutes. Trent accepted two glasses and handed me one. "Maybe this might calm you." He was still finishing his sentence when I downed the drink and reached for his. Laughing, he gave it to me and signaled the waiter. "Better?" he asked when I took a huge gulp of the second glass.

"A little," I hiccupped on a bubble.

"Just don't leave my side if you intend getting tipsy again. There are plenty of tables to choose from here." He winked, the insinuation clear and I stuck out my tongue at him. He laughed. "Come on, let me introduce you to some people." With his hand on my lower back, he guided me around what I assumed to be the foyer since there were no tables in sight.

Turned out his definition of some was a lot. By the time we met the twelfth couple, we'd moved into the gorgeous Victorian-style ballroom and I couldn't remember the names of the first couple. "How do you know all these people?" I could hear the incredulity in my voice.

The waiter arrived with our drinks. Trent took a moment to hand me the glass of iced-tea I opted for instead of alcohol. "Mostly business associates." He sipped his wine and lifted his hand to greet another person across the room.

"Mostly business? Am I to assume some pleasure associates too? Someone's wife or two." I teased.

He frowned and even with his lips curved down they begged to be kissed. "The only other man's wife I'm interested in pleasuring is exactly where she needs to be."

"And where exactly is that?"

His grip tightened on my waist, his voice low in my ear, he whispered, "In my arms." His breath tickled and burned at the same time. I shivered. "And very soon, in my mouth."

I fumbled with my glass, caressing the beads of sweat formed by the blocks of ice. "How soon?" I was being cheeky, and his brow shot up.

"Don't tempt me, sweetheart, or I'm likely to forget my speech in favor of slipping my fingers into your no doubt wet pussy while I eat you out on that balcony, right now." He gestured to the French doors to our left.

I gulped, squeezing my thighs. "You wouldn't dare. Not with all these people milling about."

"Something tells me you'd enjoy it."

I gawked at him but was prevented from saying anything as another older couple approached us. After they left, I gave up my intention to quiz him about his earlier statement and instead asked, "you haven't explained your involvement in this event."

As if sensing my redirection, he flashed me a wicked grin. "I'm one of ten founding members called Singleaders, an organization that focuses on various charitable aspects relating to kids. Children of abusive homes, addicted parents, runaway kids who lost a parent, homeless kids, and child prostitutes, are our current forte. We've raised millions over the last five years which have funded our cause."

"Singleaders?"

Trent laughed. "Ten men," he paused to point at nine men taking their seats on stage, "who lost wives or girlfriends to death, another man or incompatibility and chose to remain single. Our motto was, we don't need the stress of forming new relationships. Rather stay single, do what we want, when we want and focus our energies on someone who actually needs us, destitute kids."

"Wow." I was impressed. "And what exactly do you guys do?"

"Among other things, we employ strict processes to find those kids good, affluent homes with facilitated visits by counselors every two weeks, then monthly and every six months thereafter. The longer the kids stay with those parents, the less supervised visits are required. But we're a phone call away if the need arises for both parents and kids. Before they leave our premises, we make sure they're equipped with health insurance, college tuition and enrolments in any additional classes they may need."

"By the looks of this." I waved my hand gesturing the room. "It's a huge success."

He nodded, glancing around. "For once, it's not a group of rich people donating just to fulfil social investment obligations. These are caring, family orientated people with a genuine interest in the future leaders of our country."

He sounded proud and rightly so. I heard of mothers making a difference when it came to kids but standing in the middle of these affluent people headed up by a group of young not to mention good-looking single men was remarkable. We moved to our table and Trent stepped away to greet someone. I took a moment to watch him, aware I was the envy of plenty of women tonight. I'd seen the admiration, the drool and subtle moves to check their makeup, hair and breasts when he passed by. While the notion he was mine thrilled me, I wasn't sure for how long. Whatever happened between us since we met, some might call insta-lust. Whether it would grow into something had been a probability until I just learned what Singleaders stood for. Trent didn't want the stress of building a new relationship and I didn't wish to waste his time. Was it worth cheating on Zayne then?

"Hello, my dear."

Frowning, I turned to find a sixty-something woman at my side, her body awash in a flamboyant orange dress but it was her smile that drew me in instantly. Friendly and sincere. Almost like we'd known each other forever.

"Hi." I smiled.

"I'm Martha," she beamed. "You must be Trent's other half. What a pretty little thing you are. I'm all alone for this function. My Steven didn't want to come tonight, says he got a headache. Would you mind terribly if I sat next to you. I don't fancy sitting next to that pervert, Howard. He's got a sneaky paw and blames it on his muscles spasms," she rattled on not giving me a chance to correct her or get a word in.

Laughing, I glanced at Trent over her shoulder, and he nodded. I had no idea why but something in his expression told me she needed the attention. "Sure."

"Oh, thank you, my dear." She grabbed Trent's placeholder, scooted around the table, swapped it with hers and returned to my side.

As she took his seat and studied the menu, Trent approached me. Slipping an arm around my waist, he drew me close. "She lost her husband six months ago, hasn't accepted it yet and thinks he's still alive," he whispered in my ear.

I gasped and glanced at the old woman. Anyone looking in would think she was just a happy, easygoing person. My heart ached for what she must be going through.

"Her family hasn't been the best of support. I've got a friend trying to help ease her into the truth. You don't mind, do you?" He leaned back to look at me. I shook my head. "I have no idea where Drake is and I need to be up on stage for a bit." He glanced around the room.

"It's okay."

"I promised not to leave you alone."

"I'll be fine."

"Thank you." Dropping a quick kiss to my lips, he headed for the stage.

I lowered myself into the seat next to Martha and she immediately reached for my hand. Smiling, I caressed her hand as the emcee began speaking.

Half an hour later, after the formalities were over and just before dinner was served, Martha had found another lady her age to talk to about crocheting. I left Trent chatting to colleagues in search of the bathroom, instead, I found a door that led out into beautiful white rose gardens draped in soft lighting that probably looked even more spectacular under the sun. Needing a few moments to myself, I followed the stone pathway that curved between the bushes, stopping occasionally to smell the fresh flowers. I had barely walked a few paces when I heard a soft cry. Surprised, I glanced around but saw nothing. I paused to listen, and another soft cry sounded a moment later. Guessing it was probably a kitten, I did a three-sixty trying to pinpoint its location. Seeing nothing, I moved and rounded a corner in the pathway. I stopped short and backtracked a step yet couldn't take my eyes off the vision in front.

The sounds came from a woman. She stood about twenty feet away with her back pressed up against the glass wall of what looked like a greenhouse. Her eyes were closed, her white dress gathered around her waist and her soft whimpers were courtesy of the man kneeling in front of her, his face buried between her legs. And judging by the pure ecstasy on her face, he probably excelled at eating pussy. I was about to step back when the woman's eyes opened, and her heated gaze clashed with mine.

I balked. My breathing faltered for just a moment. To my surprise, she didn't move or let her lover know they were being watched. Instead, her gaze stayed riveted on me, burrowing itself into the depths of every nerve cell connecting my brain to my pussy. A quiver shot through me, I felt the primal heat as it started at my nape and flowed all the way down to my toes. I shuddered. Stunned by my body's reaction, some part, urging me to turn, run, move —do something to get away but stupidly my feet didn't listen, and my breathing wavered once more. When her hips bucked up against his face, I almost groaned with her, the pulse between my legs now an erratic throb. I was suddenly desperate to touch myself, to feel what she was feeling, to slide my fingers deep inside my pussy until I burst into a million shards of pleasure that would be my orgasm. I clasped my neck, fingers spread, and pressed down lightly, compelling myself to breathe slowly.

Then she came. "Oh, God, yes," her voice was low and husky, dripping with naked lust, yet her eyes stayed on mine tethered by some magnetic force that prevented me from looking away.

Giving her no reprieve from her high, her lover shot to his feet and in one quick move, lifted her with his hands under her thighs and impaled her on his cock. One of her hands on his nape, the other on his arm, she closed her eyes against his thrusts. The disconnection, however, didn't break my spell. Their sexual sounds filled the air and my breathing hitched, my pussy clenched tight. Was it possible to come just from watching? I had to get out of there but somehow my legs wouldn't move.

"That turns you on, doesn't it? Watching other people fuck," Trent's gravelly voice rasped in my ear. Instead of shock at his appearance, my body responded to the sound of him. I trembled, now desperate to have him touch me. "Is your pussy dripping right now, sweetheart? If I had to slip my fingers inside your panties would they come out wet and warm, smelling of lust and hunger?"

"Given your insolence, why haven't you fucked me, yet?" I asked, without turning to look at him, the pleading in my voice embarrassingly naïve for a woman who'd given him shit about his arrogance.

"Why don't you tell me what you want?"

I glanced over my shoulder. "Didn't I just tell you what I want? For you to fuck me?"

He stared at me, against the halo of light shading his head, his eyes were the color of midnight sin itself. "Sliding my cock inside you until we come, won't bring me the same satisfaction as you telling me what you really want. I want to see inside you, Ash. To take a peek at all your fantasies, the darkest ones, the ones you're too shy to tell your friends, your husband. The secrets I want to make come true."

A surge of arousal coiled in my belly, squeezing tight. "What makes you think I have any?" I asked, my voice almost breathless. My palms turned clammy from having clenched them each time Trent spoke. I swallowed hard to push down the nausea—the threatening queasiness of telling someone what I desired. How having someone watch me fuck myself—or better still being fucked while being watched—turned me on, made me so damn wet, it dripped down my legs in anticipation. Was I sick? Would he look down on me if I told him?

"Tell me," he urged as if reading my mind. The breath staggered in my chest, wishing to blurt it out. When I said nothing, he cupped my chin and turned my face away. "Look at them and tell me."

I watched as the man slowed his thrusts to kiss her. I wanted to see his face, to hear what he said to make her smile with such adoration when he pulled back. He began moving again. The squeals she let out and the intensity of his grip on her thighs indicated he was fucking her hard and fast. Her fingers gripped his shoulders, clinging to him as they moved in a perfect harmony I envied. Still, I kept quiet, unable to voice what I really wanted.

"Turn around." I did as Trent asked. "Look at me." I lifted my eyes to his. "Do you want me to fuck you now?"

Aware another couple was fucking a few feet away from us and other people could walk past at any time, I glanced around.

"Here?" Even though I asked, a deviant thrill crested through me and I was shaking.

As if he read my mind, he replied, "You know you want to." He moved closer, slipping his hand around my waist. "Sex is a form of art, Ash. There is nothing degrading about it. Some people just prefer a little more thrill to their pleasure. It's no different to an extreme car racer or skydiving. You just need to embrace it." He cupped my face and slowly tantalized my lips with his. "Would you like me to force your desires from you?"

Staring up at him, I was drawn into that look of understanding, of encouragement. How was it possible that this man who didn't know me, could see right into my soul where others had failed? I sighed. "About six months after I woke from the coma and while still coming to terms with my memory loss, I attended a party with a friend, a nurse at the hospital. She didn't tell me it was a sex party. Although I wasn't forced into participating sexually, I was turned on watching other people fuck and took part in the various activities. Some included dancing." I paused unsure if I wanted to divulge more.

"Hey." Trent rubbed a slow finger along my jawline. "There's no one here but the two of us and there's nothing wrong with attending a sex party or dancing at one for that matter."

I chewed my lip, realizing what he'd assumed. "You don't understand."

"Then tell me."

Raking a hand through my hair, I turned away slightly and stared up at the full moon. So bright, so peaceful, and free to rise and fall at its discretion. As crazy as it sounded, I wished for its nonchalance. "The dancing was on a stage," I explained. "It was similar to a private strip show and I agreed to it. I stripped for men I didn't know." Desire raced through my body at the memory. "On some carnal level I never understood, I liked how it felt. Having those men watch me with lust-filled eyes, wanting me, greedy to touch me—not knowing who I was or where I came from. I loved how they responded to my body, that I made them hard, made them desire me. A woman with no past and an uncertain future. I made men crave me without touching. And when they stroked themselves, it made me wet, made me delirious with want, so greedy that I touched myself while they watched, brought myself off with an orgasm so intense it made me cry while witnessed by so many hungry eyes. It was the first time since waking from the coma that I felt free, alive, different, carefree. Even though there was a moment I wanted to be fucked, filled with those hard dicks in my pussy and mouth at the same time, I chose not to, knowing I could've had any of those men. Do I regret it? I'm not sure."

I stopped speaking and moved away from him, breathing deeply and only turning when I could work up the courage to face him. While I was glad, he didn't say anything, I kept my gaze on the floor. "After that night, I put everything into some hidden compartment of my brain and never thought about it again, until now. I never went out again. Both for my safety from an unknown killer and my fear of where I'd end up if I explored my sexuality." I drew in a labored breath. "Are you judging me, Trent? Do I sound like a slut to you, knowing what's going on behind these eyes you call beautiful?"

"Look at me, Ash." I did. "I'm no one to judge but I can be your jury."

"Jury?"

"I sat on the sidelines, observed, waited, heard and now I can decide your fate, if you let me. I can give you what you want. Slow, deep, hard, fast, you say the word and I'll fuck you how you want it, but, it will come with a whole lot more."

I let out a low laugh. "How is it possible that I barely know you, yet you've got me to confess my deepest desires? A secret I've shared with no one, not even Zayne." I paused reflecting on his words. "What do you mean by more?"

Instead of the usual arrogance, his smile was lazy yet didn't detract from the passion burning in those beautiful blues, almost like watching fire grow in intensity each time fuel was added. He squeezed my arms then cupped my face. His eyes penetrated mine, looking deep. The fact that he'd cottoned on to my secrets told me his profound observation had begun on day one. Only, I didn't see it.

"Sometimes all a woman needs, is the right man to give her the freedom to be herself, to unlock her desires, to let her love, fuck and want you on her terms. The more she truly smiles, the more chance she will stay. Forever. I want forever with you," his tender words dug deep into my very soul.

"Forever?" I hesitated. "But, I barely know you."

"The heart has a way of picking the perfect love for you even if you're still on the fence about whether they are the one." His warm breath tickled my lips. "My heart chose that moment you ran out into the rain, trembling with fear yet fighting me with everything you had. Those gray eyes, rimmed by signs that danced between yes and no, pleaded for me to enter. All you needed was for someone to look past the barrier you built. I did."

"Not before?" I uttered a soft laugh. "You know the usual love at first sight cliché."

Slowly, he shook his head. "Not before. That day, that moment will stay entrenched in my heart. It's my new beginning and hopefully yours."

Then reality blinked in the distance. "I am married, Trent."

"And yet, you're here with me." There was no ridicule in his tone, only a tenderness I still had to understand, to grasp.

And like some constant death wish on my emotions, I sighed. "I don't think I'm ready for whatever this is."

Disappointment cloaked his smile. "Will you ever be?"

"I don't know."

"And if I'd fucked you last night? Would that have made a difference?"

"I'm not sure."

His jaw clenched as though trying to hold back his truths. "I'm usually a patient man, Ash, but right now I want you." The intent in his tone was crystal clear.

And we were right back where we started, I shook my head. "For a man who just spoke about the heart and what it wants, you sure as hell play the seduction card to perfection," I retorted.

His gaze roamed over my body with nothing short of unashamed hunger. "Five hours and counting." He winked. I frowned. The smile was slow but there was no doubting its decadence. "I did say two days." He licked his lips in true Trent fashion.

"Trent?" Someone called out behind him before I could respond.

He turned away. "Drake? I was beginning to think you were a no-show." Trent laughed.

I watched as a tall, well-built and judging by the streaks of gray peppering his dark hair, older man, step forward and accept Trent's hand in a quick shake. My mouth hung open for just a bit when I got a full view of his face. *Wow.* I wouldn't be surprised if Trent's gene pool was a direct descendant from Adonis himself. These were two seriously good-looking men.

"Drake, meet Ashrika." I caught Trent's knowing smile as he urged me forward with a hand to my lower back.

"Hello, Ashrika, nice to meet you." The man's deep voice coupled with those striking gray eyes must've certainly wet a few panties in his lifetime.

I grinned inwardly, wondering what Trent had told his uncle about me since his introduction hadn't come with a label. I swallowed my thoughts. "Hi. Please, call me Rika, everyone does, except for Trent that is." Jesus, was I rambling?

Drake's soft chuckle seemed to have a calming effect on my fumbling. "And what does my arrogant nephew call you?" he asked.

"Ash," Trent replied, drawing me close to him. I didn't miss the telltale look between the two men and was curious about it when Trent asked, "Where's Sianna?"

"Still smelling the flowers." Drake glanced over his shoulder. "Princess?"

Wow. He called his wife princess. I was tempted to swoon.

"Coming," she called out and two seconds later, a beautiful woman appeared beside her husband. They made a stunning couple.

Then my smile froze. *Oh, shit.* I silently cursed, recognizing the woman I'd walked in on having sex with...oh double shit. I suddenly felt like a peeping tom. God, she must've thought I was a pervert.

But my apprehension was for nothing. "Hi." Sianna held out a hand which I accepted in a soft shake. Her wide smile calmed me.

"Hi." I returned the gesture.

When Trent mentioned his uncle had married a younger woman, I didn't expect my first meeting with the couple would be of them having sex in full view of an open pathway. Damn, they rocked.

"We can get acquainted inside. Dinner is about to be served," Trent gestured to the main building.

Drake nodded, slipped a hand around his wife's waist and ushered her forward. I hung back a little and Trent noticed. "You okay?"

"I walked in on—"

"I know." He laughed. "Don't worry about it. My uncles got a wolfish sex drive for his age and I think she kind of brings it out in him more." No kidding. "Come on." Trent nudged me down the path toward the door I'd come through.

Twenty minutes later, while Drake and Trent chatted to the other men at the table, I touched Sianna's arm lightly. She sat on my right with Martha to my left. "About earlier, I didn't mean—"

"Don't worry about it." Sianna laughed. "Being married to Drake has put me in touch with my sexuality in more ways than I would've expected. Trust me, these Princeton men know how to take care of their women. I should know firsthand, I've been involved with all of them." At my widened eyes, she smiled. "No. I haven't slept with Trent if that's what you're asking, he was my boss but showed me real affection when I needed it most. I fell in love with Drake and his son, so talk about drama. Trent was my pillar then."

"Wow. Two men. How?"

"Believe me I fought it. Thought it wasn't possible. And with two men like Rayden and Drake, it was easy to fall. Some people can understand, and others can't but they don't understand what you go through. I broke. Inside. Outside. Trust me when I say, we can never understand the decisions our hearts make nor is it impossible to find two men who love you so hard, it leaves you numb, blind and indecisive."

I couldn't help thinking about my situation with Trent and Zayne. Then again, they didn't love me. Zayne was my safety net and Trent, my—my what? I blanked out. I didn't have a title for him. "You must've gone through hell."

"You have no idea. But it gets easier with time." She looked at Drake. As if sensing her eyes on him, he glanced at her and winked, making her blush. That gave me goosebumps. There was no mistaking the authenticity in their love. I could feel it in that one look. Sianna turned back to me. "By the way, Drake and I overheard your conversation with Trent. So, I think we're kind of squared on the whole knowing each other intimately thing."

Hot color flooded my cheeks. "What?" I squeaked.

She chuckled, her exuberance refreshingly honest. "We should do coffee sometime." She patted my hand lightly. "Get to know each other better if you'd like."

"I'd like that. Thank you."

I had no idea why, but something about this woman with her rosy cheeks and sparkling blue eyes put me at ease. Perhaps it was the way her husband, whom according to Trent, was almost twenty years her senior, lavished her with such affection that made her appear mature and understanding. For the first time in a long while, I actually wanted to go out for coffee and get to know someone better.

# Trent

I WASN'T EXPECTING Martha to attend tonight's ball but seeing her made her plight all that more real. That some people struggled to accept pain while others thought nothing of it. She'd been married to the same man for almost thirty years, and I could understand why it was hard for her to acknowledge Steven's death. My marriage hadn't even made the five-year mark and the loss was extremely painful to handle, Martha just needed time. I shifted my gaze to Ashrika and smiled watching her animated expressions as she chatted with Sianna and the older woman.

"So, what do you think, Trent?"

I returned Ashrika's wave and turned my attention back to the man sitting next to me at the bar. Nathan had just asked me about the proposal for sponsorship to shelter women from abusive relationships. "You know me, Nathan, anything children related and I'm all ears. There are plenty of women's shelters around New York, why would we consider taking it under our umbrella?"

"I think the idea is more single mothers with abusive boyfriends," Nathan explained. "And yes, there are plenty of those around too but given our success rate at helping children, I think those kids would benefit from the Singleaders expertise."

"Drop by the office on Monday and we can call the others in as well." My phone buzzed. I glanced at the number and frowned, not expecting to see Zayne's name flashing across the screen. "Excuse me, Nathan, I need to take this." He nodded and with my drink in hand, I walked around to the quieter side of the bar. "She's an adult, you don't need to check up on her," I answered, my tone brusque.

Zayne's laugh was mirthless. "Says the man who's gallivanting around town with *my wife*."

I frowned. Was he drunk? "What the fuck, Zayne. You were the one that offered up this deal."

"She's not a fucking deal, she's a woman, *my* fucking woman." He *was* drunk.

I wondered if he was rethinking his offer. If that was the case, I wasn't about to back down. "Would you prefer I tell her the truth?" I hissed. He cursed. "I thought so." Even though my tone was aggressive, I rubbed my brow then sighed. "Look, Zayne, I know this can't be easy for you. Fuck, it isn't easy on any of us. Honestly, I don't think I would've been this accommodating if our roles were reversed." I bit my lip. What the fuck was I doing? I exhaled on a frustrated breath. "If you want me to back down, say so now and I will."

There was a long pause on the other side. "If I said yes, would you tell her the truth?"

I dragged a hand down my face, wondering the same thing. "No." What the fuck? My frazzled brain screamed to shut the fuck up and tell him to fuck off.

"Take care of her, Trent. Don't fuck up, or God help me..." He cut the call.

I stared at the blank screen wishing I had an easier answer to this mess that the three of us had landed—no, catapulted into with no clear fucking direction in mind. I had Ashrika exactly where I wanted her—wanting me, desperate for my touch. I'd noticed her walls the first time I saw her and put it down to wariness given her memory loss.

Suffice it to say, I was in no way prepared for her disclosure. I'd nearly choked on my saliva the second she started explaining. Listening to her talk about being turned on watching people fuck, of having men watch her strip was sexy as fuck, I guess my deviant mind worked in mysterious ways. But then she mentioned bringing herself to an orgasm in front of these men. My mind warred between giving in to my selfish needs to fuck her right there or listen.

It'd taken every bit of self-control I possessed. I'd always been open to anything that would bring a little spice to our bedroom, but only if my partner wanted it. There were limitations to what Krisha had enjoyed and I hadn't pushed her. Knowing memory loss was responsible for her change in personality, I wasn't sure if I felt bad for taking advantage of those circumstances. Maybe I was just a bigger asshole than she knew.

Yet just thinking about her, I was hard as fuck. I glanced in her direction. She'd moved away to stand with the group of ladies that worked for my organization. All I had to do was give her what she needed and desired most and hope like fucking hell it would bring relief to the three of us. I wanted my wife back and I was prepared to do whatever the fuck it took.

"Is this seat taken?"

I looked up to find a tall redhead obscuring my vision of Ashrika. The woman, although not exactly beautiful, made up for her lack thereof with an alluring figure adorned in crimson satin which I was amused to discover, didn't go unnoticed by the other men around the bar.

Schooling my features into a polite mask, I gestured to the seat with a nod then signaled the bartender for another drink. After the call from Zayne, my head wasn't in the right space to approach Ashrika, I needed a couple of minutes to calm the fuck down.

The woman next to me slid into the seat and crossed her legs, her short dress riding high enough to reveal far more legs than I deemed appropriate for this event. She pulled out a long cigarette from a silver case and slid it between fire-engine red lips. Her smile engaging, she arched a brow.

"Sorry, I don't smoke," I mumbled and picked up my glass.

"Aren't you that wealthy restauranteur, what's the name..." She seemed to contemplate her question for the moment then said, "...oh yes, Mr. Shaw I believe."

I shrugged, said nothing, and made an active attempt to ignore her. I could spot easy pickings a mile away, but my heart was interested in only one woman, currently belonging to a man who seemed to be going off the rails. Could I blame him? How the fuck would I react if our roles were reversed? Still, I was concerned that he could nip his offer in the bud just as quickly as he'd made it. Then what? There was no guarantee Ashrika would believe me if I told her the truth, or worse, her reaction might not go according to plan.

"I'm sure a gentleman like you wouldn't mind buying a thirsty girl a drink?" the woman insisted on speaking. Not one for being rude, I nodded to the bartender. She pointed to my whiskey. "I'll have the same, please. Not much of a talker, are you?" She touched my hand that rested on the counter.

Short of telling her to buzz off, I moved my hand and glanced at her wedding ring. "Are you here alone?" I asked, hoping her husband wasn't some dipshit who pawned his wife off on rich guys, hoping to score. I'd seen a few of those at our previous events, given the majority of guests were affluent older men.

"Depends," she replied.

"On?"

"Whether you'd like to keep me company or not." She licked her lips suggestively.

"I'm with someone."

"So?"

I cocked a brow. Jesus. "What do you mean '*so*'?"

"I'm not fussy." Rising, she moved closer and toyed with the lapel of my jacket.

"Look, I'm not interested in whatever it is you're offering," I muttered, my tone firm. It would've been easy to push her aside, but I didn't want to attract attention. There were too many gossipmongers among the guests waiting for the slightest tidbit and I kept my private life, exactly that. The barstool I sat on, wasn't spacious and having the leggy redhead pressing against me wasn't what I needed right now. I moved slightly to ward her off.

"C'mon on big boy, don't I turn you on?"

Her persistence was shocking and before I could sufficiently react, she slipped between my parted legs, slid her hands down my chest, and kissed me. It all happened so quickly I was caught off-guard.

"Well, well, well, I'm guessing you managed to find at least one personal associate, didn't you?" Ashrika's steely voice cut through me like a laser beam.

Shoving the redhead aside, I shot up from my seat. "Ash, I—" She swung around and walked off, her shoulders stiff. "Shit."

"Her loss." The woman touched my shoulder.

"Get lost, lady," I hissed, shrugging her hand off my shoulder and no longer caring if someone noticed. Wiping my mouth with the back of my hand, I set some money down on the bar and raced after Ashrika.

I reached the elevator just as she slipped inside. She didn't see me coming and I hit the floor to the room I'd booked for us before she could press reception. Within seconds her perfect ass filled my hands and I had her up against the wall before the doors slid shut behind us. She squirmed and I gripped the back of her head, pressing her face to mine. I took her mouth, hard and fast, sliding my tongue between her plump, pink lips. I rocked into her, my cock nudging her pussy, my free hand claiming her breast, so hard I was sure she'd feel the pinch of each fingertip on her soft skin. Her soft whimper went straight to my balls. Her mouth turned greedy but mine was hungrier and our tongues battled a slick dance of who would devour whom the fastest. Her hips jerked against mine, her hands fisting my hair, telling me she wanted to lead. Unfortunately, I was no longer prepared to wait. Tonight, she'd become mine, completely, and nothing, not some stupid bitch wanting to get handsy, not Zayne's aggression, and certainly not Ashrika's resistance was going to deter me.

When I broke the kiss, she narrowed her eyes, breathing hard. "I think you'd better take me home. I've changed my mind about staying here tonight."

I let out a low laugh. "Not fucking happening, sweetheart. Tonight, you're mine." I slipped a hand between our bodies and cupped her mound. Her breath hitched. "Remember my promise." She arched a brow and I smiled, wondering just how long that sass would last. "You won't know where you end and I begin." I watched her throat work as she opened her mouth but instead of speaking, she closed it and swallowed. At the soft ding of the door opening, I felt her tense in my arms. "You have two options. Walk, or I carry you. Either way, I'm still fucking you."

Pursing her lips, she sidestepped me and walked out. My gaze fixated on her swaying ass as I followed. When I opened the door to the suite, she entered, stopped in the middle of the room, and crossed her arms over her chest, her jaw set. I smiled. This was going to be fun.

# Ashrika

I HAD NO CLUE WHY I'D allowed Trent to coerce me into staying at the hotel tonight when he fetched me. Worse, I don't know why I revealed my deep, dark secrets to him, secrets I could've acted upon at any time way before Trent. The annoying part—I wanted him. I could've gone home and wallowed in self-pity because he'd kissed another woman. Technically, it was her taking a chance, I'd seen her make a play for him and perhaps it was my inner bitch that did it. But I stood back and watched, to see his reaction. And he'd proven me right. He was selective in the women he wanted, and I, unfortunately, wanted him, arrogance and all. Call it morbid curiosity or just pure arousal but I wanted to see if he was a man of his word. He'd sparked a thousand feelings in me that I didn't know I possessed, and I wanted just one more—the slide of his cock inside me.

Keeping my scowl, I watched out of the corner of my eye as Trent shrugged off his suit jacket and tossed it over one of the two armchairs. A second later his cufflinks clinked as they hit the top of the dresser. Rolling up the sleeves of his dress shirt, he turned to face me, then tugged at his tie.

"Strip, Ash.' He slid the tie from his neck and wrapped it around his fist, drawing my gaze to the roped veins on his forearms made prominent by his flexing knuckles. A sudden vision of my hands being tied behind my back with his tie tightened my nipples. I gulped. "Now, Ash. I want you bent over that table," he jerked his chin at a glass table near the window. There was no mistaking the dominance in his tone.

Our gazes locked, and for a few seconds, we stared at each other, waiting to see who would break first, neither of us willing to back down or show submission. "Are you ever anything less than an arrogant asshole?"

His lips parted, displaying a row of perfect white teeth. "No. I always get what I want and right now I want you naked." With two quick strides, he closed the distance between us. His baby blues brilliant with promise. "If you plan on disobeying, I'm going to rip those clothes off you and eat your sweet pussy for..." he looked at his watch, "...dessert, breakfast, lunch, and dinner. You won't beg to come, sweetheart, you'll beg me to stop. And when I do, I'll fuck you into your next sleep."

I gasped. My first reaction was to argue, but something in his expression told me I'd be wasting my time. He could've been just a tad bit gentler. Even as the thought materialized, I called bullshit. Trent Shaw might be gentle, but he was a whole lot of rough too and I liked it.

Sullen, I reached for the zipper on the side of my dress. His gaze followed my movements until I stood in just my heels and underwear.

"What part of naked didn't you understand?"

Rolling my eyes, I turned my back on him. I unclasped my bra and let it fall on top of my dress, and about to remove my panties, I felt Trent's chest press up against my back. His hands covered mine on the edge of my panties.

"Did I tell you how beautiful you are, Ash?" His voice was soft and smooth, like the brush of silk over my skin, in direct contrast to his dominance of a moment ago. He sucked an earlobe into his warm mouth, and I shivered. As he trailed his tongue along the ridge of my spine, he tugged my panties down until he was kneeling behind me. "I forget just how fucking perfect you are," he murmured against my ass before gripping my thighs and sinking his teeth into one cheek. I cried out, clenching my fingers as a shameful hunger burned through me. "I want to lick, suck and nibble every piece of this gorgeous ass. So damn beautiful. So fucking tempting."

I glanced over my shoulder at him. Our eyes met and he winked while running his tongue through the cleft between the cheeks. I wasn't sure what my expression conveyed because his next words were, "Not yet." He straightened.

"For someone who is about to fuck me, you're not very naked," I muttered.

"You only need my cock for that. Now be a good girl and get your ass over the ledge." He gestured to the balcony. "I changed my mind about the table."

I widened my eyes. "You're not serious. That's like four stories down."

His laugh irked me. "I didn't say jump, Ash."

I walked across, leaned over the polished tile ledge and looked out. Trent came up behind me. His large hand feathered up my ass to my lower back, and he pushed me forward. My breasts met the cool tile, and I gasped at the contact.

"Fuck."

Trent's growl had me lifting my head, but his hand on my back kept me down. He rolled his hips pressing his crotch against my ass before his fingers slid through my slit. I shivered. My arousal slicked my thighs and anticipation lined my belly. I felt the brush of his body as he dropped to his knees behind me before his tongue glided through my pussy. Stunned by the contact, I cried out. He gripped my hips, fingers biting into the soft flesh while he bit, nipped and licked my pussy. When he ran his tongue from my pussy to my rear entrance, I shot up onto my toes, pushing me further over the ledge.

"Don't jump yet," his muffled chuckle tickled my wet heat.

Before I could respond, his finger pressed against the puckered rosette slick with my cream and his saliva. I shuddered so hard, his grip tightened on my hips, keeping me grounded. "Beautiful," he groaned as he increased the pressure, and the tip of his finger breached the tight ring.

I jerked against his touch. Sharp tingles nipped my nipples, my groan so hoarse I almost didn't recognize the sound while another part of me chided the wrongful act. Still, my body didn't care, it responded to him, trembling like a leaf on a windy day. When he straightened and moved away, I opened my mouth to beg but his lips pressed against my shoulder.

"Don't move, or you'll go to bed starving. And if you think that won't happen, think again, sweetheart. My cock is hard but it won't break if I don't fuck you," he growled in my ear.

And just like that, I was turned from a woman who'd just questioned his invasive touch, to panting like a bitch in heat. I opened my mouth to say something cheeky, but thought better of it. Instead, I stayed still and focused my gaze on the view of the hotel grounds. Trent Shaw might be a dirty talker, but he knew exactly how to control a woman, and I wanted more, craved it.

He didn't make me wait long. I felt his presence even before I heard him and as if I wasn't already in agony, he feathered his fingers up my arms, over my shoulders, and down my spine. Pure need spiked every single nerve cell and I trembled as his mouth followed his fingers in exactly the same path. My trembling morphed into a violent shake and I gripped the ledge to keep from dropping to the floor.

Caught up in the mesmeric trance of his mouth I hadn't noticed his hand drop to my ass until cold liquid slicked over my rear entrance.

I gasped more from the shock than the cold. "What are you doing!"

"It's just lube."

"What for?" I panicked. "You said not yet—"

"Shh, sweetheart. I'm going to fuck your ass. Yes, but not today. For me to do so, I need to first prepare you to take my cock. Do you want me to stop?" He rolled his finger around the entrance, his touch slow, tantalizing.

I drew in a deep breath, and any sense of sanity abandoned as my body tingled with excitement and lust. I could hardly speak and shook my head.

"I'm going to insert a small plug and then I'm going to fuck your sweet pussy with your ass filled."

*Holy shit.* I could feel my arousal slick my thighs once more. I gasped as his finger entered my ass, he pushed in and out, getting me comfortable with the sensations, then pulled his finger free and I felt the edge of something hard and cold take its place. It felt bigger than his finger, and I tried to squeeze my ass cheeks tight.

"Relax sweetheart, breathe."

I did, exhaling the breath I'd been holding and he slid the plug further in, breaching the rim until it fit.

"Oh God," I cried out, straightening. "How big is that thing?"

His soft chuckle teased my neck. One of his hands rolled over my hips and breasts distracting me from the slight burn that quickly dissipated. His other hand slipped the plug the rest of the way inside where it anchored by the flared base.

"You ready to take my cock?"

"Do I have a choice?" I snapped.

"Let's see how feisty you still are in a minute."

I didn't bother to reply because he knew he had me exactly where he wanted. By my pussy. When his body pressed up against me, all-male hardness and hot skin, I inhaled deeply. I hadn't even noticed him removing his clothes.

"I'm going to take you without a condom." He rolled his tongue over the shape of my ear. I shivered. "Can I?" Surprised he was asking, my deliberation was non-existent and I nodded. He groaned as if he'd been hoping for my response. "Lean over." His hand on my nape, he guided me back down over the ledge.

The head of his cock glided along my entrance and I lifted onto my toes. Trent gripped my hip, keeping me grounded. His hand was at my nape, tangled with my hair while his lips nipped the sensitive skin along my shoulder. I was almost breathless with anticipation and expected him to slide into me with one quick thrust, instead, he pulled back slightly and slid in one perfect inch at a time.

"Oh, God." I moaned as I felt every ridge penetrate me, the feeling of being overwhelmed rang true. My body wound tight from the two different sensations inside me, and my legs weakened as his cock filled me to the hilt.

"Fuck, sweetheart, you're so damn tight." His grip on my hair tightened and then he was fucking me.

Thrust after thrust, he pressed me to the ledge, the cold tile heightening the tension in my body as it kissed my nipples with each nudge forward. And as if that wasn't enough pleasure, he slid a hand around my front and circled my clit.

Trent Shaw played my body like an expert guitarist, he knew exactly what notes to strum to make me hum. And by God, every inch of me was singing. From the sweet notes tingling in my breasts to the hard rock thrumming in my pussy—I wanted to dance until I couldn't walk.

"Holy shit," I cried out as my entire body began to convulse. I flew higher and faster, cresting waves of bliss I didn't think possible as his essence seeped into my body, piercing my heart and shattering my soul. As he brought me back to life, my pussy pulsed, exploding with an orgasm that had me screaming his name.

And as his release chased mine, I realized he was right, I didn't know where he began and I ended.

I wasn't sure how long we stood there, his trembling body pressed up tight against mine, his grip taut on my hips, keeping me anchored. His kisses soft and tender on my neck and my shoulders as our breathing slowed back to normal.

"You okay?" he whispered into my nape.

"Yes." Even though I answered, I wasn't sure if I was okay or if I ever would be again.

His tenderness a stark contrast to his domination of my body from a few moments ago, yet no less intense. My body hummed and quivered in tune to our raspy pants, his cock still inside me, my pussy contracting voluntarily around him. I felt dizzy and light as though drunk on desire and afraid if he let me go, I'd float away over the very ledge I gripped with sweaty palms. And the longer we stayed joined, I feared I'd want more...a whole lot more.

# Trent

I WASN'T SURE WHICH was worse. Using Ashrika to enact sexual fantasies that had lain dormant for years, or not telling her the truth. She'd call me an arrogant asshole once—well, more than once and now I felt like one. Yet, somehow I didn't care. The only thing that mattered, was that she was back where she belonged—in my arms. Some might argue that I was fucked up in the way I went about it. No matter. They could call me whatever the fuck they wanted. My wife was here, with me. Naked, sated, and mine for the taking.

Only one small problem stood in my way. Zayne. How would he react knowing I'd achieved what he thought would never happen? Seriously? Was I goading? I suddenly felt like I was Nicky's age. Zayne trusted me with his wife and I was acting like it was my first schoolboy crush.

Shaking my head, I glanced at Ashrika's sleeping form. With her head on a pillow next to mine, facing me, she rested on her stomach, one hand over my chest. I shifted onto my side and ran my fingers through her thick, long hair splayed out over her back, wondering if this was the right time to tell her the truth. Then I thought of all the other people I'd impact if I was rash. My kids. Zayne. Ashrika. Her father. Admittedly, I'd gone about this in the wrong way. I should've told her the truth before that first kiss, better still, the first day I laid eyes on her.

"Fuck," I muttered under my breath.

"It can't be that bad. I'm still here," her sleepy voice cut through my reflections with her eyes closed. "Who's got your balls in a twist?"

I grinned "You."

"Me?" Her brows creased but her lids remained shut then she laughed. "I must have some potent magic then if I'm doing it in my sleep."

"You have no idea."

Her eyes opened. Even in her drowsy state, I could see them smiling. "Want to talk about it?"

How often had I dreamed of this exact moment? Waking up next to her smiling face, her eyes brilliant with sleep. Then I would remember she wasn't coming back. And when I accepted it would always remain a memory, fate brings her back to me—only, I can't talk about it. Because the woman next to me needed new memories. It would be unfair on her to remind her of what used to be, like telling her to remember someone else's life.

"Nothing important," I whispered at length.

She arched a brow at me and before I could gauge her intent, she rolled me onto my back and straddled me. I laughed when she leaned forward and nipped my chin. Yet again, I was reminded of the familiarity between us, like the last couple of years had never happened. She moved to cover me with her body, and I slipped my arms around her waist.

"Did I tell you what a sexy man you are?" She rolled a finger over the tattoo on my arm, up my shoulder and along my chin, finally stopping to trace the shape of my lips.

"Actually, you didn't." I grinned. "Promise me nothing will change between us," it was out before I could stop myself.

She frowned and lifted her head slightly. "I can't make that promise right now."

My emotions splintered with the pain of the past, the happiness of the present and the improbability of the future. I had to let it go. For her. For me and for us. "Then, I'll take the next best thing," I teased. At her frown, I winked and slid her to my side, rolled her to face her away from me and rested her back against my chest. I caressed the dip of her waist, the arch of her hip and the curve of her ass, stopping when my fingers touched the plug. "I'm going to take your tight little virgin hole. Can I?" I sucked on her neck, biting down until she whimpered. I'd fucked her hard barely two hours ago and considered she might be sore.

"Please," she moaned her consent.

Hooking one of her legs over mine, opened her pussy to my touch. I rolled the pads of two fingers over her clit and she jerked. I slipped my index finger into her pussy while keeping my thumb on her clit. "Fuck, you're soaking, sweetheart."

"Please, Trent, I want you to fuck me. No foreplay."

I stilled my fingers, needing no further encouragement. I shifted from under her, laying her on her back and moved between her spread legs. She stared up at me, her dark hair spread out around her flushed body. Her cheeks a pink hue from expectation, her nipples rosy from my hard sucks. I watched her face as I withdrew the plug from her ass. Her eyes flared slightly as her plump lips parted on a soft moan when it slipped free.

"You okay?"

"Yes. I'll be a lot better with you inside me."

Laughing, I reached for the bottle of lube on the bedstand and worked the thick liquid in and around her rear. She moaned when my finger pressed in lightly. "You like that?"

"Oh, God yes," she moaned louder when I added more lube and pushed in deeper. "Trent, please."

I pulled out my finger, applied lube to my cock and moved over her. Supporting my body on one hand, I guided my cock to her pussy with the other and rolled it over her clit. When she arched up, I pulled back slightly and slid the head toward her ass. Slowly, I eased in, loving the way her pussy dripped in anticipation, soaking her tight hole. I reveled in the look of pure awe painting her face, the way she ran the tip of her tongue over her lips and bit down on the plump flesh.

"Fuck, you're beautiful, Ash."

Her whimpers and moans sheared through my remaining shreds of control. I wanted to take it slow, to tease her to the brink, but I couldn't wait. In one quick move, I buried myself to the hilt. I couldn't move. Couldn't breathe. I was gripped by the tightest, sexiest hole my cock ever had the pleasure to know.

Krisha had never wanted this, and I'd never pushed. Now, I was going to hell for making her do this. I grinned. Whatever the case, I'd make damn sure, we both enjoyed it. It took me several moments to gather myself and hold back the orgasm already rising in my balls. I pulled back and thrust in gently on the first couple of strokes to let her get used to me. Only, she had other ideas.

"More," she ordered, gripping my waist, her nails digging into my taut skin.

"Your wish, sweetheart..."

I picked up the pace. My strokes turned aggressive. I fucked her hard. My brain short-circuited when she slid one hand down to her pussy and rolled a finger over her clit while squeezing her breast.

"Fuck." I fought to keep my orgasm in check.

Her eyes met mine, drowsy and pleading. "Harder."

I gave her what she wanted. I pulled back and pumped into her, fucking her with long, defined strokes. She bucked up and clenched around my cock, harder and tighter. Her cries grew louder, rebounding off the walls. My balls pulled tight, demanding release, yet I held back, fucking her with quick sharp snaps of my hips.

"Oh, my God," she whispered.

I could hardly hear her over the blood pounding in my ears. Leaning down, I gripped one of her nipples between my teeth and bit down. That set her off. Her body arched up, her fingers gripping my arms, she screamed her pleasure, her ass squeezing me tighter. Still, in the throes of her orgasm, I bit down on the other nipple, prompting another spasming scream.

I couldn't take it. Blood rushed, fast and furious, to my cock and my head swam. I didn't just fall over the edge, I fucking plummeted into a chasm so deep, I ironically didn't know where she began, and I ended. My heart pounded and my breath staggered in my chest. This woman would be the death of me by mind-bending fucking.

"Christ, sweetheart, that was fucking insane." I dropped my brow to hers, breathing hard and matching her gasping pants. When the air slowly seeped back into my lungs, I latched onto her lips, kissing her slowly as I eased out of her. "You okay." Her response came in the form of a lazy moan as her gaze, drowsy and sated, roamed my face. "Come on." I scooped her up in my arms and headed for the bathroom and a long soak in the jacuzzi.

# Trent

AFTER ONE GLORIOUS night with Ashrika, I was determined to take her home. How? Didn't matter for now. What was important was how I broke the news to my kids. I couldn't just arrive home with a woman who was the identical image of their mother and not give them an explanation. And how would I break it to Ashrika? That not only was I a father, but she was their mother. I decided to handle it as diplomatically as possible by bringing in the most level-headed person I knew.

Sianna.

I'd just told her everything and although Drake had filled her in, she wasn't as impartial as I would've liked her to have been.

"So, what you're saying is that Ashrika is your wife, but doesn't know she's your wife. Now you want to bring her home to meet the kids, marry her and you all pretend she's your new wife? The kids know what their mother looks like but you want to tell them that she's not their mother for now? She just looks like their mother?" Sianna appeared as confused as I felt. I nodded. "Are you freaking insane?"

"What?"

"Jesus, Trent. That's asking for trouble and you know it. Why not just tell her the truth and be done with it?"

"Because she might not accept that I knew who she was all along."

"Well crap on a cracker," she retorted. "Obviously she'll be upset. And what happens if by some small mishap she does find out the truth or regains her memory and realizes you lied to her?" I shrugged, unsure what to say. "I'm sorry, Trent but the only way this is going to work is either you tell her the truth or you make the children lie."

"Would you help me?"

"You want me to teach your kids to lie?" Her laugh incredulous.

"Not how I'd put it but they love and trust you and chances are they might listen to you," I coaxed. She rolled her eyes, not buying it.

As if on cue, Nicky and Neha ran into the room, their excitement at seeing their favorite person noisier than Independence Day fireworks.

"Hey, sweetheart," Sianna kissed Neha after the ruckus quieted.

"How's my favorite trickster." She pulled Nicky into a bear hug, the only other person he allowed to hold him besides me. "Daddy tells me you've been up to your tricks again with the nanny." She tweaked his ear.

He grinned. "It was a small trick."

"Not, according to your father," Sianna teased, looking at me. Nicky gave her a sly look and she laughed. "Come on, you two, sit with me, I want to talk to you." She patted the couch in front of her and when they were seated, she knelt between them. "So, I have a favor to ask you." They looked at each other then back at her. She threw me a cautious smile and arched her brow. I nodded, not hiding the plea from my face. "What do you guys think of daddy bringing home a mommy for you?"

"Yes," Neha was the first to respond.

Nicky took his time chewing his lip then asked, "What if we don't like her?"

Sianna rubbed his little hand in hers. "And what if she looks like your mommy? Would you like her then?"

I had intelligent kids apparently, because they both asked in unison, "How can she look like our mommy. That's silly."

Sianna hid her annoyance with me well and smiled for their benefit. "Well, there's this beautiful woman who looks like your mommy. She had an accident and can't remember anything."

I admired her approach, I wouldn't have mentioned it that way.

"Like anything," Neha asked her eyes wide in amazement and Sianna nodded.

"Will she know who we are?" I could see the caution on Nicky's face. He was always wary when there was even the slightest chance someone could tarnish his mother's name. For a child who hadn't met his mother or been reared by her, me keeping Krisha alive for them had developed an uncanny bond.

"She doesn't remember anything, Nicky and she isn't your mommy but daddy likes her and thinks she'll make a perfect mommy for you guys. The bonus is, she looks just like your mommy."

"Will we like her?" he asked.

I took the sign from Sianna to step in. "Hey, champ." I dropped into the seat next to him. "I always promised you guys that if I ever, *ever*," I placed a huge emphasis on the word so he understood, "brought home someone, she will have to be perfect. And this beautiful woman is perfect."

He took a moment to deliberate then shrugged. Okay, that was the easy part.

"But there's something we all have to do before she comes to visit." I prayed like hell they'd go for it.

"What?" both asked.

I glanced at Sianna and she nodded. "We have to hide all of mommy's photos," I said.

Nicky shot up from his seat, his eyes round marbles of shock. "All?"

I nodded. "It's only for a little while, champ, until she gets her memory back." My heart knew there was no guarantee, I was shit scared to lose her again. "And we can't mention mommy when my friend comes to visit," I explained, my insides roiling worse than a boat caught on a stormy sea.

"We have to lie?" Neha asked.

"It's not actually a lie. It's called pretending," Sianna consoled. "It's helping a friend to remember." She tossed me a scathing glare and I pleaded with my eyes for her not to give up on me. "How cool would it be when her memory comes back, and she is so happy for your help? Or, what if she falls in love with you guys and you with her, if you mention your mommy, she might go away."

The woman was a genius. Well, she'd had two men eating out of her palm. So, she must be. I grinned and Sianna scowled at me.

"And if we like her, she will stay with us?" Nicky asked, hesitantly.

Sianna nodded "First, we have to keep the secret and hide your mommy's photos."

They appeared to buy it and although I felt like crap for using my children, it was for a good reason.

"Okay," they mumbled in unison.

"Great," Sianna jumped up. "You guys meet me in the nursery, and we can check our plants, okay?" They nodded and scooted off.

Sianna had stayed on my property for about eight months and while here she'd gotten the kids interested in gardening. Whenever she visited, she made sure to make a big deal about the plants. Just to please her, the kids took their gardening project seriously.

"You owe me," Sianna nudged my knee.

"I do. Anything, you name it."

She grinned. As queen of the Princeton family, she wanted for nothing. "Raincheck for now." I chuckled and walked out with her. "You better hope like hell your plan works, Trent."

"You and me both."

# Zayne

STANDING AT THE WINDOW, I admired the view of a thousand lights pulsing in the early morning darkness, slowly disappearing as the dawn crested over the horizon.

Ashrika arrived late last night after having spent the weekend with Trent and had no idea I was home. I lied to her, saying I was traveling just to give him some advantage and I was curious to see how that had panned out. So far, she'd only mentioned Trent's name once. The morning she couldn't recall what had happened at the club. Still, I hadn't pushed. I planned on biding my time, waiting to see if she'd open up. While I accepted that she might choose him over me, I still harbored a little hope that it could go either way. After all, her happiness was the most important thing in the grand scheme of things.

I turned as her bedroom door opened. She stepped out, caught sight of me and lavished me with one of her brilliant smiles. "Hi."

"Hi." I waited for my usual hug and she didn't disappoint. When she slipped into my embrace, I tightened my arms around her, lifted her against me and inhaled the very essence of her.

"When did you get in," she asked, stepping back.

"Last night."

"You want some coffee?"

We chatted for the next fifteen minutes. She told me about the charity ball she'd attended, the work they were doing and the people she'd met. I could hear the excitement in her voice like she'd discovered a whole new world. I guess her memory loss allowed her to see each encounter from a new perspective that we took for granted. And still, no Trent.

"You've been going out a lot. Are you finally having fun?" Since she opened her door, I expected her awkwardness around me. There was none, until now. Although she nodded, her expression fought indecision. "What's wrong, Rika?"

"Nothing." She slid off the chair at the breakfast nook we sat at and moved to the window.

"You slept with him?" I asked quietly, knowing the answer to the dreaded question. She was glowing.

She nodded before her eyes met mine. "I'm sorry," she murmured at length.

I gulped down the pain and sipped my coffee to give me the strength to go into a subject I had to tackle. Now. "Don't be. You did nothing wrong."

"How can it not be wrong?" she cried out, taking me by surprise. "I cheated on you."

"Did you?" I asked, forcing her to evaluate our relationship and the boundaries I'd unconsciously placed on it by keeping away from her.

My first fuck-up.

She seemed to contemplate my words then rolled her fingers over her beloved pendant. "We've been married a long time, Zayne and I know you feel something for me. Why have you never touched me? Showed me that I mean something to you other than just the friend you married to give a future?"

The walls I'd erected around my heart cracked a little more, threatening to split wide open, warning me to tell her exactly how I felt. But I'd seen a change in her. I could see it in her eyes, hear it in her voice. Trent was bringing out a side to her I never could, no one could. I didn't want to take that from her. She needed him. I gave her away.

My biggest fuck-up.

She loved me but not in the same way I did her. I hadn't told Trent any of that—he didn't need to know until I was certain his intentions were honorable. And so far, he was proving to be an admirable adversary—the perfect man for her, the man after my own heart. Despite those thoughts, I couldn't ignore the unshakable jealousy that stained every part of me like knots on polished pine.

I sucked in a deep breath, trying to steady my thoughts, the pulse of my heart. This relationship had only one direction. "It's not you, it's me."

"I don't understand."

"There's someone else."

Hurt flashed on her face like a dagger to my heart. "Who?" Eyes the color of storm clouds searched mine as though she could see right through the lies.

*Fuck.* My random decision was adrenalin induced. I hadn't expected to provide a name. "Natasha," I blurted, silently begging Natasha to forgive me.

"As in your Assistant?" there was an icy snip to Rika's words.

I blinked. Her reaction was unexpected, given she'd never attempted to pursue anything sexual with me. Was I wrong? Had she wanted more? Had I grown so accustomed to shielding my heart against hurt that I hadn't notice the way she felt about me? The questions bounced around my head. "I didn't mean for you to find out this way, baby."

She stared at me and I couldn't read her expression. "Is it because I never came to you? Never showed you the interest I secretly hid from you. You put up barriers that would keep a Tsunami at bay, Zayne. I could never get through even if I tried."

The irony in her statement hit me like a gut punch. How had I been so wrong about her? How had I not seen what she'd wanted? More questions. Yet, I couldn't allow myself the luxury of asking.

It was too late. Against my better judgment, Trent had played his cards well and won. Rather than show my hand, it was time to bow out. "Don't be angry," I whispered instead.

"I'm not angry." She sighed. "Why didn't you say something? About Natasha."

I glanced out the window, looking but not seeing. Dead but breathing. Fuck, it hurt. Like the prick of a thousand fucking knives, I didn't see coming. Squeezing my fucking lungs until I gasped for what little air I could quickly inhale. "Sometimes the beat of the hearts around us is so deafening, we can't hear the music of our own or the message it's sending us," I replied, hoping she'd understand it had always been her my heart wanted, craved.

Her next words told me she didn't and probably never would. "I've been keeping you from the life you deserved, then. Saddled you down when you could've had so much more with Natasha."

"You haven't." I ached to take her in my arms and show her just how much I loved her, what she meant to me since that first moment she opened her eyes in the coffee shop. Deep grays staring at me, lost, scared, and insecure. Telling a tale that had no beginning and desperately searching for an ending. I gave her as much of that as I could, only I didn't give her what she'd wanted. My heart.

I finally looked at her. "Fuck." Every anguish known to mankind twisted the knot that had become my insides at her wounded expression, more so the tears rimming her eyes. Not the tears.

"What were my shortcomings?" her words so soft, I almost missed them, cut so deep, I took a moment to exhale the crushing pain shooting through my body on its way to my heart.

She'd wanted more and I hadn't seen it or chose not to. Clenching my fingers until my nails bit into my palms, I hoped it would draw blood. Hadn't I vowed never to hurt her? What the fuck was I doing to her? I hated myself. "Christ, baby." It took five steps before I stood over her. Giving no thought to my actions, I wrapped my arms around her and brought her in tight to my body. "Rika," I sighed against the top of her hair. "Fuck, baby, you think I didn't want to be with you? God, I'd go to fucking hell for the things I thought of doing to you." I should've mentioned that night she was drunk but I held back. That was my memory to keep seeing as goodbye was now imminent.

"Then why?" she cried into my chest.

I squeezed her tighter. If it were only that simple. "Not every question has an answer."

She leaned back, confusion masking her wet cheeks. "What are you saying?"

My smile was slow to form as I wiped away her tears. "Some paths are like memories, they bring us back to where we began with the slightest direction, while others take you to a fork, leaving you with a decision. Make the wrong one and the journey may be precarious. Yet sometimes even the right choice comes with its own heartaches."

She looked at me, trying desperately to understand what I was saying, and I longed to tell her the truth, to tell her to forget about Trent and love me for the rest of her life. But I couldn't do that to her, I couldn't take away her chance at the happiness she deserved. I'd rather die than do that.

She palmed my cheek. "Sometimes you find a lifetime of love in a moment."

My heart crumbled at the words. "And sometimes a lifetime is not enough to find a moment of love." I rolled a gentle finger along her jawline. "You've found yours, baby. Go to Trent and live happily. He will love you like I never could."

Tears glazed her eyes as she stared at me. "I'll never know, will I?"

I inhaled sharply and before I could say anything, she turned and walked away, out of my arms, out the door, and out of my life. And for the second time since Trent's arrival, tears rolled down my cheeks, my heart ripping in two. She'd handed it back in pieces just like I'd predicted. I'd done everything I could for her. Now, she needed to live. It was time to move on.

My phone buzzed. Wiping the corners of my eyes, I fished the phone out of my pants pocket and opened the single text.

**Target acquired.**

*One down, three to go.* I waited for the image and coordinates to download, dropped the phone and crushed it with my foot. Inside my bedroom, I slipped the folded sheet of paper out of my jacket pocket and reached for the *'The Starry Night'* painting.

Five minutes later, I poured my third Macallan and scowled. A bit early to be drinking but I didn't care. Usually I could hold my liquor, today I needed a reprieve from my pain. I glanced around the apartment. I was accustomed to spending nights alone when Ashrika chose to sleep at her apartment above the restaurant. Initially, it'd been a safety measure for the late nights then she began spending more time there and I fucking let her. The difference tonight, she wasn't coming back.

"Fuck!" My glass flew across the room, crashing into a vase. Feeling a smidgen of comfort at the resounding shatter, I reached for the bottle. I drained its contents before it smacked into a glass table, sending chips cascading across the tiles. My laugh was maniacal, my pain even more so.

# Ashrika

"WHERE TO, RIKA?"

"Just drive, Jenson," I replied to my driver, leaned my head against the backrest, and stared out the window, my mind in a whirlpool. I hadn't anticipated leaving the apartment this early, so I had nowhere to go, yet. The passing scenery failed to elicit any interest when Jenson headed out of the city.

For so long, a small part of me thought I'd meant something more to Zayne. I assumed he'd stayed away because of his promise to not take advantage of me and all this time he'd been seeing his assistant. The long overseas trips made perfect sense now. It was their time away. Still, a part of me refused to accept it. If that was indeed the case, why keep it a secret. Why not just tell me the truth? Our relationship wasn't that of a typical married couple. And if he did tell me, it would've just made the earlier confrontation a lot easier to deal with.

Why couldn't I get rid of the feeling that Zayne was keeping something from me? If he'd had thoughts of wanting me, why not mention it? He knew my relationship status and until Trent arrived, I had no reason to reject him if he'd tried anything.

I blew out a frustrated breath and closed my eyes. Maybe a little time would help settle my frazzled brain.

"Rika?" The soft call pulled me out of my sleep I didn't want to leave. "Rika?" I opened my eyes to find Jenson looking at me, his smile gentle. "I've been driving for an hour."

"Oh, shit, I'm sorry, Jenson." I covered my yawn.

"It's okay. Where can I take you?"

"Back home, please." I needed more answers.

I still had no idea what I intended to say when Jenson drew to a halt outside my apartment building. Chewing my bottom lip, I paused outside the elevator to the penthouse suite. Zayne had given me a way out and I should be in that car on my way to Trent. "This is stupid." Inhaling, I rotated to step back inside the elevator. The abrupt sound of muffled music filtered through the large black doors and had me spinning on my heels. Curiosity got the better of me. It was only when I turned the key in the lock and pushed the door open, did my first stirrings of unease begin. Backstreet Boys *'Show me the meaning of being lonely'* blasted my ears the second I stepped inside. That song. I hesitated. Did I break Zayne's heart? He asked me to go.

Four steps in and I blinked. The sharp smell, like someone had washed the apartment in alcohol, hung in the air, attacking my nasal passages. Frowning, I took another couple of steps. The music was way too loud. Clamping my hand hands over my ears, I rounded the wall that divided the living area from the foyer.

"What the—" I stopped short, my eyes round balls of shock as I scanned the room. My breathing peaking to hard pants with each discovery.

Shattered glass littered the gleaming black tiles scattered with a knocked-over lamp and cushions from the two overturned couches. I gasped taking in the baby grand piano in the corner of the room. Now a thrashed version of its former glory with a heart-wrenching fissure down the center. My gaze shot to the bar. Five empty shelves absent of its mirrored wall and rows of alcohol more for display than actual consumption, stared back at me. I took a step forward, crushing glass under my foot. I shifted my gaze to the bottle of Macallan, the only one left standing next to Zayne's discarded shoes.

Anxiety roiled in my stomach at the same time an indescribable shiver raced through my body. I took another tentative step in between the overturned dining chairs and several occasional tables.

"What the hell happened here," I muttered under my breath. "Zayne," I called out. Realizing he couldn't hear me above the music, I crossed the room, jumping over upended furniture, to the stereo and killed the music. An eerie silence filled the apartment. I shivered, clasping a hand to my chest as panic began a slow ascent up my spine. "Z-Zayne," I stammered his name, fearing the worst. Only, I didn't know what *'the worst'* was because I had no damn idea what Zayne did for a living. It could've been any number of things that would produce these results.

I surveyed the room once more, looking for signs of...I immediately blanked out the thought. "He's safe," Even as I mumbled the words, I couldn't stop the sudden flow of tears. I bit my lip, trying to curb them but the tears were relentless. My eyes darted around the open space, willing Zayne to appear. I had to do something. Moving on tiptoes, I headed for his bedroom. I peeked in at the door before stepping inside. Except for the *'The Starry Night'* painting now lying on his bed, the room was tidy. Maybe he was in the bathroom. "Zayne," I stammered on a sniffle.

"What are you doing back here, Rika?"

I screamed at the same time as I swung around. My yell died immediately when I came face to face with Zayne...or rather a poor representation of the put-together man I knew.

He stood at the door, swaying from side to side, clutching a half-empty bottle of whiskey in one hand and a framed picture in the other. I stared, but couldn't make out the photo from where I stood. I clasped a hand over my mouth, taking in his disheveled appearance. One tail of his charcoal shirt opened three buttons down, hung out of his pants. His hair looked like he'd raked his hands through it one too many times and his beard somehow took on a deeper shade, giving him an ominous look.

Dark, broody eyes narrowed to slits as he tried to focus on me. I couldn't decipher whether he was angry at me or just hated me for whatever the reason was for the tornado that had blown through our apartment.

"You haven't answered my question, Rika." A deathly quiet, one I'd heard him use on the phone before, lined his tone. "Have you come back to taunt me, baby," he mocked, staggering toward me.

I took a step back, frowning. "Taunt you?"

He ignored my question. "Or have you come back to see the pathetic shit I've turned into." I flinched at the contempt in his voice.

"What's wrong, Zayne. What's all this?"

In response, he took a swig from the bottle then sent it flying across the room. It smashed into the wall above his bed. I jumped, my shrill scream piercing the room.

Whether it was my horrified expression, the jump, my scream, or all three together it startled Zayne and he stepped back. He threw the frame on the bed and held up his hands, palms out in apology. "I'm sorry, baby," he consoled.

My fear palpable, I shook my head. "Why?" I needed answers—and fast—or I was likely to go scurrying out the room if I could get past his large frame filling the doorway. "Why are you drinking? Why the mess?"

He lifted his shoulders in a slight shrug. "It blocks out the pain."

"What pain?" I asked. "Trent and I?" He just looked at me, eyes blank, emotionless and I wasn't sure what to read in his expression. Frustrated, I swiped at the tears blurring my vision. "You told me to leave, told me to go be with Trent. Why all of this then? If it made you angry why didn't you stop me from leaving? Why the hell didn't you just fuck me, then?" Breathing hard, my fear took a back seat.

He gritted his teeth. "I don't fuck, Angel. I steal hearts and yours is not available."

"What do you mean?" I shouted, annoyance coiling the tension between my shoulder blades.

"He loved you first."

"You're not making sense. Who loved me first? Trent?" His irritated grunt was all the answer I received. "How can he—"

"Just go, Rika before I do something I'll regret."

"Is that a threat?"

"No, Angel. I'm letting you go."

"Just like that," I goaded.

"You don't fucking understand." He glared at me.

I didn't back down. "Then make me." Still, he said nothing. "Why didn't you tell me that you had feelings for me, Zayne?" I finally asked what I should have when Trent first appeared in my life.

He raked a hand through his hair and a string of curses flew from his mouth before he pinned me with a look so volatile, I feared I'd lose myself in there. "Because I never felt the need to tell you. I took it for granted that you would see it," he muttered.

I covered my gasp, staring at the man I'd longed to hear words of affection from while he'd done the same. "It's true what they say, that when you hold something too close to you, you're blinded by what's in front of you."

"If I'd told you before, would you have agreed to date me, sleep with me?"

Strangely, I couldn't find an appropriate response. Given my relationship with Trent had moved to the next level, it would've been an easy answer. Apparently not. "Why are you asking me that, now?"

"Because I won't be at peace if I don't know." He took a step closer, his gait unsteady, yet his voice remained softer, calmer.

"And if I do tell you now, what difference would it make?" My vision blurred with fresh tears and I fought to control the tremor in my voice.

"Your life doesn't come to an end when a loved one leaves you, Rika." He sighed as though he was tired of fighting some inner demon. One I longed to meet, just to see if I could help give him the peace he deserved.

"And what if it gives you an excuse to ruin your own life? It would be an insult to your loved one, would it not?" I pushed. "I'm sure you won't ever insult me."

His laugh was low, almost mocking and I reared back. "Don't you see, baby. You and I would've never worked," he scoffed.

My brows drew together in a frown. "Why?"

He turned his back on me, cupping his nape. I wondered what irked him. "Because my life has always been fucked up." He faced me, leveling me with an accusing stare. Was he blaming me for his misfortunes? "Nothing good ever comes my way and if it does, it's short-lived," pure steel edged his words. "You're my weakness, Rika and that's wrong. I'm not allowed any weaknesses."

"What are you talking about?" I cried.

"When a man shows weakness, he's taken advantage of and that advantage can ruin him, to kill his spirit. Drop him into a pit so dark it would make the fucking devil envious." My chest tightened at the agony in his words.

Still, I was confused. "You're not making sense," I hiccupped on a sob.

He shook his head. "And I never will, not to you anyway. I can't give you the love you deserve, Rika. I can't allow it. Go. Go be with Trent. Because he's the only other man that can love you as much as me if not more." His eyes swam with sadness before he shielded them from me. "Every life has a story to tell. Don't be afraid to start all over again. You might love your new story," he repeated the words he'd told me once before.

"Why are you doing this?" I swallowed the lump thickening my throat.

He turned away, his muscles rigid against the strain of tension coating his frame.

"I always trusted you when you said no one would ever hurt me again." My voice broke but I pushed through. "It's been a lie all this time. Because the one person I trusted with my life, has caused me the most amount of pain," I flung the words at his back, not caring whether they hurt or not.

He swung around, eyes glaring holes through me. "Get the fuck out of here, Rika and don't come back," he hissed.

I should've feared him, I should've backed away from the sheer fury in that clenched jaw. But I didn't. Because some part of me didn't believe he meant it.

Cold brown eyes clashed with mine before he pointed to the door. "Go."

I thought about arguing with him, but his aloof, almost menacing expression dissuaded me. Standing my ground, I debated my next move. This was a situation to which I was unaccustomed. Another new moment, experience, suffering? It had no label right now but added to my ever-growing bank of memories. Maybe I'd known how to handle it in my past. Right now, not so much. My heart dropped to the pit of my stomach, begging to be held, to be consoled. I didn't know how to.

I turned and walked away from the only man I knew and cared for enough to make me cry. Tears I might've shared before, with whom, I had no idea and I never would, but I was certain that what I'd just felt would be forever entrenched in my heart and my soul.

And that, I feared only happened when you loved someone. If that was the case, what then, did I feel for Trent?

It was simple.

While Zayne gave me life, Trent gave me freedom. And yet with both, I'd become a woman. Not just a girl without a memory, floating from day to day in the hopes that something would change, but a truly emotional woman who now understood love, pain, and hurt that inflicted so much more than a physical wound would.

Tears streamed down my cheeks as I climbed into the car.

# Ashrika

WHEN THE CAR DREW TO a stop outside Trent's apartment, I had no idea why I decided to go straight to him. I had my own place above the restaurant. For now. Until Zayne kicked me out of there too. Everything I owned belonged to him, so it was safe to say that I had no guarantee of him leaving the restaurant in my complete care.

"Rika?" I glanced at Jenson and smiled. "Shall I just drive?" For a man of few words, he seemed to pick up on my distress.

I shook my head. "Thank you, Jenson. This is perfect."

"Should I wait or come back to fetch you when you're done?"

I debated whether to tell him not to. He was, after all, employed by Zayne. I sucked in a deep breath. "I'll call you." I stared out the window at Trent's building wondering what was in store for me in there.

A couple of minutes later, the door opened, and Trent's welcome smile was like a beacon of hope to a ship about to go under. "Hi."

Before I could stop myself, I fell against his chest and the tears I'd managed to hold back in the car, gushed like a dam that had just broken a wall. I balled his shirt in my hands and clung to him.

"What's wrong, Ash?" I could hear the alarm in his voice.

Trent slipped his arms around me and held me tight to his body. His pure maleness blanketed me and rendered me helpless. And for just a moment, it was all that I wanted or needed until the shitstorm that represented my brain had a chance to abate.

"What happened, sweetheart," he asked when my body finally settled from the jerks of unashamed wails to silent sobs. "Did Zayne say something?" he gently pushed before his grip tightened and anger chased his next words, "Did he hurt you, Ash?"

I sighed and leaned back to look at the man who'd made me step out of a shell I didn't think possible. "We argued," it was all I could manage for the moment.

"Does this have something to do with us and you sleeping with me?" He wiped my wet face with his fingers. Not sure myself, I hesitated. "Come on." He walked me to his kitchen, sat me down at the modern breakfast nook before placing a glass of freshly squeezed orange juice in front of me. "Drink," he ordered when I just stared at the orange liquid. "You want to talk about it?" he asked after I downed the drink.

I ran my finger along the rim of the glass, debating what I should or shouldn't say. Trent and I had never discussed my marriage or the impact us sleeping together would have on it. In his eyes, I was just cheating on my husband. In mine, I had no idea what the hell to think anymore.

After a lengthy silence, Trent cleared his voice before speaking. "Come home with me, Ash."

My head snapped up. "Home?"

"Yes. My home is in Brenton. I stay here when I need to work in the city." At my baffled look, he added. "It's a two-hour drive."

"Why? My place is here." I wasn't sure if I sounded wistful or not.

He came around the counter and took my hand in his. "Because I want to share everything with you. Show you my life. Tell you everything about me."

"I don't think I should," I responded without thought.

He frowned. "Why?"

"Because..." I hedged, not sure what explanation to give. Zayne sent me out of his life without much of an explanation and while I was falling for Trent, if I hadn't already, a part of me wasn't ready to say goodbye to Zayne. "I think I need to give Zayne a chance. He was there for me when—"

"When I wasn't?" Trent stared at me, his thumb drawing slow circles on the back of my hand.

"I'm sorry. We can't continue this. Zayne and I—" I broke off unsure what to say.

"You slept with him last night?" he asked. Was that regret or disbelief in his tone?

Pulling my hand out of his grasp, I walked away and stared out the window. Manhattan was awash in a light drizzle and I wished for some of its cleansing to befall me. Still, I didn't want to answer, hoping my silence would convey the message I couldn't say out loud. Because in my heart, I knew it was a lie. Keeping my gaze riveted to the floor, not wanting to see his hate, his disgust, a thick lump of despair wedged in my throat.

"Look at me, Ash." There was a rigid tightness to his words and my heart sank. One traitorous tear, followed by another, slid down my cheek, splashing to my laced fingers. I tried to swipe the drops before he could see. But he did. He crossed the room, slid a finger under my chin and lifted until my gaze met his. "I don't hate you. I can never hate you," he whispered, gently using his thumbs to wipe my tears. My shock slipped out in a soft gasp. "You're right, sweetheart. He was there for you when I wasn't. He took care of you like I never could. And I can only try to give you everything he did, if not more. But." He paused, his blue eyes searching mine, his smile tender. "Don't leave me because you can, leave me because you want to."

"What are you saying?"

"Every relationship has boundaries, Ash and I'm willing to cross any of those for you. Whatever it takes."

"What about—" I turned and walked away, swallowing my shame for lying.

Trent came up behind me, slid his arms around to my stomach, drew me tighter to him and leaned his chin on my shoulder. "I don't care. He is your husband, and he has a right to you that I never will." He turned me around and walked me backward until a wall touched my rear. Slipping his hands to my butt, he lifted me, and I wrapped my legs around his waist. "But I'll be damned if I let you walk out of my life without a fight."

I gaped at him, not sure I'd heard right. "Why?"

"Because I love you."

"What?" I croaked. Shock erupted inside me, shadowing my body with unchecked goosebumps.

His response came in the form of a kiss. A decadent melding of lips that spoke a thousand words and unleashed a flood of emotions. The kiss was slow and passionate. I clung to him, desperate for clarity, guidance, knowing that I was stuck in a vortex that had the possibility of spinning my clockwise thinking in an anticlockwise direction within seconds. Question was, would I find the balance to withstand the spiral?

"Do you believe in us?" he asked when we broke for air.

My euphoria flattened to dejection as a sense of betrayal took residence inside my belly. To whom, I had no idea. "Honestly, I don't know what to believe right now." I squirmed out of his hold. And when he set me down, I turned away to face the window again. "I lied to you just now, Trent."

"About?"

I glanced at him over my shoulder and pulled in a deep breath before facing him. "Zayne and I never slept together."

He frowned. "Last night?"

Slowly, I shook my head, embarrassment tainting my cheeks. Not from lying but my inability to make my husband sleep with me. "Ever."

Incredulity sharpened his gaze. He stared at me as though contemplating his next words. "I don't understand."

"Neither do I. Apparently he's been in love with someone else."

His jaw tightened, emotions I couldn't read fast enough, flicked across his face. "He hurt you?" he gritted through clenched teeth.

"He didn't." I sighed. "He married me in name only to give me stability, security."

Trent didn't respond immediately. He rubbed his jaw, studying me. "Yet, you desired something more, didn't you?" he said at last.

Hating his perception, I looked away, hoping to hide my disappointment. I shouldn't have said anything. Did I come across as wanton? Maybe. But I couldn't blame Zayne, nor could anyone blame me for my feelings for him. He'd been honest from the start and now I'd allowed Trent to fall in love with me. If my heart secretly yearned for Zayne, why then was I feeling like I'd just betrayed Trent instead.

"Hey." He ran a slow finger along my jawline, bringing my gaze back to his, the liquid blues I'd come to love, filled with the usual, sincere affection I'd seen so often. There was no disgust or hatred as I'd expected. "It's only natural to expect something more. You've been married to the guy for a while and you've known no other family."

I closed my eyes, inhaling on a long breath. Tears pricked the back of my lids. How was I blessed with not one, but two distinctly different yet caring men who had my heart in a twist, my mind on a rollercoaster, and my pussy clenching with lust when they were around me.

"Have you discussed this with Zayne?" Trent pulled me from my reflections.

My laugh was mirthless. "We did a lot of things that would've eventually led to sex," I recoiled at the memory of Zayne's stiff features. "In another lifetime perhaps," I mumbled.

And once again, Trent had the uncanny ability of picking up on my innermost feelings. "Did he ask you to walk away?" the question was quiet but the disbelief behind it, an indication he already knew the answer.

"He doesn't believe I can make him happy."

"Why?"

I looked at him, my laugh just short of caustic. "That there is the million-dollar question. You would think that being married to the man for a while, I would know him. Honestly, I don't." I sighed. "Would you believe I don't even know what he does for a living?"

Trent didn't look surprised, and I wondered if he knew something that I didn't. "Do you want me to speak to him?"

"No."

"Do you think he has feelings for you?"

"I would be lying if I said yes with conviction." I fidgeted with my nails, remembering the confrontation. "You should've seen him, Trent. He's one of the most put-together men I know, but today, he looked so..." I searched my brain for the right word. "Unhinged. Like whatever he was telling me was lies. I didn't want to believe him, I couldn't. Maybe I'm just reading too much into this whole thing and Zayne is only pushing me away because he is in love with this other woman he mentioned."

"Do you have feelings for him?"

I wasn't expecting that question and when our eyes met, I wasn't sure if what I read in his was distress or understanding, perhaps a bit of both. My heart somersaulted at the possibility of breaking the hearts of two men within hours of each other.

"I can't answer that, Trent, I'm sorry."

To my surprise, he laughed. "I wouldn't expect you not to, sweetheart. The man was a stranger when he found you and he gave you a second chance at life. I don't think there are many men out there who can pull that off, myself included."

Wow. "That was unexpected."

"It's the truth." He moved closer. "Falling in love isn't easy, Ash. At times it can drive us crazy and makes us do irrational things. Sometimes those that tread the path of love, never find their goals or they gain nothing, but pain. Still, love is something we can never truly understand, no matter how hard we believe we can. But how it makes us feel, will determine whether we survive it or not." He sighed. "Does that make sense?" I nodded. He cupped my face, dropping a soft kiss to my lips. "I'm not sure what I can say to make this right for you but if you're up for it, come home with me. Use it as time to decide your next step. If you feel you want to return to your life with Zayne, I'll bring you back, no questions asked. Just give me a chance to show you that I can give you the life you need."

I shifted from one foot to the other. Whichever way I looked at it, this situation would never get easier. The safest option was to walk away, from *both* of them. Zayne had already made his intention clear. Why then could I not just take Trent up on his offer? See where it led. My heart, however, was adamant that Zayne deserved a fair chance. I had to give him time. What then? If Zayne laid bare his feelings what would become of Trent? Undoubtedly, there was nothing but heartache at the end of this journey. Someone would end up getting hurt.

"Ash?" Trent touched my shoulder. "You okay?"

"Would you mind if I took a raincheck? I don't think I'm ready for anything other than solitude right now." What I didn't say was that Zayne had broken a little bit of my spirit today, and I wasn't prepared to lose anymore. "Every new emotion is a first to me, I have to learn how to handle it if I am to survive." On my own.

"When you're ready." He dropped a light kiss to my brow. "Join me for dinner?" My expression must've conveyed my feelings. Before I could answer, he smiled. "Raincheck?"

I nodded. "I won't be the company you deserve." I kissed his cheek. "I'll call you."

As I walked to the door, Trent called out, "Ash?" I turned. "I don't allow the people I love to wallow in self-pity for too long. Three days max, sweetheart."

Love and an ultimatum in the same statement, what more could I ask for from a man who'd dominated my body and by the looks of things my heart pretty soon. His phone rang and he held up a hand, signaling me to wait.

"Neha?" I picked up on the tenderness in his voice. "Yes, baby."

I was suddenly wary. Was he talking to his ex-wife? He did mention they were still friends, judging by his expression, very good friends. Even as a prick of jealousy stung my heart, I had to acknowledge one fact. If he treated his ex in that manner, how would he treat a new woman in his life?

Sighing, I let myself out the door and requested an Uber. When I walked out of the building, Jenson stood next to his car, waiting.

He opened the door as I approached him. "I did say I'd call."

"Got a call from the boss, said to make sure I become your shadow." His countenance showed he wasn't about to take no for an answer so I should quit objecting before I even began. If Zayne's phone call wasn't an indication of his feelings, then my name wasn't Ashrika Morrone.

## Trent

"STILL NOT TALKING TO me?"

I turned to find Tia at my side, her usually brazen smile now hesitant. I'd just stepped into the restaurant and she'd come down the passage from the bathrooms. "What makes you think that?"

"Oh, I don't know. The fact that you've ignored me every time you've been here after the club incident." When I said nothing, she took a step forward. "Look, I know you're angry but someday you'll understand that I do care deeply for Rika. I love her like a sister. And yes, I fucked up that night but I was just trying to get her to unwind."

"By leaving her with a pervert?" I snorted.

"That wasn't supposed to happen."

"But it did." I wasn't sure if I trusted her yet. "Where's Ash?"

"Upstairs. She hasn't been down since Monday."

I frowned. "That was three days ago."

Tia nodded. "She walked in here on Monday morning, told us she wasn't feeling well and said not to disturb her. I tried going up, but she won't open the door." She eyed me quizzically. "What happened?"

"Zayne," I muttered and exited the door, leaving her to decide whether she wanted to question him. Because I sure as fuck wanted to. I had no idea what went down that morning Ashrika arrived on my doorstep, dejected and crying but I'd promised to give her time. That time was up and I wanted answers, especially from Zayne. When I reached the rear, I tried her phone first before pounding on the door.

She answered on the fourth ring, "Hi." She sounded tired.

"Hi. Were you sleeping?"

"No. The restaurant's been hectic, just tired," she lied.

"It's day three, sweetheart and I haven't heard from you. My cock's taken offence that you just used him with no follow up," I tried to lighten the tension I could hear in her voice and I was right.

Her laugh lacked its usual spark. "I'm sorry, I should've called."

"Well, all you have to do, is open your door and I'm sure he'll give you a little happy twitch when he sees you."

"You're downstairs?"

"Yes."

There was a long pause before, "So, you know I lied just now?"

"Yes. Now open the door or I swear I'll get a locksmith or the 'jaws of life' out here, if I have to," I warned. She muttered something before cutting the call. A few seconds later, I heard the deadbolt slide before the metal door clanged open. She looked tired and melted into my arms the second I stepped toward her. "Tia says you've been holed up in this place since Monday. You ready to talk to me?" I kissed her brow when she leaned back.

"I'm in this weird situation I don't know how to handle. I just needed time, I guess." She sighed. "Do you want to come up?"

I shook my head, knowing she could do with some air. "Let's stand out there for a bit." I pointed to the rail overlooking the harbor.

She nodded and together we walked toward it. There, I leaned over the rail and studied the ripples in the water. Since she walked out of my place on Monday morning, it had taken extreme effort not to go after her. Now that she was right next to me, looking like a little lost girl, I was determined to get answers.

"Did the time alone help?" I glanced at her. She shook her head and I caught sight of the first tear as it rolled down her cheek. "Hey, there's no need for these." I wiped her cheek. "I'm here and I'm not going anywhere until you want me to. Even then, you'll have to force me out at gun point." That earned me a watery laugh. She leaned into my chest. I held her tight and I kissed the top of her head. The faint smell of her citrusy shampoo teased my senses. "I can't say I know what it feels like to have my heart broken, Ash but I have been hurt before. Pain, big or small can have disastrous effects on our emotions and it kills me that I can't help you because you won't let me."

I felt her tense before she leaned back to look at me. "I can't let you because I don't know how to help myself either." There was the slightest trace of irritation in her voice and I got the feeling it wasn't directed at me. She stepped away, drew in a deep breath and fidgeted with the peeling paint on the rail. "Zayne married me in name only, I get that. He promised he'd never take advantage of me, I get that too and there were plenty of opportunities to let me know how he felt. He never did. Then that morning the riddles that spilled from his mouth left me so confused, I wasn't sure what to think, believe, feel, and accept. It's just one big giant ball of inexplicable 'I don't know what the heck to do.' He's a closed-up type of person and I have no idea how to handle him or what he's going through." She glanced at me, chewing her bottom lip.

"What do you want from Zayne?"

She leaned an elbow on the rail and massaged her brow. "I don't know."

"Then how do you expect him to give you an answer? Unless you think he's hiding something from you."

She looked out across the water, her mind distant. "I get the feeling he is," she said at length, without looking at me.

Dragging a hand down my face, I prepared myself to ask the one question sitting at the forefront of my mind since the day Zayne gave me permission to pursue her. "Do you love him?"

She bit her thumb, keeping her gaze on the water. "Is it possible to love two men?"

I sucked in a deep breath. "Do you?" I guess that was something I could never fully prepare myself to hear. The question remained. What would I do? "If I said I can help you, would you let me?" That's not what I should be doing, right? I should be coaxing her to go home with me. I couldn't.

"How?"

"I'll speak to Zayne."

Immediately her face clouded with trepidation. "What makes you think he'll entertain the notion?"

"Because I slept with you?" I asked. She nodded. "I'm a man, I'll force him to listen." Fuck, I sounded like a fucking hell-bent lover set to take on any enemy that came between him and his lover. Wait. I was. I grinned inwardly.

"Not to make you appear inadequate, but have you seen Zayne fight?" She mistook my frown for hesitation. "I have, Trent, he's no easy pushover. Trust me. And anyway, I don't think it's a good idea."

"I'm a man who picks his battles, Ash, and trust me. This one is worth every blow." I gave her a reassuring smile. "Whether he's a pushover or not, is not the point. He needs to know."

"How are you so caring when I could just as well break your heart?"

"Then don't break it."

She closed her eyes, pulling in deep breaths, causing my heart to stop and start in tandem. Doubt suddenly poured over me. What if she chose Zayne over me? Would I be able to handle it?

*You went into this with your eyes open and your heart in a grinder.*

I reminded myself. Either way, I had to be prepared for the inevitable. She finally opened her eyes, the flecks of black piercing through her gray irises—her gaze heavy, unreadable. I held my breath.

"You asked me what I wanted from Zayne, what do you want from me, Trent?"

"Come out with me tomorrow."

"That's it?" She gaped at me. When I nodded, she sighed. "I don't think I should."

I turned her to face me and gently squeezed her shoulders. "Whether you love two men, isn't the issue here, Ash because one of them is willing to give you the world. You just need to reach out and grab it with both hands. You already took the risk. This time I'm asking you to jump without looking and I promise I'll catch you, every single time." She nodded and in this single moment, I knew my life was about to change.

# Trent

DURING THE DAY, INCOGNITO looked like any other fancy hotel on Fifth Avenue. The eye-catcher was the elaborate sign above black revolving doors that beckoned you to come take a peek. The second you stepped inside, the sophisticated atmosphere, opulent luxury created by the black and red décor, and the security guard standing at the door, changed your perception. Three hallways branched off as soon as you stepped past the black velvet rope. One to a five-star restaurant, the other to the dance floors and the last to the sexier side of the club. All this I'd learned courtesy of Tia.

"Welcome to Incognito, Mr. Shaw, will you be staying long?"

I grinned. The fact that the young blonde receptionist recognized me by name after one visit meant Zayne hadn't lied about putting me on his guest list. "Thank you, I'm here to see Zayne. Is he in?"

She smiled and nodded to an elevator marked private. "Go on up."

The second I entered the car, it automatically shot up and when it opened, I exited into a mini lobby flanked by two beefy security guards. I took a minute to gather my thoughts. When I'd left Ashrika an hour ago, I had no idea what I intended to say to the man who'd started this ball rolling, who'd given me Ashrika back until I walked through the door one security guard held open for me. Inside I stopped short when I spotted Zayne standing at a window.

Without turning, he said, "We're done. You got what you wanted, what are you doing here?" his voice as cold as the sudden rain pissing outside the window he stared through.

"What the fuck's wrong with you?" I yelled, not caring that my voice vibrated through the room.

Slowly, he turned. His eyes, frosty daggers, speared me. "I'll warn you to watch your tone. You don't know me."

"Like I fucking care." His scowl did nothing to intimidate me. I took a step forward. "My first night here, you warned me not to hurt her, that there would be limitations to what you'd allow her emotions to suffer. So, what the fuck do you call what you're doing to her? Do you fucking think I'm going to stand by and watch you kill the spirit she's just discovered enough to start living again without worrying about her past? Fuck, that. Do you even know your wife?"

I wasn't sure what I said that got his attention but he took a deep breath and shook his head. "What the fuck do you want from me? I've given you everything," his words quieter, calmer.

"Everything?" I stared at him, contemplating his words then it clicked. "You love her, don't you?

He folded his arms across his chest, leaned back against the window and studied me with eyes full of mystery that had me once again wondering about the man behind the name he'd given Ashrika.

"But you never told her, did you?"

"What's it to you?"

"Christ, Zayne. Wake the fuck up. She's hurting, don't you see that?" His silence annoyed the shit out of me. "I don't know what the fuck you did to her, but she's hardly eaten anything in three days."

That seemed to get his attention. He straightened and took a step forward. "I told her how I felt."

"You probably had a shitty way of telling her, if it's had this kind of effect on her. But trust me, there's no way in fucking hell I'd let you hurt her."

"It was never my intention to hurt her, Trent." He slipped his hands into his pants pockets and turned his back on me. I cursed and was about to leave when he began speaking again. "Time changes you. Marriage changes you. Life changes you. Sure, she stayed with me all this time, because it's possible she thought she had to. She's a stunning woman who got caught in an unforeseen situation with the two of us and she's now trying to make amends. We created this and she's trying to fix it. But not everything is meant to be fixed." He turned to face me, his face a mask of pain I hadn't thought possible for a man with his demeanor. "I'm tired of fighting this. She chose." He moved and took his seat behind the large black table. Still, he was a formidable sight against its size.

And for the first time since meeting him, I realized that Zayne Morrone wasn't just someone with money and mysterious background, but he held immense power to make and break people. Only, he hadn't expected a woman like Ashrika to weaken him to the point that he'd chosen anger over love. Whether or not I judged well, one thing was certain, he loved Ashrika deeply.

I dragged in a long inhale, readying my mind for the inevitable. "You're wrong, she didn't choose. You gave her an out, forced her hand. I mean you didn't even sleep with her. She thinks she wasn't good enough—"

"You know about that," he cut me off.

I nodded, taking a step forward. "If you are her something special and that was meant to be, I won't come between you two, Zayne. Maybe a fresh start." He looked up, surprised. I continued, "we never have to tell her how this all started. I'll walk away. Before that, I'll give her whatever she asks for and whatever she wants to take from me. Then, I'll walk away. You have my word."

"You'll give up your wife just like that?"

"Whatever it takes, remember." I reminded him of our first conversation.

"You're an admirable man, Trent and someone who'll love Ashrika whether her memory returns or not, but you can't make this decision for her. As you said, she's hurting because I pushed her away, imagine what it would do to her if you also pushed her away. She has to choose." There was no aggression in his tone and his words made perfect sense.

I had no idea what he had in mind, but I intended going ahead with my plan. "Tomorrow, I'm bringing her here." At his frown, I shook my head. "No. Not to see you. I'm giving her a chance to be who she wants to be, for one night."

"I don't understand." He looked genuinely staggered.

I raked a hand through my hair then dropped into a chair. "Have you ever taken the time to talk to her? Do you know anything about the woman you've been married to for the last three years? Her likes, dislikes, her favorites, her cravings. Her desires perhaps?"

He shook his head. "Some. Circumstances—"

"Fuck circumstances. You took the woman under your wing and chose to give her a life. The least you could've done was gotten to know her, make her feel more of a person than an empty vessel floating around until her memory came back." I snorted. "She describes herself as incognito, living a day-to-day existence under pretense, to make others happy. Why is that, if you gave her a life and everything she needed?"

"Quit the twenty fucking questions and tell me what you're planning," he barked but wasn't quick enough to hide his shock.

I stood. "Everything is not always black and white, Zayne. Sometimes you need to dig a little deeper to understand a woman. I don't know if you told her about this place or not, if you do happen to see her here tomorrow, you need to decide what you're giving her. I know I already do." I walked out, leaving him with a deeper frown than the one I'd walked in on.

# Ashrika

CLIMBING OUT OF THE car, I surveyed the tall, glass building, my eyes falling to the subtle nuance of glowing gold that made up the name. "Incognito," I whispered. It didn't strike me as your typical nightclub, not with those tinted revolving doors, red carpet and black-suited security that manned the entrance. No. It looked like some high-end restaurant, hotel, or even a private casino for a specific brand of people. I turned as Trent rounded the car. "What is this place?"

He merely smiled and looped my arm through his. When we pushed through the main doors, cool air drenched my skin and my senses perked up at the blend of lime, mint and something sweet, almost like Indian incense I'd smelled at a spice shop. The combination had an almost drugging effect.

"Good evening, Mr. Shaw, we've reserved the VIP suite for you," a young blonde with a friendly smile, greeted him.

"VIP suite?" I looked at him as he led me down a semi-dark hallway filled with sultry tones of soft music. "You've been here before?"

Trent poured heaps of himself into a sexy smile. "Not in today's capacity."

I frowned when he didn't elaborate but had no time to question him. We reached the end of the hallway. Another young woman greeted us and pointed to an elevator. A tight black dress I would've probably called slutty on me gave her a very sexy but classy look. I glimpsed a club setting behind her before Trent directed me toward the elevator.

"Still not telling me what we're doing here?" I asked as he hit the only button on the chrome wall. "Is this some fancy dine-in-the-dark restaurant?" I persisted when he still didn't answer. "Are we having dinner?"

"Are you hungry, Ash?"

"No," I snapped, suddenly irritated that he wouldn't give me answers. However, when the elevator doors opened, I gawked, my gaze darting all over the place. "Whose...what is..." I trailed off, taking in the dark space.

On my left stood a very large bed draped in dark bedding. With the top half set in an alcove, and a wider base so low, it was like it had none. Opposite to that and the only other piece of major furniture, a long black leather couch faced the bed flanked by two small tables. One held two glasses and a bottle of something in a bucket of ice, while a tray of fruit and chocolate sat on the other. Blank walls adorned the room completed by a dark charcoal carpet. The only light came from a ceiling that looked like a clear sky at night.

"Where are we? I finally asked. "Better yet, what are we doing here?"

Trent walked me into the room, poured us what I now noticed as chilled wine and handed me a glass. "You once told me that you called yourself incognito. And I figured with what you're going through right now, what better place to bring you than to Incognito."

He picked up a small remote and pressed a button. Portions of the two walls opened. I gasped, taking in the view on the other side of the glass partitions. I stared fascinated as two rooms with distinct color and lighting, came into view. One red and the other blue. But it was the couples in the room that drew my attention.

The blue room hosted two women and a man. One woman was spread-eagled and shackled to a table. The other woman feasted on the woman's pussy while the man, with his hands tight around her neck, face-fucked her. I groaned. My pussy was beginning to feel the effects.

The red room hosted a couple performing a reverse cowgirl while three other men watched, stroking their cocks.

Trent walked up behind me and slipped his hands around my waist, his fingers drawing slow circles over my stomach. "I'm giving you the freedom to be yourself, to fulfill your deepest, darkest fantasies. No questions, no judgments, no boundaries and only one decision."

"Which is?"

"To be whoever you want to be." He dropped soft kisses to my nape and from one shoulder to the other. "You don't need yesterday to make today, sweetheart, because you have tomorrow to make yours forever."

"And what if my memories don't return." His growing hardness against my ass hitched my breath and my legs trembled.

"I'm hoping it doesn't."

The slightest tension touched my body. "Why?"

Trent massaged my arms, wooing my anxiety with decadent nips to my neck. "Then we can create a whole lot of new ones together," he whispered, releasing the zipper at the back of my dress. It slipped down my body and pooled at my feet, leaving me in lace underwear.

For just a moment all the air was sucked out of my lungs as I wondered what I'd done to deserve a man like him. Crude. Arrogant. Sexy. Poetic. I angled my head to meet his lips, pressing my back tighter to his chest, allowing his kiss to consume me, to stoke the fire building low in my belly. His hands snuck around my waist and climbed to my breasts. He alternated between rolling and pinching the nipples between his thumb and forefinger. Pain and pleasure blended in perfect harmony, shooting pinpricks of need through my body.

"Touch me, please," I demanded when he broke the kiss.

He turned my head to look at the couples. "Do they turn you on?"

"Yes."

"Do you want them to watch me fuck you?" He slid his hands over my shoulder, one caressing down my arm while the other curled around my throat and tightened.

"Can they see me?"

"If you want them to."

"Later," I whispered, hypnotized by the thought of all those men watching me. "Now, I just want us to watch." His hand on my neck squeezed tighter while the other rolled over my stomach and slid into my panties. I groaned, keeping my gaze on the couple in the red room. The men watching, picked her up and while two held her in their arms face down. Another man fucked her ass, while the fourth man fucked her mouth.

Trent turned slightly so that his back leaned against the wall and we faced the elevator. I closed my eyes, relishing the caress of his fingers. Slipping a hand behind me, I massaged his hard arousal, delighting in the way it twitched against my touch every time I squeezed. I groaned, my hips bucking as he pressed down on my clit.

"Open your eyes, sweetheart," he coaxed a minute or so later.

I did, blinking until my vision focused. I gasped. With his hands in the pockets of his dark pants, one shoulder pressed into the elevator outer frame and one ankle crossed over the other, Zayne watched us. His gaze skimmed my body before coming to rest on my face again. Our eyes clashed. The intense look there, one I'd only seen once, the night of Nina's bachelorette—the night I was desperate for him to say, *'don't go, stay and let me fuck you, Rika.'*

It never happened. Now, as his gaze tracked Trent's hands moving over my body, my glass of wine churned in my stomach, instead of surprise though, I wondered if he was ready to give me a little more of himself.

I made no move to acknowledge his presence or go to him. I merely stared, silently willing him to come to me. Trent pressed down on my clit and with my eyes still latched to Zayne's I jerked against Trent's fingers, moaning as the need that began as a slow burn threatened to flame out of control. Sensing my need, Trent bit down on my neck. Another second and I was coming, crying out as my body shook, my gaze still connected with Zayne's. My orgasm was so intense, I could feel it coat my thighs.

"Go to him," Trent whispered in my ear.

Those simple words should've elicited everything from trepidation to *what the hell, to is this for real.* Instead, it tapped a profound beat of desire from my nipples to my pussy. I needed no further encouragement. My legs unsteady, I slowly crossed the room to Zayne, his expression like the veneration I needed to keep upright. When I stood an inch from him, we stared at each other. Sexual tension reverberated between our bodies, so tangible, I was conscious of my shallow breathing, booming heart and an unbridled ache in my pussy. Considering I'd just climaxed, I was surprised. He was just as affected. I could see his pulse jump just below his jaw. I felt his heavy, minty breath on my face, hard and fast. I knew if I touched him, I'd feel his arousal. Tentative, I reached out a hand, but he beat me to the draw and cupped my face.

"What the fuck do you want from me?" His breathing labored as if this was taking a lot out of him.

Instinctively, my body clammed up with panic, sparring between nerves and need. Swallowing down the anxiety, I whispered, "Touch me."

His groan was so soft, I almost missed it. "I want whatever this is more than my next breath, angel, but you need to be sure."

*I'm sure.* I wanted to scream staring into those pleading amber eyes. Without a smidgen of reservation, without a thought of the consequences, I nodded. "I want you."

A growl escaped his barely parted lips, his hands tangled in my hair at my nape. "Fuck, baby, I've wanted this for so fucking long, so many nights dreaming of what it would feel like to hold you in my arms." His warm breath teased my lips, making me dizzy with want. Every nerve pulsed, alive with need for him.

"I want to belong to you even if it's just for tonight."

"No, angel." He glanced over my shoulder, his nod to Trent so slight, it was almost non-existent. Whatever silent message passed between them, one thing was certain, they agreed. "You belong to us tonight."

I should've panicked. One alpha was a handful. Two? I didn't want to know. Because while one possessed me and the other infatuated me, all that resounded in my head was, 'you belong to us.'

Zayne placed the tip of his finger on my shoulder, his touch spiraling an already raging inferno through me, and slowly he dragged his finger up the column of my neck until it rested at the pulse point under my jaw. I moaned low in my throat. He replaced his finger with his lips and trailed it all the way back to my shoulder. His breath fanned across my neck as he placed a kiss there and another at the edge of my jaw. I shivered.

The room was silent and dark, and even though unchartered waters surged over us with every passing second, this moment that these two men had chosen to give me, was worth more than a thousand lost memories. Because Zayne was giving me something priceless. Himself. And Trent, he was giving me something precious. Himself. And I feared I'd need both. Always.

Zayne took my mouth, kissing me deeply. I moaned low in my throat. Having desired his kiss for so long, I wasn't prepared for the sweet seduction of his tongue. How it glided and danced with mine. His hands slid down to palm my breasts, a gentle massage while the roughened pads of his thumbs skimmed and flicked over the taut buds. And just when I thought it couldn't get any better, Trent came up behind me and with his hands on my hips pressed his body close. He'd removed his shirt. I felt his heated abs against my back and his hard cock pressing into my ass. A small whimper fell from my lips.

Zayne dipped his head, and tongued a nipple through my bra, the white lace heightening the friction and greedy arousal rushed through my blood. My pussy muscles clenched in anticipation. Lifting an arm, I snaked it around Trent's neck, craning mine so that I could capture his mouth. My tongue chased his but he only gave me what he wanted—slow, drugging seduction while I slipped my other hand into Zayne's silky soft hair, pressing him tighter to my breast. In return, he unclasped the front clip on my bra and sucked a nipple into his mouth while squeezing the other. Molten heat gushed through me, slicking my pussy and tightening my stomach.

I ripped my mouth from Trent's. "Oh, God, Zayne," I groaned when he bit down harder on the nipple blurring the lines between pain and pleasure.

Trent trailed his tongue down my spine leaving a burning path in its wake as he sank to his knees behind me. His fingers on the edge of my panties, he dragged the white lace down my legs and helped me out of them. I tried to focus, only Zayne's tongue wreaked havoc on my nipple while he pinched and rolled the other. When Trent ran a finger from my pussy to my rear entrance, I shuddered so hard, Zayne grabbed my hips to keep me still.

Trent's soft chuckle teased a cheek before his hands caressed the round orbs firmly and moved down my thighs to lightly skim the backs of my knees. I shivered. He planted open-mouthed kisses down the insides of my thighs, closer and closer to my dripping pussy, and sucked on the tender skin near the apex.

"Trent, please," I whispered, my voice breathless, needy, and I barely recognized myself.

"Do you want this, sweetheart?" He spread my pussy lips and blew warm air across the wet folds.

"Yes." I pushed my bottom back, shamelessly begging for more. He didn't disappoint.

The bold sweep of his tongue over my folds had me gasping. *Oh, fuck.* With Trent's tongue in my pussy and Zayne's mouth switching between my nipples, piquant sensations I never thought possible ripped through me as they both alternated with sucking, licking and nipping my tender flesh. I tried hard to concentrate, to differentiate between the two distinct rhythms. One hard and painful, the other soft and gentle, yet combined they were mind-blowing. I cried out, fisting my hands in Zayne's hair. My legs shook and almost failed me. If it weren't for his hands on my hips, I would've fallen.

"Oh, God, yes," I whimpered with each deliberte movement, fast losing myself in their seduction. My orgasm built, hard and fast, chasing their beats and ready to explode.

Trent laved my clit one last time and eased two fingers into my pussy as he stood. "You're dripping, Ash. So fucking wet." He began pumping his fingers in and out in a slow cadence to Zayne's tongue on my nipple.

"You guys do this to me," I groaned.

"Do we, angel?" Zayne moved his mouth to capture my lips, swallowing my answer while one of his hands glided down my belly and two calloused pads rubbed my clit.

My breathing sped up and I yanked my mouth from his, trying to keep upright, trying to breathe, forgetting to think. His pace, the pressure, in perfect harmony with Trent's pumping fingers. Two hardcore men, both strumming parts of my body that made me wanton. The friction weakened me, destroying everything but the ability to ache with greed. I could do nothing but hang on, exulting in the fiery sensations charging through my body.

Trent's free hand curved around my jaw and angled my head so he could kiss me. I tasted myself on his lips and tongue. My pulse echoed in my ears, a staccato beat that begged direction. I couldn't give it what it wanted because I was too caught up in these two men who owned my body and possessed my hammering heart.

Zayne nipped one shoulder while Trent broke the kiss and sucked the other. There was nothing more beautiful than having these two gorgeous men's bodies pressed up close to mine, surrounding me, filling my senses with their distinct scents yet both just as powerful in their offering.

"Come for us, Ash," Trent whispered.

My body bowed to his command. It took barely a few seconds before an orgasm, so intense, so bold and so fiery, tore through me, scorching every inch of my heated skin. My body vibrated, my pussy muscles clamping onto Trent's fingers, my own fingers gripping Zayne's hair as he bit first one then the other nipple. "Oh, God," I gasped for air as every nerve ending ignited and in dire contrast, goosebumps teased my skin. Yet the storm raged inside me. Hot. Potent. Delirious.

"That's it, angel," Zayne coaxed, pressing down on my swollen clit.

Then he was kissing me, a hot melding of lips I couldn't grasp while Trent's fingers continued to pump in and out of my pussy, drawing out my orgasm to the max. And if I thought my climax was satisfying, I was surprised my body was still on a high and each of these men's touches seemed to be awakening another tempest rather than calming me down. My body trembled. My heart pounded. My pussy throbbed. Heat danced over my skin as my body begged a different kind of satiation.

When Zayne broke the kiss, I leaned back into Trent's body as he withdrew his fingers. "Open your mouth, sweetheart." I did. He slid his wet fingers into my mouth. "Suck," he ordered. My eyes on Zayne, I ran my tongue in between Trent's fingers, tasting my arousal until he pulled out his fingers.

Zayne leaned forward and licked my lips. "Beautiful."

"I want to be fucked now," I demanded.

Zayne sucked in a sharp breath when I wrapped my fingers firmly around his erection. He was long and thick in my hand, and I wondered how he'd react if I dropped to my knees to take him in my mouth. I squeezed him harder, and he groaned.

"Should we give her what she wants, Trent," Zayne asked, keeping his gaze fixed on mine.

"Are you ready to take us both, Ash," Trent nipped my shoulder, rubbing his hard cock along the cleft of my ass.

Lust crashed in my belly. I turned in his arms, pulled his face down to mine and kissed him, sucking and biting on his tongue and lips until I couldn't breathe. "Is that a good enough answer?"

He chuckled. "She's ready."

When I turned to face him, Zayne was undoing the last button on his shirt. I watched as he parted the dark material, revealing the toned body and defined abs I'd wanted to touch so often. This time I did, and he let me. I skimmed my fingers across the hard lines and smooth skin. When I leaned down and sucked on his nipples, first one then the other, his breathing sped up and his skin pebbled beneath my mouth. I smiled at my power over him. I tugged at the button on his pants, and he stopped my hand.

"Please."

Instead of giving me what I wanted, he moved away and reclined on the bed. "I want your cunt on my face, angel."

With his words, another flush swept through me. My heart pounded but my pussy clenched, anticipation shortening my breaths. I glanced at Trent.

"Give him what he wants, sweetheart."

If Zayne's voice was the command of sin, then Trent's was the penance itself.

I climbed onto the bed, straddling him, and inched my way up to his face, my movements awkward. I'd never sat on someone's face before but considering I'd never fucked two men either, there was a first time for everything. Zayne cupped my ass cheeks with both hands and I tensed just a little, but any hesitation other than my hitched breath was wiped from my mind when he tongued my clit. I shuddered, gripping the top of the upholstered headboard for balance. He ate me out like a man possessed, his tongue spearing my soaked channel, biting down on my clit before sucking it between his thick lips.

"You taste so fucking good, baby," he muttered against my pussy.

My body tightened, the unwinding coil in my lower belly springing to life once more as a shocking burst of sensation tingled through every sensitive point in my body. I squirmed trying to escape the onslaught his teeth inflicted. He was having none of that. Digging his fingers into my cheeks, his firm grip kept me in place.

As if summoned by my desire, nothing prepared me for the stomach-quivering pleasure that ratcheted through me when Trent's hands slid around me to cup my breasts. "Don't come, sweetheart, not yet," his husky whisper caressed my ear. With his knees anchored into the mattress, he straddled Zayne behind me. I released my hold on the headboard and leaned my back into Trent's chest. He bit the sensitive skin at my neck then soothed it with his flattened tongue. I shuddered.

Zayne slid his mouth lower, his tongue pushing into my pussy. Where Trent's mouth earlier had been soft and gentle, this time, Zayne's was abrasive, more demanding. He nipped my clit, his teeth pulling on the folds before he used his tongue to suction the swollen bundle. As if he sensed my need, Trent pinched my nipples between his thumb and forefinger. Pain and pleasure blended, sparking flames of need I wanted sated. I cried out, "Oh fuck, yes. I need to come."

"Not yet," Zayne echoed Trent's words against my pussy.

I moaned. *God help me.*

Moving one hand to my jaw, Trent angled my head up to his, teasing my lips with soft licks while his fingers unleashed torture on my breast. That tightness between my legs, the one I felt with Zayne's predatory stares and Trent's touches, started to pulsate, spreading rapidly through my limbs like a resonant beat. "Oh, God." My words were swallowed by Trent's hungry mouth eating away at mine. His hand dropped away from my jaw and feathered over my skin from my neck all the way to my asshole. He turned away for barely a second before he returned and rolled a finger cool with lube over the puckered rosette. "Please...I can't," I panted, my second orgasm already spiraling its way down my spine.

"Only if you come harder than you just did." Trent nipped my earlobe.

I had no idea whether I responded or not because every nerve ending kicked into gear as he began to push his finger in. "Oh, fuck," I could hardly speak, barely breathe as my skin ignited, my body floated. Drowning in pleasure my toes curled. I couldn't recognize the words falling from my mouth. And just when I couldn't hold on, Trent thrust his finger deeper at the same time as Zayne's teeth scraped my clit.

"Come, Ash," Trent ordered.

"Oh, God," I wasn't sure if I screamed because my body convulsed, ripping my second climax from me leaving me a shaking mass. Trent's finger worked my ass faster while under me, Zayne groaned, lapping me up, with quick sharp strokes, squeezing my hips to keep me still.

I was still shaking when Trent lifted me off Zayne and laid me on the bed. And just when I thought I couldn't be pleasured anymore, Trent leaned over me and kissed me. His lips were slow, flirty, and wicked in the way his tongue danced with mine before nipping his way down to capture a nipple in his mouth. As if taking his cue from him, Zayne slipped down to the other side of me and latched onto the other nipple. Both men squeezed my breasts while their tongues teased and nibbled the hard buds. Having just come twice, I didn't think it possible to get wetter than I already was, yet the sight of these two hot men lapping at my breasts like it was the best damn meal on the menu, had my juices dripping down my thighs and my fingers biting into their scalps. When I cried out, they pulled back, their lips wet, pink and kissable.

"What's wrong, sweetheart?" Trent asked.

"Please," I didn't care that I begged, I was so ready to have their cocks fill me.

"Not yet," Zayne said. I rolled my eyes and they both chuckled. "You want us to fuck you, angel?" I nodded. "We will." He rolled a slow finger through my drenched slit then licked his finger. I shivered. He dipped it in my slit again. "As soon as you use this pretty little mouth to suck our cocks." This time he pushed his finger into my mouth. "Suck it, Rika, show us what that clever tongue can do." Drawing his finger all the way into my mouth, I curled my tongue around the digit and sucking hard. I flicked a gaze between them as they watched me, their faces glowing with arousal. Zayne groaned and withdrew his finger.

Licking my lips, I watched them straighten and remove their pants. I had no idea if they'd discussed tonight but the way they matched each other's movements, was like watching a well-coordinated opera and sexy as hell.

They stood at the edge of the bed, their expressions expectant. I rolled up onto my knees and moved closer, positioning myself between both. I ran my gaze over the length of their bodies, admiring taut muscles, slabbed chests, and defined abs. A girl could get used to this sight, daily. I hadn't seen Zayne completely naked before and I took a moment to appreciate his heavily veined cock. I looked up and he quirked a brow. I ran the tip of my tongue over my lips telling him I liked what I saw and in response, just the tiniest of smiles teased his mouth. I reached for Trent.

He backed away, sat down on the leather couch and spread his legs. His eyes on me, he stroked himself. "You want me to fuck you, Ash," he demanded.

Immediate need flushed my skin, the burn potent. "Yes."

"I will, sweetheart. First, I want to watch you suck his cock. You want that, don't you?" The man had it in him to make me beg and he knew it. My gaze dropped to his long fingers as he squeezed and pulled on his shaft.

Need pulsed, hot and heavy, in my belly. I nodded and looked up at Zayne. He took hold of my nape in a light grip, fisted his shaft with his other hand, and guided my head toward his cock. Only when I closed my mouth around it did I feel the slightest intimidation. They were both big men who'd be filling and stretching me in a matter of minutes. A hundred erotic images filled my head, each one filthier than the last, and I had the sudden urge to touch myself. When I dragged my tongue across the swollen head of Zayne's cock, he groaned low in his throat. Trent echoed the feeling.

I laved Zayne's dick once more with the flat of my tongue and he hissed in a breath. Watching his thighs draw taught, I swirled my tongue around the ridge, then dragged my tongue from tip to hilt. His low growl resonated through my heated sex, more so the salty taste of him leaking across my tongue. I groaned and it excited him.

"Fuck, angel." He fisted his hands in my hair and began pumping into my mouth in quick, short snaps of his hips. Breathing through my nose, I bore down on him, swallowing quickly when he hit the back of my throat. I almost gagged when my nose pressed into his groin, and a primal growl ripped from his lips. "That's it," His voice was so deep and husky, it vibrated through my body, teasing me until I shook. "Touch your pussy," he ordered. I complied, rolling two fingers over my clit, I moaned around his cock. Zayne was breathing hard now. I glanced up. Nostrils flared, brow creased, he was beautiful. A thrill surged through me, knowing I did that to him "Push those fingers into your sweet cunt for me, Rika. Feel how tight you are."

I could hear myself, the wet suck of my fingers plunging inside my aching pussy, but it only propelled my pleasure higher. I whimpered and closed my eyes against the carnal pressure in my groin.

"Open your eyes, Ash," the sharp snap of Trent's words sliced across my flesh like the lash of a whip. Opening them I glanced at him. He was staring at us through eyes that burned a fiery blue. His eyelids lowered, his next words were filled with longing, so potent it shot straight to my pussy but there was no mistaking the command. "Look at him. Add another finger." I did as he asked, realizing I was now facing the two alphas I'd come to know. They wanted me at their mercy and I willingly obliged. God, I was desperate to come. As if he was privy to my thoughts, Trent growled, "don't come, Ash."

My gaze snapped to his trying to convey my irritation. He merely cocked a brow as if to say, you wanted this, now deal with it. His sly smile confirmed my suspicion.

"Suck me harder." Zayne drew my attention. His grip on my hair tightened almost painfully, and as if sensing how close I was, he said, "stop touching yourself, angel."

Moaning, I pulled my hand away, aware of the flow of juices down my thighs. Deciding I wanted in on their pleasure, I doubled my efforts to suck Zayne off. Locking my tongue and palate around his cock, I hollowed my cheeks, taking him all the way to the back of my throat and swallowed his demanding strokes, letting him control the speed to ride me, hard and fast. And it worked.

"Fuck, Rika, that's fucking hot," he growled. "Jesus, Trent, I'm not going to last."

I wasn't sure if that was his signal to Trent to come as well but I glanced his way. Trent was breathing harder now, his grip so tight on his cock, his knuckles looked pale. The beginnings of a climax fluttered inside me. I whimpered, desperate to come. I clawed my thighs to stay the need and focused. Zayne swelled in my mouth. He grew harder. I could feel the tension radiate through his tight grip on my scalp. He was close. Three more hard thrusts and he pulsed on my tongue.

"Oh, fuck," he cried out, his hips jerking. His hot cum, filled my mouth, thick and salty. I barely had time to swallow before Trent's roar punched the air. I glanced his way as thick spurts of cum painted his abs. Zayne pulled out of my mouth and leaned down to kiss me. "You're fucking amazing, angel."

Trent arrived at his side. "Clean me up, sweetheart." He pointed to his stomach lined with milky drops of cum. Gripping his hips, I ran my tongue along his heated skin, making sure I got every drop. After, he also kissed me. "Zayne's right, you are fucking amazing."

Although their words were sweet, frustration shadowed my joy and having two pairs of sexy as fuck alphas devouring me with their eyes wasn't helping the pressing need between my thighs. I glared at them hoping they'd get the picture.

"Judging by that look, I'd say she isn't happy," Trent said to Zayne, a twitch of smile told me he was only too aware of what he was doing.

"If you two are done with your psychoanalyses then either fuck me or let me go," I snapped, every inch of me on fire and desperate for their attention.

"Feisty, aren't you?" It was Zayne's turn to smirk. I glowered as he climbed onto the bed, stroking his cock.

My need suddenly pulsed as I noticed Trent doing the same thing. Blood rushed through my veins as my mouth watered.

"Come here, baby." Zayne reclined on the bed. I neared him. "Straddle me." I did as he asked, and he pulled me to him. "Trent is going to come in that sweet ass of yours, while I come in your hot little pussy." I quaked. Lust burning a ravenous fire through my body. "Do you want that, angel?"

"Yes." I moaned.

His fingers drifted into my hair tightening as his tongue traced the seam of my mouth. I opened for him, inviting him with hungry licks and soft moans. He slipped two fingers into my pussy. "You are so fucking wet." He was right. I was soaked, and so damn needy. I wanted so much more of the two of them. Angling my head, his mouth teased and wooed me into parting mine, his tongue sinking deeper and swirling faster. Sweeping with expert strokes, he controlled the pace while his fingers created their own magic. A growl resonated from his lips and I devoured it, biting down hard on his lips and unable to catch my breath. And just like that another flood of arousal bathed my pussy. "Fuck, you're so damn sweet." He pulled back, licking his lips.

I didn't notice Trent climb up behind me until Zayne released me and eased me down his body into Trent's grasp yet he kept his fingers inside me, in slow deliberate strokes, as if preparing me.

Trent pulled me back toward him and the tip of his well-lubricated cock rolled over my rear entrance. I gasped.

"Ready to take us, sweetheart?" Trent nipped my shoulder.

An avalanche of hunger crashed through me, I could only nod. My skin turned molten as rapid heat spread through every nerve cell. Trent cupped both my breasts as he slid pass the seam of my asshole, slowly inching his way inside, yet his thick fullness pulsed, demanding I give him what he wanted—hard and fast.

Moaning at the feel of him stretching me, I pushed down and he stilled my movement. "Trent," I closed my eyes, breathing out his name on a long exhale.

"I'm right here," he hissed before jerking his body forward, snapping my eyes open. He was seated fully inside me, the length of his erection buried deep, his balls tickling my pussy. "Fuck," he growled.

The feeling of him tunneling through the forbidden passage had me purring in contentment, begging for satiation. But he didn't move even when I wiggled my ass. I figured he was just savoring the moment. He dropped soft kisses to my shoulder blades before rocking his hips slowly. Groaning, I surrendered to the guidance of his body, losing myself in the delicious sensations it started.

I stared down at Zayne, who watched me as though mesmerized by the strain on my face. "You're fucking beautiful to watch, baby." His warm words seeped through me. He pulled his fingers from my pussy, sucked my juices making my mouth water. He smirked knowingly and lifted a finger to my mouth. I swallowed the digit whole, tasting myself. Groaning, Zayne removed his finger and ran his hands over my breasts, down my curves and rested them on my hips. Positioning himself at the entrance of my soaked pussy, he rolled the head of his cock through the slit and I bucked.

"Holy fuck," Trent's groan mixed with Zayne's grunt and my whimper.

Zayne gripped my hips tightly, ensuring I didn't move again, then flexed his pelvis and inched in a little. The penetration stole the breath from my lungs. I shuddered when he thrust inside.

"Jesus, you're fucking tight." He pushed his way in quickly, past the resistance made tight by Trent's cock at my rear, the unexpected jolt of arousal wrenched a sharp cry from my throat.

"Oh, my God." They were killing me, and I loved it. The burn of their cocks stretching and filling me, shoved my senses into a combustible overload, and powered me back to a mind-blowing thrill that stole my breath. Gripping Zayne's shoulders kept me grounded and entrenched in the reality of what was happening to my body—the ecstasy of being wanted and taken by these beautiful men.

And then they began to move. Anyone looking in would assume that we'd done this before, that these men knew each other. With every second that passed, I discovered they were more in tune than I'd first noticed. They knew exactly how to touch me, exactly what would make me moan and flood my body with pleasure. They learned my body in a way I could've never dreamed of. Within minutes they found their rhythm—Trent thrust in, while Zayne withdrew and vice versa—like a beautiful ballet with all the dips, flips and highs—they moved in perfect harmony, choreographed for the ultimate ruination of my senses.

Yet with that beauty came pleasure. I'd never had every single pleasure-point in my body pulsating at the same time—a sensory overload. And just when I figured my body could sing no more, Zayne rolled the pad of his thumb over my clit.

"Oh, God, yes," I bucked hard, clamping both my pussy and my ass.

"Fuck," they both moaned.

"So fucking tight, sweetheart." Trent reached around me and cupped a breast, squeezing the plump flesh and pinching the nipple.

I cried out and he picked up his pace. Zayne gripped my hip to keep me in place while his thumb worked my clit. Another two seconds and I didn't just fly, I skyrocketed off the edge, flooding my pussy and squeezing my ass as I came.

"Fuck," Zayne moaned. "So hot. So wet and all ours." He picked up his pace, matching the cadence of Trent's beat.

My moans pitched higher, and the little bit of air I was able to regain was forced right back out of my lungs leaving me a panting mess sandwiched between two overtly sexual alphas. All I could do was buckle down and hold on. But they were having none of that.

"One more time, Ash," Trent growled. "Give us more of that sweet cream, sweetheart. Fuck her harder, Zayne. I need to feel her ass squeeze my cock again."

"Jesus, Trent, any harder and we'll break her."

I had no idea why but hearing them talk dirty shot my arousal through the roof. As if sensing my need, Trent pushed down on my back directing my breasts toward Zayne. He latched onto a nipple, rolling his tongue over the taut bud while dragging his finger around my swollen clit again. And once more as if they'd written this seduction on a play-by-play basis, Zayne bit my nipple, the same time Trent bit down on my neck. Pain ratchetted through my body, clouding the lines of pleasure but so intense, I felt my toes curl.

I exploded. My pussy spasmed and I clenched my ass. I came so hard, white spots danced behind my eyelids. My body floated. I felt myself fall like the effect of a mind-blowing drug. If it wasn't for the two of them holding me up, I would've happily sunk into oblivion.

"Oh, fuck yes." Trent groaned.

"So close, baby." Zayne pulled my head down, capturing my mouth in a delicious kiss that shot tingles all the way down to my clit. I could barely breathe but he refused to let go. I dug my nails into his shoulders to keep from catapulting into the euphoria that hung on the sides.

When he finally released me, those golden ambers roamed over my face, so sensual and tender I had no idea I'd whispered the words, "I love you, Zayne."

Until he responded too, "I love you too, Angel."

I felt Trent tense and his grip on my hips tightened. Somehow that had the desired effect and I clamped down hard on both cocks, sending them spiraling out of control. Both men cursed as they came with me, holding and caressing me in their own special way and taking a piece of me with them—a piece I willingly handed over.

For the first time in my short life, I felt completely free, unhinged, and happy. I could go on describing how I felt. Even with the bumps and bruises, I'd experienced since waking up from that coma, this moment right here, held my heart over a spindle. Whether it fell or not, I knew that whatever life threw me, it would be worth the pricks of pleasure I'd just endured.

I had no idea what would happen when the three of us walked out of Incognito, but one thing was certain, I had finally stepped out from behind that mask.

# Trent

SOFT MUSIC FILLED THE room, shrouding the aftermath of an act I never thought I'd participate in, ever. And I had. Was it good? It was fucking awesome. Would I do it again? I had no idea. But for her, I'd walk a mile, naked just to see that smile on her face again.

I glanced down. With her head on my chest, her hand on my stomach, Ashrika slept cocooned between Zayne and I. Millions of tiny lights shining down from the ceiling, sparkled over her black hair curled around her creamy skin. She appeared peacefully serene and ignorant to my palpitating heart or the butterflies that decided my stomach was a good place to visit.

Why was I nervous? Because when the night began, I'd hoped it would end the way I wanted. With Ashrika uttering the sentiment I longed to hear. She had. Only, it wasn't my name at the end of those three beautiful words, but the man who currently slept with his arm draped over her waist, his body curved to hers, keeping her just as protected as I would.

I knew the second I mentioned my plan to Zayne to bring her here, he might want in. I never expected him to go through with it, though. Nor had I let on that I intended telling her the truth tonight. Whatever the outcome I was going to grin and bear it, even if she hated me. I figured I'd secured a tiny niche in her heart and she'd forgive me. Unfortunately, that niche was so tiny, it was easily usurped by another man. Yet, I felt no anger toward him. I never would.

Taking care not to wake her, I slid out from under her and stood. In less than two minutes, I was fully dressed and reaching for my watch when Zayne climbed off the bed. The man wasn't family, neither was he a friend, and I expected some awkwardness after what we'd just done to the woman we both loved. There was none. I wasn't surprised and by the expression on his face, neither was he.

He pulled on his pants, turned to me and raked a hand through his hair. "Where the fuck are you going?" he whispered.

I glanced at Ashrika who'd rolled onto her stomach. Clipping my watch around my wrist, I looked at him. "Take her home."

He frowned. "What do you mean?"

I slipped one hand into my pants pocket and shoved the other through my hair. "I gave her what she wanted. Now it's up to you to give her what she needs."

"Isn't that the same fucking thing?" he was trying hard to keep his voice down.

I moved away from the bed and he followed me. "She needs to live, Zayne. She opened up to me, told me things about herself that you needed to know. But that's up to you how you get her to tell you everything. She loves you. So now it's up to you to make her not only believe but fully accept that Incognito was just the title of a club where she got what her body desired. That the woman in her can step out from behind that mask she's worn for so long. Am I making sense?"

I hoped like hell that I was because walking away from her tonight would be the biggest test I'd face in my lifetime. Ashrika Morrone had stolen the heart that belonged to Krisha Shaw and surprisingly, I didn't feel bad, I didn't feel remorse, nor did I feel it was wrong. She might be the same person but who she'd become now, was someone I never met then yet would love forever. Only, her forever belonged with Zayne.

I dragged air through my aching lungs. "Look, what we did tonight, might be fucked up on so many levels but when love is involved, fucked up is how you live until the right end is in sight. I don't regret it. Not when I made the decision, not during the act and not now that it's over. You wanted her to choose. She did. She chose you."

"And what? You're just going to walk away?" he scoffed, disbelief lining his tone.

"That's what we agreed to."

"We agreed to nothing," He turned away and gripped his brow then looked at me again. "Fuck, Trent, I had no fucking clue what you intended when I walked through that door tonight." He gestured to the elevator. "And like you, I don't regret it but what do I tell her when she wakes. You can't just walk out of her life without an explanation."

"I did just walk in, remember?" I shrugged. "And it's put us all through the wringer." I shook my head no less convinced than he was. "Look, make me the bad guy if you must but for fuck sakes, make her live again."

With that, I hit the open button on the elevator and when I reached the exit, my heart dropped so far down to the pit of my stomach, I wasn't sure I'd be able to drive off. I gripped the roof of my car, bent over and hurled the contents of my stomach onto the sidewalk. And with it, every emotion I could, hoping it would free my body of the bone-numbing pain I'd felt the second she uttered those words. When I could finally stand without heaving, I walked around to the driver's side and retrieved a bottled water. I rinsed my mouth, my hands and downed the rest of the warm liquid, wishing for the burn of a stiff drink instead.

I shot off down the street the second the engine roared to life, leaving behind my heart, my soul, my life.

# Zayne

"ANGEL," I CALLED OUT to Ashrika. We stood in an art gallery two weeks after our...I wasn't sure what to call what happened at Incognito. When Ashrika woke to find Trent gone, she seemed fine with it until two nights ago when I walked in on her crying in the kitchen. I tried asking her what was wrong, and she merely put it down to too much spice in the chili she'd just tasted. She'd moved into my bedroom and we made love a few times since but after the first three times, I sensed her restraint.

Thinking she needed to get away from the norm, I'd driven us to the countryside. So far, she appeared to be enjoying herself, to the point where she shared a full-on kiss with me after lunch and there was no reticence.

"Do you like it?" she sidled up to me and stared at the painting of a little girl pointing at something.

"I can't decide if I love it." I grinned, admiring the way the painter had captured the little girl's expression as if she was desperately looking for something.

"Don't buy it."

I glanced at her. "You seem sure about that."

She shrugged. "I mean if you're going to have to look at it every day or often, you should love it without any reservations."

"You feel that way about relationships too?" I asked without thinking.

"Who said anything about relationships?" She looked away but wasn't quick enough to hide her wistful smile.

"Show me your favorite painting, angel." I changed the topic, for the moment, yet in my heart I knew I had to address it at some point.

Nodding, she directed me to a painting on the opposite wall. It was one of a little girl sitting on a fence. The look on her face indicated she appeared to be contemplating on which side of the fence she needed to get down. "Fitting," I whispered not realizing Ashrika heard me.

"Why?" she asked.

Slowly, I turned to face her and linked my fingers with hers. "You miss him, don't you?"

She frowned. "Who?" even though she asked, I could tell she knew to whom I referred.

"I won't break, baby." I brushed the back of my fingers gently down her cheek. "You don't need to hide your true feelings from me."

"I'm not."

Sighing, I turned to the painting and scanned the bottom to find the name of the artist. I looked up as a woman around fifty or sixty, I couldn't be sure, walked through an inner door.

She smiled at us. "That's the last of the two paintings I have left of the artist."

Curious, I asked, "Which is the other one?"

She pointed to the other one with the little girl I was indecisive about.

Next to me, Ashrika laughed. "It's the same painter. So, you can take either one."

Smiling, I turned to the older woman. "Are you the gallery owner?"

"My daughter is, I just help out. She's off on a week's holiday with her husband. I'm Mary by the way and unfortunately, these two paintings are not for sale."

"Oh, no," Ashrika moaned.

I gave her hand a gentle squeeze. "Why are these the last two paintings?" I asked Mary.

"The artist was a young woman who supplied our gallery with beautiful countryscapes. They always included that little girl." Mary pointed to the two paintings. "Then one day, we stopped receiving her artwork. We figured she'd either moved, got married, or something worse we didn't want to think about. Pity. Her paintings were popular with tourists. They said there was an authenticity to her art as though she painted from either life experiences or she knew the little girl."

"That's so sad," Ashrika sighed.

"Was she a local artist?" I asked, noting the DC initials on the artwork.

Mary shook her head. "Honestly, I don't know. Never met her. A guy would bring the pieces once a month and collect the payment."

"Why are these paintings not for sale," Ashrika asked.

"I'm not sure." Mary glanced at the painting. "I might be wrong, but I think my daughter may have met the artist and kept these as mementos."

"Would your daughter be interested in selling one of them?" I offered her a charming smile.

Mary laughed. "Leave me your card, I can ask her to give you a call."

"Sure. I'll grab one from the car before we leave," I replied. Mary nodded and walked away.

"Do you love this painting?" I asked Ashrika.

She studied the artwork then smiled. "Reminds me of me." At my raised brow, she added, "I'm sitting on the fence at the moment."

My heart rate sped up. "With Trent and I?"

She looked at me, hesitated then sighed. "No. With my past and present. A part of me wants to know my past and the other part says, 'let it go.'" Although I nodded, I didn't believe her.

Three hours later I sat up against the headboard and watched as she walked out the bathroom. She placed a foot on the edge of the bed and applied cream to her leg.

"See something you like," she asked without looking up.

"Always." Grinning, I set aside the book I'd been trying to read for the last hour. I could no longer concentrate on anything, worrying more about her heart than mine. Exhaustion wore down my belief she'd be mine forever. I had to give in. "Come here, baby."

She closed the lid on the bottle and crawled across the bed. When she reached me, she straddled my thighs and ran her hands up my chest. I wanted nothing more than to fuck her but I needed to address the emotions she was trying to hide from me.

"I need to ask you something." I slid my hands up and down her arms, squeezing lightly.

"Sure."

"Do you love Trent?"

I felt her tense in my arms before her expression shuttered and she tried to shield her eyes from me by looking at my hands.

"Where's this coming from," she asked then squirmed to move off me.

"Don't, angel." I tightened my grip on her arms, keeping her in place. "I need you to be honest with me."

Her body sagged before her gaze met mine. "He walked away." Her bottom lip trembled before she sucked it in between her teeth.

I drew in a deep breath. "He didn't."

Glazed eyes stared back at me, filled with confusion. "I don't understand."

"He loves you." Even though pain battered my heart like a sledgehammer's wicked blow, I pushed on. "He didn't walk away."

"You lied," she cried and tried to wiggle off me. Flipping us, I used my elbows and knees to pin her under me. "Get off me, Zayne." I shook my head. "Why would you lie?" she was breathing hard from the exertion of fighting me.

"I didn't, baby," I consoled, keeping my voice low so she would hear me. "He asked me to lie."

"I don't understand. You said, he didn't want anything to do with us, with me and that whatever we had was over."

"I did." I swallowed against the shards of agony thickening from my throat. "Trent asked me to lie. He asked me to make him the bad guy so that you would stay with me."

"Why?"

I went in for the kill. "Because when you uttered 'I love you, Zayne' during your orgasm, I told him he needed to leave, to give us a chance. He'd just be in our way if he stayed, and he agreed."

She closed her eyes and the tears leaked down her temples, mixing with her wet hair. "Why would you do that?" She opened her eyes and stared at me but there was no hatred just pain.

"Because I wanted to give us a chance, see if we could make it work. But I've watched you for the last two weeks, Angel. You love him. You're in denial because I made you believe he doesn't want you. I'm sorry."

She wriggled to pull her arms free, and I let her. Sighing she palmed my cheeks. "Don't you see, Zayne. I do love you. Ever since that day I met you in the coffee shop, I have felt everything for you. Yet, you have never, in all the time you've known me, been able to say how you feel about me. You're not one for emotions, I get that, but you denied me your love and I settled for second place to your travels and Natasha. Then Trent walked into my life. Like a raging winter storm, he blew through my life one night and refused to leave until my heart froze for him. I love you Zayne but I love Trent more."

I was a man who could make grown-ass men cry. However, that right there, made me the weakest son-of-a-bitch to walk the planet. It took the very air I needed from me and I knew that right then if I didn't step aside, I was setting us on a path for absolute failure. It was better if my heart hurt, alone.

I reined in my emotions like I'd trained my mind to do for years and smiled. "Then go to him, baby."

She hiccupped on a sob. "And what about you?"

"I'm not going anywhere. I'll be right here whenever you need me. I'll always live in your heartbeat and you, in mine." I kissed her and she let me. It wasn't goodbye, yet. Goodbye would come only when I was certain she was safe.

# Trent

I STARED AT THE DOCUMENTS in my hand, having read the same line repeatedly for the last hour as my mind drifted. Over the last two weeks, my heart continuously bounced around my chest like an aimless ping-pong ball thinking of Ashrika. I had to move on. I'd done it once before, the second time around could be easier. Snorting out a laugh, I stood and walked over to my office window. How could I have lost the same woman twice? First to death, then to life—a life with someone else. Twice to fate. If there was any possible way, I could change her mind, it didn't exist. Shaking my head, I sat again realizing I had to quit stalling and tell the kids. It wasn't going to be easy—but loving someone never was.

"Trent?"

I glanced up and frowned. "What the fuck?" was my first response as I stared at the man who'd broken my mother's heart and turned me into a rebel at the age of twenty-one. "What the fuck are you doing here?"

"I know I'm the last person you want to see but I'm sorry, son—"

"Son?" I barked, my laugh incredulous. "That title is reserved for a father, something you probably can't even spell."

He sighed. "Look, I'm not here for your forgiveness, I don't expect it. I brought you this." He moved further into my office and set a brown envelope on my table.

"What the fuck is that? A peace-offering," I scoffed. "You know where to shove it—"

"For fuck sakes, Trent quit being a whiny bastard for once and just look at the contents," he snapped. And that there was the

Princeton affluence I'd come to expect of the family name. It was sired into their bloodline. He might be in his fifties, but Joshua Princeton still carried himself with the same regal air as his brother. Same eye color, same rugged handsomeness and his hair a lot grayer than Drake's, but that's where similarities ended. Drake had a heart, my father, not so much. Shaking my head, I stared at the envelope. "If not for you, then for Krisha's sake," he muttered.

My head snapped up. "Why would anything you have, concern her?" I leapt up from my seat. "You've never met—"

"Because it's not from me. Read the goddamn contents," he pushed. "I tried to give you this before, but you refused meetings with me. So, here I am, forcing you to read it. Seeing as Krisha is back in your life, this might answer a few questions."

My irritation slipped just a notch. "You know about her?"

"There's nothing I don't know about you, Trent," his voice lowered an octave and I almost believed the fatherly concern. I knew better.

I didn't bother asking him to elaborate. My eyes on him, I reached for the envelope, opened it and tipped the contents out onto the table. The quicker I read it the sooner I could tell him to get lost. Several documents fell out. I picked up a letter and scanned the first couple of lines. My muscles tensed, my grip tightening on the page. I looked up at him.

"Read all of it." Joshua, my biological father and the man who'd cheated on my mother and fathered a child, lowered his tall frame into a chair, uninvited, and stared me straight in the eye. I might not know the man but the sudden sincerity in those gray eyes was genuine. Somehow, they reminded me of Drake's eyes.

"Does Drake know you've been around?"

He nodded. "I met him a couple of weeks ago. Told him of my intention to give you this." He pointed to the letter in my hand. "Drake asked me to postpone it for a bit, said you were going through some shit. That's how I found out Krisha was back in the picture. Read." He jerked his chin at the letter.

"Have you met your daughter?"

He shook his head. "She's not ready to see me."

I smirked. My sister had just discovered he was her father a few months ago. I didn't blame her. She wasn't likely to entertain him either because the man she called father, gave her a life worth living.

I continued reading. As the father of two kids, it took a lot to shock me. A couple more lines and the shiver running through my body shook me like the blast of an unexpected gut punch. I wasn't sure I wanted to read more, but the very next line had the blood crystalizing in my veins. I was shaking so badly, the letter fell from my fingers. I dropped into my chair. Tugging the knot on my tie to loosen it, I stared at my father. Confusion, anger, irritation all snowballing into one gigantic ball of nausea. I was ready to hurl. "How?" I finally muttered after several deep swallows.

He stood. "I'm at this address if you want to talk." He set a business card on the table and as he walked away, I caught sight of the company name.

I saw red. "What the fuck's wrong with you?" He turned at my shout. "You waltz in here almost twelve years after your shit, drop this fucking bomb, and now expect me to wait?" I held up the card. "How?" I bit out. I was in no mood for his shit.

And he probably knew it. Sighing heavily, he took a step toward me. "I was given a proxy by the old man and have been managing his affairs for the last nine odd years," he explained.

I frowned, still not understanding how this man who'd never met my wife, or her family for that matter was running her father's company. "You were given a proxy by who?"

"Mr. Singh." *Krisha's father.*

I blinked a couple of times. "How the fuck did that happen?"

"If you're interested, it will take more than a few minutes to give you the full story. Coffee? Lunch?"

As much as I was against having any type of social interaction with him, my curiosity was a little more than piqued. I ignored the invite for the moment. "How do you know Krisha's father? I'm sure you don't need coffee to answer that," I grimaced.

"I met Mr. Singh at your wedding."

I was flummoxed. "You were at the wedding?"

He nodded. "I wasn't invited but I came anyway." He stared at me, his expression contemplative. "I sat at the back of the church so no one would see me. On my way out, I bumped into Mr. Singh. Somehow, we got talking and when I told him I was your father, he invited me to a drink after the reception. We became friends." He shrugged.

"Well, fanfuckingtastic for you then," I scoffed. "But seeing as I've lost touch with your benevolent side, which I'm inclined to think never existed in the first place, how the fuck am I to believe this shit?" I waved a hand over the spilled contents on my table. "If you're here for forgiveness that's probably never going to happen," I barked. "So I'd start with the truth, right about now."

He slipped his hands into his pockets. "Look, this isn't what you think it is." At my arched brow, he took a deep breath then continued, "clemency aside and this might be a bit late, but I'm sorry, genuinely sorry for your loss. You seemed so happy with her—"

"Don't make a mockery of my love. Something you probably never understood, or you wouldn't have..." I swallowed the acid sluicing my throat.

He stared at me for a moment, deliberation shadowing his taut features. "I might've fucked up as a father, but I tried to do right by watching over you, even if it was from the sidelines. I was at Krisha's funeral. You never noticed because I made sure to stay out of sight.

You're a heck of a father, Trent, someone I could probably take a lesson from, but this," he pointed to my table, "it's all legal."

The solemnity of his countenance made me question whether I was being too rash. "In what sense."

"Time is imperative, otherwise his estate goes to the wrong people."

I frowned. "The old man's not dead why would— "

"There's a case pending evidence to declare the old man incompetent, to declare my proxy null and void and to declare his daughter missing."

That got my attention. I stood. "Are you telling me someone knows she's alive?"

"It looks that way. Either that or they think she's dead and now want to make it legal. After seven years, a court will declare her a missing person. I've stalled indicating I have evidence to the contrary. She has to come forward."

That for me was a red flag. If someone filed the case, chances were the attacker could be the same person, or not. "Who filed the case?"

"It was done by a third party using a company name. They have proof that they're entitled to the old man's estate."

"What about Easton?"

"As a minority shareholder, Easton currently has no leg to stand on. His father was in the process of changing the will to make Easton a majority when the accident occurred."

I stepped away from behind my table and poured myself a drink, then as an afterthought offered him one. "Drink?"

"Sure."

My whiskey burned down my throat quickly while he sipped his. "How long do we have before you need to present your case?"

"Two weeks."

"A lot can fucking happen in two weeks," I grumbled before pouring another drink.

"For what it's worth, you now have the answers about how she's alive. Does she know the truth yet?" he asked. I looked at him wondering how much he knew about what had gone down. "Look, you don't have to tell me anything." He finished his drink and set the glass on the table. "Just call me when you're ready to talk."

"Have you been following me all this time?" I asked as he walked away.

He turned to face me. "Since the day I fucked up, I've made sure someone watched over you, your mother, Krisha and the kids. I might not have a heart, according to you, Trent but no harm will come to my son and his family while I am alive." With that, he was gone.

I stared at the closing door, still on the fence about whether I believed the fatherly sentiment. Massaging my brow, I glanced at the letter on my table and uttered a caustic laugh. Once again, fate played me for a fool. The good thing was, I didn't need to tell her the truth anymore. It no longer mattered now that she was with Zayne.

# Ashrika

I STARED AT THE LARGE modern house with its glass finishing set against a beautifully landscaped garden and climbed out of the car.

"Thank you, Jenson."

"Do you want me to wait?" he asked.

"Yes, please." My nerves were in tatters since yesterday evening after Zayne told me what happened. I didn't hate him. I couldn't. I accepted love made us do unexpected things. If Incognito was anything to go by—very unexpected. Even as I pressed the buzzer, I wasn't sure how Trent would react to my appearance. I didn't tell him I was coming and hoped that the surprise factor I was aiming for, would work in my favor. Several seconds later, the door opened.

"I'm coming, Neha, I just—" Trent's words trailed off when his gaze met mine. If he was surprised, he didn't show it.

"Hi," I hesitated. *Neha?* Was he entertaining his ex? "Um, did I come at a bad time? I can come back if you want," the words spewed from my mouth. God, I felt like an idiot. I should've called first. "I'll just go." I turned to leave.

He stopped me. "Ash." I faced him once more. "Hi." He smiled before I noticed the white powdered patches on his cheeks and brow.

"Hi. Um, you have something—"

"Something?" He frowned.

"On your..." I reached up and wiped the white spots then glanced at my fingers, recognizing the texture. "Is that flour?" Then I noticed his black t-shirt was covered with the same powder. "Did I come at the—"

"Daddy! It's burning," a child's voice yelled behind him.

I blinked. "Daddy?"

"Come on in, give me a sec," he called over his shoulder as he raced off down a hallway leaving me at the entrance, flabbergasted.

"Trent is a father?" I mumbled. *Oh shit.* Why hadn't he mentioned it? Perhaps the child lived with his wife and she was visiting. "I should leave." I turned to go.

"Mommy?"

I froze. Pulling in a deep breath, I slowly rotated and came face to face with a handsome little boy. Sparkling cerulean eyes, immediately reminding me of Trent's baby blues, dragged a slow gaze over me before coming to rest on my face.

"Hi," I greeted but he just stared. I dropped to my haunches. "Hi," I tried again. To my surprise, he neared me and even more bizarre, palmed my cheek. Still, he didn't smile. Something in the way he looked at me kept me smiling and not moving.

"You came back, mommy," he whispered.

I had no idea why my skin suddenly pebbled with goosebumps. "Um—"

"Nicky?" Trent's soft call had the little boy swiveling on his heel and hurrying up the stairs that led off from the foyer. "I'm sorry about that." I was still looking at the top of the stair when Trent neared me.

"Your son?" I finally found my voice.

He nodded before offering me one of his charming smiles. "I'm sorry you had to find out this way." He looked genuinely apologetic. "After the charity ball, I wanted to invite you home to meet them then the whole Za—"

"Them?" At his frown, I repeated, "you said them. How many kids do you have?"

"Tw—"

"Daddy?" I glanced behind him to see a little girl peeking at me from behind a pillar. She hid when she saw me looking.

Trent held out his hand gesturing to the hallway. "Would you like to come in or are you afraid of kids?" The corner of his lips twitched.

"Sure."

I moved away from the door, waited while he closed it then followed him. I checked behind the pillar as we walked by. The little girl was gone. I glanced around, impressed by the soft décor and the sheer size of the place. When we entered the kitchen, I stopped short, my nose assailed by the sweet aroma of pancakes at the same time I took in the mess. Amid the flour and chocolate-covered counters sat the little girl. Deep blue eyes framed by thick, dark lashes and pitch-black hair stared at me.

I smiled and she returned the gesture before her father called to her. "Come here, Pixie." She stood, straightened her pretty pink dress, and neared him. He crouched next to her. "This is Ashrika, say hello."

"Hello," she greeted shyly then to her father, "she has such a pretty name, daddy just like her."

I blushed and Trent grinned when he noticed. "Ash, meet my daughter, Neha."

"Hello, Ne—" I paused, and his brow quirked up. "Neha." So, if this was his daughter, I was curious about the wife.

"Earlier you met Nicky, her twin," he offered, straightening.

"Twins? Wow. That must be so cool," I said to the little girl.

"Sometimes it is and sometimes not. You know when other children say I look like my brother or my brother looks like me. Then we fight because Nicky wants me to look like him. But he's my brother," she rattled on her tone matter-of-fact. "Please, say you're staying with us. You can sleep in my room. We can do all the girly things daddy can't. Will you show me how to wear make-up, please. I want to dress up all pretty just like you and then..."

I met Trent's gaze and he mouthed, "Sorry." I shook my head, trying to convey it was okay.

"Would you like a flapcake?" Neha asked, drawing my attention again.

Curious, I glanced at Trent who'd moved to the stove where he poured batter into a pan. "Flapcake?" I asked him.

"Yes, daddy's made more because he burned the others," Neha's gentle pout had me smiling.

"I have a British butler." Trent looked at me over his shoulder. "He would occasionally interchange the words flapjacks and pancakes. One day he made the mistake of calling them flapcakes while joking with the nanny and Neha picked up the word. She was three at the time. It's stuck ever since."

"Flapcakes it is then. I'll consider adding that name to my menu at the restaurant." Trent laughed at my suggestion. I looked at Neha. "Thank you, Neha, I'll have some flapcakes, please. Are they any good or does daddy burn them a lot?" I teased.

She giggled while setting a plate on the table. "They are so good. You have to try the one with chocolate ice cream and sprinkles, it's the best."

"Thank you, I will." I slipped off my jacket, hung it on the back of a chair, and waited. She began helping me assemble the sweet treat on the plate. I looked up to find Trent watching us and I winked. He grinned. I'd thought he looked delicious in a suit, but nothing beat knowing that the gorgeous man cooking in the kitchen was also a father, it gave me the shivers.

Trent finished up at the stove, moved closer to me and slid an arm around my waist. "You want me to save you?" he whispered in my ear. I shook my head, making him smile. "How did you find my home?" this time he spoke at a normal level.

"Jenson's a pretty...oh shit." I slapped a hand to my mouth when Neha looked up from her artwork. "Sorry," I blanched. Shaking her head as she walked off. Puzzled I turned to Trent. "I'm sorry, I didn't mean to."

"It's okay." He laughed. "As long as you have five dollars, you're good.

"Five dollars?" I frowned as Neha returned with a jar in her hand.

"Five dollars, please." She lifted the jar to me.

At my baffled look, Trent responded, "it's a swear jar. Each curse word costs you five dollars."

"I haven't heard of that before, limited memory and all that." I grinned. "Am I right to assume that all that money belongs to you?" I gestured to the almost-filled jar and reached for my purse.

Laughing, he nodded. "Guilty as charged. Although the majority are due to phone calls. I don't curse unnecessarily in front of my kids. Well, I try not to and quite a bit belongs to my cousin, Rayden."

"Hmm, will ten dollars do, I don't have a five," I asked Neha.

"I'll keep it as a credit. Daddy does that sometimes for his next curse word." She took the money and walked away.

I burst out laughing. "Oh, my God, she's precious. Credit for my next word? How old is she?"

Trent grinned. "They're seven."

"You have beautiful children, Trent. Why did your son run off?"

"Come on, we can talk while you dig into your pancake. Coffee?" He gestured to a chair at the kitchen table.

"If you're the owner of the Crystal Oasis, how do you find time to take care of the kids, prepare meals and run a successful business?" I asked, sitting down.

"I don't." He chuckled. "I wish I did, though." He shrugged and I got the feeling he wished to spend more time with his kids. "I have a nanny, a butler, a cook, and a grandmother who visits occasionally. Together they all make me look like Captain America." He set down a mug of coffee in front of me. "I couldn't do any of this without them, and today I gave all of them the day off so I could be at my kid's beck and call."

"Wow, that's generous of you." I laughed, then remembered Jenson. "Oh, shit." I quickly covered my mouth and glanced around. Trent noticed I was looking for Neha and grinned. I'd never had children around me other than diners. "Jenson's outside. I forgot all about him. I should—" I moved to stand, and Trent stopped me with a hand to my shoulder.

"Relax, eat up and I'll go invite him in. There's plenty of room."

"Room?" I frowned.

Trent moved closer and before I could gauge his intention, he leaned down and palmed my cheeks, dropping a quick to my lips. I sighed, having missed his touch. When he stood back, he dropped to his haunches. "I'm hoping you'll stay even if it's just for tonight—" he hesitated. "And if it freaks you out having to stay with the kids being here, Jenson can stick around, in case you need a getaway car." He winked and I dissolved into a fit of laughter.

"They're just kids, how bad can they be?"

"Trust me. You haven't met my son—my real son." He got to his feet with a chuckle then turned and walked out.

I wasn't sure what he meant by that and chose to ignore it. Pulling the plate Neha had decorated toward me, I dug in. I had no idea how long I sat there when I had an uncanny feeling of being watched. Twisting in my seat, I glanced around before my gaze fell to Trent's son. He stood at the door, his face wearing an expression I couldn't read.

"Hi." I smiled. He didn't say anything. "Would you like some pancakes?" I offered. Still, he said nothing, just stared and I was beginning to wonder if Trent's teasing was a little more than that. "It's okay, honey," I tried one more time, keeping my voice low and friendly. "I won't hurt you," I coaxed. That seemed to work. He took a tentative step forward and another when I held out my hands. And before I could anticipate his next move. He flew into my arms, rested his head on my shoulder, and held me tight. Stunned, I said nothing and caressed his back. We stayed like that for another minute or so and just when I thought I heard a sob, Trent's footsteps coming down the hallway had his son pulling away from me. Baffled, I touched his cheek, and in return, he fingered my hair. Then he turned and ran off, passing Trent on his way out.

"Did Nicky say anything?" I immediately picked up on the anxiety in Trent's voice. I shook my head. Sighing, he dropped into a seat next to me.

I reached for his hand. "Why do I get the feeling, Nicky misses his mother?"

Trent stared at me, his blue gaze tender. He opened his mouth to say something, seemed to think twice, and leaned back in his seat. I'd only ever met the arrogant, cocky side of him but looking at the man sitting in front of me now, something in his expression told me he had a story to tell. I hoped I could perhaps be the shoulder he needed.

"You okay?" I gave his hand a light squeeze.

"I lost my wife to childbirth."

I gasped. "Oh, God. That means the kids..."

"Never met their mother," he finished for me. "Over the years Neha adapted but Nicky sort of acted out. He'd see his friends with their moms and often ask me questions about his. As much as I tried to give him the affection he needed, I think he longs for a mother."

At his words, I now understood Nicky's reaction to me yet couldn't understand why he would call me mommy. Perhaps the idea of any friend of Trent's being something more, appealed to Nicky and I wondered how many women Trent had introduced to his children. "Why have you never remarried?"

He shrugged. "I didn't see the need. Women can be callous with stepchildren. As a Singleader founder, I'd seen my fair share of these cases. I couldn't put my kids through that. You're the first woman I've brought home—what I mean is, wanted to bring home to meet them."

Even as I now understood Nicky's reaction to me, warmth spread through me as Trent's words sank in and I couldn't stop smiling like an idiot.

"About the night at Incognito. Why?" He knew what I was asking.

"You needed closure."

"Closure?"

"Zayne never touching you despite being married to you, hurt you more than him asking you to leave. You felt incomplete. I could see it. As a woman without memory, and him being your only family had double the impact on your emotions. I tried to help the only way I could, by giving you what you needed. Him."

Emotions I couldn't describe tightened my chest and I sucked in a deep breath. "You knew he would agree?"

Trent shook his head. "I had no idea what to expect. I didn't exactly tell Zayne what I wanted to achieve, only that you were hurting, and he needed to fix it. He had to understand you both had feelings for each other."

Wow. God, this man was heaven-sent. "So, what happened wasn't planned?"

He nodded, not bothering to elaborate because he didn't have to. What he'd done had almost sacrificed his love for me. It took guts. No. It took a man like Trent—the only copy that would be impossible to duplicate and he was all mine for the taking.

He leaned closer. "I'll do anything for you, Ash. Don't leave, please. I can't lose you." He gripped my hand on the table, squeezing. "Fuck, I'll cut off my left testicle rather than give you up."

"What about the right one?" I bit my lip to keep from laughing.

He frowned before throwing his head back in a belly laugh. "I'll cut that one too," he said after his body stopped quaking.

# Ashrika

WHILE TRENT ATTENDED a conference call, I made a quick call to Zayne, letting him know I was safe and that I was staying the night. I'd no idea how I found myself smack bang in the middle of two men, who treated me like a damsel in distress and, handled me with kid gloves, yet still made love to me like I was on a runaway train. Either way, I couldn't complain.

Sighing, I strolled into the dining room and pushed through glass doors that led to a sunroom—a cozy one with white wicker furniture and pale lemon curtains. Large picture windows overlooked an immaculate garden and poured sunlight into the room, all built around a beautifully carved circular staircase that hung with creepers and little pink flowers. The space was so airy and radiant, I couldn't help stretching out my hands, twirling on my toes like a ballerina, and smiled while singing *Somewhere over the Rainbow,* ironically the first song I'd heard after waking from my coma.

I was in the middle of another twirl when my eyes landed on the glass doors. Pushing a stray of hair from my face, I stopped. Nicky stood there, a set of dimples bracketing a wide smile. Since that embrace in the kitchen, he hadn't made another appearance.

"Hi."

"Hi," he greeted shyly.

I moved to the seat carved into the wall below the window ledge, sat, and patted the cushion. "Would you like to sit with me?"

To my surprise, he moved closer and slid down next to me. Although I was glad he'd come back, I wasn't sure how to break the ice. He sat for a minute then stared at my neck until I fidgeted, before he broke the silence.

"Daddy has one like that."

I frowned. "Like what?"

He reached up and fingered my pendant. "Like this one."

Surprised Trent hadn't mentioned it, I rolled a finger over the pendant. "It's my lucky charm." I smiled.

"Why?" He appeared genuinely interested.

"Well, some time ago, I lost my memory. And this was the only thing I had left."

"Did it hurt?"

"What?"

He tilted his head to look at me, reminding me of Trent. "Losing your memory."

I uttered a low laugh. "Did you ever have something you liked and couldn't remember where you left it? And then after days of not finding it, you decide to give up looking?"

He nodded, his face glowing with childish exuberance. "I had this toy daddy brought me from Africa. One day I was playing with it, then we had to go visit grandma. When we came back home, I couldn't remember where I left it."

"Did it hurt?"

"No. It sucked because I liked it and wanted to find it. Maybe it's still at grandma's and I'll find it one day." He shrugged, his smile so innocently sweet.

"So, losing my memory is just like how you felt when you lost your toy and just like you, I hope I find it one day."

"And if you don't find it?"

I'd often wondered the same thing. Before meeting Trent, I'd become a recluse and desperate to get my memory back. Now, I remembered his words at Incognito when I thought about the loss. "I'll make new ones."

He reached for my hand and held it in both of his. "But you won't leave us if it comes back, will you?"

Startled, I stared at him. And the glow from a moment ago was replaced with earnest, almost begging me. God, how did I answer a child I barely knew and who'd oddly latched onto my heart in barely a day? "I'll try."

He shook his head vehemently, his grasp on my hand tightening. "You have to promise."

I palmed his cheek and dropped a light kiss to his brow. "I promise." As the vow left my lips, I sent a silent prayer that I'd never break his tiny heart.

He beamed and immediate warmth spread through my chest. "Will you read me something, please?"

I glanced at the rows of books sitting on the shelves against a wall. "Sure. Do you have any favorites?"

Instead of answering, he reached into his pocket and slid out an envelope. "Can you read this, please?" He held it out.

Curious, I turned the envelope over. Other than his name, it had nothing else. "What is it?"

"It's my mommy's letter."

My heart clenched. "Your mommy?" He nodded. Was this little boy so desperate for a mother that he'd written a letter to her? I took the envelope and pulled it out. As I opened it, I realized it was written to him and wondered what had gone through his mind prompting him to write a letter to himself. I began reading out loud.

*"My sweet, sweet, Nicky, You're seven today and one more year older since we last met. That means you're officially a big boy. Have you been a good boy too?"* I laughed at his creativity. *"I'm sure you're bathing by yourself now. My big, sweet boy. I'm going to tell you a little secret. Always make sure you bathe every day because you never know when you're going to meet a pretty girl. And if you do, you want to be smelling perfect for her. If anyone tells you it's okay not to bathe, don't believe them, baby, people do smell. Yup, they do. You're a hand-*

*some boy now, so make sure you have those girls eating out of your hand, okay? Oh, and don't forget to wash behind your ears. And yes, clean underwear is a must. Promise me."*

"I promise." Nicky's whisper drew my gaze. He stared at me, put a hand over his heart and nodded.

A lump formed in my throat. I blinked to clear my suddenly hazy vision and resumed reading. *"School is going to get tougher with each year, baby. You might meet some nasty kids that will bully you."* That gave me pause. Had Nicky encountered bullies? Was that why he'd acted out? I continued reading, *"if they do, baby, never back down, punch them in the nose or in the nuts. It always works so you can escape if you have to. Shh, don't tell daddy I said that."* I laughed and so did Nicky. I glanced at him. He wasn't looking at the letter, but at my face. Was he watching my expressions? I suddenly wondered just how real the letter was.

He touched my hand. "Read some more, mommy. Your voice is pretty."

My eyes watered again. I didn't let him see it and hid my expression behind a smile. *"And if that doesn't work and they still bully you then go tell daddy to help you. You know you're mommy's little boy, right?"*

"Yes," Nicky replied.

It was only then that I realized that the reason he'd asked me to read the letter was that he wanted to share the emotions of his mother by having a direct conversation. I tilted the letter slightly, so I could look at him while reading. *"You'll always be my little boy, but daddy is your friend, Nicky, he will do anything and everything to make you smile and keep you safe. Don't forget that, okay?"*

"I won't, mommy."

*"And now that you're seven, it's okay if you want to go riding on daddy's bike."* Trent had a bike. Why wasn't I surprised? *"I know I told him you can't, but I want you to do everything you want with*

*daddy. I wish I could be there for you but I can't. Plus, heaven is a really cool place, and the angels keep me busy. They look down on you and Neha sometimes and come tell me that you're being a naughty boy. I can see you smiling, Nicky. You're mischievous, sometimes, right?"*

He giggled, shaking his head. "No." I smiled, loving his look of innocence.

*"Because I can't be there, you, Neha, and daddy need each other. You need to take care of each other. Don't forget, okay."* He nodded. *"Now that you agreed and you're a big boy, I need your help with daddy too. Don't tell him this, but he's a big baby."* Nicky giggled. *"Sometimes he forgets things and I know he'll miss mommy too just like you. Will you help me with daddy, sweetheart?"*

"Yes, mommy."

*"Okay, this is what I need you to do. First, I'm going to explain something to you. Daddy and I were soulmates. I know, your little mind won't understand this now. When you're bigger, however, you can read this letter again and you'll understand. Soulmates are two people who find and love each other forever. Unfortunately, I had to leave your daddy, so he is all alone now because I know your daddy. He won't bring you guys another mommy. Am I right?"*

Nicky smiled and nodded.

*"If I am then I need you to find a soulmate for daddy, sweetheart."* My heart staggered in my chest. She wanted him to find love again. *"Because I don't want daddy to be alone for the rest of his life. He's the perfect daddy and he was perfect to me too. And he needs someone perfect to take care of him. Will you help me, sweetheart?"*

"Yes, mommy."

*"If you're nodding then you just made my heart dance like the colors of the rainbow. All bright and airy."* The first tear fell and I didn't wipe it away. *"Is your heart dancing too, Nicky?"*

He nodded.

*"Then let's make daddy's heart dance too. Let's find him the perfect soulmate who will make his heart dance and sing. If you're worried, don't be, you're his bestest son and you will know who she is."* I paused, my heart sat in my chest, realizing that somehow this handsome little boy was older and wiser beyond his years than anyone could see.

He pulled in a deep breath. "How will I know, mommy? How will I know his perfect soulmate?" His eyes stayed fixed on my face and my tears now flowed freely. I stared at the writing, trying to imagine how he'd put all these words together. Who'd helped him? Trent perhaps? A teacher? Then I began reading once more.

*"Because she will smile like the sun. She'll cry like the rain. She'll dance like the breeze. She'll sing like a nightingale and most importantly, she'll make you a promise without knowing you."*

*Oh, my God.* I swallowed my gasp. The spookiness of that description hitting me square in the chest just as Nicky murmured, "Just like you when I was standing at the door, mommy?"

Not sure what to say, I stared as those innocent blues roamed my face, his expression expectant. What did I say? "Will you be my daddy's soulmate?" He grasped my hand. "Please." His eyes glazed over, and my heart dropped through my body to my toes.

"I—"

"Nicky?"

We both looked up. Trent stood at the door. Once more, anxiety laced his small smile. Nicky let go of my hand and hurled himself at his father's body. Looking at me, Trent hugged his son, silently asking me what had happened?

Nicky answered by tugging his father down to his level. Trent crouched and looked at his son while I wiped my wet face with my palms. "She's going to be your soulmate, Daddy."

Trent looked up, his brow tight with shock. I shrugged, offering him an unsure smile. There was nothing else I could do. He opened his mouth to say something but Neha running into the room distracted him. Nicky walked over to my side and held his hand out for the letter. Smiling, I handed it over, even though I was curious to finish it.

"Daddy, can we take Ashrika to the farm please?" Neha asked as Trent neared me.

"Farm?" I asked.

Laughing, he dropped his large frame into the seat next to me. "I own farms that grow the produce for my restaurants. That way I get to say what fruit, vegetables, and dairy products are used.

"You're serious?" I was enamored.

He nodded. "Want to take a drive? It's about an hour out in the countryside. We'll be back in time for dinner or not."

"It's so cool." Nicky slipped in between me and Trent.

I caught his surprised look over his son's head and hid my laugh. It seemed like I had two Shaw men vying for my attention.

# Ashrika

"OH, SHIT, NO!" I YELLED, hopping from one foot to the other. "Gross."

Trent rounded the corner of the dairy, took one look at me and burst out laughing. I glared at him. "Not funny."

"It's just a little shit, sweetheart."

"Really! Just a little shit. My boots are covered in the crap! Pun intended. I can't get out of here, because this whole place is like one big giant yard of poop. Get me out of here."

Trent and the kids had taken me on a tour around the farm which turned out to be acres and acres of thriving fruit and vegetables. Only, I ended up visiting the dairy part of the farm and walked right into cow shit that literally covered the whole yard. While they were suitably dressed and I wasn't one for fashion, Prada boots and cow shit didn't see eye to eye.

Nicky and Neha chose that moment to come riding in on horses and burst out laughing as they watched my dance of shit.

I glowered at them. "I'll get you guys."

Immediately Nicky's face turned somber. "Sorry, mommy."

I felt bad and surprisingly I calmed down, took one look at my boots and began laughing. Nicky's smile returned.

Trent walked toward me and I grinned. "I thought you said it's just a little shit." At his cocked brow, I added, "then why are you walking around it like they're landmines." I folded my arms waiting for him to reach me.

"If I can avoid it, why not?" He grinned, stopping an arms-length away. The hot steamy cowpat between us was huge. He held out a hand. "You're going to tramp more, nothing you can do about it, sweetheart. What are you doing this side, anyway?"

I gave him a sheepish smile. "I followed a piglet and it ran, I didn't realize what I'd walked into until it was too late." Laughing I reached for his hand and stepped tentatively toward him trying to avoid the softer piles.

It happened so quickly I didn't see it coming, neither did Trent. I thought he had a firm grip on my hand and as I stepped forward, I slipped and without thinking, jumped toward him. Trent was a strong man, but no man was prepared for cow shit. He slipped.

"No..." I yelled the same time he cursed.

"Fuck!" He fell backward, ass-first into a pile of shit with me safe on his lap.

We sat there for a full minute, looked at each other then burst out laughing, making the kids giggle.

"You could've just laughed about it," Trent mock scolded me. He pushed me up and stood.

"What's the damage," I asked, looking at his jeans.

"Just my ass, fortunately." He grinned and walked us back out of the mess. "I've got a pair of shorts in the truck." He checked the back of his pants. "It's not a lot."

Five minutes later, I gave up trying to get the stuff off while he went to change into his shorts. When he returned looking just as sexy as he'd done in jeans, I followed him around.

"Wow. It's beautiful." I shielded the sun from my face with a hand and glanced around. We stood, leaning against a wall that separated the rich fields from the dairy farm at our rear. "I've never been to an actual farm before. Okay, maybe I have and I don't know." I grinned. "Although, a fair warning that 'you're going to trample lots of shit, Ash' would've been appreciated," I smirked, glancing down at my boots covered in crap.

Chuckling, Trent grabbed me around the waist and hoisted me up onto the wall to face him. "I'm sorry, I should've warned you." He unzipped my boots. "It's called cow dung and surprisingly, it's used as agricultural fertilizer."

I gawked. "Wait. You use that." I point to the shit, "On that?" I jerked my thumb at the crop fields behind my back." He nodded, laughing. "Holy cow." We laughed at my choice of word. "Honestly, I knew about the fertilizer, but I didn't do in-depth study of what went into it."

"Consider it another learning experience for that ever-growing bank of memories." He pulled off my boots.

"Another?"

"I taught you how to fuck." He winked before turning away.

My cheeks grew warm before I realized I was stuck on a wall without shoes. "What are you doing? I'm not walking around barefoot in this place."

"Hang on, sweetheart." He called over his shoulder and walked up to a metal structure. I couldn't see what he was doing until he returned. "All pretty again." He slipped on my boots, now clean, and zipped them.

"Thank you."

Keeping me on the wall, he inched between my spread legs and circled my waist. "And thank you, for coming to my home today and out here. It means a lot."

"And to think I almost didn't."

"I'm glad you changed your mind. You'll stay tonight?" I nodded. "And I'll keep Jenson around just in case I become a handful." He winked and I laughed.

"But I don't have any clothes."

"Easily remedied." His heated gaze dropped to my chest while he licked his lips.

I swatted his hand. "Behave, you have children."

"So?" He moved closer, his hands painting slow circles on my lower back. I immediately felt the burn through my skirt. His face drew closer, our noses almost touching. "They need to know their dad is in love," his soft words brushed across my lips.

I gasped, loving the way he was looking at me. The kids came bounding back from the stables and Trent leaned away with a soft groan making me laugh. "What their naughty dad needs to know is that sex only happens behind locked doors with kids around," I whispered as Nicky pulled Neha's cap and ran off. Squealing her irritation, she chased after him.

"Locked doors are for beginners, sweetheart and quite clearly you haven't grasped the fact that I'm a master manipulator," he kept his voice low then shifted putting his mouth right next to my ear. "Deepest, darkest desires. I aim to make them all come true." He stepped away before I could react. That, however, didn't stop the abrupt heat scorching my pussy. I squeezed my thighs with an inaudible moan. Master manipulator indeed.

"Come on, I want to show you something," Trent lifted me off the wall and set me down on the ground. "Nicky, Neha," he called. When they came running back to where we stood, he leaned down. "Can you stay with Fanny please? I'm taking Ashrika to the factory?"

"Ok, daddy," they replied in unison.

Hearing her name, their nanny appeared from behind the shed and gestured for them to follow her.

"They like it here?" I asked as I followed him.

"It's the animals. The kids consider them their pets and with each visit they get to spend time with a different animal. This way."

I frowned as he steered me away from the buildings that I knew were the factories. "Where are we going?"

He glanced at me, his smile reminding me of Nicky. "Quick roll in the hay."

"You can't be serious."

"What's wrong, sweetheart?" He slipped a hand around my waist and drew me tight to his side. "Not afraid of people watching me eat your pussy, are you?" I blushed so hard, the skin on my cheeks felt like they'd been seared. "Relax, I have something else in mind that would look perfect between your legs."

What the hell kind of statement was that?

Another two turns down the path brought us to a shed. Curious, I waited while he unlocked the large doors and pulled them open. He gestured for me to enter. As I did my glance fell to a large—very large black and chrome bike. I knew nothing about bikes or cars for that matter. How did someone keep such a large machine upright on two wheels? I laughed realizing I'd sound stupid if I asked.

"Care to share the joke?" Trent came up behind me. Before I could respond, he turned me around sharply to face him, grabbed the back of my neck, and claimed my mouth. I clutched his arms to keep from falling backward. Despite the wolfish hunger lurking in his kiss, his lips were warm and soft. His tongue pushed past my teeth, coaxing my mouth open. Once I gave him access, the intensity changed, hungrier, more demanding, stealing my breath, weakening my ability to keep upright. I tilted my head to deepen the kiss and his fingers tightened at the back of my neck. Every inch of my body pulsed, pouring liquid heat into me from my belly to my thighs, and searing the very core of me. I wasn't sure if the low growl emanating between us, came from me or him.

He pulled back slightly, his eyes no longer tender but a sexy invitation to get downright dirty. "I've wanted to do that since you walked through my door this morning looking like fucking sex in boots." He kissed me again, this time softer, sweeter. His hand dropped from my neck to my ass, pressing me tighter to his body. "I need to fuck you now, Ash."

"The kids—"

"They're busy," his lips brushed mine. "Fuck, sweetheart, you're like that extra drop of cream in a warm mug of hot chocolate, the one you shouldn't want but must have." His hand crept under the hem of my skirt bunching it as he slipped inside my panties. I shuddered when he pushed two fingers into my pussy. My grip on his arms tightened. "Trent, we shouldn't," I gasped as his thumb brushed my clit.

"But you know you want it, right?"

I shut my eyes tight as my orgasm raced down my spine, my pussy muscles clenched in readiness. My knees buckled and I clung to his arms.

The sudden sound of approaching footsteps running toward the shed, had me pushing him away. I barely had time to straighten my skirt when Nicky and Neha barreled through the open door, breathing hard.

"Shit."

I caught Trent's mumbled curse and grinned. He scowled when he snagged my 'I told you so smirk."

"Can we go for a ride, daddy?" Nicky brushed past Trent and went to investigate.

"No. You know you can't—"

"But, mommy says it's okay," he wailed.

Trent frowned. "What are you talking about, champ?"

"Tell him, mommy."

I balked, realizing Nicky was talking to me before catching Trent's look that hinged between surprise and I could've been wrong but I was sure it was anger.

"Ash," Trent gestured for me to follow him outside. "Nicky, Neha, stay put," an unusual tightness tinged his words, a far cry from the sexually excited man from a few minutes ago. "Want to explain?" he said when we rounded the corner of the building.

"Did I do something wrong?" I was seriously out of my element here. I knew nothing about parenting kids.

He opened his mouth to say something then he closed it, his expression softening. "Why is Nicky calling you mommy?"

"I have no idea. He came into the sunroom while I waited for you. Asked if I could read him a letter he'd written to look like it came from his mother—"

"He asked you to read the letter?"

"Yes. Why?" What was the big deal over a child writing a letter to himself? Granted, some of the things were a little too adult for a seven-year-old, I saw nothing wrong with it.

Trent sighed. "That letter was written by my wife."

"You said your wife died at childbirth?"

"She knew she wasn't going to make—" his voice cracked on the words and he turned away. For the first time since meeting him, I watched the cocky man I'd come to know, appear almost vulnerable. I stayed silent unsure how to handle something this emotional, this intense. When I finally couldn't take the silence, I touched his shoulder and he began speaking again. "She wrote each of the kids seven letters. One for each birthday. Every year, I'd read the letters to them until the last one. Both kids decided they were big enough to read it themselves." He turned to face me. "I'm sorry I came across a little harsh just now."

"You didn't." I palmed his cheek. "You're a great father and you were just concerned. I know I'd be if they were mine. Nicky's right, she did say he could ride with you. And he wants you to find a soulmate. You presenting me to them has opened up that door for their introspection since you haven't given them any other options. They're just following what their mom asked them to do. And I'm so sorry Nicky called me mommy without—"

He placed a finger to my lip, slowly shaking his head. "I want them to call you mommy if you're okay with it."

I smiled, nodding. He lowered his head and drew me in for a slow kiss.

"Yuck."

"Gross."

Two distinct voices shouted, drawing us apart.

I laughed at Trent's 'I give up' look. "What did I say about staying put?" he scolded.

"But, daddy—"

"No buts. When I say stay put, I mean it, champ," he chided Nicky then to me in a whisper, "We need to set some ground rules or my cock's not likely to get any action."

I laughed. "What was that, about locked doors and master manipulator, again?"

He cocked a brow, scowling then slid an arm around my waist, guiding me back to the shed. "If I don't have you under me by nine tonight, my name isn't Trent Shaw," he whispered in my ear.

"Would that be deep throat or deep pussy?" He stopped moving, shock dropping his jaw. I carried on walking, giving him a sweet smile over my shoulder.

When he caught up with me he gripped my waist again. "Now I'm more inclined to get you home than have you straddle my bike."

I stopped and cupped his face. "How about I straddle that bike now and do the same to you later."

"Bold and beautiful, aren't you?" He chuckled.

"I am but a friend said riding a man's bike gives your pussy the best damn vibrations ever. And I want to test it." I walked away leaving him gaping.

"Fuck. I've unleashed the fucking devil." He groaned.

# Trent

ASHRIKA ARRIVING ON my doorstep was an unexpected distraction, but a welcome one, nonetheless. Whether Zayne sent her willingly, I hadn't asked, I just hoped it was a long-term thing, not a once-off. We had yet to have that discussion. All three of us or just me and her remained to be seen.

It seemed like I'd worried for nothing where the kids were concerned. Watching them with her at the farm and now in my kitchen, preparing dinner was a surreal experience. Something I'd longed for and never thought would happen. While my heart sang, I dreaded the moment she found out the truth. A part of me, the logical side, wanted to tell her. To sit her down and open my heart to her, let her know that everything I'd done was because I loved her. The other part, the vulnerable one, the one afraid she might leave and never come back, resisted.

Whatever happened, I had to take it in stride. I just wished it was as easy as the pizza dough Ashrika was teaching the kids to make.

The sudden slap of something cold to my neck jolted me out of my reflections. "What the—" I broke off in time and put a hand to my neck. It came away with a piece of pepperoni sticking to my fingers. I glanced up.

Ashrika's guilty smile followed with a questionable, "oops." She didn't look apologetic.

I arched a brow. The kids' eyes, round saucers of surprise, bounced between the two of us. "You were daydreaming, I had to get your attention." She shrugged as if it was the most natural thing to do.

I set my whiskey glass on the center counter we all sat around and stood. "And flying pepperoni was your best method of communication?" I prowled to her side grabbing a handful of flour on my way.

She anticipated my intention. "No!" she yelled, ducking around the corner. The kitchen erupted with squeals, giggles, and mumbled curses as I gave chase.

"Get her, Daddy!" Neha shouted.

"Run, Mommy!" Nicky counted.

Ashrika wasn't fast enough. I cornered her, dumping the flour over her. Standing still, she gaped at me then flicked a glance to her black sweater now a perfection of white haze. She raked a hand through her hair and coughed as flour coated her face.

Scowling, she narrowed her gaze at me. "You're so dead."

"Come and get me, sweetheart," I taunted. Moving next to Neha, I grabbed a handful of pepperoni and sausage and set it down in front of my daughter.

"Can I, daddy?" Neha picked a couple of pieces.

"Let her have it, Pixie," I yelled, unleashing meat saucers.

Ashrika's hands shot up, defending herself, "Ooh, I'm going to get you, Trent."

Doubled over with laughter I didn't see Nicky move until the first piece of sausage caught me square in the brow. The next in the chin.

"I got you good, Daddy." Squealing, Nicky let loose pieces of meat as fast as his little hands could, defending Ashrika.

"You're supposed to be defending me." I charged him with a handful of flour, sinking it into his hair. Squirming, he darted away, straight into Ashrika's arms.

Laughing uncontrollably, they both fell to the floor.

"Shit." My hands on my hips, I gaped around the messed kitchen.

"Five dollars, daddy." Neha was still giggling.

"That was so worth it, baby." I winked at Neha, then smiled watching Ashrika dust the flour off Nicky's head.

"Did a bomb go off in here?"

We all turned. My grandmother stood at the door. *Oh, fuck!* I panicked. She didn't know about Ashrika yet.

"Nana!" Both kids flew across the room, straight into her arms, not caring that they were messed.

"What are you doing here, grandma?"

She had a key to the house, so she could come and go as she pleased. Problem, this wasn't the ideal time. I was trying to think of the best way to distract her when her eyes fell on Ashrika. I saw the recognition in my grandmother's eyes, my insides churned and my mind spun.

*Fuck.*

"And you must be the lovely Ashrika." Gran neared Ash and palmed her cheek. "You're just as beautiful as Drake mentioned. Welcome to the family, my dear, hopefully, you'll stay for a long time to come."

I was still trying to digest what had happened and caught my gran's teary gaze as she turned, her knowing expression all the comfort I needed that my secret was safe. Behind her, Ash blushed, giving me a 'why didn't I tell her' look. I offered her a comforting smile.

"To answer your question, young man, I came to take my great-grand kids home. It's the week of the Disney fair in Granger Valley. Sianna was supposed to fetch them tomorrow but I had an errand in the city for your grandfather. I told her I'd fetch them. If that's okay with you?" Her raised brow told me I shouldn't bother arguing.

"Yes," the twins responded before I could.

"Then it's settled. Go get cleaned up kids," Gran shooed them toward the door.

Nicky did a one-eighty turn around her and ran up to Ashrika. "Will you help me, mommy?"

"Sure." She took his hand as he led her away.

The minute Ashrika disappeared around the door, gran let out a slow exhale. "I really can't believe this is happening, Trent. How? When Drake told me, I was shocked. Now seeing her for myself... God, I don't know how to describe what I feel right now."

"I know, it takes some getting used to."

"And Nicky's calling her mommy?"

I nodded. "Long story, grandma, and not the best time to explain."

"Do you plan to tell her the truth?"

I shoved both hands through my hair. "I have no idea if I should or shouldn't." I still hadn't decided on a plan of action.

"Well, the kids won't be here, so make the most of that time and tell her," she said, her tone matter-of-fact. A clear warning to do the right thing.

Twenty minutes later, I watched the taillights of Gran's town car recede before I closed the door, my mind in a whirl. I walked into the kitchen to find Ashrika tidying up. Silently, I helped her and when we were done, she turned to me. "I can make something quick for dinner." She smiled. "But I need a shower first. I smell like a deli."

"Shower yes, dinner no, we can order take-out. What's your preference?"

She licked her lips. "You."

I laughed. "That was a given."

She rolled her eyes. "Always cocky, aren't you?"

"Would you have me any other way?"

"No. But I am going to have you my way, Mr. Shaw."

My eyes flared. "What have you done with the real Ashrika?"

"Let me show you." A cheeky grin flashed around her pink lips before she ate up the distance between us and backed me up against a counter. She pushed up onto her toes and cupped my face. And in dire contrast to the untamed look in her eyes, her lips moved over mine in a slow seductive dance of tongue, teeth, and lips. My cock, hard and impatient strained against my shorts.

Gripping the counter on either side of me, I gave her free rein, letting her lead. I drank her soft moans as they flowed from her mouth to mine. She stepped back and with her eyes on me, lifted my t-shirt and pulled it over my head. Her lips soft, wet and warm, she kissed my chest, rolled her tongue around my nipples, tasting and teasing before using her tongue to explore every inch of exposed skin.

She bit down on a tight bud. "Ash," I hissed.

I struggled to breathe as her mouth and hands blazed a heated path down my chest to my stomach and up my arms. I leaned back against the counter, the boom of my heartbeat filling my ears, louder and faster with each exhale. I didn't want to say it—I shouldn't have thought it—but I had to. Krisha was fading away into the background as this woman, slowly lowering to her knees in front of me, took her place. She stole my heart with all the right words, manipulating my body with the perfected touches, and blinding my emotions with only a smile. Was it wrong that I wanted every single one of those feelings, every minute, every hour, and forever?

When she pressed her lips against the front of my shorts, over my cock alternating soft, gentle kisses with tiny nips of her teeth, I sucked in a breath. When her teeth grazed the soft fabric and bit down on the head, I stopped breathing. Grabbing a fistful of her hair, I yanked her up and crashed my lips to hers. The erotic slide of her tongue against mine as she deepened the kiss had me grabbing her ass and crushing her body to mine. For just a moment, she allowed me to devour her mouth, sucking, biting and nibbling before she pulled back, her ragged pants matching my strained breath.

"No. My way or no way," she rasped.

"Ash," I growled. "I need to fuck you now."

She arched a brow at me. "What? No foreplay?" Her lips curved in a decadent smile, her gaze dropping to the bulge in my crotch. Watching me, she slid her hand inside the edge of my shorts and wrapped her fingers around my hard cock, slowly gliding back and forth and coaxing another hoarse groan from my lips. The slither of my shorts as it fell to the floor, barely registered. She shifted her gaze to watch the crazy wildfire her hands ignited over my shaft and I was ready to fuck her on the counter I leaned against.

I grabbed her hips and pulled her back to my body. "Ever played with fire, sweetheart?"

"No," came the quick reply following with a cheeky smile.

I inched my hand under her skirt, dragging slow fingertips up her thighs until I reached her pussy. I paused when I felt her wet heat. No panties, just her drenched pussy leaking onto her bare thighs. "No panties, Ash." She gasped and thrust her hips when I slid a finger between her soaked folds and pinched her clit. Her fingers frozen on my cock as a low moan escaped her lips. And just when I thought I had her where I wanted, she stepped back trying hard to hide her arousal but she knew I knew better.

"Come here, sweetheart."

Instead of moving, she ran a slow gaze over my naked body. "If I don't get my way, you'll have to tie me down if you want me."

"I don't need to tie you down." At her arched brow, I shrugged. "I just have to touch you." I grinned, loving the invite. I lunged for her and she stepped out of reach.

Then with her eyes on me she slipped her fingers inside the edge of her skirt and in a provocative twist of her body, she slid it down her thighs, giving me a generous glimpse of her shapely ass. "What say we up the ante?"

"I'm listening." I folded my arms over my chest and waited.

She took a step toward me while sliding her top off, leaving us both naked except for her bra. A thin tease of black lace I wanted to rip off with my teeth. Standing in front of me, she pushed gently at my chest until I sank backward into the bench seat that skirted the table behind me. I allowed her to guide me, wanting to see what she planned to do. Leaning forward, she placed a knee on either side of my thighs, her gaze holding mine steady.

"Would you explode if I touched you?" Her tongue peeked out to lick her lips.

I probably would. "Not likely."

"Rest your hands on the table," she instructed, and I did. My eyes on her, I spread out my hands on the table. With her kneeling over me I was hard-pressed not to grab one of those creamy breasts and suck hard until she cried out. "No touching," she warned, and I grinned.

Her subtle control intrigued me and the ache in my balls made me impatient to take her. She surprised me when she gripped my cock and slowly lowered her body, widening her knees with each inch down. Anticipation forced my hips to jerk upward to meet her pussy. She restrained me with a press of her knees, her eyes scolding me. Then with a seductive roll of her hips, she rubbed the head of my cock over her clit. The subtle sensation had me clenching my fists to prevent grabbing her hips and impaling her on my cock.

"God, Ash."

Her husky laugh, low and sexy threatened my control. She rolled my cock around her pussy lips once more, this time letting just the head slip inside the heat of her slick entrance, and I moaned with her. She leaned forward and nipped at my neck, then ran her tongue over my nipples. She bit down hard before soothing it with her tongue flattened against my skin. All this, while her hips slowly undulated over my cock, the sensitive head French kissing her pussy and begging for more.

I sucked in a breath. Liquid heat pumped fire through my veins. The wicked sensation of her riding just the head of my cock was enough to make me want to force her down. "Ash," I muttered, closing my eyes against the sexy torture. I didn't know she had it in her to manipulate me into obeying her request not to move.

Gripping me tighter with her pussy lips, she sank down a little more, and picked up her pace. I groaned, wanting all of her. Still in control, she reached for my hands and placed them on her hips. "Now, you can touch," she whispered before slanting her mouth over mine.

This time our mouths connected softly, almost testing each other's control to see who'd give in, and I was tempted. Greedy, I drank from her lips, stroking my tongue over hers in mind-drugging licks that left us panting when we parted.

Our gazes locked, I slid my arms around her, supporting her full weight. "Ash, please," I moaned. She nodded then she sank down on my cock, sheathing me fully. I inhaled sharply, loving the feel of her slick heat encasing me, holding me snug. Gripping her ass, I guided her back and forth, letting her feel the slide of my cock, the position allowing me to go deeper.

"Oh, God, Trent, I need to come," she begged, her seduction forgotten.

"I've got you, sweetheart."

Taking her cue from me, she gripped my shoulders and in tantalizing erotic rhythm, rolled her hips, creating pinpricks of pleasure that sabotaged my control to stay upright. Fighting restraint, I watched as she tossed her head back, closed her eyes and arched, pushing her tits up and taking my cock deeper. With my hand on her hip, keeping her in place, I cupped a breast with my free hand and sucked the rigid nipple through her bra.

"Trent," she cried out.

I picked her up with my cock still in her, turned and laid her on the table. Throwing her legs over my shoulders, I gripped her neck and almost bending her in half as I leaned forward and rammed into her, hard and fast. She cried out, clutching at my arms.

"Come for me, Ash." I pressed my thumb down on her clit.

"Oh, God." Her body jerked.

I didn't let up, instead I increased the pace and fucked her harder. Only, the abrupt clench of her pussy muscles robbed me of my restraint and pushed me over the edge. I groaned my release, pumping all of my cum into her until my legs turned wobbly and I gripped the table to keep upright. She quivered under me, making me smile.

"Damn, you're sexy, sweetheart and so fucking beautiful." Moving her legs off my shoulders, I kissed her with everything I had. This woman *owned* me.

"I could say the same thing about you." She laughed.

I grinned. "How about that shower now?"

She nodded and scooping her up in my arms, I carried her upstairs and into the bathroom.

# Ashrika

I DIDN'T EXPECT MY one night's stay at Trent's home to turn into three. Shifting from under his arm, I stood and pulled on his shirt then headed for the kitchen. His sexual prowess was amazing, more so his stamina. I could barely breathe by the time my third orgasm hit and he'd had no intention of slowing down.

Laughing, I turned away from the refrigerator at the sound of approaching footsteps. "You want something—" My smile faltered, and the words stuck when instead of Trent, a younger man entered the kitchen.

"What the fuck." He stopped short, the look on his face morphing from friendly to mild curiosity then outright shock in quick succession.

Realization dawned and I smiled. "Hi. You must be Rayden." Trent had mentioned his cousin tended to visit unannounced. Something in the way he stared at me, made me slightly uncomfortable. The back of my neck tingled, shooting the tiny hairs to attention and embarrassment replaced my smile. Tugging the hem of Trent's t-shirt and glad it ended mid-thigh, I took a tentative step forward.

"Where the fuck did you come from?"

I reared back from the unmistakable snarl that hurtled across the room. "Excuse me?"

"You're supposed to be dead."

"Wha—" Disbelief caught me by the throat.

"You heard me." He took a step toward me. "Dead. As in six feet under. How the fuck are you alive?"

Clutching the shirt front, I pulled in a deep breath. Anxiety I'd buried a long time ago surfaced, gripping my heart in deadly grasp. "I-I don't—"

"Fuck."

We both turned as Trent walked in. His face pale, his gaze shifted between me and the other man.

"What are you doing here, Easton? You were supposed to call before coming out." There was no mistaking the threat in Trent's tone or the sudden anger masking his usually calm features. "Outside. Now." He pointed to the door.

"But—" Easton's words died at the look on Trent's face. "Fine," he muttered and walked out, leaving me baffled.

"Are you okay?" Trent asked, nearing my side, his smile hesitant.

"Who...um...what did he mean?" the flustered words rushed out as I struggled to grasp what I heard.

"Can you give me a second? I just need to have a quick chat with him?" I wasn't sure if he was pleading with me. I nodded. "I'll be right back. Wait here, okay?"

The second the door shut behind him, I opened it slightly and peeked out. I could hear their voices coming from the dining room. I tiptoed there and put my ear to the door.

"I don't fucking understand," Easton grunted.

"Keep your voice down," a vicious warning tainted Trent's hard tone, something I never thought I'd hear. My curiosity morphed into anxiety. What was he keeping from me?

"What the fuck, Trent. Your fucking wife is alive."

What the— I frowned. How?

"It was an accident. She doesn't know," Trent muttered.

Who doesn't know? I wiped my clammy palms down the shirt front. What the hell was happening?

"You..." a pause, "...killed your wife?" Easton sounded shocked.

Trent moved because I couldn't hear what he was saying. Then, "She survived."

I reared back. Panic eating into the air I needed to breathe. Did Trent kill his wife? Oh, my God. I balled my fists. My phone and purse were upstairs. I was miles from Zayne even if I called him. I was alone. Was I really sleeping with a killer?

"So that woman in your kitchen is..." I couldn't hear the rest of Easton's words.

Who was I to Trent? Judging by Easton's tone, I was someone he knew. I stood back and glared at the door. What was going on? Why were they talking about me and Trent's wife? Was there a connection? I raked a hand through my hair, tempted to burst through the door and demand—a sudden movement told me they were coming back. Quickly, I tiptoed back to the kitchen and paced for a moment before the door opened and Trent walked in. Nothing in his expression indicated he'd just had an incriminating conversation with the other man. Was I in danger?

"You okay?" He reached for me and I jerked away from his touch. Startled, he dropped his hand.

Swallowing down the sour taste in my mouth, I fought for control. I shivered so badly, I couldn't even muster my voice. He stared at me for a lifetime before his hands came together and cupped his neck. My trembling grew frenetic in the pregnant silence. I was afraid I'd hurl the contents of my stomach if I didn't say something.

"Who was that?" I finally managed, glad I sounded relatively normal.

"Don't worry about him."

That got my hackles up. "You can't be serious! Did you not hear what he just asked me? A man I don't know, that I've never met, is asking me why I'm alive and you're telling me not to worry. What kind of dumb do you take me for, Trent? Who is he?" *Wow.* Was that me speaking with such conviction, belying the chaos my head had become the second Easton opened his mouth?

Trent stared at me, his complexion pale. Dragging a hand down his face, he paced to a chair and perched on the edge. He leaned over his lap and with his fingers steepled, his leg bounced. His stiff shoulders showing his inner battle.

"Trent?" The single word was calm, contradicting the tempest raging in my lungs, threatening to wipe my very existence with a quick snap of the oxygen I desperately needed.

He stood and faced away for just a fraction of a second then turned with his hands on his hips. A muscle ticked in his jaw before he blew out a frustrated breath. "He's your brother, half-brother, actually," he muttered.

Shock massacred my breathing. I gulped air like a fish out of water. "B-brother?" I stared at Trent, waiting for him to elaborate. When he said nothing, I swallowed. "How?"

"Let me show you something?"

A knot twisted in my stomach, and I was suddenly uneasy on my feet. The fear of the unknown combined with my usual distrust had me teetering on a razor-sharp edge. I nodded, too shaken to form words. Even though I agreed, I couldn't ignore the trepidation sitting in my chest. I followed as he led the way to his study. He opened a drawer at his table and drew something out, only when he held it out to me, did I realize it was a photo.

My gaze locked with his as I took it, then glanced down. "This is a picture of us standing in front of your car. Is it supposed to mean something?" We took the picture just before we left for the farm.

"Look closer, sweetheart."

I studied the image again. I heard myself gasp. "No. It can't be." My stomach felt like someone had just dropped a sack of rocks into it. "There's snow behind the car," I whispered, noticing the barely visible timestamp at the bottom. It was taken almost nine years ago. "Am I—" I couldn't say it. My heart thumped harshly in my ears and my palms grew damp.

"That's my wife," Trent's soft words wrenched my gaze back to his face.

"I'm your wife?" My throat suffocated on a fist of dread. Slowly, he shook his head. "I don't understand. This is me." I waved the photo.

"No, sweetheart, that's Krisha. Your twin sister."

"Twin sister?" I couldn't breathe beneath the incapacitating shock. My knees buckled and I gripped the table to stay upright. The photo slipped from my fingers as I clutched my chest, disbelief spiraling through every cell. Trent caught me as I fell and lowered himself to the floor with me in his lap. "I have a twin sister?"

"Had."

It took a moment before the full implications of his words registered. My heart crumpled like a piece of paper. A wicked fear grabbing hold. Did he kill his wife? I pushed out of his embrace, crawled away, and sat against the table. I hugged my knees to my chin rocking back and forth, to control the sudden trembling that crept over me and tried to understand. Even without memories, my past and my future collided, holding me prisoner once more. Sharp pains stabbed my chest, devastating my heart.

Then it hit me. A chill slithered up my spine, and my blood turned to ice. "You knew?" I whispered. My skin tingled and bewilderment swept through me as I turned to look at Trent. The tremble began once more in my chin and rippled inward, bulldozing me. I leapt to my feet, gripping the table to support my suddenly dizzy body. "All this time, you knew who I was?" It wasn't true. Yet it was the only explanation for the sudden need to empty my stomach. "How could you?" I glanced down at my shaking hands. My head throbbed, the pain shooting me right between the eyes, like a misguided bullet. "All this time, my past lay right at your feet and you chose to blindside me into your bed." I panted, gasping breaths from a chest too tight to heave. It didn't make sense. It wasn't real. Soon, the real Trent would wake me up and take me in his arms, and comfort me like he knew how.

He stood. "Please, Ash, calm down."

I stared at those cerulean eyes that could make my body burn with just a look. Now, all I felt was contempt. Tears gathered at the corners, clinging to his dark lashes. The sight of his agonized expression sucked all the oxygen from my lungs. Then I paused. No. Those were not real tears. He lied. I backed away from him, stumbling as my unsteady legs fought to keep me upright.

"Don't you dare, Trent." A sob escaped my lips and I swallowed down the next one. Everything inside me turned cold, unfeeling, miserable. "Don't you dare tell me to calm down," my steady voice morphed into a scratchy whisper. "You lied to my face. Wait—was your whole family in on this? Your children?"

"Don't, Ash, you're hurting," he took a step toward me.

"Hurting," my laugh was caustic, dry, brittle. "You once told me to jump without looking and guess what, I did. Right into your devious arms." My heart sank at the improbable realization. Fresh tears blurred my vision and I buried my face in my hands. I winced at its attempt to make me appear pathetic. I was, wasn't I?

"You're right. I lied and I have a lot of explaining to do." Trent's voice broke and I almost believed the sincerity of his emotions. "Just give me a chance, Ash. Let me explain. Please." The tortured words coming from him threatened to drop me to my knees.

I hardened my heart and glared at him. "You had your chance, and you made a mockery of my love for you. There are no second chances in love, not in my lifetime. Because of men like you, real women with real pain are afraid to love."

I turned away and he came up behind me, gripping my shoulders. He pulled my back to his chest. And just for a moment, I melted against him before my brain intervened. "No!" I twisted out of his embrace and staggered away, my hands and legs shaking violently. "How could you do this to me?" I gaped at him, silently begging him to tell me that it was all a sick joke. Any second now he'd spring the truth on me.

"I'm sorry, sweetheart."

*No such luck.* "I can't deal with this right now, I need to get out of here. Now!"

"I'll drive you—"

"Stay the fuck away from me, Trent. Or God help me..." I threatened and hurried from the room. Instead of going upstairs, I headed out toward the main door, knowing I'd find everything I needed. As I reached the end of the hallway, I could hear Trent coming after me. Grabbing his trench and car keys from the table at the entrance hall, I raced out the door. In two seconds flat, the car purred to life and as I sped down the driveway, I glimpsed Trent in the rearview mirror, his face unreadable.

I'd driven all of five times since living with Zayne, only because he wanted me to get a feel for a car should the need arise. Well, thank fuck. However, the sedan I'd driven was no match for the Lambo and I struggled to keep the vehicle steady for a bit. Why the hell had I sent Jenson back home? Oh, wait because I had no idea Trent was a deceitful bastard at the time. God, how did I fall for such innocence, such lies? He'd lied with a straight face, every single time he kissed me, touched me, fucked me. And I'd craved more of his devious intentions.

"Fuck." I hit the wheel then grabbed it with both hands as the car slid from my grasp. If I didn't make it back in one piece, lying would be the least of Trent's problems. Zayne would kill him and think nothing of it. I might be blind to his occupation, but I was no idiot. Some of his phone calls alone, which I'd overheard by chance, told me he wasn't all that innocent. It seemed the same could be said for Trent, apparently. At least, with Zayne I knew where I stood. He hadn't lied to me—he just never told me anything and I never asked.

I had no idea how I made it back home in one piece, but I did. As I reached the building, I looked out the window and gasped. Zayne was waiting for me on the curb, the thunderous look on his face a clear indication Trent had called him. I barely put the car in park before I jumped out and staggered into his arms.

"Fuck, Angel, I've been going out of my mind since Trent called me. Are you all right?" He caressed the back of my head as I bawled against his shirt. "What happened, baby? Please, tell me." His arms tightened around me. "Where's your purse, your phone?"

"Trent lied to me," my muffled words slipped out between the tears.

"About what?" he asked, rage filling his tone.

I leaned back to look up at him. "He knew," I sobbed.

"Knew what?"

"Who I am." I sagged against him.

Without a word, Zayne scooped me up into his arms and carried me into the building as I fell apart. Inside the apartment, he strode into the kitchen and set me down on a countertop. He walked away for a moment and returned with a glass of water.

"Drink this." When I shook my head. He held it to my mouth. "Drink, baby," he coaxed. I gulped down a large sip and hiccupped on a sob. "Tell me what happened." He set the glass aside and gently wiped my wet face with his palms. "Does this have something to do with your past?"

"Yes. Trent's wife died at childbirth. I didn't even know he had kids, he never told me." I hiccupped. "I'm not mommy material."

"Ashrika, listen to me, baby." Zayne cupped my face. "You will be a perfect mom. Tell me what happened."

"His kids are seven which means she died around the time I was attacked." Realizing what I was saying, a fresh bout of tears started up. "I'm his wife's twin."

"What!" His shout hit my eardrums like a slash of a whip. I'd seen him angry before, it had nothing on the current look on his face.

"I didn't bother with letting him explain, I had to get out of there," I cried, my hands fisting the front of his shirt.

"Shh, baby, it's okay."

"How could he lie to me, knowing I was desperate to find out about my past?" I was shaking hard, the tears relentless.

He palmed my cheeks. "I need you to calm down, Angel. Can you do that for me?"

Pain seared my head, my heart. "I had a life, I had a sister. I had family and he knew, but he didn't tell me. Why?"

Zayne tightened his grip and dropped a soft kiss to my lips. "I will find out the truth but first, I need you to calm down, okay?" I tried to squirm out of his hold. "Rika!" his voice boomed around the room. I quieted down to soft sobs. "Have I ever lied to you?" I shook my head. "Then listen to me when I say this. There must be a perfectly reasonable explanation why Trent lied and I'm going to find out everything. Once you've had some rest, you'll feel better and we can discuss this with him."

Before I could argue, he lifted me into his arms and headed for his bedroom. Expecting him to leave me there, I waited while he pulled back the covers, crawled into bed, and turned when he settled down next to me. With my head on his chest, Zayne ran gentle fingers through my hair. Exhausted, I closed my eyes to the soft echo of his beating heart against my ear.

# Zayne

I SLIPPED OUT OF BED an hour after Ashrika drifted off, my body coiled tight. When Trent called to let me know she'd driven off from his place without her phone, I went completely nuts on him. Still, he hadn't mentioned the shocking revelation Ashrika divulged. She was his wife's twin? How the fuck did he make that fucking error? Regardless I had one intention when I saw him, knock the bastard to his knees and put a bullet through his head.

"Fuck. What the hell am I thinking?" Shaking my head, I reached for my phone and scrolled down to his number the same time the intercom buzzed. I walked over to the door. "You better have a damn good reason for fucking up?" I growled as soon as Trent answered the phone.

"I'm outside your apartment," he replied.

"I'm coming down," I cut the call and headed outside. The second I caught sight of him in the lobby, I clenched my fists to keep from hurling him across the floor. "What the fuck happened?"

He raked a hand through his hair, his countenance a mixture of anguish and concern. "Is she okay?"

"She finally calmed down, no thanks to you," I grunted.

"I need to see her."

'She's sleeping, and no I'm not waking her or allowing you anywhere near her until I know what the fuck happened at your place."

"Can we sit?" He gestured to the visitor's couch.

I nodded and followed him. When we were both seated, he leaned his elbows on his knees, linked his fingers, and bounced his knees. I could tell he was fighting his own internal battle, his own hell.

"I'm waiting, Trent."

His shoulders slackened and I suddenly realized that this was the first I'd seen him this unhinged. The usual cockiness was hiding behind a man sunk in despair. Surprisingly, I felt sorry for him. The notion caught me off guard and I almost snorted out loud. The fucker was on the cusp of taking my wife from me and I was feeling sorry for him. What the fuck! Either all this love shit was making me soft or I'd just fucking lost my marbles. I looked up as he began speaking.

"Ashrika found out she's my wife's twin. Her half-brother visited before I could brief him and went apeshit."

"You told me she was your wife." I gritted out. "Did you lie just to get into her panties?"

He pinched the bridge of his nose and leaned back in the seat. "I had no idea."

"And you expect me to fucking believe that? Do I look like a fucking fool to you?" my voice rose.

"It's not what you think." He looked at me.

"Then spit it out because I sure as fuck got better things to do—"

"Two weeks after Incognito, I received some documents from her father's attorney. Trust me when I say this. I was just as shocked to find out Krisha had a twin sister who was kidnapped at birth. My wife didn't know either. Her father was in the process of bringing Ashrika to meet her sister when Krisha..." he trailed off and for some reason I could tell he was being sincere, I believed he was telling me the truth.

"Does she know that I knew?" When he frowned, I added, "that I'd known she was your wife and I helped your plan to get her back?"

"She knows nothing other than she's my wife's twin. I never got a chance to explain."

"Do you intend to telling her about my involvement?"

"No," came his quick reply.

I deliberated for a moment before I stood. "If you want this to work in your favor, then I suggest you do exactly what I say. Agreed?"

"I don't understand."

"You will. Just meet me at the club in a week. Agreed?"

Rising, he nodded. "Would you give her this?" He drew out an envelope from inside his jacket pocket. It's a letter from her mother. It might explain a few things to her."

I took the envelope. "A week, Trent, and don't call her." He nodded and I turned away.

When I entered the bathroom, Ashrika was stepping out of the shower. I held out a large towel and she stepped into it. Slowly, I wiped her body. "You okay?" I stood behind her and massaged her arms.

She leaned back into me on a long exhale. "I'm not sure. It feels weird finding out I had a twin sister. I have so many questions and the only person who can give me answers betrayed my trust." She turned in my arms and slipped her arms around my neck, tightening the space between our bodies. "Don't leave me, please."

"You know I won't." Every inch of me screamed not to make a promise I couldn't keep, because she'd chosen to be with Trent. Then I remembered. She was my wife too. I happened to be her source of comfort now. I kissed her brow and gave her the comfort she needed.

An hour later, I sat in bed, with her head on my chest. I held out the envelope to her. "Trent had this dropped off." She leaned away from me. Her gaze flicked between the envelope and my face, her doubt evident. "It also contains a letter from your mother."

Taking it, she settled back against my chest and began to reading the letter out loud.

*My dear Krisha*

*If you're reading this then it means your father and I are no longer around. It pains me to bring this news to you via a letter when I should've told you about this the second you were old enough to understand. If by now you haven't learned the truth or found her, then please take my words to heart, I am sorry.*

*You, sweetheart, have a twin sister who was unfortunately kidnapped two days after you were born. We never stopped looking for her, and there were days when your father and I were so distraught we couldn't give you the affection you deserved. We eventually decided it was better for you if we never told you the truth. It was never our intention to keep it from you, we just did it out of love.*

*Wherever Ashrika is, yes, that's the name we'd given her, we pray and hope she has had a good life and hopefully one day you get to meet her. And if you do, please tell her that we never forgot her. Everything we've done in life for you has always been a plus one. If she needs to see the extent of our love for her then daddy's attorney will provide her with a key to a storage facility that will show her.*

*I am hopeful that you two will meet and both daddy and I receive both our girls' forgiveness, even in death.*

*Lots of love,*

*Mum*

"Oh, my word," Ashrika turned and sobbed against my chest for the second time that day.

"Does it help knowing the truth, Angel?" I asked when her body finally stopped shaking.

"Some. If Ashrika is my name and I never met my family, how did I remember it? When did I hear it? God, I have so many questions."

"And we will get you the answers. Get some rest now and when you're ready to talk to Trent, you tell me, okay?" I settled her in the crook of my arm.

She nodded and as she drifted, I hoped that within a week, she'd make a final decision for her life.

# Ashrika

"YOU OWN INCOGNITO?" I gawked at Zayne.

He stepped back as I climbed out the car and stared at the building. During the day, it appeared a lot less glamorous, yet still retained a certain charm.

He nodded. "I figured it's time you knew who you were married to."

"Really?" I arched a brow, not meaning to come across as sarcastic, but I couldn't help myself.

Zayne chuckled. "I deserved that." With a hand on my lower back, he walked me into the club. "There's no one here during the day, except for my admin staff. I thought I'd give you a tour," he explained as we entered the foyer.

I was doing a slow three-sixty when my gaze fell to the entrance and I balked, taking in the rugged appearance of the man who'd betrayed me. "What are you doing here, Trent?"

A week ago, I was all set to kill him, today not so much. Today my frazzled brain, which Zayne had tried hard to soothe since that night, needed a reprieve. I was less likely to fight, and more inclined to ask for answers. But that didn't mean I couldn't make him sweat.

"I warned you about hurting her, Trent," Zayne's voice was low, firm and deadly.

"It wasn't intentional." Trent looked at me. "I should've told you sooner, Ash. I'm sorry."

"Yes. Like the first day you met me and decided to fuck your wife's sister." A lump formed in my throat and I peeled my gaze away to focus on Zayne whose ticking jaw showcased his anger.

"That's not what happened." Trent blew out a frustrated breath. "Give me a chance to explain. Please."

"You had your chance, and you blew it. I think you should leave," Zayne warned before he turned to me. His gaze, hard and searching, swept over every inch of me as though looking for physical signs of my pain. Then his icy stare cut back to Trent. "You have two seconds to get the fuck away from her before—"

"Fuck you, Zayne." Trent's lips pressed into a hard line. "Do whatever the fuck you want to me but I'm not leaving until she listens to me. I owe her an explanation and she's damn well going to get it. Whatever it takes," he hissed out the last part.

Zayne cursed taking a step forward. I clutched his arm, hoping I had the strength to stop him. My gaze shifted between both men, each wearing murderous scowls ready to kill if it came down to the wire. Trent might've hurt me but the fact he was willing to take on Zayne spoke to his desperation to save whatever we had, no matter how fucked-up it appeared. Fists clenched, Zayne yanked his arm out of my grasp and took a step forward. I had to stop them before someone got hurt. Chances were it would be both if their body language was anything to go by.

"Zayne." I touched his arm again. "It's okay. Let him speak."

"You sure, Angel?" he asked without breaking eye-contact with Trent.

"Yes." I dragged in a deep breath. He stepped behind me giving Trent room to move forward.

"Ash," He reached for my hand. I pulled it away and he sighed. "I honestly never meant to hurt you and yes I should've told you the truth from the beginning, but I wasn't thinking. Please, sweetheart, you have to know that despite my lies, I love you. Not because you look like my wife or I wanted you to be my wife—"

"Would you have shared me with Zayne if I was your wife?" I snapped.

He reared back like I'd just slapped him. "Yes," he whispered, looking absolutely destroyed.

I didn't want to feel anything for him. "Why don't I believe you?" I uttered a caustic laugh. "You used me, Trent, to fulfill some fucked up fetish you had. Perhaps you wanted to share your wife before?" I was being nasty, but I didn't care.

"For fuck sakes, Ash," he growled.

Zayne took a step forward and I had no idea why I put out a hand to stop him. "Why the hell should I believe anything you say, Trent? You lied to me, lied about a past I was so desperate to find out about. Do you have any idea what I've been through, not knowing anything?" I held out my hands, beseeching. "Give me one good reason I should believe you?"

He said nothing for a long moment, simply staring at me with that intimidating gaze. Frustration tightening my stomach muscles, I shook my head and turned my back on him, gesturing to Zayne I was ready to leave.

"Because I had no idea," his words stopped me from walking away. Turning, I arched a brow at him. "I had no idea you weren't my wife until after that night..." he trailed off and looked at Zayne.

I knew to which night he referred. None of us mentioned it and strangely, I felt no shame, no embarrassment. Was it weird that each of these men held a piece of my heart that I'd be willing to repeat that night—willing to share myself with both of them at the drop of a hat? Sianna was right, sometimes we didn't understand the decisions our hearts make, nor was it impossible to find two men who loved you so hard, it left you numb, blind, and indecisive.

"Two weeks after we came here," Trent spoke again. "I received an envelope with all the details. Your father knew his life was in danger and hired an attorney to make sure his children each received their allotted share. I had no idea Krisha had a twin sister until that morning." The ache in his voice crushed my heart.

Still, I stayed firm. "Why didn't you call me, then?"

"Because," he hesitated and I might've been mistaken but hurt flashed across his face. "I didn't expect to see you again."

I frowned. "At your home?"

Raking a hand through his hair, he turned away cursing. His fists clenched and unclenched as though he was holding something back. I tried to ignore it, but I couldn't because every inch of me knew I could never stop loving him. I glanced at Zayne over my shoulder. He gestured to Trent with his chin as if urging me on, pushing me to talk to him.

"Trent?"

He swung back to face me. "Because I thought it was over, that you wanted to be with him." He pointed to Zayne. I gasped, shock eating through my confusion. "I told him I had to walk away, Ash. I should've—"

"Asked me what I wanted," I accused, my tone hard. "Is that the real reason you left without saying goodbye. Nothing to do with the closure you spoke about?"

"That too."

As he responded, something clicked. "Wait. You only found out after that night?" He nodded and I swallowed against the rising lump. "You were willing to sacrifice your love because you thought I was happy with Zayne?" Again, he nodded, staring at me through eyes that dripped undisguised affection. "You were willing to give me up..." My heartbeat quickened, railroading my emotions, bursting through my veins. I clutched my chest. "Even though you believed I was your wife?" I whispered the last part, realizing the extent of his sacrifice.

"Falling in love is easy, sweetheart, having sex, even easier, but meeting someone who can spark a flame in your soul, ignite a burn in your chest and stutter the beat of your heart, is extraordinary, rare, even. You did all of that to me, Ash." He took a step closer and cupped my face in his palms. "I wasn't lying when I said I fell in love with you that moment you ran out into the rain and into my arms. Something told me you weren't her and I began to believe it. Even when it was confirmed, I felt nothing but pain because I thought I'd lost you. You gave me a chance to fall in love with you. You. Ashrika Morrone, not Krisha Shaw. Whether you believe me or not, I fucking love you, more than life itself. And if Zayne is the man that made you complete, then I'd gladly step aside. I might be an arrogant bastard who takes what he wants, your happiness, however, means everything to me."

Tendrils of warmth unfurled through every inch of my soul, my body, my mind, yet my heart remained divided. Part of me knew I couldn't have one without the other. Part of me knew that if I chose I'd be miserable and living a lie. I had to ask. "And what if I want both of you?" I heard Zayne's sharp inhale behind me.

Trent didn't even flinch. "I'll give you anything you want, if I can have just one lifetime with you, Ashrika." I don't think I'd ever heard him use my full name before.

"Just one?" I asked, stepping back so that Zayne was standing next to me and now part of the conversation.

The two men shared a look I couldn't even comprehend before they both glanced at me. "Whatever it takes. For however long," both men whispered together, flooding my body with a sweet warmth I couldn't describe.

Some people had beautiful memories and some people had none at all, just like me. Yet, I had two gorgeous men wanting to give me beautiful memories, together. What more could I ask for?

I came out of my daze realizing that both men were no longer looking at me. Their attention pulled to something behind me. Before I could turn.

"Zayne, gun!" Tia's scream pierced the air.

One minute I was standing and looking at the two men, the next, both Zayne and Trent grabbed my arms and shoved me behind them into Tia's arms.

"Keep your head down, Rika." She dropped us to the floor. I was too distracted to worry about what she was doing there.

Gunfire erupted all around us, echoing painfully loud against the walls and furniture. Against Tia's advice, I lifted my head in time to see Zayne and Trent drop as well. I couldn't see who was shooting. Then in a coordinated move, I'd only ever seen in a movie, both Tia and Zayne pulled guns from the back of their pants, leapt to their feet, and opened fire. I screamed.

Trent looked over his shoulder at me at the same time as Zayne yelled at him, "Go to her!"

Crawling between couches, chairs and around pillars, Trent reached my side and pulled me into his arms. He tucked my head to his chest and covered my body.

The next few seconds happened so quickly, it felt like a dream. I squirmed from beneath Trent's grasp and looked up. One minute Zayne was standing, the next, he dropped clutching his side.

"Zayne," I screamed.

He rolled his head to look at me and in that single moment, I knew my life was about to change once more. Before either Trent or I could go to him, he mumbled something to Tia and raced out the door.

She turned to us. "Trent, he needs you. Go. I've got her." Even in all the haze around him, I realized I'd never heard the authoritative command in Tia's voice before. She stopped him as he raced for the door. "You're going to need this." She tossed him a gun and mumbled an address.

He stared at the gun for a second then looked at me. "I'll be back soon, sweetheart."

"Trent," I called out.

"Don't worry, I'll bring him back with me."

"I love you," I shouted but he was already gone.

"Come on." Tia lifted me to my feet. "You hurt?"

"No," I mumbled on an unsteady breath, yet it had nothing on my shaking body. Tia noticed, and she pulled me into a bear hug, caressing my back. When we finally stepped back I inhaled deeply. "Should I even ask?" I pointed to the gun in her hand, trying hard to sound normal. She merely smiled. "They're going to be all right?"

She nodded. "Zayne's one tough bastard, babe."

If I wasn't worried about the two men I loved getting killed, I would've drilled her for answers, but I couldn't focus.

# Zayne

IF I HADN'T CAUGHT sight of the bastard in the back seat of the car when I raced out of Incognito, I would've assumed the attack was meant for Ashrika. Did he think I wouldn't see him? When I gave chase, I hadn't thought of my actions, just that I wanted to nail the asshole. Not for sending armed men into my club to take me out. I didn't care if they did. But his hit put Ashrika in harm's way, and she was my Achilles heel, whether he knew it or not. Only, he'd gotten away.

The second the engine died, I was out of the car and heading up the stairs not caring that one side of my body stung like a bitch. I crept through the building knowing someone was going to die today and it sure as fuck wasn't going to be me. If there was one place I'd find him, it would be here. After all, this was where it all began and where it would end.

It was fucking amazing how life spun its mighty web on unsuspecting prey. I'd waited years for this, knowing he'd come for me. What I hadn't expected was for him to show his face, to be so brazen and to challenge me. He had just upped the stakes of the game. A true narcissistic fucker, but he had ultimately played into my hands without realizing it. I was two steps ahead of him. Always.

My side twinged and I glanced down, ignoring the burn, nothing was going to stop me from killing the motherfucker. Tonight!

The sound of the key card sliding into the door resounded around the silent hallway. I inched the door open and peeked around it. All clear. I slipped inside, closed the door, and with quiet steps crept further into the room. I dragged a chair to the middle, sat, and did what I always did well. Waited.

I didn't have to wait long. The familiar sound of the key card clicked the door open. I glanced at my watch. I'd sat there for eleven excruciating minutes. My breathing intensified as pain clawed through my side. But it was agony that I would gladly tolerate. It was worth every wince. Drawing in two deep breaths, I leaned back in the chair, gripping the barrel of my gun hard as I listened to the door open on a squeak and close with a bang.

He didn't notice me. Then again, he was as cocky as he was stupid. He'd always been that way, thinking nobody or no one could get to him. He believed his face was too innocent. He wouldn't harm a fly, that's what people said, according to him. Sadly, I had probably assumed the same thing, never once believing he'd be the man. The fucker I was there to end. Had he not had shit for brains, he would've known something was wrong the minute he entered.

He'd been considered my shadow, yet always trying to outdo me. He failed. Couldn't keep up. Still, I'd shown him, taught him how to be evasive and wary. He'd gotten the evasive tactic right. I mean he'd blindsided me for years. As for the wary, not so much. He'd become too brash for his own good. Ultimately it would be his downfall.

He moved further into the room. My fingers twitched to end him right then and there. He wouldn't see the bullet coming. A quick end. Only, I needed answers.

"Would you look at what the cat dragged in?" I scoffed from my position in the middle of the room. I didn't lurk in the shadows. I was a man you saw coming from a mile away and knew your time was up.

Easton Daniels, once a friend, now a foe. His smile was all the confirmation I needed he'd expected to find me there. That's what swimming in your own shit would do to you. You knew sooner or later, someone would flush you down the toilet. He was a gem when he'd started. I figured with time, the diamond had lost its sparkle. Now he was just looking for the next jeweler, to give him another polish. Well, fuck that. A forty caliber was all he needed. Straight through his brow, I wouldn't miss.

He slipped his hands into his pants pockets and leaned back against a wall. At least his dress sense was up to standard. I'd taught him that too. His pristine baby blue shirt was tucked into fitted navy slacks like he was ready to meet his maker.

"Took you long enough." He shrugged. "Seven odd years to be precise." His grin triumphant.

"Would you like a medal of honor to go with that headstone?" my voice was deathly calm. Something he didn't know how to read.

"Judging by that," he pointed to the growing red patch on my white shirt. "You'll be needing the headstone long before I do."

"You and I both know they spent a lot of money teaching me how not to die after they were done training me how to kill twisted fuckers like you."

He snorted a laugh. "That's swell, coming from you. I must say, you did a fine job hiding her from me."

What the fuck? I nearly dropped my gun with that reveal. *So, he was after her.* I gripped the barrel tight. How the fuck had I not seen that? What was his connection to her? Keeping my expression blank, I cut to the chase. "Why Ashrika?"

"You mean Davina?" He blinked. "Ah, yes, the memory loss, I forget. Didn't see that coming."

*Davina?* What the actual fuck? I was growing impatient for answers. I drew in air through my nostrils, letting it calm me. "Why?"

He lifted his shoulders in a shrug. "She was a means to an end. A very lucrative means that would set me up for life. No more shit."

I saw nothing but fury as I braced myself, allowing my breaths to even out. It would be easy to end his life right now. A bullet to the head. Done. The end. No. That would be too fast. He deserved the opposite of that. He deserved a slow death—a slow mutilating death. He fucking touched her. Hurt her. He'd almost killed her the first time. Took away her memory. He was going to kill her again. I wanted to take my time. Kill him slowly, the way he'd tortured her. I calmed my temper.

"What do you mean?" I asked, my tone would impress a priest.

"Her daddy's money."

I frowned. "How would killing her get you her father's money?"

"Look, as much I'm enjoying this little chit-chat, I've got places to be, people to kill, and money to claim. So, if you could just do us both a favor and drop dead, I'll be forever in your debt. Oh, wait, you don't need favors where you're going, right." He snorted out a laugh.

I pulled the trigger, the sharp sound vibrating around the room at the same time Easton jumped, grabbing his ear or rather what was left of it.

He howled for a second before glaring at me. "What the fuck? You shot my ear," he screamed as blood gushed down his neck, quickly turning his shirt bright red.

"It's only the start," I gritted out. "Now, answer the fucking question."

Groaning, he reached for his jacket he'd thrown on the counter next to him and bunched it against his ear. "Dav—Ashrika is my half-sister. Her father, my mother. Do the math." He sneered.

I thought back to my conversation with Rika. She hadn't known her father until that night she discovered the truth at Trent's place. Her mother's letter said she was kidnapped at birth.

"I can see the brain fry from here." He laughed. "You're trying to figure out this shit. Would you look at that, for once the mighty

Zayne Morrone is stumped," he scoffed. Well, kill me if you want. You're not getting anything mor—"

I pulled the trigger. He howled as his other ear joined its twin on the floor. "Wrong answer, asshole." The pain in my side flared. I bit down on the inside of my cheek to stifle it. "I will kill you, but slow torture is far worse than death and I have time. Plenty of it."

"Not if you're fucking dead before me," he snarled. "I can see you biting down on the pain. I know you, remember. We've been through far worse shit than this."

"True, but that doesn't stop me from watching you bleed to death." I cocked a brow. When he said nothing, I blew out a frustrated breath and leaned forward. "Tell me what I want, and maybe I'll grant you some mercy. Kill you faster."

He clenched his jaw then as if recognizing there was only one way out of his dilemma, answered, "I duped Raj Singh, Ashrika's biological father."

"I got that, move on."

"I was ten when Daniels, my father, kidnapped Ashrika the day after she was born. He wanted revenge on Singh for sleeping with my mother when I was six. She never got over him and Daniels took it hard and became obsessed with Singh and his family. Then he found out they were going to have twins."

"So you're not related to Ashrika?" I asked. He nodded. "She lived with you and your parents?" He nodded again. "Did Daniels hurt her?"

"No. The bastard fell in love with her. Treated her like a daughter and me like shit. Sent me to go live with my mother's sister. I swore I'd get revenge on Ashrika and I did."

Rage spiked my blood. "How?"

"I presented myself to Singh as his son. Told him I was the result of his affair with my mother. Bastard didn't even bother with a DNA test, just accepted me. Said he was sorry he hadn't done it sooner. I never told him about Ashrika. She was to be my leverage if I ever needed one," his maniacal chuckle filled the room. "It happened a lot sooner than I thought. My mother developed cancer of the pancreas. Just before her death, she told Ashrika about her true identity and wrote a letter to Singh, telling him about Ashrika and begging his forgiveness. Shocked and excited, Singh told me about it."

"Did Singh meet Ashrika?"

"Two coffees or luncheons, who the fuck cares?"

"I do. Now answer the fucking question. Or one of your balls will bat between those ears or what's left of them." I gestured to the scattered pieces of cartilage next to him.

"Yeah, Singh met with her. When he returned was blabbing about telling her name and giving her some fucking pendant. Their next meet was for him to bring her to meet her sister."

"What happened?"

"He couldn't tell Trent's wife. With the pregnancy complications crap, he feared the anxiety might be detrimental. I had to act fast." Wincing against the pain, he sank to the floor and alternated the jacket between his ears. "I hired an assassin. Arranged for the father to be incapacitated, not killed because I knew he hadn't changed his will over to me yet. Only thing was, Singh, the fucker, gave his attorney proxy and told him about Ashrika which meant she had to die. I had to wait for her to be declared dead before I inherited everything as the sole heir. That fucking attorney kept stalling, presenting evidence she was alive. All in all, I'd done well. Pretty smart, don't you think?"

"Yet here you are. About to die. Ironically, by my hand. You didn't anticipate she'd live, did you?" I mocked.

Narrowing his eyes at me, he yelled, "Fuck you, Zayne. Why the fuck did you save her? You were never the sentimental type.

Losing your touch, are you?" If it were possible for looks to kill, I would be splattered on the wall behind me.

I uttered a caustic laugh. "Maybe if you'd dumped her somewhere else, you might've gotten your way. Did you actually think setting me up would work?"

"The assassin I hired was supposed to take her out as well, then I found out you were around. That you'd finally made your presence known. I decided to take care of her my way. One stone, two birds," he grunted, wincing in pain. He closed his eyes, pressing his hands to his ears. "First, I prettied her up a little. After the boys busted her up a bit too much, it didn't look like a random attack. Heroin overdose made her look like an addict," with each word he uttered, I clenched my fist tighter and tighter until I drew blood.

"You, barbaric fuck," I snarled.

Easton looked at me, eyes wide then he snorted out a laugh. "Jesus, Zayne, did you fall for that pussy."

I replied with another bullet. His knee jumped from the impact and he wailed like fucking a bitch in heat. I smiled. "How did you find me?"

He ignored me and I cocked the gun. "A mutual friend."

There was only one mutual friend who'd give him my details, not out of spite but merely because he didn't know what a fucked-up piece of shit Easton had become. We'd been friends, the three of us—in another lifetime.

That answered the burning question of how Easton had found me, and knew in which building to dump Ashrika's body. Now the *why*? I shifted to ease the dull throb that now settled over my body. I could feel it shutting down. The bullet had either hit a nerve or some major fucking organ. If my time was up, so be it. I had no qualms about dying.

"Why me?" I asked.

Easton gritted his teeth, his eyes were wild. "Are you seriously fucking asking me that? You have no one to blame but yourself."

I sighed, the blood loss making me weaker. "Was it the money? The power? Why would you want to go down this road?" I waved the gun around the air. "This place has been empty for so long, you neglected it. You chose to walk out."

"Because of you. We had a bro code. You should have never fucked my wife and knocked her up with what was supposed to be my son." he roared.

My head jerked up, I straightened in the chair. "Is that what they told you?" Then I shook my head. "You dumb fuck. You could've just asked me—"

"Fuck you, Zayne. She was a virgin!" He yelled, his body shaking. "I was trying to respect her wishes, respect her father. And she, apparently, gave herself to you."

Before I could gauge his intention, he lunged to his side behind a table. I dropped to the floor just as he opened fire, hitting the chair. Wincing, I rolled to get out of his line of fire. I hissed when a bullet scraped my leg. I got off a couple of rounds. Then silence. I stayed down, listening for movement. Nothing.

Then, "Zayne? You okay?"

Frowning, I lifted my head and cursed. "Trent? What the fuck are you doing here?" I tried to sit up but the pain slowed my movements. Panting, I laid on the floor as Trent leaned over me. I looked at the gun in his hand. "You killed him?" incredulity lined my brow.

Slowly, he nodded. His expression a clear indication he was in shock. I doubted he'd killed a man before.

# Trent

CHEST BURNING, LUNGS heaving, heart in a palpitating mess and hands shaking, I surveyed the scene around me. When Tia threw the gun at me and rattled off the address, I hadn't expected to walk into World War fucking Three. I stared down at the man I'd just shot and paled. What the fuck was Easton doing here and why the fuck was he shooting at Zayne?

I glanced over at Zayne's still body and called out. He lifted his head, saw me and immediate shock breached his usually stiff countenance.

"What the fuck are you doing here, Trent?" he repeated when I didn't hear him the first time. The boom of my heartbeat had taken over my ability to hear.

"I have no fucking clue what I'm doing here," I finally muttered and walked over to him. I stared down at the man I'd just saved. By killing another man. "What the fuck did I just walk into, Zayne and no bullshit. I want the truth." I glanced at his white shirt now the color of red wine on one side of his body. "First, I need to get you to a hospital."

He shook his head. "Go to Rika. She needs you more than me. You're the perfect man for her."

I paused, debating whether to haul him to his feet or not. When he shook his head again, I sighed. "As much as I want to agree with you, I can't. I lied to her. Your plan to pretend you were angry with my arrival at Incognito today was impressive, I don't think it worked, though. I should've told her who I was from the get-go. She hasn't forgiven me yet." Even as I uttered the words, I wondered if I'd heard her scream 'I love you' before I ran out of Incognito, or if it was just my imagination.

"My plan worked, she bought that I was angry. Her responses told me that and she didn't get a chance to forgive you. Hell blew over, remember?" His laugh was strained, something between a chuckle and a cough.

"Don't remind me." I was still in shock that one of us, if not all three, might've been killed today.

"Look, after what we've been through, I'm not surprised at her reaction. She loves you, Trent, she just needs time to adjust. Trust me. Your lies were far holier than mine. It's better this way. She's rid of the devil before meeting him."

"What fucking devil? You're not making any sense."

He tried to push up. I crouched to his level and helped him to sit up against the wall. "I married her to get revenge."

"Revenge?" Baffled, I sat down next to him. "I don't understand."

"I'm not who you think I am, neither does Rika know for that matter."

"Why am I not surprised." My tone dripped sarcasm, but I was impatient to hear his story.

He almost knocked me on my ass when he said, "I was paid to injure her father."

"What the fuck? A killer? Are you fucking kidding me right now?" I ranted, disbelief tightening my chest.

"I was hired—"

"I got that part, move on to the why and the how or better still by who?"

"Him." He gestured to Easton's lifeless body. Somehow the revelation wasn't as shocking as I expected. In the time I'd known him, my brother-in-law's concept of family had been severely lacking.

"Shortened version. Easton is not related to Singh. His mother had an affair with Singh. His father kidnapped Rika out of revenge for the affair when Easton was young. Angry with Ashrika for taking his place, he saw an opportunity. He approached Singh and claimed he was the result of Singh's affair with his mother. Singh never questioned him. You getting all this?" Zayne rasped. I nodded. "When your wife died, he thought he'd get Singh's money but then Singh learned of Ashrika's whereabouts just before your wife's death, through a letter sent by Easton's mother."

"Jesus fucking Christ." I shoved a hand through my hair. "Sounds like a fucking family saga gone fucking weird."

"It gets worse." The look on Zayne's face told me I wouldn't like what I was about to hear. I cocked a brow. "Singh met with Ashrika. That's how she learned her real name and he gave her that pendant. The only two things that stayed with her memory. Singh planned to bring Rika to meet your wife. Easton knew his time was up. He hired an assassin to injure Singh.

"Because the estate hadn't been put into Easton's name yet?" I asked. Zayne nodded. "He needed the old man alive." I surmised as the puzzle pieces began clicking into place. My father's warning now made perfect sense. Ashrika had to come out of hiding to claim her shares.

"Only, some fucking attorney got proxy and knew about Ashrika." Zayne winced and shifted slightly. "She became a problem and—

"Let me guess, Easton hired you to kill her?" Even as I said the words, incredulity tightened my chest and I didn't want to believe it.

"I'm a trained sniper, Trent. Circumstances, I won't go into, made me a killer for hire."

I reared back. His words were like a double punch to the face. "You're fucking kidding me," I exploded, shooting up from the floor. My hands on my hips, I glared at him. "A hired killer? Jesus Christ. You're a sick fuck." My anger too far gone to care that the man was on his deathbed. "How the fuck do you live with yourself, knowing you almost killed her, knowing you were part of the reason she doesn't have a memory?" I seethed, pacing the room. Rage, vigilance, and possessiveness flared inside me.

"Easton wanted me dead and had no fucking idea I was the assassin he hired, until today," Zayne attempted pacification.

"And that makes what you did to her, fucking okay?" I bit out, my jaw ached from being clenched too tight.

"No, it doesn't." His shoulders sagged in despair.

I ignored it. My heart swung on a fucking wrecking ball. I wanted to kill him, squeeze the fucking life out of him. "I should tell her, let her know her beloved Zayne is not all that he's made out to be," I sneered.

"Don't, Trent." He held up a hand, his tone pleading. "Not for me but for her sanity."

I expelled a volatile breath. "What do mean?"

He dragged air through his mouth and exhaled through his nose. I could tell he was winded. "Don't you see? It will destroy her. The hurt will be too much. She just began living again, Trent. You gave her that. You gave her a new lease on a life that was just an empty shell. You gave her kids, a family. She's finally accepted her memory will never return and she's made peace with it. Don't take that away from her. Even though she might appear strong, deep down, she's still fragile. If her memory returns, she might handle the truth better and you can tell her then..." he trailed off, his expression desperate.

While I found it surprising that the strong man I once knew had been reduced to begging, I ground my teeth to keep from agreeing with him. But he was right. "Why the fuck would you concoct such a fucked up story about the way you found her?"

He shook his head. "I didn't. That part is true."

I frowned. "I don't understand."

"A day before I planned to take her out, Easton pulled the plug. I figured he had a change of heart. A week or so later, I found Rika in my building in the condition I described. At the time, the woman I was meant to take out ending up in my building almost on her deathbed, was too much of a coincidence not to notice the obvious. Someone planned the whole fucking thing to take me down while getting rid of her. I just didn't know who he was until today." He glanced at Easton.

"And that's where the whole fucked up idea for revenge sprung?" I asked, sarcasm spiking my words.

Zayne nodded. "Easton and I have a history not worth mentioning. He didn't know I was the assassin he hired and canceled the contract because he learned I was in town. Dumb fuck." Uttering a caustic laugh, he glared at Easton's body. "He planned for me to get caught with a dead body. Diabolical fucker that he was, he hadn't anticipated me finding her before..." Zayne broke into a coughing fit.

Regardless, my anger hadn't dissipated. "So when did your gallant side make an appearance? Or were you just biding your time then got all mushy and decided not to kill her?"

He shook his head, pulling in a raspy breath. "Sometimes, to catch a wolf you need to sacrifice the lamb. Selfishly, saving her provided me with the perfect bait to reel him in. I figured if I kept her around, whoever set me up would come looking for her. Nobody double-crosses me and gets away with it." His jaw tightened, there was no mistaking the poison in his words.

"And what happens to the bait?"

He shrugged. "Depended on whether I like them or not."

"And I'm guessing Ashrika blew your fucked up rules to kingdom come?"

We stared at each other, an avalanche of tension bubbling beneath the surface before he sighed. "I didn't anticipate the coma, memory loss, and worse. Falling in love with her."

"Is this like the confessions of a dying man," I snorted. "You use her and expect me to believe you love her. I must look like a real dick to you if you think—"

"You have every right to be angry, to hate me," he grunted.

"Angry doesn't even begin to describe what I feel right now, Zayne. Unlike you, I don't go around killing people. Although, looking at your face right now and this dumb shit." I pointed to Easton. "I wish I did."

"I know." He paused, leaning his head back against the wall. Closing his eyes, he dragged in lungsful of air.

Part of me wanted to help him, rush him to the hospital, but the other part, the one wanting to strangle the life out of him, fought my restraint.

"That first meeting after she woke from the coma," he began speaking again. "When I found her in that coffee shop, scared and desperate for someone to help save her from her own blank mind, I fell in love." He opened his eyes and I read the sincerity in them. "All thoughts of revenge fled. I gave her a secure life, kept her close so I could protect her for when he came for her, even if I couldn't have her the way I wanted. Only, Easton was under the impression she was dead. Then you appeared..." he trailed off, staring into space.

I dropped to my haunches again and his gaze met mine. "That night at the club, was it a setup? Did you arrange it?" His hesitation was all the confirmation I needed. "Why?"

"For seven years, I heard from no one. The people who worked for me had no leads as to who set me up. Then you arrived out of the blue. I had to test you, make sure—"

"I wasn't the person who hired you?" I scoffed. "And you gave no thought to her safety. The fucker could've—"

"I had it covered."

"How?" I cursed.

"Tia—"

"Seriously, you trust that fucking woman—"

"With my life," he snapped.

I wondered about their relationship. The fact she had a gun on her at the club and the way she used it, told me there was more to her than just a waitress at the restaurant. Still. I didn't question him. "She was following your instructions that night?"

He nodded. "The bouncers as well. If the fucker took it too far, they..." He appeared to rethink his words. "Let's just say he did and became fish food real quick."

My shock must've shown because he smirked like an evil son of a bitch. "You killed him?" I muttered.

"I didn't have a choice."

"What do you mean, you didn't have a choice?" I snapped. "There is a justice system that can take care of fuckers like him."

"No," the vehement shake of his head gave credence to that single word. "I had to make sure he'd never get another chance to touch Rika again. I had to make sure he didn't walk out of here alive today even if it meant my death."

I shook my head, surprised. "Even at the risk of being caught?"

"I made it my mission in life to never get caught, Trent." His gaze held mine, unblinking. "I'd do it again if I had to. Would you?" He gestured to Easton.

I glanced at the dead man. I hadn't hesitated to pull the trigger because of the threat to life. Every inch of my brain knew the answer. No. I'd done it to protect Ashrika. And I'd do it again. "You do love her, don't you?"

His laugh was low, strained. "I might possess the face of a saint and the heart of a sinner, but when it came to Ashrika, she was the light that encased my darkness, the angel that lured my pain, turning it into pleasure with just her smile alone. I'm not her hero neither am I her villain, both just fell in love...with her."

Our gazes met. And in that pregnant silence, an unspoken conversation like the night at Incognito passed between us. His look read 'it's over for me' and mine, 'not yet.' "Get the fuck up, Zayne. I'm taking you to the hospital," I grunted, leaning toward him.

"No. This is it for me."

"For fuck's sake, don't be a pussy! You're not fucking dying—not on my watch."

He snorted out a laugh, breathing hard through his nose while panting through his mouth. "You know something, Trent. I'm the kind of man mothers warn their daughters about. The kind of evil children hate in fairytales," he rasped. "I'm nothing but a cold-blooded killer. I deserve to die."

"And yet you were innocent once, I'm sure." Giving him no chance to respond, I pushed a hand under his arm, slid it along his back, and gripped at the same time pulling him to his feet. "No one is born evil, Zayne. Sometimes bloodlust is forced upon you by circumstances you can't control." Supporting his full weight, we staggered to the car. As I pulled away from the curb, Zayne reached inside his pants pocket for his phone.

A few seconds later, his instruction was pointed and terse. "Yeah. I need a clean-up, stat." When he was done giving the address, he cut the call and looked at me.

I shook my head. "I'm not even going to ask."

"You don't need to do this, you know."

My laugh lacked mirth. "I just fucking killed a man. Something I would've never thought myself capable of until I met you. Fuck, the last time I broke a law was before I married and that was fucking child's play compared to this." My hands tightened around the wheel in a vice grip. What the fuck was I thinking? I was a goddamn father. I didn't go around killing people.

"Hey," Zayne touched my arm. "Nothing's coming back to you." I shifted my gaze from the road for a second. "I won't let it." I caught the sincere promise in his eyes before he broke into a coughing fit.

"You good?" I asked, stepping on the gas.

Breathing hard, he rested his head back against the seat. "Yeah. Promise me you'll take good care of her, Trent?" he demanded but his tone lacked the usual hardness I'd become accustomed to.

"Where the fuck do you think you're going?" I barked out instead. His attempt at a laugh was weak. "Look, I have no clue what you're up to, what demons haunt your past, and what kind of evil you are, but to Ash, you're her knight in shining armor. Don't take that from her. If nothing else, live for her," I urged.

"You're her happy ever after," he replied, yet there was none of the usual sarcasm in his voice.

"But you loved her first," I countered. Our gazes met briefly. As fucked up as this situation might be to the average man, it was the truth. As simple as night became day with every sunrise, he'd loved her long before I arrived.

"And you'll love her enough for the both of us." Zayne turned his head to stare out the window, his breathing taking on a harder, faster pace.

I hit the gas, clocking speeds that would probably get me locked up but I didn't care. It was a matter of life and death. I couldn't let a piece of Ashrika die before she had a chance to live, fully and unconditionally. He was a part of her as much as I was, if not more.

# Ashrika

MY FIST PUNCHING THE palm of the other hand, my butt perched on the edge of the seat, and my legs bouncing non-stop, I stared at the corridor leading toward the operation theater. I'd been sitting there for the last thirty minutes, my head a nervous wreck since Trent's call that Zayne was hurt. Tia got me to the hospital in time but when the doors opened and they wheeled Zayne in, I could no longer breathe. Just watching them rush him off for emergency surgery, shredded my control and the tears poured, blinding me to Trent's embrace and Tia's calming words.

"Here, drink this." I looked up into those serene blues filled with tenderness. "Please, sweetheart," Trent coaxed.

I took the bottle of orange juice and slowly sipped. The cold liquid did nothing for my calm but sated the burning dryness in my mouth.

"He's going to be fine." He took one of my hands in his and brought it to his lips.

"What did the surgeon say?" I'd been too nervous to sit still when they were chatting earlier. Then, too, I'd also blocked out the conversation, not wanting to hear.

"Gunshot to the abdomen and a punctured lung. Zayne lost a lot of blood but the surgeon's confident he'll survive." Trent stood and pulled me up. He guided me to the couch at the back, sat, and patted the seat. "Come on, you need to get some sleep."

I dropped down next to him and put my head in his lap. The soft caress of his hand through my hair pulled me under. My eyes fluttered open to blinding fluorescent lights. Squinting, I turned slightly. His eyes closed and head against the backrest, Trent slept with my head still on his lap. I sat up and he moved but didn't wake. My throat was so dry it felt like I'd swallowed shards of glass. Rising, I made my way to the bathroom. When I returned, the nurse we'd met on arrival came through a door and smiled.

"He's out of surgery," she whispered.

My heart jumped. Excitement stealing my breath. "Can I see him?"

She nodded and gestured for me to follow her through another door. A few minutes later, I stared through a window at Zayne.

"He's sedated but once he comes around, you can go in." She patted my arm.

I had no idea how long I stayed outside his window pacing until I feared I'd wear a hole in my shoe when a familiar sound filled my ears. No! I'd been in a hospital long enough to recognize it. Code blue! My pulse soared. Startled, I watched as nurses and doctors hurried past me. I followed them. Silently, I prayed. Not that room. Please. I froze. My mind switching to code blue, my heartbeat matching the cadence of the resounding alarm through the hallway. Then they were dashing into Zayne's room.

Adrenalin pushed fear into me. I clenched the front of my dress in my fist. "No," it came out as a whisper. Then another much louder scream, "No!" "I grabbed one of the nurse's arms as she flew by. "What's happening."

"Cardiac arrest," she called over her shoulder, ducking into Zayne's room.

I tried following but another nurse barred me from entering. Moving to the window looking into his room, I balked. Nurses and doctors crowded his bed.

"Please, please, please," the incessant prayer filled my ears as my clenched fists pounded the glass. Pinpricks of heat stabbed my skin. Sweat pooled in my arms, beaded my upper lid and brow. "Don't you leave me, Zayne," I mouthed over and over.

I was close to dropping to my knees when I felt Trent's arms snake around me. I spun around and the warmth of his embrace closed around me, shielding me, offering me protection, comfort. Tears burned down my cheeks, searing my skin with pain. Several minutes passed and calm begrudgingly settled over the ward, he sat me down on a chair.

"Wait here, I'm going to get an update, okay?" He lifted my chin to look at him. "Okay, sweetheart."

I nodded, staring into eyes filled with tenderness. My body was ready to drop from exhaustion, looking at Trent, I could tell he was dead on his feet. This was taking its toll on him too. I covered his hand. "Thank you for being here."

"There's nowhere else I'd rather be." With that, he went after the nurse who'd brought me to Zayne's room.

Fifteen minutes later, I walked into Zayne's room. I stood taking in everything. I heard the soft beep of the heart monitor, the melancholy drone of the ventilator, the muted buzz of the air-conditioning, and finally the soft breaths of a man I loved. I clasped my neck, telling myself to breathe, to clear my vision of tears so that I could see him. I blinked, letting the final pool fall.

Eyes, red and puffy, stared up at me, his breathing labored. His expression nothing like the austere man I knew. "Hi," he whispered.

I balked, my insides on a crazy rollercoaster I couldn't stop even though I held the controls. This man owned a piece of my heart and he was taking it with him. I swallowed and covered his hand with mine, gently squeezing. "Don't you dare leave me," words finally came.

His laugh was low, almost non-existent. "I wouldn't dream of it."

"Why?" I whispered. "Why did you have to go after that man?" My heart spasmed once more even as I tried to ignore the pain.

"You could've been hurt," he murmured.

"And this is so much better?" I scowled making him smile as a nurse approached.

"I just need a minute to administer some medication, if you'll just wait outside, please."

Her stern façade was infuriating. Regardless, I nodded, squeezing his hand before I left the room. Trent was waiting for me as only immediate family was allowed inside.

"How's he doing?" He pulled me into a tight hug that I needed.

"I'm not sure. They say it's too soon to tell and they'll know more in an hour." I sighed and turned as someone approached.

Natasha, Zayne's assistant stood there. Having only met her a few times, when she dropped by to pick up stuff for him, I didn't know her. Zayne made sure his work-life never crossed over into his personal life.

"Hi," she greeted us both as another woman walked in behind her. "How is he, Rika?"

I scowled at the familiarity she didn't deserve and shrugged. "They're not allowing visitors yet."

Not sure if she mistook my irritation for pain, I was surprised when she gestured to the woman next to her. "This is my partner, Stacey."

I gawked, she was bringing her partner to see her lover. How cruel. Wait. Her partner was a woman? What was I missing?

"I know that look, Rika." At my frown, she added, "he told me what he did. It was a lie. We never had a relationship. I'm happily married enough to speak in front of Stacey."

My jaw dropped so hard it actually bounced back with a snap. "Zayne lied?" She nodded. "Why?"

"You'll have to ask him that. I do know, though, he's been in love with you for years."

Next to me, Trent stiffened as much I did. I glanced up at him but there was only tender affection in his smile.

Several minutes later when I could go back into Zayne's room, I asked, "Why did you lie about Natasha?"

"Because I needed you to be happy."

"But I was happy."

He sighed. "Were you, baby? Happy being my friend? Happy being in a marriage that was in name only?"

"Yes, and you could've changed all of that," I mumbled. "You could've made it something more but you chose not to. Why?"

He smiled. "The morning I put that ring on your finger." He pointed to the jade ring I wore. "I was going to tell you how I truly felt. Then, Trent walked out and I noticed the way you looked at him. Almost like you recognized him and something told me to wait, to find out who he was and I did."

"But you should've said something, I deserved to know," I cried. "We were married long before he arrived, yet you gave me up without a fight," I didn't keep the accusation out of my voice. "I loved—love you Zayne."

"And what about Trent?" I stared at him, unsure what answer to give, never expecting my heart to split me in two. How was it possible to have such strong feelings for both?

"You love him, Rika and he loves you. After all that has happened, and even if I kept the truth from you. You don't have to admit it, it's written all over your face." He coughed and I startled. The tears in full force, blurring my vision. "It doesn't matter how long we've lived, baby, what matters is how much we've lived in that lifetime."

"Don't you dare say that to me, Zayne. You were...are my life...don't you dare leave me, I need you."

"You have no idea what you gave me, unknowingly. You made me live. You gave me a second chance at life."

I looked at him, confusion creasing my brow. "I don't understand."

"You don't need to." He swallowed, searching my face. "I love you, Rika. Always have and always will. Don't you ever forget that, okay?"

"That's unfair. How can you tell me that now?" I cried, the tears relentless.

"Because I needed you to find love on your own. I couldn't have you settling just for my sake." His breath came out short raspy pants. He closed his eyes, his grip tight on my hand.

"Zayne, please."

"I need you to leave now, Miss. Please."

I turned to the male nurse behind me. "He is going to be all right, isn't he?"

The man's expression remained blank, but his eyes spoke a thousand words. He couldn't make that promise to me. I looked at Zayne once more.

He opened his eyes again and smiled. "I need to see Trent, Rika." He looked at the nurse. "Please let him in, it's important." The nurse nodded. "Go get him, angel."

I did.

# Trent

I GLANCED UP AS ASHRIKA came running down the passage. Shooting up from my seat, I caught her in my arms. She collapsed against my chest, her sobs uncontrolled. "What's wrong, Ash?" I held her tight.

She leaned back, her red-rimmed eyes searching mine. "He's dying, Trent. He's leaving me."

*Fuck.* My wistfulness dropped like an anvil, and all that was left was anger. *He can't fucking die.* I reined it in. "I'm sorry, sweetheart." My fists clenched at her back, squeezing hard as though I could wipe away her pain.

"He wants to see you," her voice cracked on the words.

"Let's go."

She stepped back, shaking her head. "He wants to see you alone."

"Are you going to be okay?" After she nodded, I wiped her tears with my palms and kissed her brow. "He's going to be fine, sweetheart." Her silent gaze roved over my face, and I wished to God my words hadn't lacked conviction just to ease her pain. Together we walked back to his room. She clasped my hand tight just before I opened the door. I glanced back at her, turned, and pulled her into an embrace, caressing the back of her head a moment longer. "Better?" When she nodded, I kissed the top of her head and released my hold.

"Trent?" She stopped me. I looked at her. "I love you." I blinked, not sure I heard right. "I love you," she whispered again, and every inch of my body tingled.

I wasn't sure if it was the right moment to be happy. But I was. I took a step closer to her. "I love you too."

She palmed my cheek. "If you're wondering why now it's because I screamed it out before you raced off at Incognito. I wasn't sure you'd heard me. I needed to say it again, just to make sure. He found a friend in you. Let him see it."

I dropped a light kiss on her cheek and left. Inside the room, I stared at the man swathed in the pale grasp of pain. "Zayne?"

He opened his eyes. "You good?"

My laugh was low. "You're asking me that?"

"Trust me. Takes a lot to take this fucker down." His smile was weak. "There are times we set out on one path and inevitably end up going down another, one we don't see until that fork is upon us and we change direction at the last minute. That's what happened to us and I wanted to say thank you."

I was still confused. "For."

"In some weird fucked up way, we became friends, something I rarely do. I know it's not how we started but I'm glad to have met you."

"I guess you never can predict what tomorrow will bring, no matter how much planning you do. And for what it's worth, I'm glad I met you too."

"I know I don't need to ask this of you, but promise me, she won't cry. That her heart will know no sorrow?"

"That's one tall order, considering you're the one making her cry and feeding her sorrow with this bullshit plan to die," I scoffed.

He chuckled. "And there's the 'say-it-like-is-Trent.' That's the one thing I admired about you. You go in guns blazing, take whatever the fuck you want, others be damned, yet you have the fucking heart of a lover."

Grinning, I shrugged. "What can I say? Women want me, and men want to *be* me. Unfortunately, there's only one woman for me and she's got me by the balls."

"I'm glad to hear that. That said, I need to ask you a favor."

"Sure."

He gestured to the chair. "Take a seat."

## Ashrika

**ONE MONTH LATER...**

"Ash?" I turned at the sound of Trent's voice and smiled. "You okay?"

I nodded. "I'm sorry."

He frowned. "For?"

When he reached my side, I slipped my hands around his waist and rested my head on his chest. "For locking you out. Neglecting you. Acting like you didn't count, like you didn't exist."

"Hey." He held me away from him. "If you'd done this sooner, then I would've believed you either felt nothing for him or you were pretending you'd stopped grieving." He palmed my cheeks. "I'm not going anywhere and for however long you need, I'll wait. Zayne wasn't just some random hookup or a guy you dated for a month. He saved you, gave you life, I wouldn't expect anything less from you. You can take as much time as you need."

"How do you always know what to say?"

He shrugged. "When you truly love someone, words and emotions come naturally, without thought, without direction, without pretense. I want to spend the rest of my life with you, Ash even if that means keeping a part of Zayne with us, I don't care. Fuck, the man weaved his way into my life too and I guess I'm standing here today because of him. He brought you to me the day he saved you and then he gave you to me fully when he left. He will forever be part of our lives."

"I don't understand."

"Ashrika Morrone Shaw."

I blinked. "You're asking me to marry you?"

"Yes. When you're ready."

Realization dawned. "You're asking me to keep Zayne's name as well?"

"Yes. When you're ready," he repeated before he lowered his head and captured my lips in a slow, tantalizing kiss, meant to coax and calm. "For now, are you ready to do this?" he asked when he pulled back.

I glanced around. We stood in the apartment I'd shared with Zayne. Trent brought me there to show me something. "I still don't understand why we're here." I sat down at the breakfast nook.

Trent stepped away from me and picked up the Van Gogh *'The Starry Night'* painting he'd retrieved from Zayne's bedroom since I refused to go in there. "He made me promise that you got this painting before you sold the apartment."

Still frowning, I stared at the artwork. It'd been a month since I'd come back home. A month and one week since Zayne's funeral. A month and two weeks since he took a bullet meant for me. He'd left me. My tears had long since dried up, but that didn't mean my heart couldn't cry. It did.

I shifted my gaze to the man holding the painting. The other man in my life. The one who'd stayed. My pillar of strength. The man who'd held and consoled me every day that I'd shared tears for another love. I smiled at him. My savior, my liberator, and more importantly. My first and only true love.

Can a woman love two men at the same time? Yes. Without a doubt. I did. And they loved me back, loved me hard, and loved me unconditionally. Yes. A woman can love two men at the same time. I did. I loved Zayne Morrone but I loved Trent Shaw more. And he'd not only just asked me to marry him but to keep Zayne's name. What man did that? I guess the one that loved you just as hard.

"Sweetheart?" the husky call gently coaxed my attention.

Standing, I neared him and stared at the painting. "I don't understand why this was important."

Trent held up the artwork. He checked the front then examined the back. "Get me a knife."

I retrieved a small knife from the kitchen drawer and handed it to him. He laid the painting face down on the dining table and with gentle manipulation, lifted the canvas cover at the back. When he pulled it back, a note was stuck inside the edge of the frame. Trent pried it free, gave it a quick scan, and held it out.

"It's for you."

Frowning, I took the note and read it.

*Hey, baby.*

*If you're reading this, chances are I'm dead or running behind a woman far less beautiful than you. Either way, I'm sorry I left you before I had a chance to give you what you truly desired. Your past. While I can't promise to give you everything, I hope the little I have managed to uncover will give you some peace. Remember what I said, though. 'It's time to write a new story. You might enjoy it.' And I'm sure Trent will give that to you. He's gold where I was just silver.*

*If after reading this, you're still sitting on the fence of whether you want to know about your past or not—go back to that place where we saw the little girl sitting on the fence. She might have a story to tell.*

*I love you, angel—always have and always will—wherever I am.*

*Zayne*

I flipped the page over as though it had more and looked up at Trent. "Can you take me?"

He nodded and lifted the painting. "What do you want to do with this?"

"Put it back in his room for—" I broke off as my gaze fell to the bottom right of the artwork. I frowned.

"What's wrong?"

I pointed to the bottom. "These initials, DC, they shouldn't be here. I'm no expert but this is a Van Gogh painting. It costs an arm and a leg, if not a whole body to buy."

"It's another Zayne secret we will never know." Trent gave me a gentle smile. "You want to go?" I nodded.

An hour or so later, I stood outside the quaint gallery Zayne had brought me to visit. I hesitated on the first step, swallowing back the dryness that settled there the second I'd read Zayne's letter.

Trent placed his arm on my lower back and gently massaged. "You okay." It was amazing how he knew exactly what I needed and when.

"Yes."

When we entered, my gaze automatically snapped to the wall where the painting of the little girl had hung. It wasn't there. Disappointed, I neared the counter at the back.

"Hello, dear," Mary looked up.

"Hello, Mary, do you remember me. I was in here almost two—"

"Of course, I remember you." She beamed. "Zayne came back, you know," she said then noticing Trent for the first time, offered him a pleasant smile. "You must be Trent."

I blinked. "How do you know?"

She chuckled. "Zayne said that the next time you came back here it would be with your husband, Trent."

I blanched and Trent gave my waist a gentle squeeze, drawing me closer to his side. "How did Zayne know I'd return here with Trent?" I asked. "And when did he come back?"

With one hand on her hip, she tapped her lip, trying to remember. "I think it was the week after your visit if I'm not mistaken. He met my daughter. Hang on a sec, let me get her." She stepped through a door at her rear.

"You okay?" Trent leaned in to whisper.

I nodded and a minute later the door opened and a younger woman stepped out. The second her gaze landed on me, she froze. Shock evident in her wide eyes and I immediately tensed. She knew who I was.

"Davina?" She approached me, her steps slow. "Oh, my God, it's been ages since I've seen you?"

"You know me?" I asked, apprehension and excitement quickening my pulse.

"Yes, oh, wait. Zayne mentioned the memory loss. Come on." She gestured to a sitting area to one side of the room. "I think you might have a few questions for me."

I glanced up at Trent and he gave me a reassuring smile. We followed her and after we were seated and Trent and I declined her offer for a drink, she leaned toward me.

"So, I'm Susan by the way and you must be Trent?" She smiled at him and he nodded before her gaze returned to me. "Zayne mentioned you'd suffered memory loss and that you'd come looking for answers. I must say, Zayne and Trent are a huge step up from that lowlife you had to put up with." At my baffled look, she slapped a hand to her brow and chuckled. "I'm sorry. Let me start from the beginning. So, your name is—was Davina."

"Davina," I whispered the foreign name.

"Does it ring any bells?" Trent took my hand in his giving it a gentle squeeze.

I shook my head, surprisingly not disappointed.

"You're an artist," Susan drew my gaze.

"An artist?"

"The paintings you loved of the little girl. Those are yours."

I blinked. That revelation struck a chord. Now, I understood my keen eye for art. "They are?"

She nodded. "You wanted to make it a career, but he held you back."

"Who?"

"Easton Daniels."

At the name, Trent cursed.

"My brother?" I said with a shaky breath.

"He was never your real brother. He just duped your real father." His voice tight, he gave my hand another gentle squeeze.

"I don't understand. Why? How?" I was at a loss for the right words.

Mary arrived with a tray. She handed me a cup. "Drink up, love. It's chamomile, it will help soothe that pain you're carrying. It's a recent loss, isn't it?" I stared at her, surprised by her perception, and nodded. "Time." She palmed my cheek. The motherly gesture overwhelmed me and my eyes watered. She handed Trent a mug. "Coffee."

"Thank you," we both said together.

I looked at Trent. "What did you mean about Easton not being my brother?"

"Easton's mother had an affair with your father. Filled with jealousy, Easton's father kidnapped you the day you were born. Instead of hurting you like he promised his wife, he fell in love with you and raised you as his daughter but ill-treated his son. That made Easton jealous. He presented himself to your father and lied he was the result of your father's affair with his mother. Your father, gentleman that he is, believed him and began treating him like a son. Then your father discovered you were alive when Easton's mother, on her deathbed, sent your father a letter. Easton found out and planned your death."

With each word Trent uttered, cold fingers of fear and shock wrapped themselves around my lungs, squeezing until I couldn't breathe. Noting my struggle, he sat forward and rubbed my lower back.

"It's over, sweetheart, no one is going to hurt you, ever. Zayne and I made sure of that."

I frowned but the look on his face told me I shouldn't ask him anything. With all the happenings surrounding Zayne, I'd neglected to ask what had gone down. I'd been too caught up in my misery of losing him to think about anything else. My love for Trent grew with each passing day and now looking at him I acknowledged just how good he was for me, and just how much he loved me in return. Not revealing those horrid details sooner meant he gave me time to grieve. I nodded, swallowing to gain back my control.

"Before Easton approached your father, he made you work for him," Susan said.

"Work for him? How?"

Leaning back in her seat, her expression tense, I had the feeling I wouldn't like what she was about to tell me. "He made you forge expensive paintings, which they sold on the black market."

"What?" The cup rattled in the saucer I held. Trent took the china from my hand.

"I'm sorry to be the one to tell you this, Davina." Susan gave me a small smile. "Easton belonged to a crime syndicate involved in the theft of artifacts and expensive artwork. When he discovered your talent for painting, he and his buddies decided to use you for their gain."

"Oh, my God, I'm a criminal." My hands trembled and my lungs closed for a second time.

"Not by choice," Trent's soft words caressed my anxiety. I looked at him and his gentle smile coaxed me to calm down.

"If that was the case, why didn't I go to the police? Seek help?" I whispered, my heart in my mouth that I'd soiled beautiful art pieces with my skill.

"He threatened to kill your parents." My shock must have registered on my face because she leaned forward and grasped my hand.

"They were his parents too?" I gasped.

She nodded. "He was involved with some rough people so scaring you into believing he'd kill them was easy for him until he decided to approach your real father and pretend to be his son."

"Easton hired a killer to have your father incapacitated and you killed," Trent added.

"Wow. This is all sounding like a dramatic crime movie and I'm the main character." I shook my head, trying to drink it all in.

Noting my distress, he handed me the cup of tea. "Drink."

Slowly, I sipped the tea, trying to digest everything I'd just heard. When I set the cup and saucer on the side table, I looked at Susan. "How do you know all of this? Were we friends? How did you get my paintings?"

She smiled. "You agreed to do what Easton wanted, provided he allowed you to paint. He decided to make more money off you by selling your artwork. The first time he brought me your paintings, I fell in love with all five and it so happened that day we had an event here. Some tourists saw your paintings behind the counter as I hadn't put them up yet and they asked if they could buy them. And that's how I started selling paintings of an unknown artist until one day, two years later, you arrived here. We had tea, seated in these very chairs and you told me what happened. I wasn't sure how to help because it meant putting you and your parents in danger. Then six months later, I stopped receiving your paintings and I couldn't get hold of Easton."

Hearing my past unfold, should've elicited a more passionate response than the simple deflated look on my face. I figured I owed my calm to Trent's firm fingers laced with mine. The occasional squeeze as she spoke reminded me he was there for me and that I should just treat her divulgence as a story. It was Davina's story, not mine. I was Ashrika Morrone and no longer possessed Davina's mind, or past for that matter. Zayne asked me to write a new story and I had, with two beautiful men at the helm. Even with the slight edit that took one away from me, I still had one beautiful soul at my side. Trent and I had plenty of blank pages to fill. Not only had he given me freedom but love and two gorgeous children and I intended to lavish them with all the affection they'd missed from their mother.

When I could finally speak, I asked, "the paintings? Any reason why it always included a little girl in them. Did I ever mention anything?"

Susan nodded, her smile soft. "You mentioned that every time you closed your eyes, you would dream of a little girl. Each dream was different. Sometimes you two would walk in the park, sometimes sit on a swing together, and sometimes you would run in the fields. And every time you woke, you would paint a picture of that dream. The gestures of the little girl pointing, standing, sitting, smiling, looking for something in the paintings. It was you capturing her expressions of what you two did together."

"When Susan told me the story, I told her that maybe a soul or someone in your life was reaching out to you. Someone you probably didn't know in reality but existed in your subconscious. A twin perhaps?" Mary had approached while Susan spoke.

Next to me, Trent tensed. I felt the pressure in his grasp. Our eyes met and without speaking I knew what he'd felt. Krisha.

"Was there someone?" Mary asked as if she'd picked up on our silent communication.

I looked at her, nodding. "I had a twin sister. His wife. She died at childbirth a couple of weeks before I met with my ill-timed fate. Easton left me for dead, Zayne saved me, and I spent almost four years in a coma. Trent believed I was his dead wife the first time he saw me since he had no idea she had a twin and neither did I."

He sighed, raking a hand through his hair. "Krisha had the same dreams. We just didn't understand what they meant, and no one could tell her. She decided to accept it for what it was, some angel looking over her."

This time, I squeezed his hand, telling him I felt his pain too. We'd both lost someone we loved and we were both stronger for it, because of each other.

"Wow," Susan's thrill made me smile before she said, "When, and only if you want to, would you let me sell your paintings if you start painting again?"

I laughed, my first in many days. "I will, and yes, you can." Then something clicked. "The initials at the bottom of the paintings read DC and I know the family surname I lived with was Daniels, do you perhaps know what DC stands for?"

Susan nodded. "Davina *Croire.*" At my baffled look she added, "Van Gogh was your favorite artist and one of his languages of choice was French. When you began painting you chose something in keeping with both your lives. Croire is French for 'Believe' You always believed everything would turn out for the best."

"And it did." Laughter bubbled out my throat and had Trent smiling. "Wow." Fascinated, I palmed my cheeks. I now understood the forged Van Gogh painting Zayne kept. All this time a little piece of my past lived with us. I looked at Susan. "There's a Van Gogh painting at home that—"

"'*The Starry Night'* was your first forged painting. Zayne didn't provide me with the clues about how he got it, only that when he walked in here and recognized the initials on your paintings, he began piecing the puzzle together."

"Wow." I blinked. "He knew and never mentioned it."

"Because he couldn't get your hopes up without having all the facts, sweetheart," Trent said.

I nodded then reached for Susan's hand. "I can't tell you how glad I am that I met you then because of what you've given me today, I can't tell you the value you've added to my life and I appreciate you." I stood and Trent followed.

Standing, Susan laughed. "I'm just glad we were able to help. Now it's time to write your new story. You'll probably love it."

I startled. "Those words," I whispered.

"Zayne said to tell you that after I'd given you every bit of information on your past. At the time I had no idea what he meant, now I do. I wish you all the best, Davina."

"Ashrika." And at the tilt of her head, I added. "My name is Ashrika Morrone Shaw." I heard Trent's sharp inhale and looked at him. "Yes."

His smile was indescribable, more so the twinkle in his eyes. I'd missed it and now I was ready to reap its benefits along with his love. "One more stop," he whispered as we walked out.

I no longer needed to ask where. I'd follow him anywhere.

An hour and a half later, I stood back as Trent pulled opened the door to a storage facility. And as he flicked the light switch, I gasped, taking in the neatly designed room made to look like a little girl's castle. Scattered around the entire room sat gifts in all shapes and sizes, some wrapped and others not. I walked forward and fingered them. They all had labels. A gift for every birthday, Christmas, and various other school gifts ranging from age one to age twenty-two.

Laughing, I turned to Trent. "I don't understand."

"It looks like that for every gift they bought Krisha, your parents bought you one as well, probably waiting for the day you came back."

"They really loved me."

He nodded as I neared a dresser that held various jewel pieces. My gaze fell to a pendant similar to mine, only the other half. I picked it up and held it close to mine, puzzled. Trent neared me and took the loose half and did something with mine still attached to my neck. When his hands dropped, I gasped. The two halves fitted together perfectly.

"Wow."

"Your parents bought these for your nineteenth birthdays. When Krisha and I married. One half was meant for you to keep while the other half you were to give to your true love or husband."

"Krisha gave you hers?" I asked. He nodded. "Nicky mentioned you had one like mine and it's weird how I forgot to ask you about it." I unclipped the loose half of my pendant, opened Trent's hand, and placed it in his palm. "This is for you. My true love."

Smiling, he fingered the piece. "You sure you want me to have this?"

"Serendipity." Slipping my arms around his neck, I pressed my body close to his and drew his head to mine. "Kiss me, Trent Shaw."

"With pleasure, Mrs. Shaw."

As we stood there in a castle made by parents I didn't know, warmth spread through my body making me lightheaded. In a space of a few months, I found love, passion, and family. What more could I ask for? Nothing.

I remembered the day Zayne asked me to leave and never come back. He'd hurt me only to hide his love from me.

Then I remembered the day I left Trent's house after discovering the truth. He'd hurt me only to hide his past from me.

And me, I'd hurt myself by hiding my true self, my true desires.

In a way, all three of us pretended just to make the other happy.

Suitably incognito.

Not just me, or Trent, or Zayne. But all three of us.

They say the truth will set you free. In my case, lies had not only set me free. It gave me life, love, and new memories, I'd never want to forget.

# Trent

**THREE MONTHS LATER...**

"Daddy?"

I turned away from the beam I was hammering and looked at my daughter. She sat cross-legged on the grass in the shadow of the newly-erected tree house I'd finally gotten round to building for her and Nicky. More her than Nicky since he seemed to be preoccupied lately with following Ashrika around the house.

"Yes, Pixie?"

"Do you think mommy will be happy now?"

Frowning, I thought back to the conversation Ashrika and I had a week ago with the kids. I tried to explain the whole twin angle to them but because I'd initially lied about her being a friend, they didn't understand. Figuring it was best not to confuse them, we told them our plans to marry. I found it strange there were no questions about why she looked like mommy. They'd merely punched the air with an excited 'yay' and run off.

So, Neha's unexpected statement, threw me. I set down the hammer I'd been using to nail the last rung to the ladder on the tree, crossed over to her side and dropped to my haunches. "What do you mean, Pixie?"

She took a moment to lace up the rest of her doll's dress and looked at me. "You said fairytales don't come true and mommy said they can if I believe." She shoved aside her bangs and gave me one of her deep dimpled smiles. "I believed, daddy. I believed so hard and it came true."

Stunned speechless, I had no idea what to say, or what to think. When I could finally swallow against the lump sitting in my throat,

I sat down next to her and palmed her cheeks. "Can you explain to me, please, Pixie how you believed?"

She nodded. "In my last letter, mommy said that I had to help her. She said that you were the perfect daddy to us and to her. She said you needed a beautiful princess to live in your castle with you. To take care of you and make you happy."

My heartbeat staggered for just a moment as I remembered my conversation with Neha the first night I saw Ashrika. Was fate set on playing with my emotions?

"Mommy said she was your soulmate but she had to go away. She said I had to help her find you another one who would make you smile wider, make you laugh like there was no tomorrow and cry tears of happiness and sadness. When Ashrika came to visit us that first time, I knew she was the one, I knew she was your soulmate, your perfect princess like mommy said she would be."

I gulped air quickly into my lungs as I tried hard to breathe. "How, baby?" I whispered.

"At the farm when you fell in the shit—oops." She slammed a hand to her mouth. I laughed and eased her hand off her mouth, nodding it was okay. She continued speaking, "when you fell trying to help Ashrika and then when we all had the food fight in the kitchen, and you played too. You never laughed liked that before, daddy. It was fun but you were smiling and laughing differently. And when she left you and we came from grandma's you were crying, you were sad just like mommy said you would be."

I thought back to that day Ashrika found out the truth about her identity and how she'd reacted. It was the first time in my life since losing Krisha, I'd cried so hard that when the kids returned, I couldn't hide my tears from them no matter how hard I tried. Both of them had hugged me which I found ironic given I was the parent, I needed to comfort them and they'd comforted me.

"And when you told us you were going to marry Ashrika, you cried that day, you cried happy tears. You see, daddy, mommy was right and I believed for you and it came true."

"Fuck." I pulled her into my chest, holding tight until she could barely breathe.

She finally leaned back, and trailed her little fingers across my face then touched her wet cheeks too. "Are we crying happy tears?" I nodded, too emotionally stuffed to speak, and grabbed her to my chest again.

"That looks like the perfect hug, can we join?"

I looked behind me to find Ashrika and Nicky standing there, hand in hand. Their tears told me they'd heard the conversation. I nodded to them and stretched out my free arm. They both fell to grass and pushed into my embrace until we all fell over. Within seconds we burst out laughing and I pulled both my kids to my chest.

"You guys are the best and I love you with all my heart."

"We too, daddy," they mumbled in unison when they pulled back.

"Can we go see the tree house now?" Nicky asked.

"First, daddy owes me money for cursing just now." Neha held out her hand.

I chuckled at her vigilance. "Credit?" She nodded.

Laughing, they both scooted up to the house. Nicky on the rope and Neha up the ladder. With a soft sigh, I turned and pulled the woman who'd made my life complete, into the crook of my arms. "I love you."

"I love you too." She stared up at me. "It seemed like my sister was the ultimate romantic?"

"She was, and I had no idea what she'd written in their last letters now I can understand why they didn't want to show it to me. It seems like both were for me and they had a mission to complete." Grinning, I traced a slow finger over her lips.

"Yep, make their arrogant father fall in love again," she teased.

"It's because I was arrogant that you're lying here, in my arms on the grass on a bright sunny day when you would be locked in your restaurant, sweating for hungry diners."

"Hey, don't diss my diners." She punched my arm playfully. "If it wasn't for them, you wouldn't be sitting here, holding me in your arms." She laughed.

Somehow, I doubted that. "Serendipity, sweetheart." I captured her mouth in a soft kiss, knowing that fate had, in fact, had a plan for me all this time, it just hadn't told me what it was or more importantly, how intricate my love life would be. And I'd never change a damn thing about it.

# Ashrika

**THREE MONTHS AND ONE week later...**

Cleaning up the cake plates, glasses, and cutlery, I glanced over at Trent. He stood outside Enigma on the deck overlooking the port with Nicky and Neha. They were attempting to fly the kites I'd brought from a recent trip to India.

I'd come up with this idea to visit one country every month to learn new ways and cultures to build on my ever-growing bank of memories. Trent and I had drawn up a schedule that included places we could do together as a couple, a family, and me alone. I had no idea why I decided to start the whole plan with India, perhaps it had something to do with my heritage. Whatever it was, it had heightened my adventurous streak and I couldn't wait for the next visit.

We'd just celebrated my real birthday, my first since waking from the coma. We'd never known my actual birthday and Zayne had made me pick a random date I liked, and we'd celebrate it as my birthday. Laughing at the memory, I stacked the last of the dishes in Leah's hands and headed for the bathroom.

"Can I go in alone? Please. I won't be long."

I frowned as I came upon a beautiful dark-haired woman around my age begging a burly guy to let her use the bathroom alone. "Excuse me," I tapped his shoulder. "Can you read the sign? It says, ladies. And you don't look like a lady to me, mister."

"Move along, lady, this here got nothing to do with you." He turned away to push the woman into the bathroom.

"The fact that you're standing in my restaurant, makes it my business. So I'll ask nicely. Step aside and let the lady do her lady business or I'll be forced to kick you out on your ass." Jesus, was that me? When had I become this fearless? I held back my chuckle.

"You and which army?" he sneered, turning away.

"Ever heard the one called Help! Rape!" I matched his sneer.

He faced me again and I caught the distinct flare of his eyes as he looked over my shoulder. "Fine. Ladies it is." He took a step back, hands up, palms out in apology. "I'll wait here for you," he said to the woman.

Frowning, I glanced over my shoulder. There was no one there. I could, however, have sworn the sudden sense of being watched floated over me. I did a full three-sixty and came up empty. The bathrooms were designed such that you had to walk out of the dining area into a glass-encased structure. It overlooked a portion of the harbor and the open water.

Ignoring the feeling, I pressed my thighs together to hold in my pee with a little chuckle and entered the bathroom. Done, I exited the stall to find the other woman washing her hand.

Our gazes met in the mirror and a tentative smile hovered around her lips. "Can I ask you a favor?" she whispered.

At my nod, she leaned closer. I sensed her fear even before she spoke. Without meaning to, I scanned her face and what little I could see of her body beneath a mid-thigh summer dress, for signs of trauma. There was none apart from the haunting look in her eyes. "Would you please give someone a message for me?"

"Are you okay, honey?"

"Shh, I don't have time, that man will barge in here if I'm not quick."

"Sure. Tell me."

"Tell Rayden, *where the mountain meets the seas and trees bloom orange against the night, he might find me there. Once.*"

I frowned at the cryptic message and before I could ask her for more, she was gone. Giving no thoughts to my action, I raced out the bathroom, searching for her. Quickly scanning the restaurant, I cursed when I didn't see her. My legs on speed, I ran out into the parking lot in time to see her being helped into the back seat of a black SUV. Breathing hard, I barely took two steps before the vehicle sped off within seconds of her burly companion jumping into the passenger seat.

"Ash?" Turning, I waited as Trent neared me. "What's wrong, sweetheart, you look like you've seen a ghost?" Tension immediately gripped the frown lines in his face.

Raking a hand through my open hair, I shook my head. "Would you find it odd that I was given a cryptic message for your cousin?"

"Rayden?"

I nodded and quickly relayed what transpired since arriving at the bathroom.

He paled. "Zena!" Cursing, he searched for his phone. "Come on." He grabbed my hand and hurried back into the restaurant.

"What's going on," I asked, my panic full-blown. "Who's Zena?"

"Give me a sec, and I'll explain," he grabbed his phone off the table we'd been sitting at and within seconds of dialing, someone answered, "Ray. You're not going to believe this."

After the call, he turned to me. "Sit. I'll explain. Rayden's on his way."

# Zayne

**THREE MONTHS AND ONE week later, the same day just outside Enigma.**

I watched her...Beautiful Ashrika.

The angel who'd come into my life for the wrong reasons and ended up staying for the right ones. The woman who'd given me a chance to live, love, smile, and be whole again. The woman who'd made my smoke and mirrors past, solid, defined, and acceptable. And the woman who should've been mine. Still, she was with whom she belonged.

Trent Shaw.

A formidable opponent and an admirable friend, two things I would've never hoped to encounter in my life. But I did. Our tango for the love of a woman was worth every damn step. Grinning, I stared, waiting to see his response. He looked up and glanced around as if he knew they were being watched before his gaze zeroed in on me. He smiled like he could see me.

"When are you going to start living?"

I turned to find Tia at my rear. "I am living."

"By spending every day here, watching over her," she snorted. I knew she meant well. "It's been three months, Zayne."

I nodded and smiled at the one woman I could trust with my life. Katarina Petrov aka Tia Ramone, my friend, my partner, and Ashrika's bodyguard. "I saw your little scare tactic outside the bathrooms, just now. I'm guessing Rika didn't see you threaten him." She nodded. "Did the fucker recognize you?"

"He did."

"Think he's going to be a problem for her?" I never trusted those fuckers.

"I think they've got their hands full already."

I frowned. "Who is she?"

"Zena Sen."

"The dead girl?" I asked. Tia nodded. "Do we need to get involved?"

"Let me do some digging, I'll call you. And you do know I'll call if Rika's in any kind of trouble, right?"

"I know you will."

"But, you want to make sure?" She nudged my shoulder with hers.

"She's the reason why I lived even after dying, Tia." I inhaled on a long ragged breath.

"Exactly." She smiled. "You haven't begun to live again. You need to."

I glanced away, watching Ashrika hand her daughter an ice-cream. They laughed before she dotted the child's nose with the treat. She moved around to feed Trent some as well and my heart staggered when he pulled her in for a kiss.

"He's good for her, you know."

I shifted my gaze back to Tia. "I do." I wasn't sure of the exact moment, Trent Shaw evolved from my enemy to a friend, but I was convinced he was the perfect man for her.

The inside pocket of my jacket buzzed. I frowned. Pulling out my phone—the one a select number of people had the number to and stared at the flashing number. I cursed, debating whether to answer the facetime call or not.

"Who is it?"

I showed her the call and she grinned. "Take it. You need to." With a gentle squeeze to my shoulder, she walked away.

"What the fuck do you want?" I eventually answered as the face of a man I hadn't seen in fuck knows how long, came into focus.

"Long time." He offered me one of his tentative smiles.

"Not long enough," I seethed.

"You're a fucking hard man to find," he replied, his tone just as firm.

"The fact that I'm looking at your face, I'm guessing it wasn't that hard," I scoffed, sarcasm dripping from my words.

"Fuck sakes, Gabriel, I—"

"It's Zayne." He knew why I had to change my name.

A long pause as he dragged a hand down his face and looked me straight in the eye, "Still incognito?" He cocked a brow, cheeky as shit. "Changing your name doesn't change who you were—are," he snapped out the last word then laughed. "You're looking good in your old age."

"Go fuck yourself. Call me when you're an adult. Actually, don't. Lose my number." I moved my hand to cut the call and he called out.

"Zayne, wait."

I hesitated. I never hesitated. "What the fuck do you want?"

"I need you—I mean I need you for a job. It's a big one."

"I'm not interested, Tanner. You of all people know I only work with people I trust."

"Please, Gabe—Zayne," he quickly corrected. "Meet me for a drink, so we can talk this shit out. I'm in New York."

I blinked. "What the fuck are you doing here?" We'd agreed a long time ago to never meet—it was safer that way. The fewer people saw us together, the better.

"Meet me and I'll tell you all about it. I'll text you the address." He cut the call before I could decline.

I stared at the blank screen for a moment longer, wondering where we'd gone wrong. I scrolled down the contacts list and found his name. My thumb hovered over delete and block before moving up to slide over his name. Declan Tanner, my good friend. My confidante, my spotter, my handler until he committed the ultimate betrayal.

He killed my wife.

And I had to walk away.

Then.

# Afterword

Hi Lovelies

If you're here at the end. Thank you so much for reading Trent and Ashrika's story. If you want to see more of them and how their HEA progresses, they will appear in Rayden's story, coming soon!

And keep a lookout for the broody Zayne, you never know around which corner you're going to meet him too – he needs an HEA, right.

Lotsa love Charlene

## Other book in the Series

Intoxication

"Take a risk. Just for the pleasure of it."

My past:

He was my lover

My present:

He's my future father-in-law

My future:

Who do I choose? Promises are not meant to be broken.

Are they?

NOTE: Please be aware that this book deals with sensitive topics like cheating.

Printed in Great Britain
by Amazon